To: Allen H
Shell Is!

Best Wishes!

DIRECTIONAL WARNING

by

Joseph A. Whaley, Jr.

Joe Whaley
5/15/5

Llumina Press

ISBN: 1-932047-84-0

Printed in the United States of America.

DEDICATION

DIRECTIONAL WARNING is dedicated to the memory of my Mother and Father.

ACKNOWLEDGEMENTS

The author acknowledges with grateful appreciation:

- My Father, for providing me with an education and for introducing me to the "great outdoors";
- My Mother, for instilling in me a love of reading and creative writing;
- My Mother and Father equally, for their constant nurturing;
- My Wife, for her love, and for her encouragement of my writing of this novel—and for her tolerance of my periods of seclusion in doing so;
- My children, for their love, and also, for letting me know that I am the kind of father that they are proud to call their Dad;
- My editor, Dawn Richardson, for her tireless efforts to make this novel a better literary work;
- My publisher, Deborah Greenspan, for her encouragement of my efforts to complete this novel;
- To Marilyn Brannen and the entire Llumina Press staff, for their efforts in publishing this novel.
- To Dana Bryan, wildlife photographer, for the use of his photograph from the St. Marks Wildlife Refuge website (saintmarks.fws.gov).

ABOUT THE AUTHOR

Joseph A. Whaley, Jr.

Born in 1948 in Pelham, Georgia, Joe Whaley graduated from the University of Georgia with a B.S. Degree in Chemistry and in Pharmacy. Whaley currently serves as Director of Pharmacy for Southwest Georgia's Public Health District in Albany, Georgia.

The author is married to the former Sharon Waller of Lynn Haven, Florida. They have two children, Kristen Leigh, born in 1980 and Kevin Carter, born in 1982.

Joe Whaley was appointed by two Georgia Governors to serve two five-year terms as a member of the Georgia State Board of Pharmacy. During his second term, Whaley was elected to serve on the Executive Committee of the National Association of Boards of Pharmacy. As a member of the Georgia Board, he was affiliated with the Georgia Drugs and Narcotics Agency. His association with the GDNA created his interest in narcotic diversion, drug addiction, and drug smuggling.

A member of the Georgia Pharmacy Association, Whaley is a Lifetime Optimist Club member and active in numerous health related agencies and organizations. An active member of Georgia's state disaster planning and response committee, Whaley has authored a pharmacy disaster relief manual that has been distributed nation-wide as a template for providing drugs, biologicals, and medical supplies in times of natural and man-made disasters. Whaley is a member of Porterfield United Methodist Church and coached Dixie youth baseball for the nine years of his son's youth baseball career.

Whaley's hobbies are hunting, fishing, golf, and scuba diving. During his youth, his family owned a beach house at Alligator Point, Florida and his formative years were spent fishing and exploring the shallow water flats of the Apalachee Bay. At least twice each year, the author, his son, and best friend and son speckled trout fish on the saltwater flats offshore of the St. Marks Lighthouse.

Information for much of this novel came from the author's recreational, vacation, and professional life experiences, and from diligent research.

CHAPTER ONE

Appearing robust and physically fit, Edward D. Walters looked much younger than his 62 years. Walters conscientiously watched his diet and exercised regularly to maintain that healthy image and to sustain the energy level that was required to perform his duties as leader of the free world. Despite his healthy lifestyle, the President noticed that his coordination and endurance were slowly waning. He began to tire more easily. In the past, a short afternoon rest period was usually sufficient to overcome any fatigue. Now, his lethargy persisted even after a restful night's sleep.

On this Monday morning, Walters found it challenging to maintain focus and coordination as he performed even the most menial of his daily tasks. That afternoon, the sudden realization he had neither the dexterity nor the stamina to complete his usual exercise routine was troubling. Yet, to rationalize his health concerns, the President attempted to attribute his loss of coordination, strength, and energy to the rigors of his first term in office.

Alarmed when she noticed her husband's slumped shoulders and fatigued look, the First Lady voiced her concern when the President sat down to dinner that evening.

"Edward, dear, I'm really worried about you," she began. You look very tired. You seem to have so little energy. Aren't you feeling well?"

Walters recognized his wife's genuine concern. She usually addressed him as 'Eddie'; she reserved 'Edward' only for moments of anxious conversation. In an attempt to appease her anxiety he replied, "Oh, I'm fine, Claire. It's really nothing to worry about. I'm just tired. You know how demanding my recent responsibilities have been."

The President had spent a wearisome weekend coping with another crisis in Iraq. Despite repeated warnings from the United Nations Security Council, the Iraqi dictator had yet again unleashed a plague of biochemical warfare on the Kurdish villages of northern Iraq. CNN satellite reports conveyed a carnage of extermination not seen since the atrocities of the Holocaust. The entire civilized world was horrified to witness this latest barbaric attempt at ethnic cleansing.

Dealing with the political aspects of this potential threat to world peace had left the President both physically exhausted and emotionally drained. Only a few weeks ago, Walters thought, even the stress of an international crisis of this magnitude would have had little or no affect on my health. Though he tried not to worry, he was becoming increasingly alarmed.

To add to his concerns, Walter's political adversaries jockeyed for prime-time coverage to voice their opinions about how the President should handle this crisis. Walters could already hear the criticism from those who would find condemnation in whatever path he took.

And then there was Congress. "The President must take swift military action to stop this atrocity!" the liberal activists avowed.

These Congressional partisans believed the United States should serve as peacekeepers for the world. Never would they hesitate to appropriate millions of U.S. dollars or deploy America's Armed Forces and weaponry to foreign soil to settle national disputes. Foreign wars, Walters thought, in which America had no economic interest, no direct threat to its political sovereignty, no clear and present danger to homeland security, and in fact, no legitimate reason for military intrusion.

In an effort to respond to these political adversaries and propose a resolution to halt Iraq's senseless acts of inhumanity, Walters had spent two sleepless nights trying to decide what course of action would be in the best interest of America, and most helpful to the oppressed Kurds inside Iraq. His Joint Chiefs had proposed a direct and decisive military strategy, while the Secretary of State cautioned him, arguing, at least for the present, for a more diplomatic resolution.

The President knew that neither the American economy nor its people would tolerate another predominantly U.S.-funded overseas military conflict. Especially a conflict in which, for other than humanitarian concerns, the United States had no purposeful political interest.

With characteristic conservative insight, Edward Walters invited the leaders of the free world to convene a summit in Washington to develop a global strategy to deal with Iraq's deployment of these weapons of mass destruction against its own citizens. He knew he must remain focused to host this summit and attend to his other presidential duties and responsibilities. Yet, he could not.

Admittedly tired, he knew the mental stress of the presidency was not his cause for concern. He was certain he had a serious physical health problem. Frightened to learn the truth, yet anxious for a definitive answer, Walters confided in Dr. James B. Atwood, his life-long friend and personal physician.

Immediately following the summit, Atwood scheduled a series of medical tests for the President at George Washington University Hospital. As soon as the results were in, Atwood met in seclusion with top medical specialists at University Hospital to confirm a diagnosis. Test results were conclusive, the diagnosis undeniable.

The doctor then called the Oval Office to inform the President that he was ready to discuss the results. "I would like to meet with you, Eddie. The sooner the better," Atwood added, a sense of urgency in his request. The President asked his Executive Secretary, Ester Hinman, to schedule the doctor for the next day's first half-hour appointment. A half-hour would prove an insufficient allotment of time. Jim Atwood would be there much longer.

"Good morning, Jim." The President greeted Atwood the following morning.

"Mr. President." Atwood smiled cordially as he fondly shook hands with his friend. Though his demeanor was meant with genial sincerity, he could not disguise his genuine discomfort at having to meet with the President under these circumstances. The doctor's warm greeting had belied a pretense of pleasure to see his distinguished friend on this occasion.

The First Lady was called to join them.

"Good Morning, Claire." Atwood said pleasantly, rising to greet her as she entered the room. "It's nice to see you, again."

"It's nice to see you, too, Jim," she said, searching his face for any hint that her husband's situation was less than critical. Seeing none, she quietly sat down beside her husband, certain now that the news would not be good. Jim Atwood sat facing them across the President's desk in the Oval Office. Both Claire and Edward Walters found Atwood's uncharacteristic uneasiness foreboding. They had been friends too long for deception, and idle conversation was characteristic of neither Eddie nor Jim.

Perceiving his friend's discomfort, the President began. "Thank you for coming, Jim. Please, just tell us what you have to report."

The President and Mrs. Walters listened attentively to their friend who was obviously disconsolate with his report. Walters had prepared himself for the worse. He was glad he had done so. He learned that his political career, not to mention his life, would be short-lived.

Focusing his eyes intently on the President's, Atwood inhaled deeply and began, "I'm sorry to have to tell you this, Eddie, but your diagnosis is Sporadic ALS – Amyotrophic Lateral Sclerosis."

Claire Walters took a sharp intake of breath and began to cry softly. She knew ALS was untreatable. And terminal.

"Commonly referred to as Lou Gehrig's Disease or MND (Motor Neuorone Disease)," Atwood continued, "ALS is a rapidly progressive, fatal neuromuscular disease. It attacks the motor neurons responsible for the transmission of electrical impulses from the brain to the voluntary skeletal muscles throughout the body. These electronic transmissions signal the muscles into movement."

"Though the brain may will the muscle into motion," he explained, "with a loss of electronic signal to promote the desired muscular movement, the muscle fails to respond. Over time, as muscles continuously fail to receive these electrical stimuli, they eventually loose their strength and ability to function. They soon atrophy and die."

They learned more. In the 1930s, Lou Gehrig, the New York Yankee's famous 'Iron Man' was noted for his agility, strength, and excellent health. His baseball prowess became legendary. So did the disease that ended his career – and his life. ALS would forever be known as Lou Gehrig's disease. Likewise, it was now, Edward Walters' disease.

Still considerate of his friend's discomfort as the messenger of such news, the President thanked Atwood for his candor. "I know you must have agonized over having to be the bearer of such unwelcome news. I had hoped for a better report but was convinced the outcome might not be good." Clasping Claire's hand he continued, "With God's help and your guidance, Jim, we'll make the best of these circumstances I have been given."

Walters knew he must carefully consider his options to remain in office. In a quiet, almost imperceptible voice the First Lady asked, "Eddie, what will you do now?"

Thoughtfully, the President spoke. "Claire, it is in the best interest of this country that I make the right decision concerning my responsibilities as President, and it is a decision I must make quickly." He turned back to the doctor.

"Jim, help me to understand what will be the short term effect of this disease." He understood the long-term prognosis. Death, usually within three years.

"Eddie," Atwood began, "you are in the early stage of ALS. The loss of motor coordination and weakness you are now experiencing will be progressive. How rapid, I can't say. Because ALS attacks only motor neurons, the mind remains virtually unaffected. I would expect you to remain mentally competent and retain full possession of all your perceptual and cognitive senses. Your hearing, sight, smell, taste, and touch will remain essentially unchanged. I fully expect your ability to focus on your duties and responsibilities as President will remain unimpeded. Only your skeletal muscles will be affected."

Knowing the short-term political spin that would necessarily follow a public pronouncement of the President's present health problem, Atwood attempted to ease the impact of his diagnosis. "At this point in your disease progression, Eddie, there is no reason for anyone to doubt your competency to continue to serve as President. But," Atwood continued, "I must make you aware that in the progression of the disease, you will eventually end up in a wheelchair."

Hoping to offer his friend more encouragement, Atwood hastily added, "As you know, this is not unprecedented in American history. Franklin Delano Roosevelt, America's 32nd President, was stricken with poliomyelitis prior to his election as President. Paralyzed in both legs, he served his entire Presidency confined primarily to his wheelchair. Despite his physical infirmity, FDR was elected for an unprecedented four terms of office."

Knowing that his friend was trying to lessen the impact of the devastating diagnosis, the President thought for a moment. Then he spoke. "Yes, Jim, but FDR's infirmity was not as immediately fatal as will be mine. I can no longer consider the possibility of another term of office. I only hope that I can just finish out my present term."

Despite his best attempts to encourage his friend, Atwood's outward demeanor confirmed what the President already knew. ALS would assuredly deny him an opportunity for a second term.

In just two years of office, Edward Walters was recognized as one of the most productive Presidents in American history. James K. Polk, the 11th President, was noted as perhaps the strongest politician of the 19th century. Historians already considered Walters an equal.

He was trusted by the American people, revered by America's allies, and feared by its enemies. As Chief Executive Officer of the United States, Walters managed the U.S. government through decisions based not upon political correctness, but upon what he felt was in the best interest and welfare of America.

The President rose from his chair to look out across the White House lawn in the direction of the Washington Monument. He stood silently for a few moments, reflecting on all that had been said and what impact it would undoubtedly have on his family and on the country. It took him little time to reach a decision.

Returning to his desk, Walters calmly said, "I think it is in the nation's best interest that I immediately hold a press conference and make full disclosure of my diagnosis. Jim, I think the announcement would be less conjectural if you accompanied me. I will ask that all medically related questions be directed to you."

Confident, Walters continued, "I will announce that, so long as it is possible, I will remain in office for the balance of my term. I will also pledge that, should my medical condition worsen to the extent that I am incapable of competently continuing to serve as President, I will resign immediately."

He knew this was the right decision. For Claire, for himself, and for the country. He had resolved he would continue as Commander-in-Chief for as long as was physically possible. He had many items on his political agenda yet to accomplish. Walters wanted to leave the nation in the leadership of the Republican Party. To accomplish this he knew he must work diligently in the time remaining to smoothly transition Charles Douglas, his loyal Vice President, into the Presidency.

With absolute resolve and, oddly, renewed strength, he was prepared to face his disease. Walters rose, shook hands with Jim, hugged Claire, and then called in his Chief of Staff, his Executive Secretary, and the Vice President.

Eddie Walters' political success could be attributed in large part to those he had chosen as his inner circle of political advisors. The Vice President and Cabinet ministers were all Washington outsiders, thoughtfully selected from corporate and academic America for their individual management skills, political knowledge, and intense desire to help manage the economic and political affairs of the country.

Vice President Charles K. Douglas was the President's best friend and strongest political ally. Walters had lured his 56-year-old friend away from academia to serve as chief foreign policy advisor. As Vice President, Douglas formally served as President of the U.S. Senate. From that chair, he managed the Senate's legislative agenda with a firm hand and vigilant eye.

Douglas was profoundly successful in getting the President's legislative agenda passed through the Senate. Whenever a dissenting Senator considered opposing the President on a key political vote, Douglas would threaten to use the local newspapers within the Senator's district to inform his constituents that their Senator intended to vote against a key issue that was of vital local political and economic importance to them. Usually just the threat of doing so led to a fear of not being re-elected which usually proved sufficient to change a Senator's voting consideration. Douglas's use of bribery-through-intimidation tactics to achieve what was in the best interest of the nation worked flawlessly. The American people respected him.

When he accepted Edward Walters offer to serve as his Vice Presidential running mate, Douglas knew he would only be a heartbeat away from the presidency. Yet, he had given little thought to the fact that the President's last heartbeat might be this close. A student of world history and economic affairs, Douglas was well prepared to assume the presidency in the event of Walters' death or incapacity.

Three people in particular would listen to the evening news conference and receive the President's message with great pleasure. The first was Democrat A. Bixby Lane. Lane was the U.S. House Majority Leader, aspirant for the Presidency, and Walters' most outspoken critic. The second was CIA Deputy Director Wayne Payton Clark. And third, but certainly not the least receptive of the President's message was Juan Carlos Diego, South America's biggest, and most profitable drug lord.

A. Bixby Lane would not hesitate to resort to innuendo and deception for an opportunity to promote his candidacy for Edward Walters' job. True to his character, as soon as he heard the opening remarks of the President's press conference, Lane put his plan into action.

The President had conveyed to Ester Hinman that the two days following his press conference would require an open calendar where he could receive the many calls from foreign heads of state and congressional well-wishers that customarily follow such a press conference. All but the most critical of the President's appointments had been canceled.

Even before the conclusion of the President's speech, A. Bixby phoned the White House to schedule an appointment to "express his condolence and extend the President his best wishes."

"As soon as possible," he cajoled. "I must let the President know he has my full support."

A. Bixby was given a 9:00 AM appointment the next day. Upon learning of Lane's appointment, the President was certain that if he did not wake up feeling nauseated, he was sure to feel that way after spending only a few minutes alone with Bixby Lane.

"Humph!" Ester Hinman exclaimed to Chief of Staff, Carter Martin. "I'm sure Lane will find some way to exploit this situation. I have no doubt he will call the national press corps to announce his own press conference." Neither could stand the arrogance of the man.

The media loved A. Bixby Lane. He was never too busy for an interview, and they were never too busy to accommodate him.

"I can just picture him on the eleven o'clock news," Martin said mockingly, "standing solemn faced beside by the American flag, assuring all of America that despite the President's illness, all will be well."

"Most assuredly, the media will announce importantly that A. Bixby Lane has expressed his deepest concern for the health of the President and for the country in the President's time of illness," Hinman predicted sarcastically.

"Furthermore," she continued, "certain of the biased liberal media will be sure to put a deceptive spin on the fact that A. Bixby was appointed the first meeting tomorrow morning at the White House to meet with the President, perhaps to receive more personal and detailed information."

"I'm sure their media report will conclude that with A. Bixby now involved, America should have less cause for concern for its future and for the President's health," Martin sarcastically interjected.

Lane was dialing the national press corps even as they spoke.

Ester Hinman and Carter Martin were accurate in their predications, almost to the word. Lane would attempt to debauch the President's illness to his own advantage. The man had no conscious. The national television networks complied with his request to televise his press conference. The media thought Bixby was infallible. "A great American," they often called him. They knew Lane would quell the nation's concern - reason enough to oblige him with the airtime.

As CIA Deputy Chief for Caribbean and Latin America Analysis, Wayne Payton Clark was single, but married to the CIA. Responsible to the Director of Intelligence, Clark provided the President and his senior advisors with timely, accurate, and comprehensive intelligence regarding national security issues in the Caribbean.

An expert in his field, Wayne Clark was considered the CIA's greatest authority on Caribbean drug smuggling intelligence. He had studied and chronicled every proposed route of entry into the U.S. and worked extensively with the Immigration and Naturalization Service and its U.S. Border Patrol to help plan drug interdiction strategies.

Clark's drug smuggling knowledge and intervention expertise served him well in more ways than one. Wayne Clark led a carefully contrived double life; in addition to his CIA intelligence work, the consummate professional also directed the largest drug smuggling ring within the United States. Deposited in an offshore bank in the Cayman Islands was a fortune Clark had amassed from the profits of cocaine sales distributed through his U.S. pipeline.

Head of the largest and most powerful drug cartel in Latin America, Juan Carlos Diego was also number one on the FBI's 'Most Wanted' list. Drug traffickers in Bolivia, Columbia, and Peru realized an estimated $12 to $14 billion in annual cocaine sales. Managing 65 % of Columbia's cocaine operations, the Diego Cartel had annually deposited an average of $2.6 billion, revenue greater than the mid-90's profits of the Cali and Medellin Cartels combined.

Banks in Panama, the Cayman Islands, and Switzerland protected the millions the Señor Diego had deposited from the illicit sale of cocaine in the United States. Before Edward D. Walters took office, Juan Carlos Diego had been a rich and happy man. As the Republican Presidential candidate, Walters had campaigned relentlessly, promising the American people he would drastically reduce drug smuggling into the United States. Walters had a plan to do so. The American people were sufficiently impressed. Not so was Juan Carlos Diego.

In the past 10 years, Diego had smuggled more than 12 tons of cocaine into the United States through Panama, 17 tons across the Mexican border, and another 18 tons across the Caribbean into Miami. Neither the Drug Enforcement Administration nor the federal agencies of the U.S. Coast Guard, the U.S. Border Patrol, and the U.S. Customs Agency was sufficiently staffed, funded, or equipped to intercept such a volume of illegal drugs.

As a Presidential candidate, Edward Walters had promised he would commit the manpower, funds, and technology necessary to change this. As President, Walters had kept that promise.

Past administrations' efforts to reduce drug trafficking had achieved only limited success. Previous anti-drug smuggling interventions had focused on reducing the source of illicit drugs within Latin America, targeting the manufacture of cocaine and harvest of marijuana plants. In theory, destroying coca-leaf and marijuana fields and their processing facilities would substantially reduce the illicit drug supply.

Congress had passed Senate bill 2365, creating the Western Hemisphere Drug Elimination Act and providing $5 billion dollars to be spent over a three-year period in this drug interdiction effort. Supplied predominantly to local drug enforcement agencies within Bolivia, Columbia, and Peru, these funds provided military equipment and surveillance technology to aid in locating and destroying crop plantings and processing labs.

Many of the surveillance aircraft, land transport vehicles, and military weapons and munitions ended up the in control of the underground paramilitary. Ostensibly provided to reduce the amount of illicit drugs smuggled into the United States, this armamentarium was used more to repress human rights than to curb illicit drug production.

Congress appropriated an additional $100 million to South American governments for the express purpose of paying Andean coca-leaf and marijuana farmers not to plant their crops. This fallow enticement program proved a dismal failure. Most of the money quickly made its way into the numbered accounts of South American government officials. Little Andean drug crop eradication was realized.

In actuality, the costly programs achieved a paltry 10% reduction in drug trafficking. Displeased with such wasteful give-away programs, the American taxpayers demanded better planning, greater success, and more efficient leadership from their President. The electorate had displayed their displeasure at the voting booth by voting in support of Walters' campaign platform.

In his first State of the Union address to Congress, President Walters introduced his own four-year plan with its realistic expectation to reduce drug smuggling by 75%. He spoke with certainty. "My administration's strategy takes a pragmatic approach to reduce the quantity of drugs smuggled into the Unites States. As long as there is a demand for drugs," he said, "there will always be someone who will attempt to smuggle them into our country."

"First, it should be understood that there is no quick fix to this problem. It will take time, but my administration has devised a strategic plan that will achieve results. These results will not come cheaply. This plan will succeed only if Congress appropriates the funds necessary to implement the first year of my program."

Aware of public support for the President's mandate, Congress complied. Walter's first Federal budget proposed $7 billion for anti-drug smuggling efforts in Latin America. Congress approved $6.9 billion. Neither A. Bixby Lane nor any congressman dared publicly oppose the President on this budget line item. Americans were enraged over high crime rates, increasing school violence, and the decay of family and moral values, all of which they attributed to the accessibility and aggrandized use of illegal drugs.

Once funding was appropriated, Edward Walters quickly began to implement his war on drugs. In a prime time press conference, he unveiled the details of his plan to the nation. "Past administration's efforts to reduce drug trafficking into the United States by attempting to decrease drug production and supply within Latin American borders have proven unsuccessful," the President began. "I rather propose to strengthen and use the U.S. military and Federal enforcement agencies in a unified effort to stop drug smuggling at the U.S. borders."

"Effective tomorrow, we will begin a new initiative in America to stop the influx of illegal drugs into the United States," Walters announced. "I am forming a new U.S. Border Surveillance and Drug Interdiction Agency, the BSDIA, whose primary goal will be to intercept illegal drugs at the U.S. borders before they can be smuggled into the United States."

The President continued, "For the first time in U.S. history, the military branches of the Army, Navy, Air Force, and Marines will work concertedly with the U.S. Coast Guard, Border Patrol, Customs Service, INS, FBI, CIA, and Drug Enforcement Administration, in a unified effort to stop illegal drugs from entering the United States. Congress has appropriated $6.9 billion this year to begin this initiative. In this border war on drugs, I plan to strengthen the military and BSDIA both in the air and on the sea with new drug interdiction and surveillance equipment."

"First, at a cost of over $6 million each, 500 new S-76 Hawk series helicopters will be purchased to patrol our U. S. borders."

Based on the performance of the Army's Black Hawk and Navy's Sea Hawk helicopters, the dependability of this impressive aircraft had been proven with over four million flying hours. Manufactured by Sikorsky Industry in Connecticut, this was a welcomed announcement to the employees of Sikorsky Aviation watching the President's speech. The Black Hawk's purchase would prove to be a boon to the state's economy.

In his efforts to select an aerial surveillance and intervention aircraft, Edward Walters had read with interest the avionic capabilities of the S-76 series helicopters. As promotional consideration for their craft, Sikorsky emphasized the Hawk's ESSS (External Stores Support System), which made the S-76 capable of cruising at 5,000 feet at a maximum speed of 162 knots and for a distance of 1,150 nautical miles.

Prior to his press conference, the President had asked his Army Chief of Staff to explain the significance of these figures to him in layman's terms. The Army General responded, "A one-knot speed is equal to one nautical mile per hour, and one nautical mile is equal to 1.15 statute (speedometer) miles. Thus, the Hawk series helicopter can cruise at a sustained speed of 185 miles per hour and cover a distance of over 1,300 miles in a little over 7 hours. The deployment of these helicopters will make it much easier to patrol America's borders."

Walters continued his press conference promoting the aircraft's usefulness, stating, "Few of the fixed wing aircraft used in drug smuggling efforts can outrun and out-distance, and certainly not out maneuver Sikorsky's Black Hawk helicopters. Their purchase will enable the BSDIA to provide a formidable air cover over America's borders."

Walters stated further, "In addition to the investment in these superior aircraft, I plan to increase our maritime surveillance and interception capabilities as well. At a cost of $1 million each, the budget will fund the purchase of 1,000 high-performance offshore power-racing boats. Retrofitted with the most technologically advanced surveillance and detection equipment, these craft will be used to patrol the Atlantic, Pacific, and Gulf of Mexico coastlines."

Manufactured in Aventura, Florida by National Marine, the taxpayers of Florida and employees of National Marine would celebrate this news.

In his quest to select a marine craft, the President had asked the Navy Joint Chief for his recommendation. Admiral J. Paul Simpson answered informatively, "At 38 feet in length, the new Twin-Step hull design by National Marine boasts a 260-gallon fuel capacity. Capable of cruising at 120 miles per hour, these offshore cigarette-style racing boats can cover 100 miles in moderately heavy seas in less than one hour. With a diminished draft of only 27 inches, these powerboats can patrol in shallow water depths of less than 3 feet."

Walters' continued his press conference, "Purchase of these offshore powerboats outfitted with modern surveillance equipment, assures that few drug smuggling vessels will be able to avoid detection and interdiction. These powerboats are ideally suited for both offshore rough-water, high-speed pursuits as well as for shallow inshore coastal water patrol."

The President had asked all associated Agency Heads and Military Joint Chiefs to attend the press conference. There had been much speculation as who would be selected to direct this new agency. President Walters had kept his choice a closely guarded secret. Unprecedented in U.S. history, no person outside the President had ever been authorized so much power to make policy that would affect so many individual federal agencies and direct personnel from within these agencies as would the new BSDIA Director. The President had been lobbied by most members of Congress as well as from inside the Pentagon for one choice or another.

"Surely an officer of the Armed Forces would be chosen as BSDIA Director," the Joint Chiefs surmised. Who would be better qualified than a military officer to direct this military-style interdiction agency?"

Similarly, the FBI and CIA Directors each speculated that surely the President would consider him or one his Deputy Directors to head the BSDIA. Both thought their respective agencies had the most qualified personnel to manage and organize the President's new agency."

Edward Walters surprised them all when he announced to the nation that he had chosen present DEA Director, Richard A. Tolbert, as Agency head.

"I have the greatest faith in Director Tolbert's ability to command the BSDIA. Likewise, I am confident this new agency will meet America's highest expectations of protecting our homeland from cross-border drug smuggling," the President said.

"As promised during my campaign," Walters concluded, "with the initiation of the Border Surveillance and Drug Interdiction Agency, a new day has dawned in America. With all federal investigative and enforcement agencies working in concert with the American military, our nation has declared a new war on drugs. And this is a war we will win! Thank you, and good night. And may God bless these United States."

After the press conference, Walters met with the agency heads and joint chiefs in attendance. "Because so many federal agencies are involved in this new initiative," he said, "to help Director Tolbert assume a smooth initiation of the BSDIA, he will report directly to my office daily through Vice President Douglas. I expect the full cooperation of each federal agency involved in meeting the new agency's vital goals and objectives."

The BSDIA was Edward Walters' priority project. He did not intend to let this program fail.

Earlier, he had emphasized this point to Vice President Douglas, "Charles, as you know, an increased drug interdiction success was one of our primary campaign platform proposals. The American people's desire to get illegal drugs off their streets elected us. We must not let this program fail. If we do not stop it now, illicit drug use will undermine the economic and moral fiber of our country."

The President was adamant; this program would be his legacy. The success or failure of the BSDIA could also prescribe the future success or failure of Charles Douglas to be elected as President, something of which both men were acutely aware.

"Because of my health," the President told Douglas, "I feel it best to have Tolbert report directly to you. I want you to have direct knowledge and oversight of all program activity. I am relying on you to resolve any inter-agency problems that may arise."

As President of the U.S. Senate, Charles Douglas was both feared and revered. The President knew he would apply the same no-nonsense approach to managing problems within the BSDIA as he did managing legislative agenda within the Senate. The Vice President was given total oversight of this new federal agency. It would be his stepping-stone to the Presidency.

"Thank you for the opportunity, Eddie," Douglas said. "You can rest assured, I will let no one within any branch of the military or in any involved federal agency undermine this program's success. Protecting America from the ravages of drug-related crime is far more important than pacifying a bruised ego."

Douglas concurred with the President's choice for BSDIA Director. "I too, have faith that Rick Tolbert is the right man for the job," he said. "I will see that no obstacles in Washington stand in his way."

A quiet, unassuming man, Tolbert had seldom been mentioned in the news unless it was in reference to a DEA story, and then only in the context of his role as DEA Director. Washington insiders and the national press corps knew little about him. Now they wanted to know more.

Juan Carlos Diego knew much about Rick Tolbert. He loathed his success as DEA Director. As Diego would soon learn, as head of the new BSDIA, Tolbert would bring much stress and discontent into his life.

CHAPTER TWO

DEA Director Richard A. Tolbert was born in Valdosta, Georgia, in 1946 into one of the city's most influential families. His parents knew the value of hard work, and Rick had been taught that virtue at an early age. His mother was a college professor, and his father a successful realtor who owned much of the property on the north end of Patterson Street, the city's fastest growing business district.

Working alongside his parents as a young teenager, Rick quickly learned the business and personnel management skills that would prove invaluable to him later in life. He also learned that with hard work came rewards.

His father taught him to love the great outdoors. Many family weekends were spent at their lake house in nearby Twin Lakes or at their beach cottage on Alligator Point Peninsula, at Panacea, Florida. Isolated from the more popular Florida beach resorts, the peninsula's most frequent visitors were its few residents and area sports fishermen. For his parents, the weekend retreats served as a solace from work. For Rick, they served as a life-skills learning experience.

Welcoming the cool Gulf breezes, he often walked along the beach at night, enjoying the peaceful solitude of the seashore. To his right, he could see the nearby red blinking buoy light marking the channel dividing Alligator Point peninsula from Dog Island. Further to the left, on a clear, moonless night, he could see the rhythmic signal of the lighthouse beacon marking the entrance to the St. Marks River.

Peering out across the Gulf of Mexico, the bright stars seemed to disappear into the dark waters. Except for an occasional passing shrimp boat, the Gulf waters appeared tranquil and lifeless. In his youth, Rick Tolbert could not have imagined the drama that would unfold on these waters later in his adult life.

In his childhood, Rick had become an outdoors adventurer whose favorite activity was speckled trout fishing on the Ocklocknee shoal flats off Panacea. On most trips to the cottage, Rick's parents allowed him to bring along a companion. He always brought his best friend, Lincoln Knox.

By age 13, they were competently skilled to take the skiff out by themselves. Up before daybreak, they waited patiently until Rick's father woke to drive them to Crumb's Landing on Wilson's Beach where they would launch their boat.

Rick's mother prepared for them a picnic lunch that was always the same. She packed three peanut butter and jelly sandwiches each, two bags of Fritos, six iced bottles of Cokes, a quart jar of water and chocolate chip cookies for dessert. She knew they would be gone all day. Weather permitting, they always were.

Outfitted with their Zebco 808 saltwater reel and rod combo and tackle boxes filled with assorted hooks, weights, and Salty Dog curly-tailed jigs, they set out to fish. The 50 horsepower Evinrude outboard skimmed their 18 foot V-Hull Alumicraft powerfully along on the glassy calm bay. Even as young teenagers, they could both maneuver the sand and oyster bars with the familiarity and skill of local fishermen.

On the incoming tide, they would drift across the sawgrass flats just inside the first sandbar east of the Ocklocknee shoals. At an early age, they learned that fishing was always best on a rising tide.

Shrimp and other small crustaceans drifted in on the incoming tide to feed off the zooplankton stirred up as the sawgrass whipped back and forth with the waves. Pintails, croakers, ballyhoos, and menhaden baitfish fed on the shrimp. The larger game fish fed on the baitfish. Rick and Lincoln knew where to locate the baitfish.

Their most challenging and favorite fish to catch was the speckled trout. Apalachee Bay fishermen simply called them 'specks'. Other Gulf coast fishermen commonly referred to them as spotted weakfish or spotted sea bass. By whatever name, Rick and Lincoln soon learned they were difficult to catch, for the hook tended to easily pull loose from their paper-thin lips. Successfully landing a speck was a challenge.

Challenging these fish was their passion. Rick and Lincoln developed the skill of alternating their retrieve with a jerk-and-reel motion to best entice a strike. As the bait falls after the jerk cycle, the speck hits the lure with a forceful attack. Impatience in not allowing the fish to swallow the bait before setting the hook was a common mistake made by even seasoned anglers. Impatient, less skilled fishermen lost many large trout. Rick and Lincoln caught their limits.

Mid-April through May was always the best time to fish for specks on the Ocklocknee shoals. Speckled trout and Spanish and king mackerel could readily be caught as they schooled northwestward in the Gulf of Mexico in late spring. Migration began in the late winter months as the schools migrated north from the warmer winter waters of southern Florida. Reaching the Big Bend area during April and May, they would at last arrive in the deeper and cooler summer waters off the coasts of Texas and Louisiana by mid-June.

On the Gulf's saltwater flats, for two hours after the ebb of an incoming tide, fishing was fast and furious. In this pelagic ecosystem, a delicate balance existed between the predators within the food chain. At the end of this two-hour feeding frenzy, the crustaceans would suddenly retreat to safety with the rising tide surge. All feeding activity up the food chain virtually stopped. For a period of four to six hours, until the tide began to fall, there was little feeding activity and little reason to fish.

During these changing tide intervals, Rick and Lincoln often explored the coastline. They knew every brackish water feeder steam, rock pile, and coastal indentation along the Ocklocknee River basin. They explored east past Shell Point, across the St. Marks River, past Gray Mare, the Aucilla River, and beyond. It became their weekend and summer backyard. They knew it well.

On Valdosta High's football team, Rick was a star halfback. Lincoln was his blocking fullback. They were an unstoppable backfield tandem and the nucleus of the kind of team about which every coach dreams. Legendary among college football recruiting coaches, Valdosta High held the winningest record among high school football teams in the country.

Rick and Lincoln's team did not lose a single game during their high school career. Four years in a row, from 1961-1964, they were the AAAA National Champions. They were tough and disciplined young men, and football taught them the value of teamwork, a merit that would prove equally invaluable later in life.

Lincoln Knox was heavily recruited out of high school for both his running and blocking skills. He chose to play college football at Florida State University. Despite his toughness and athletic ability, Rick Tolbert lacked the physical size to move up to the college ranks. He attended his hometown Valdosta State College where he majored in criminal justice.

After high school, Rick and Lincoln spent time together whenever Lincoln returned home from FSU. As a college athlete, he had little time during the year to do so. During the summer, the two always returned to the saltwater flats of Ocklocknee Bay for a long weekend of trout fishing. Here, they caught up on happenings in both their lives and reminisced about their past. They were closer than even most brothers.

After receiving his Masters Degree in criminal justice from Valdosta State College, Rick Tolbert joined the Navy. With a high draft number, he could have deferred service to work on a doctorate degree, but he did not. Tolbert completed his basic training at the Great Lakes Naval Training Center in Illinois. He finished 2nd out of a class of 150. As an elective basic training course, Rick received his advanced open scuba certification.

Scoring high on his aptitude test, and meeting the age, physical, and rating requirements, Tolbert was encouraged to apply for the Navy SEALS (Sea, Air and Land) training program. He applied and was accepted for consideration. Rick Tolbert would be required to pass both a comprehensive mental evaluation and his most demanding physical assessment even before he could be accepted into the training program.

SEAL candidates endured a strenuous physical challenge. First, they were required to swim a distance of 500 yards within a 12 minute and 30 second time-period. After a 10-minute rest, they had to perform 42 push-ups in less than 2 minutes. Following a short 2-minute rest, they had to complete 50 sit-ups - again, in less than 2 minutes. After another 2-minute rest period, they had to perform 8 pull-ups, but with no specified time limit. As a final test of endurance, after a 10-minute rest, wearing heavy combat boots, they were required to run a mile and a-half in less than 11 minutes and 30 seconds. This pre-SEALS acceptance test was a physical trial few could endure.

Rick Tolbert's perseverance saw him through. He was accepted into the Basic Underwater Demolition/SEALS (BUDS) training program conducted at the Naval Special Warfare Center on the Coronado Peninsula at San Diego, California. Graduating with his BUDS class of 30, Tolbert served four years as a Navy SEAL attached to an amphibious landing assault unit in Vietnam.

During his tour of duty, Tolbert received the Navy Distinguished Service Metal and was awarded the Purple Heart. After his honorable discharge, Rick married his high school and college sweetheart and moved to Washington, D.C. where he joined the Federal Bureau of Investigation.

His distinguished service record brought him to the attention of FBI Director, S. Tullis Faulk. Within 12 years, Tolbert had been promoted to Southeastern United States Deputy Director. His territorial responsibilities included the Gulf Coast and Atlantic Ocean border states extending from Texas eastward through the Carolinas, including the adjacent Southern states.

When elected President, Edward Walters had quickly recognized Tolbert's leadership abilities and management skills. President Walters appointed Tolbert as Director of the Drug Enforcement Administration. A dedication to hard work, tenacity, and intra-agency cooperation earned him the respect of the various other federal agency directors with whom he worked.

Rick Tolbert had the reputation of being a tenacious and successful operative. There was no better candidate for Director of the U.S. Border Surveillance and Drug Interdiction Agency. In the two years that Rick Tolbert had directed the DEA, Juan Carlos Diego's drug trafficking profits had noticeably diminished. It was an omen. As the BSDIA became active, Diego should have had a foreboding that Tolbert would put even more pressure on his drug smuggling operation and cause constant anxiety in his life.

Washington's Cherry Blossom Festival commemorates Japan's gift of 3,000 cherry trees to the people of the United States. In 1912, Tokyo's Mayor, Yukio Ozaki presented the gift as a memorial of national friend-ship. The April blossoming of the cherry trees surrounding the Tidal Basin highlighted the natural beauty of spring in the nation's capitol, Bixby Lane thought.

Heading towards Independence Avenue and the U.S. Capitol, the Senator enjoyed the spectacular view of the blossoming trees fronting the Jefferson Memorial and West Basin Drive. It was a pleasant April Satur-day morning. A. Bixby asked his limousine driver to roll the windows down so he could enjoy the fragrance of the cherry blossoms in full bloom.

A. Bixby was a happy man, pleased in the acclaim that he was the Democratic Presidential frontrunner for the primaries that would start in less than 11 months. He speculated that he would occupy the Oval Office in 21 short months. With the timely announcement of the President's ter-minal illness, A. Bixby was convinced the President had implicitly deliv-ered him a victory.

Certain of the biased liberal media all but acknowledged it so.

Arriving at the Capitol, Lane was ceremonially ushered to his confer-ence room in the House Majority Leader's office wing. Waiting there was the nucleus of his election advisory team, all Democratic Washington insiders who attached themselves to whomever was the prospective winning party nominee.

Lane's entourage immediately encircled him. With the obligatory pats on the back and fervent handshakes, his supporters lauded effusive complements for his apparently successful press conference.

"Fine job, Bixby!" shouted one advisor encouragingly. "Most assuredly, you effectively locked up your nomination with last night's press conference."

"You really hit a homerun, Champ!" said another supportively.

"Very Presidential!" lavished U.S. Representative C. Terrell Sheffield, chairman of the House Appropriations Committee and speculated to be Lane's choice as his running mate.

"I did think my press conference went rather well, didn't you, Terrell?" A. Bixby boasted. But for the lack of media exposure, the affable and well respected Terrell Sheffield would himself, be a formidable contender as the Democratic Presidential nominee. A. Bixby Lane knew as much.

"Very impressive, A!" Sheffield answered. "The media really honed in on your concern for the President and expounded upon the importance of you meeting with him to discuss the health of the nation. Nice ambiguity, that."

"You did appear so genuinely sincere." Sheffield continued. "Quite a nice added touch, too, seated at your desk with the American flag just off your left shoulder. The entire press conference came across as very Presidential!"

"I had rather thought it might," gloated A. Bixby.

"By the way, Bixby, how long were you in conference with the President?" Terrell asked.

"Only about five minutes," Lane said regrettably. "Walters soon asked that I please excuse him because suddenly he wasn't feeling very well." With his pious, egotistical attitude, five minutes in the presence of A. Bixby Lane was indeed more than the President could tolerate.

About Lane, Walters' was fond of quoting John Bright; "He is a self-made man and worships his own creator!"

Bixby addressed the group. "The reason I asked you here today is to seek your advice on campaign strategy. I'd like for each of you to tell me if you agree with my preliminary assessment."

"Obviously," A. Bixby began, "the President won't be here for another election. To retain the White House, Republicans will have little choice but to support the Vice President as their Presidential candidate. He may have some opposition from Senate Foreign Relations Chairman, Maxwell, but I think it will be weak. It's a big risk for Maxwell to announce he will run. Because he narrowly won a close reelection bid two years ago at home, if he does decide to run, and loses the nomination, it's likely that he would loose his Senate seat as well. I don't think he will take that chance, though I wish he would."

"We need someone to challenge Douglas and create discernable Republican in-fighting. Since it's unlikely that will occur, because of Walters' illness, we've got to find a way to depose a potential sympathy vote for the Republicans." A. Bixby continued. "I fear though, that the Vice President will be the leading candidate in the Republican primaries."

"Do you agree, Terrell?" Lane asked as if this was some brilliantly deduced theorem.

"Most assuredly, I do," C. Terrell cajoled, nodding vigorously at this obvious political deduction while looking around the table to invite nods for the others. "Most perceptive." the others stated, nodding their affirmation.

"I'm equally concerned," said Lane, "with the perception of the President's announcement that the Vice President will be responsible for oversight of this new drug smuggling agency. If Tolbert demonstrates even a modicum of success, I'm convinced media endorsement will boost Douglas' leadership appeal."

"Because of widespread public support for this program, I feel that at the moment there is more public attraction to the Republican platform than to ours. We need to conceive a Democratic platform ace card of our own." Lane surmised.

"I agree," quipped C. Terrell. He knew it would be difficult for Lane to surmount any credible campaign against the Vice President without a similar socially appealing stratagem.

A. Bixby continued, "We know drugs are pervasive in the streets of America, and the people have resolved to purge them from their neighborhoods. Terrell, do you have any thoughts on a strategy that we might adopt which might dilute the relative importance of the Republican's focus on drugs?"

C. Terrell gave careful thought and responded. "The decay of family moral values has always stirred the American emotion," he offered.

With eyebrows raised, heads nodded in approval. Terrell continued as

Lane assessed his proposed campaign philosophy.

"Bixby," Terrell said. "I believe that if you adopt a platform focused on your advocacy for an ideology supporting strong family values, this would definitely increase your perception as a family man of character concerned with the moral decay of our country and its seeming persistence for drug abuse."

"Additionally, we need to promote the fact that you have raised four children in a steadfastly religious family circle. This will further encourage your image as a family man with strong character and moral values. Each time the Vice President is interviewed concerning the success of a particular BSDIA initiative, you could counter with, 'I agree that reducing the supply of drugs is an issue of importance to Americans, and I support that. It is equally as important to remember, however, that we must build a strong moral fiber into American family values. This is just as important, if not more important, than reducing drug use. Take away the demand for drugs, and the supply will necessarily decrease."

Terrell continued informatively. "I suggest that one of your campaign strategies should be to continue to remind Americans that by building a family unit supported with strong moral values, principles, and character, the market for illegal drugs will decrease. Strengthen the family unit until there is no demand for drugs, and the supply will reduce itself."

"What do think, A?" Terrell asked at last. He knew this was the only strategy Lane might employ to overcome the positive press that would be heaped upon the Republicans for any BSDIA success in drug interdiction.

"Brilliant strategy, Terrell! Brilliant!" A. Bixby exclaimed. He applauded his fellow Democrat. Those around the table added their approval.

Lane anguished even as he applauded Sheffield's proposal. Despite his exuberance, Lane felt a growing sense of anxiety. A dark secret from his past gave him great cause for concern. He had hidden this secret well for thirteen years. If ever disclosed, A. Bixby knew his political career, and possibly his marriage, would be over.

Terrell's strategy for promoting a strong moral family value unit was indeed brilliant; only its proclamation would be flawed. Lane's concern was that he had five children, not four. He also had a son in Jamaica born out of wedlock.

Fourteen years earlier as a member of the British West Indies Trade Relations Committee, A. Bixby Lane and three other U.S. Representatives had attended a trade conference co-hosted by the Jamaican government and the Jamaican liquor export coalition. Promoted as a 'trade relations

fact finding mission', the conference had included a taste of Jamaica's finest recreation, cuisine, and libations.

Flying into Kingston, the committee had been welcomed by Jamaican
President Eduardo Cardara and the American Ambassador to Jamaica, Jer-
emy Farley. In Kingston, they had begun their royal wine and dine retreat.
At Ivor's, they had feasted on various tropical rum drinks, a smorgasbord
of gourmet delicacies, temping desserts, and Jamaica's famous Blue
Mountain coffee.

Montego Bay had provided relaxing rounds of golf at the Tryall Golf
Club, Jamaican host of the PGA World Championship of Golf. A full
day's charter, deep sea fishing for marlin and bonito was scheduled. They
had sampled Jamaican seafood at the famous Margueritavilla, Ltd., where
they imbibed drinks of its namesake.

As they toasted their surroundings, A. Bixby had expressed disap-
pointment to his companions that their wives were unable to make this trip
with them. "Were this not a whirlwind fact finding mission, it would be
great fun to have the wives with us," he had exclaimed.

As they swirled their fourth cocktail of the evening, they solemnly
acknowledged their agreement. All profusely confessed that it was so. In
actuality, it was the first time in four days that they had even thought
about their wives.

Their final stay brought them to Ocho Rios and Runaway Bay. They
were treated to a hotly contested polo match at the Chukka Cove Eques-
trian Centre, where the Ambassador had explained the fierce competition
between the local and international riders. Polo was Jamaica's national
pastime. While they professed great interest, they admittedly preferred
football. After dinner, the American contingency noted that as yet, they
had not gathered sufficient facts about Jamaican nightlife. Dutifully, Farley escorted them to the Jamaica Me Crazy lounge at the Jamaica Grande
Hotel.

By midnight, they concluded that perhaps that they had gathered an
abundance of facts for the evening, so they stumbled off to their rooms.

Lane could not sleep. He was aroused from the near nude floor show
he had watched at the Jamaica Me Crazy lounge. Stripping off his clothes,
he dressed in the opulent cotton robe provided in his luxury suite. Still
hungry, he placed an order with room service for a midnight snack with
champagne.

Simone Arrelia Mariquez delivered his order. She was 22, with the
sculptured body of a goddess. Her white cotton button-down shirt and

white shorts did little to cloak her bronzed beauty. With jet-black hair, hazel eyes, and teeth as white as the Jamaican sand, she was as beautiful as any model Lane had seen on a postcard.

His body was inflamed from the alcohol, and with lustful desire. A. Bixby undressed her with his eyes while he engaged her in aimless conversation. Flattered that such a handsome and distinguished American dignitary would pay her any attention, Simone accepted his repeated offers to share the champagne.

When at last she asked, "Was there anything else she could do for him?" the fervor of the moment took over and Lane told her his carnal desires. With her inhibitions diminished by the alcohol, Simone had surrendered to him passionately.

He awoke alone, late in the morning. His head throbbed from a nasty hangover, yet he remembered with clarity every passionate detail of last night. Rising slowly, he noticed strains of her long black hair clinging to his pillow. As he packed, he knew he must be careful to leave behind this and any other evidence of his infidelity. A backward glance as he left the room assured him there was no remaining evidence of this chanced tryst. He smiled, confident it would go undetected.

Upon arrival at Washington National Airport, members of the press corps met A. Bixby and company. Naturally, an interview upon their return had been scheduled far in advance of their departure. They never missed a photo op.

Even as a junior Representative, A. Bixby had been the focus of media interviews. When asked to describe the trade relations venture, he said with a wry smile, "In our short trip, we discovered much of Jamaica's natural beauty. Though we were rushed from locale to locale, we are now better able to understand Jamaica's travel and tourism opportunities and obstacles; the understanding of which should lead to better trade relations between our two countries."

"Nice whitewash," he thought. What was really on his mind was his unforeseen opportunity to delve into one of Jamaica's most beautiful natural resources. Oh, what a sacrifice he made in service for his country!

Exactly 284 days later, he would better understand the full fruits of his service.

It was a typical cold January evening in Washington, D.C. Lane sat beside his den fireplace enjoying the warmth while watching the early evening C-SPAN report. The news anchor extolled the significance of the House Appropriations Committee's decision to recommend full House funding of HB 2196. "The importance of this legislation, which would grant the U.S. Virgin Islands a total of $14.5 million dollars over a 3-year period, would be to improve port facilities and refurbish the island's hurricane-damaged interior."

The anchor continued, "The entire U.S. Virgin Island economy would benefit from these funds. St. Johns and St. Croix would rebuild their harbors and revitalize their waterfronts. Deeper harbors would provide for greater export opportunities and generate increased port tax revenue. Revitalized waterfronts would facelift the communities and attract greater tourism, a benefit to all of the Virgin Islands."

Lane smiled as he listened to the announcer laud the virtues of this federal expenditure. As an Appropriations Committee member, A. Bixby Lane determined that at least once each winter, it would be his responsibility to check on this revitalization progress. He felt it was his duty to the American taxpayers that he do so.

He had heard the islanders were friendly and quite beautiful. Not unlike the Jamaicans. Perhaps he would take time again to enjoy another late-night room service.

The ringing of the phone goaded Lane back from the islands. It was the American Ambassador to Jamaica, Jeremy Farley. He wondered if he might have a word with the Representative early the next morning. "In private," he said. "It is a matter of extreme personal urgency."

Perhaps, A. Bixby thought, Ambassador Farley wanted to seek his advice on arranging another trade relations assessment. By his reckoning, the last had certainly been a success.

"Perhaps you can come by my office around 10:00 AM?" Lane responded.

"Earlier." stated Farley, who explained he had an early flight back to Kingston.

After the perfunctory handshakes and greetings from Lane, Jeremy Farley, was ushered into A. Bixby's private office.

"Why don't you close the door?" Farley suggested.

A. Bixby was puzzled. He had thought the Ambassador had come to discuss trade relations, and that they could discuss that with the door open. The House press corps had assembled to report on A. Bixby's important meeting with the Jamaican Ambassador. He would prefer that the press be able to see them in conference. Their report might require pictures.

He closed the door, feeling a bit apprehensive. With a dry mouth, he asked, "What can I do for you, Mr. Ambassador?"

"I am here to discuss your son."

A. Bixby was taken aback. He had three daughters and a five-year-old son. "What could he possibly have to discuss with me about my son?" Lane thought.

"My son?" He asked questionably. "I didn't know you knew my son." Bixby said, squirming in his seat.

"I don't know the son of whom you speak, and neither do you know the one of whom I speak." Farley quipped. He was intrigued watching Lane squirm as he tried to comprehend this parody of words.

Lane was losing patience. "I don't think this is very amusing, Farley. Get to the point."

"Okay. The point, Bixby, is your seducement. Remember the game of seduction you played when you were in Jamaica?" He was having fun with the usually unflappable, A. Bixby Lane.

Bixby was visibly shaken. How did Farley know, he wondered. Had the girl talked?

As he spoke, he envisioned his marriage and political career slowly vanishing. The news media would attack this infidelity unrelentingly, unmercifully. Oh, how he suddenly loathed the press!

Unconvincingly, he tried to bolster his voice. "Jeremy, the only game I played in Jamaica was golf. I don't know what you are talking about."

"How could you forget about your little game of 'entice the room service delivery girl into bed'?" Farley asked. "Did you forget about that little dalliance?"

Lane remembered. Every moment suddenly flashed back in vivid detail. Suddenly, he felt nauseated. He stared at Farley open-mouthed.

Having achieved part of his mission, the Ambassador attempted to lighten the situation. "Well, congratulations, Mr. Representative. I'm here to report that you are now the proud father of a healthy 7 pound 9 1/2 ounce, baby boy! Shall I send out for cigars?"

Lane sank into his chair, pale and catatonic. "Should I call for the House doctor, Bixby?" Farley asked amusedly. "You don't look so well."

Raising his hand in a faint gesture of 'No.', Lane was now certain that his career and marriage were over. At this particular moment, Lane appeared a defeated man.

Despite the January weather, A. Bixby Lane broke out in cold sweat.

His voice began to tremble, "Is this true Jeremy? Are, are you sure? Say it's not so!"

"I'm afraid for your sake, Bixby, that it is." "At least that's your name listed here on this birth certificate." Farley exclaimed.

The ambassador passed a certified copy of a Jamaican birth certificate across the desk. Name of child, Santiago Betisto Mariquez. Name of Father, Augustine Bixby Lane.

Lane stammered, realizing all pretense at innocence was useless. "I, I'll admit that we had sex, but how do you know she's telling the truth about my being the father? How do you know that I'm not being blackmailed?"

"I've seen the child, Bixby. Blond hair, blue eyes. Only Caucasian in the nursery! Oh, I'm quite convinced that it's yours all right." Farley quipped. "Simone said sex with you was her first time and that she has been with no other man since."

Reaching into his briefcase, he pulled out a manila envelope. "Here are samples of the baby's hair and blood. Have them DNA tested against yours. I'm certain they'll be a match."

Lane intended to do so, but he already knew what the results would be. He had remembered her saying, "Please take it easy." He regretted having taken her at all!

"You're not being blackmailed, Lane." Farley retorted. "Simone is not asking for any birthrights. Only child support. That's why I'm here. She and her mother and father came to talk with me after the child was born."

"No one in America other than you and I know of this. They intend to tell no one as long as you provide support for Simone and Santiago. She wants to raise the child in a home for unwed Mothers in Ocho Rios. She only asks that you pay her expenses and support for the child."

"The Maraquez's know you are an important American politician. They intend to do you no political harm. I was asked to personally bring you this news and make arrangements for the support of Simone and your son. All things considered, I think you are getting off pretty lightly. What do you think?"

"If this is my child, and I believe that it probably is, I know I am very fortunate to get off this unscathed. You well know that just a rumor that I could have fathered an illegitimate child could ruin my career. I'll have the DNA tests run just for my own edification, but regardless of the outcome, I will support Simone and the child financially, for whatever needs they have."

"Have you thought of a plan to provide this support?" Lane asked.

"I have." Farley responded.

"I know you are a wealthy man, Lane, and I'm sure you can identify at least one of your corporations that would have an intense interest in supporting global human rights efforts."

"I can." Lane said with assurance, some of the color and bravado returning to his voice as he realized he just might survive this incident.

The Ambassador continued, "It would be a very simple matter for a monthly donation to be made to the Sister Margaret Child Care Mission in Jamaica, would it not?"

"Yes, Jeremy, of course it would. That's an excellent plan." Lane said respectfully. "How much will they need monthly?"

"A dormitory suite is $1,500. Food, clothing, doctor bills, medicine, and incidentals, say another $2,500. Perhaps add another $1,000 as a charitable donation to Sister Margaret for the Agency's general expenses, and I'd say $5,000 would be sufficient."

For the first time in his life, A. Bixby Lane was a humbled man. Jeremy Farley was returning his political career to him, and he knew it.

"So it shall be done, beginning tomorrow. Tell Sister Margaret she can expect a monthly check from Northeastern Export Company, Ltd. in the amount of $7,500 for the care of Simone and Santiago. She is free to use the extra funds in the support of her mission work."

"I wonder if I might ask an additional favor of you, Jeremy?"

"Certainly."

"I would appreciate you setting up a savings account in the name of Simone and Santiago Mariquez at Sister Margaret's bank."

"Consider it done."

"Likewise, please inform Sister Margaret that she will receive an additional check in the amount of $2,500 that I would like deposited into their savings account. That is for Simone and Santiago's future."

"Jeremy, please tell Simone and her mother and father that I am sorry and that I wish them and my son well."

Though Farley thought Lane's generosity was probably offered more out of guilt than responsibility, nevertheless he thought it laudable. Despite A. Bixby's generosity though, Farley could not bring himself to like Lane. He still had little respect for this 'man who would be President.'

Incidentally," Farley exclaimed, "this trip's expense is on you. I'm not billing this excursion to the taxpayers."

"You will be handsomely rewarded for your efforts," A. Bixby said.

"I don't want anything from you, Lane, except for you to pay the expenses for this trip." Farley retorted.

"There's one other thing I am supposed to tell you, Bixby. Simone and her parents request that you sign this document promising to take care of Santiago financially in the terms we have discussed until he is 21 years of age, or until age 25 in the event of Simone's death. They have requested that I act as the executor of this promissory contract."

"That, sir, is not a problem," replied Bixby. "You have my promise and my signature."

A. Bixby's swagger was gone. He had suddenly lost his desire to schedule a revitalization assessment trip to the Virgin Islands.

CHAPTER THREE

Wayne Clark's Miami office on Brickell Avenue faced eastward, overlooking Biscayne Bay and Miami Beach. From this office, with little fear or danger of detection Clark had contrived his counter-interdiction plan to successfully move illegal drugs through his U.S. distribution pipelines. A numbered overseas account attested to his success. No one in the drug smuggling trade other than his supplier, Juan Carlos Diego, knew his identity. Clark's communiqués were encrypted; his voice, electronically disguised. In his drug smuggling pipeline, he was known only as "The Commander."

With the formation of the BSDIA, Clark knew he must move his operation center out of Miami. To stay would jeopardize his illicit drug empire. He must give careful thought as to where to relocate the operation and distribution center to reduce his risk of discovery.

As Caribbean CIA Deputy Chief, Wayne Clark had access to the names of government officials and business and communication system information throughout the Caribbean as well as Central and South America. With this information at his disposal, selecting the best offshore location would be a relatively easy task.

He knew he would have to choose a politically sovereign country – one where his operation would remain undetected with little risk of political anarchy. The next base of operation had to be centrally located on the Andean cocaine pipeline, accessible from the sea, and within his territory of CIA surveillance responsibility.

He chose Belize.

Of all the Central American and Caribbean countries, Belize seemed the logical choice. There was little fear of military or civilian insurrection in the stable Democratic nation. A member of the British Commonwealth and an independent nation since 1981, Belize was governed by a parliamentary democracy that was supported by a Constitution and Bill of Rights. Its largest port city, Belize City was situated directly on the Caribbean coast and connected directly to Miami via American Airlines.

Politically stable, near his drug supply, and readily accessible to the sea, Belize was the ideal offshore location to headquarter Clark's smuggling operation.

From his Miami office, Wayne Clark began his covert plan to move his operation to Belize.

Rick Tolbert convened his inaugural meeting with the Armed Forces Chiefs of Staff and all federal agency directors assigned to the BSDIA initiative. Each director was asked to present an agency report on any present drug smuggling interdiction programs or activities.

The President felt it important that he and the Vice President attend this first meeting to assure that each department head fully understood their responsibility for cooperation with the BSDIA. The White House Situation Room was appropriately chosen to accommodate the meeting.

Tolbert began with an overview of his perspective on drug smuggling.

"Gentlemen, let me begin by stating that we most assuredly are in a national drug crisis. Drug use was once thought to be only a nuisance in America. What was considered only an experimentation by the 'Peace Generation' of the Vietnam era has now grown into a crisis that affects the entire nation."

"Every community in America is affected. Every neighborhood in the country is venerable. From the inner city poor to affluent suburbia, every family in America has either been directly impacted or knows another who has been negatively affected by illicit drugs."

"Legal drug misuse and illegal drug abuse are having a devastating effect on America's youth. A staggering 17,500 drug related deaths each year, principally among young people, can be attributed to drug abuse."

"Illegal drugs have an equally devastating effect on American economics. It is estimated that one-fourth of a trillion dollars is lost in the American economy each year as a direct result of illegal drugs. This is just the economic effect. These figures do not take into account the human toll in terms of families destroyed as a result of these drug-related deaths."

"Presently, there are nearly 2 million persons imprisoned in America. Of these, almost 70% are incarcerated because of drug-related crime. The crimes they commit and the loss of life and property in commission of those crimes establishes this as a national disaster. Most assuredly, this drug-related crime is as much a national disaster as are floods, fires, tornadoes, and hurricanes."

Tolbert resumed his account. "This Agency's goal will be to prevent illegal drugs and narcotics from entering the United States. America shares over 2,000 miles of its southern border with Mexico and 4,000 miles of its northern border with Canada. With an Atlantic coastline of over 28,000 miles, a Gulf Coast greater than 17,000, and a Continental U.S. Pacific coastline of over 7,000 total miles, success in drug interdiction at our 60,000 mile border seems a daunting task."

"We have achieved some degree of deterrence, but it has certainly been a difficult task for any one agency to attempt on its own. Under the BSDIA umbrella, we now have the men, the equipment, and the technology to better accomplish this goal."

Tolbert continued, saying, "Gentlemen, we will now hear the reports on your individual agency's strategies and activities to deter drug smuggling."

Particularly to the Joint Chiefs, Tolbert prompted, "As you listen to these reports, consider where your department can play a supportive role." Rick Tolbert had his own ideas, but knew it would be best to allow these brilliant military strategists the opportunity to offer their own.

Each assured him that they were certain they could devise military tactics to incorporate their men and equipment into the operational plans of the federal agencies whose primary goal was drug interdiction. Though they liked to take the front on implementing military strategy, they would, nevertheless, cooperate fully in the BSDIA's overall goals and objectives.

Beginning with the Immigration and Naturalization Service, Tolbert asked each agency head to update the BSDIA on any ongoing or planned interdiction programs. INS Director Jason Gonzales Alvarez began with a review of his agency's goals and objectives. "The Immigration and Naturalization Service operates under the U.S. Department of Justice. Our enforcement arm is the U.S. Border Patrol. Our goal is simple - to manage a cross-border program that will allow legal migration into and out of the country, while deterring illegal migration, alien smuggling, and drug trafficking - a worthwhile goal whose objective is not simple to achieve. If it were, we would not be here today. The greatest challenge for the INS is along the 2,000 mile Mexican border, particularly along the Southwest corridor."

Alvarez had more to say. "The INS has focused most of its agency funding in recent years on equipping its agents with enhanced surveillance and detection technology," he explained. "Night-vision goggles and infrared spotting scopes have aided in detection, while underground motion sensors and field laptop computers have aided in both the detection and identification of alien smugglers."

"Border enforcement infrastructure has been improved. The INS has funded fence installations, constructed anti drive-through barriers, and improved patrol roads along the common passageways of illegal ports-of-entry. In areas where we have concentrated these efforts, deterrence has been effective. Our strategy to have all INS agents working under a single framework of detection, but with plans individualized on different ports-of-entry has proven effective in border drug detection and arrests."

Alvarez continued, "INS multi-year operational strategies include three well-defined plans for drug interdiction – Operation Rio Grande, in Texas and New Mexico; Operation Safeguard in eastern and central Arizona; and Operation Gatekeeper in western Arizona and California."

"Operation Rio Grande" he explained, "focused on the Rio Grande crossing into McAllen, Brownsville, and Laredo, Texas. Growing out of the successful 'Hold the Line' interdiction project in El Paso, Operation Rio Grande has decreased illegal border crossings by 35%."

"Operation Safeguard effectively redirected illegal entry attempts away from the urban ports of entry near Nogales, Arizona, to the more open and more easily detectable areas of southern Arizona."

"Operation Gatekeeper is the INS's best example that organized deterrence is effective. This operation focused initially on a 5-mile stretch of border near Imperial Beach, California, that was responsible for nearly 25 % of all the nation's illegal entries. Increased surveillance and interdictions decreased these illegal crossings by 45%."

Director Alvarez concluded, "We have had success, but our capability to do more has been hindered by budget cuts. We welcome the additional support we will receive from our allied federal agencies and from the Armed Forces."

U.S. Customs Director John Frank Buckley next gave his report.

"The U.S. Customs Service is the primary enforcement agency protecting the nation's borders. As the primary border interdiction agency, Customs is the only border agency with an extensive air, land, and marine interdiction force and with an investigative force supported by its own intelligence branch."

"On a typical day, Customs is responsible to examine 3.1 million passengers, 2,261 aircraft, 60,196 truck/container conveyances, 348,205 vehicles, 552 ships, and almost 60,000 cross-border entries."

"From these examinations, 65 arrests and 118 narcotic seizures are made. These seizures include an average of 4,302 pounds of narcotics and $32,200 in arms and ammunition."

"Can we do more?"

"Yes." Buckley stated, answering his own question.

"Do we have the funds and manpower to do more?"

"No."

"U.S. Customs, likewise, welcomes the opportunity to work collaboratively with other federal agencies to reduce the illegal import of drugs."

Tolbert now turned his attention to the Armed Forces Joint Chiefs.

Speaking directly to the Army, Air Force, and Marine Generals, Tolbert stated, "I would expect from listening to these two interdiction agency reports, you can devise a single military strategy that will utilize your manpower to deploy two-thirds of the 500 Black Hawk helicopters that were purchased to patrol U.S. borders. Our responsibility will be to support these drug interdiction plans already in existence along the Mexican border." The Generals acknowledged that the task would not be difficult to accomplish.

General McAlfred of the Army spoke up. "In our preliminary discussions here today, I propose moving some of our routine training exercises to the Mexican-American border. A mere presence, particularly along the Arizona and New Mexico borders of 100,000 American troops should pose a formidable barrier to border smugglers."

"I agree with the Generals' perception, said Tolbert. "I feel we need a mighty military presence along the southwest border. Detecting and deterring drug trafficking through Mexico is my greatest concern. Mexico has become the sieve though which 60-75% of all narcotics and other illegal drugs are channeled into the U.S. As DEA Director, it was my greatest concern. Because of the Mexican government's unwillingness to address this problem internally, interdiction along the Mexican border has become increasingly difficult."

"The Mexican government has failed to sign the maritime agreement that would allow American military and enforcement vessels to patrol and interdict those vessels off the Mexican coast that have been identified by American intelligence sources as illegal drug transports," Tolbert said. "Further, despite repeated requests, not one drug cartel member arrested in Mexico has ever been extradited to the Unites States to stand trial. These are just a few examples of the frustrations we face in dealing with the Mexican government in drug interdiction efforts."

"Interdiction along the Mexican border has also become increasingly dangerous. As DEA Director, I asked for additional funding to protect our agents abroad, particularly in Mexico. Were funds allocated?"

"No."

"Were there consequences?"

"Most assuredly."

"I only need to refer to the Enrique Camarena Salazar story to support my contentions. Salazar was a DEA special agent working undercover with Mexican drugs lords. After gathering intelligence information and evidence, his undercover activity was discovered. He was subsequently kidnapped and executed. Camarena's torture prior to his death was horrible. Brutal. It defies description."

"These drug lords are ruthless. They have no respect for human life."

"Can we better protect our agents?"

"Yes, with the help of the Armed Forces we can."

"We must."

"The FBI and CIA can attest that corruption within Mexico is pervasive. Any agent who crosses the border into Mexico does so at risk. There is little or no protection from Mexican law enforcement."

"All levels of enforcement have their palm out - the local police, the state police, and the Federales. They either take the bribe offered by the drug cartel and look the other way, or they die. It is a way of life in Mexico. They learn fast."

"The 'Mexico Narcotraficanteto' has little effect on illegal drug portage through Mexico. "Mexico is ruled by a President; but most assuredly, it is run by narcoterrorism."

"We have tried and failed to deter drug trafficking from the supply source. We have learned it is difficult, if not impossible, to deter drug trafficking in route to the United States. Therefore, we must stop the drug smugglers at our borders."

Tolbert resumed discussion with the military agency heads.

He looked toward the Navy Admiral. "Admiral Simpson, you will have responsibility for the personnel and deployment of the 1000 offshore power boats that have been purchased for this program. I am certain you can devise an operational strategy to work directly with U.S. Customs and the Coast Guard to patrol the U.S. borders along the coast."

"Additionally, I am requesting that the President authorize the Navy to use the shipping lanes along the Atlantic and Pacific coastlines and particularly the Gulf of Mexico for training maneuvers. The mere presence of Naval vessels near coastal shipping lanes should pose a significant threat to drug smugglers."

President Walters intervened, "For fear of threatening our international commerce, past administrations have discouraged such a near-shore naval military presence. Effective today, I am authorizing our Navy to proceed with the coastal training maneuvers as Director Tolbert has recommended."

Tolbert gave each agency head sufficient time for comment.

Vice President Charles Douglas had been asked by Tolbert to conclude the meeting with a synopsis of what had been presented and discussed and to challenge the BSDIA operatives to achieve results.

"The BSDIA initiatives proposed today are doable." Douglas began. "The goals and objectives are achievable, and most certainly, would prove to be effective in protecting the American homeland from cross-border drug smuggling. The President is committed to this endeavor and it is what the American people want, expect, and demand of their federal enforcement agencies and of the armed forces. Gentlemen, everyone understands their role and what is expected of them. Let's get to work."

Tolbert's inaugural meeting of the BSDIA had been successful. He had given the Agency heads and Armed Forces Joint Chiefs the proper respect needed to recognize their agency's importance to the overall success of the project. No one felt slighted or offended. Rick Tolbert had earned their respect.

Departing comments and well-wishes to the President for the success of this program left no doubt that Walters believed he had chosen the right man for the job.

Although still mid-April, it was hot and humid when Wayne Clark stepped off American Airlines Flight 2103 at Philip Goldson International Airport in Belize City. Had the weather not been humid, Clark's anxiety level was sufficient to cause him to perspire. Reading the new BSDIA interdiction memorandum that crossed his desk the day before, Clark knew he must find an alternative method to smuggle his drugs into the U.S.Modern warships of the U.S. Navy and a myriad of offshore power-boats flying the BSDIA emblem now patrolled his routine traffic lanes into Miami.

From his office window, it appeared America was at war. Last week, Clark had seen Iowa class battleships and Areligh Burke and Spruance Class destroyers patrolling offshore beyond the Port of Miami. This week he had counted 5 Ticonderoga class cruisers, 14 frigates, and one Nimitz-class aircraft carrier just offshore in the shipping lanes.

Seeing such a close in-shore armada of naval vessels was unprecedented. Clark also noticed that a flotilla of BSDIA powerboats was on active patrol within Biscayne Bay. He was plenty worried. His previously successful smuggling scheme involved the use of fast running powerboats to transport bundles of cocaine offshore of Miami. As local trawlers came alongside, drug bundles of cocaine were dropped overboard where they were retrieved in the trawler's nets, then hidden aboard the vessels. Clark had successfully smuggled tons of cocaine into Miami using this drop-and-retrieve method.

Now it seemed doubtful, even in the dark of night, that his drug runners would be able to offload their cargo without detection. Every square mile of water around Miami and across the Gulf of Mexico from Florida to Texas was either under BSDIA surveillance detection or directly patrolled by a military craft.

Florida's water lanes were seemingly locked tight. Clark knew he must devise an alternative conduit into the U.S or he would be out of the drug smuggling business.

As Caribbean CIA Deputy Chief, it was not unusual for Clark to visit every Central American and Caribbean island country at least once each month. Neither was it unusual for him to arrange a meeting with local government officials when he visited their country.

Clark had called Tao Lopez, mayor of Belize City, to notify him that he intended to pay a visit to Belize the next day. "Papa," as Lopez was known to his friends, "can you pick me up at the airport tomorrow? I will arrive on the 12:35 PM American flight from Miami."

"Certainly, Amigo," Lopez was quick to reply. "It will be good to see my old friend Wayne Clark again. I will be glad to meet you tomorrow." Lopez liked Clark, for he always brought him huge bags of pecans and peanuts—two commodities not readily available in Belize. Lopez met him at the airport then drove to his office at Government House in the Belize City.

"Is this a business call, Wayne?"

"No, Papa. This is strictly a social call. I am interested in finding a rather isolated beach location, someplace away from the routine tourist areas where I can relax when I return for my vacation. Do you know anyone who might give me a tour around the outer islands where I can search for the perfect place for rest and solitude?"

"I know just the man. If he does not already have a charter, he would be glad to take you around. No one knows more about the cayes than Pepe. We will look for him in a moment. First, let's sit here on the veranda and cool off."

The veranda overlooked Regent Street and the Belize Harbor. As they drank a cold Coke, Papa told of the restoration plans for many of the surrounding homes in the historic South sector. All had been damaged by the recent hurricanes that had caused so much devastation in Belize and the Mexican States of the southeast Yucatan Peninsula.

After their rest, they leisurely strolled the eight blocks north from Government House until they reached the Swing Bridge at Haulover Creek. Divided into a North and South sector by Haulover Creek, Belize City utilized the Swing Bridge, a pedestrian footbridge and two-lane auto expanse of Queen Street, to connect the two halves of the city. Twice each day, the bridge was hand-cranked and swung around to open the creek for the larger boat traffic headed northwest through the city and southwards to the cayes.

Crossing the Swing Bridge into the North sector, they turned right onto the docks of the Marine Terminal. Here the Caye Caulker Water Taxi Association chartered boats for transfer out to the cayes and Turneffe Islands. Lopez quickly spotted Pepe tending his mooring lines.

"Hey, Pepe!" he shouted over the din of boat traffic along Haulover Creek to attract his attention. Papa introduced Clark to Pepe Decileo Santos, one of the caye tour operators who docked his boat alongside the Marine Terminal. "Buenos dias, Señor Clark." said Santos.

"Buenos dias, to you, Pepe," Clark replied.

"This is an important U.S. government man, Pepe," Lopez said. "Señor Clark is my friend. He wishes to engage your services. He is looking for an isolated offshore caye or beach where he can rest when he returns for vacation."

"I know several secluded places that I can show Señor Clark. Don't worry. I will take good care of your friend, Papa."

"Thank you, Pepe. Can you leave in about an hour? We would like to get some lunch first."

"I will be ready, Señor. Take your time."

Leaving the Marine Terminal, Papa and Clark re-crossed the Swing Bridge. "I will take you to the Blue Crab restaurant just on the other side of Haulover Creek." Papa said. "Here they have the best fresh seafood in Belize City."

After lunch, Lopez walked Clark back to Pepe's mooring.

"Ready to go, Pepe?" he asked.

"Si, Señor. Full tank and extra cans of gas. I wish to take Señor Clark north towards the Corozal district. I know several places around there where tourists do not often go."

"That's just what I'm looking for. Someplace where I can have some peace and quiet." Clark said. What he couldn't say but was thinking was, some isolated location where I can disguise my drug smuggling operation.

Pepe rounded the Fort George lighthouse and headed north towards the leeward side of Ambergris Caye. As he sped up his Pursuit Center Console, the offshore breeze helped to cool the oppressive afternoon temperature.

Capable of maintaining a cruising speed of 55 mph, with his 100-gallon built-in fuel tank and four 12-gallon portable reserves, Pepe could easily cruise the northern length of Belize and return in the five hours of daylight they had remaining.

Travel agents often refer to Belize as the jewel of the Caribbean. Clark could see why it was so nicknamed. They sped past miles of sugar-white sand beaches and colorful azure and pink coral heads. The turquoise water was crystal clear.

With the outer islands serving as a wind barrier for the inner island reefs, water visibility often approached 180 feet. Clark shouted to Pepe as they sped closer to the southern tip of Ambergris Caye, "What is the depth of the water here, Pepe? It doesn't look very deep. I can easily see the coral formations on the bottom."

"The depth of the clear water is very deceptive, Señor. Here, the water averages around 40 feet."

Good, thought Clark. "The deeper the better."

"Señor, Clark, are you looking for an isolated resort where you can hide away from the usual tourist traffic? If you are, Captain Morgan's Retreat is just ahead on Ambergris Caye. It is a very nice vacation place."

"No, Pepe. I'm not looking for a resort. I would prefer a location which has only a few haciendas and not too many people around."

"Then we need to head further north towards Sarteneja in the Corozal district."

"What's up that way, Pepe?"

"Corozal is the sugarcane district. Near Cerros. It used to be an ancient Mayan trading center. Now there are only isolated fishing villages on the bay where few tourists ever go," Pepe said.

"Do we have enough fuel and time to get there and back by dark?"

"Si, Señor. Plenty gas. Plenty time."

"Good, then let's go there," Clark said.

A half-hour later Pepe veered north-northwest past Sarteneja towards Cerros. The water suddenly turned ink-black which characteristically noted very deep water.

"Pepe, how deep is this water here?"

"About 450 feet, Señor. It runs this deep close to shore until just past the old sugarcane factory around the bend."

Clark was inwardly excited. He couldn't wait to glimpse what was waiting ahead.

As the boat rounded the mangrove point, Clark asked Pepe to slow down as he noticed the remains of a not-so-ancient sugarcane processing plant that obviously had taken the full force of a recent hurricane. Rather than incur the expense of rebuilding, it appeared that the owner had simply abandoned it. Clark was ecstatic.

He suspected that, for next to nothing, the owner would be glad to sell the remaining shell of the once productive sugar processing plant. It would serve him well as a disguise for his drug smuggling operation.

An isolated building with a deepwater egress leading through the cayes and into the Caribbean—it was exactly what Clark had been hoping to find.

Not wishing to appear too excited, he calmly said to Pepe, "This area along here looks like a good place for a vacation. Plenty of deep water for fishing and scuba diving. Nearby beaches. Anywhere close by for lodging and food?"

"Cerros is just a mile further north, Señor. Good food and lodging. Nobody disturb you there." That's just what Clark wanted to hear. The salt air had made him hungry.

"Let's land and eat an early dinner, Pepe. We'll get a beer too, to celebrate our friendship."

"Si, Señor. We eat. We drink. Then we head home. Take us 'bout two and a half hours running with the wind and the tide."

When they reached Belize City, Pepe dropped Clark off at the Fort George pier in front of the Radisson Fort George Hotel where he had an overnight reservation.

Clark thanked Pepe with five hundred-dollar bills, worth $1000 in Belizean exchange. Pepe was speechless. It was more money than he made in one month!

"Gracias! Gracias, Señor!"

"Next time you need go out in boat, you let Papa know day before. He will tell Pepe you come, and Pepe will wait for you."

"Muchos Gracias, Amigo!"

Now that Clark had found the ideal place to camouflage his smuggling operation, he needed to devise a plan to buy it and convert it into his needs. He would call his compadre, Juan Carlos Diego, to ask if he would be interested in becoming his partner in this offshore smuggling venture.

His call would be timely. Juan Carlos Diego was soon to feel the sting of the BSDIA.

CHAPTER FOUR

Diego had prepared three separate cargo containers for shipment. Though it was the prime coca leaf harvest time in Colombia, his Andean coca fields had realized their lowest productive spring yields in a decade. Juan Carlos expected to make a fair profit this year. Fortunately, his protection payoffs had been the lowest in two years. The Americans, it seemed, had lost interest in crop eradication efforts, and there were few attempts to destroy his fields and his processing labs.

Juan Carlos divided his small production of cocaine, marijuana, and heroin into three shipments for distribution through his routine disguised smuggling routes. These would be his first shipments in six months. This would be his only source of revenue this year.

Each shipment contained two tons of cocaine, two tons of marijuana, and one ton of heroin with a total combined street value of $118.8 million. After distribution costs, Diego expected to realize a $300 million profit.

His first shipment was to be ferried by freighter across the Caribbean past western Cuba and into the U.S. freighter lanes running around the Florida Keys and northwards up the Atlantic. Off the Miami coast, under cover of darkness, bundles of drugs would be dropped into the ocean where a shrimp trawler would wait to retrieve them in its nets.

Neither Customs nor the Coast Guard previously had sufficient manpower or budget to check every shrimp boat that returned to port for illegal drugs. Some were searched, and a few drug busts were made. But not nearly enough. Diego had been very successful smuggling his contraband in this crude, yet highly effective manner.

An occasional bundle not snared could be found floating free in the Gulf Stream along the Keys. It was not unusual for a sports fisherman or dive boat to spot drug bundles floating along the reefs. Locals knew better than to risk a pickup, even to turn the contraband over to authorities. There was always the very real chance that a pirate drug smuggler awaited an opportunity to hijack the bundle for the money that could be made from its easy sale. A 50-pound pot bundle could bring a quick $4,500. Fifty pounds of coke would net the pirate an even larger windfall of $450,000.

With so much money at stake, if a drug pirate spotted a pleasure boat hauling a bundle out of the water he would attempt to stop the vessel to confiscate the drug. To make some quick, easy money, drug pirates had no reservation about killing every passenger on board. Much like the pirates of old, they held the firm belief that dead men don't talk.

Many unsolved maritime murders still remained on Coast Guard record. Often a lone vessel would be found drifting in the Gulf Stream. Sometimes drug pirates left the dead on board; sometimes not. Many times the passengers and crew just disappeared overboard. Sometimes even the vessel disappeared. Drug pirates played for keeps. They had no respect for property or human life. Neither did Clark nor Diego.

Diego's second and third shipments would be transported overland across the Colombian border into La Palma, Panama. Panama was a country rich in copper and molybdenum ore deposits. Mined ore was a major export. After mining and transport to the La Palma seaport, the raw ore was loaded into cargo containers and shipped overseas to refinery plants in California and Texas.

Diego paid the loading and shipping company $10 million to load and transport his drugs within their ore cargo containers. Before secretly marked containers were filled with ore, wooden crates of Diego's drug shipment were loaded into the lower section of the containers. Hundreds of tons of ore were then loaded into the containers to conceal the drugs hidden within.

The La Palma western shipping route crossed the Gulf of Panama and followed the Pacific coast northward to the San Diego shipyards. Diego's second shipment was secreted into select containers bound for California. The Texas bound shipments passed through the Panama Canal and up the western Caribbean freight lines into Galveston. Diego's third drug shipment was hidden into a Texas bound ore shipment.

Upon arrival in the U.S., these secretly marked containers were temporarily diverted into recovery warehouses where the drugs were uncovered and removed. The ore was replaced and the container continued its overland transport to an ore smelting facility. None but the well-paid container transport driver was the wiser.

Once reclaimed, the drugs were then channeled through Wayne Clark's distribution pipeline throughout the U.S.

Another simple smuggling plan - simple, but effective. Diego knew there was little risk of his drugs being detected while hidden under tons of copper and molybdenum ore. He had never been caught trafficking in this manner before, and he had every expectation that he never would.

Juan Carlos knew neither the U.S. Customs nor the INS had sufficient capability to x-ray through a 15 by 50-foot cargo ore container to check for smuggled drugs that might be hidden within.

Thus far, Juan Carlos Diego had been lucky. With the initiation of the BSDIA, his luck was about to change.

Each of Diego's two ore container shipments was scheduled to travel about 10 days before reaching its destination point. For Juan Carlos, it was always an agonizing wait before he could expect to receive word of their safe arrival and retrieval into Clark's East and West coast underground storage facilities. As soon as the shipments left Columbia, Diego would monitor television newscasts to see if there was any report of a confiscation.

He anticipated the occasional nuisance report; "Today, the U.S. Customs Service reports that they have seized 1,000 pounds of cocaine, heroin, and marijuana coming into Miami. This drug bust exemplifies Custom's success in protecting the U.S. borders from drug traffickers."

"Got a half-ton. Missed 4.5 tons." Diego laughed. Juan Carlos could easily accept those losses. "Just a cost of doing business." He had joked.

This time the CNN report would be different.

"This late-breaking news in the world of law enforcement just in from Florida." Diego sat up stiffly, sipping coffee, intent on every word. He turned up the volume. "Let's go to Miami now with correspondent Bob Hannington. What can you tell us, Bob, about this news bulletin just coming in on the wire from the Miami feds?"

"Good evening, America, this is Bob Hannington reporting live from the FBI building in downtown Miami. The FBI reported tonight that agents of the new Border Surveillance and Drug Interdiction Agency have just made the largest maritime drug bust ever."

"Held in Federal custody here at FBI headquarters are Reymundo Jorges Alejandro and Erisela Lozano Ortiz, arrested for the attempted smuggling of an estimated two tons each of cocaine, marijuana, and heroin into Miami. BSDIA officials have estimated the street value of these confiscated drugs at $100 million."

Juan Carlos Diego let out a string of expletives, flinging his coffee cup across the room. The expansive plate glass window fronting his recreation room shattered, raining glass down onto his lower pool deck and into his pool.

"How could that happen?" he shouted to no one in particular.

He was about to find out.

Hannington continued, "Rick Tolbert, BSDIA Director reported earlier that the unwary drug smugglers were detected by U. S. Navy helicopter pilot, Capt. Gus Wilson, who spotted the drug bundles as they were being dumped overboard from a Colombian freighter. Waiting nearby to pick up the load was a shrimp trawler out of Miami."

"Though it was a dark, cloudy night here in Miami," Hannington reported, "Captain Wilson, piloting one of the BSDIA's recently purchased S-76 Black Hawk helicopters, stated that the entire smuggling effort was vividly displayed on the helicopter's FLIR screen. Wilson explained that the craft's FLIR, or forward-looking infrared radar, could detect any object that gives off heat."

"It was as though the smugglers were operating in broad daylight." Hannington quoted Wilson's earlier comment.

"Within minutes," Hannington continued, "the Navy Destroyer, 'Marathon,' and a squadron of BSDIA power boats stopped and boarded the two vessels, arresting both boat captains and their crew."

Diego was incredulous. Again, he cursed and shouted to his lieutenants, "I have lost more money today than in all my smuggling years combined. That was one third of the drug supply it has taken me all year to produce!"

CNN continued, "Vice President Charles K. Douglas, who has executive oversight of the BSDIA program, stated that he and President Walters are proud of the concerted effort of every agency and Armed Forces department that took part in this drug bust tonight."

Diego screamed. " I promise you, Mr. Vice President Douglas, and you, Mr. Rick Tolbert, if I ever get the chance, you are dead men!" Diego shook his fist at the television in a fit of rage, screaming, "At least you bastards didn't get my other two shipments!"

He drank himself to sleep. Had he known what was to come tomorrow, even the tequila would not have been much of a sedative.

He awoke feeling terrible. "I feel like I've been run over by a bull," he said to no one in particular. "Someone get me some coffee and cocaine to stop this pain."

Despite the attempt to ease his hangover, by mid-afternoon he would grow to feel much worse. At 2:12 PM PST, every network suddenly issued a news bulletin. "We interrupt our regularly scheduled programming to bring you this special news bulletin just in from the FBI office in San

Diego," stated a CNN announcer.

"Juan Carlos, you had better get in here quick. This doesn't sound good!" one of his lieutenants advised. In a cocaine daze and barely able to focus, Diego stumbled into the den.

The news report continued, "This morning, BSDIA agents on routine patrol in U.S. waters northwest of the Baja Peninsula stopped a San Diego bound Panamanian freighter transporting containers loaded with copper ore. Using the Navy's sophisticated and previously top secret, landbased sonar technology, agents checked the contents of randomly selected ore containers for smuggled drugs and contraband."

"While the Navy would not release detailed information on their new detection device called the Orca Wave Sonar, they would say that the device used sound wave technology rather than X-rays to visualize the contents of these ore laden containers. Until today, drug smugglers were totally unaware that this detection technology existed."

The reporter had been briefed by the Department of the Navy with an explanation of the device's scientific principles of detection. "The device works by pulsing sound waves through the cargo container. A computer records the speed at which the sound waves pass through the mass density of its contents. When the contents are of a consistent mass throughout, sound waves are registered at a constant speed. But, for example, when drugs are hidden within the container, the mass is different and the waves pass through at different speeds. The computer can detect even minute differences in content densities and identifies the exact location within the container where the drugs are hidden," the Navy spokesperson stated.

The reporter was impressed.

He continued his report. "In layman's terms, the Orca Wave Sonar device works on the same principle that surface ships use to detect heavier, more dense objects, like submarines, under water. Only the reverse is true of land-use sonar. The sonar detects the less dense object, in this case, drug bundles, hidden in and surrounded by the more dense ore. This sonar detection device alerted BSDIA agents that something was hidden within the ore."

"Before the Navy joined forces with the BSDIA, this technology was unavailable to drug interdiction agencies. Now use of the Navy's land-application sonar will greatly increase the Agency's ability to detect illegal drugs hidden within shipping containers."

The reporter continued, "During a routine check, one container showed different wave readings. When a portion of the ore was excavated, huge drug caches were discovered. FBI officials report that the freighter was ordered into port in San Diego where all the similar containers were sound wave tested. Customs and the INS reported again, that, an estimated two tons each of cocaine, marijuana, and heroin with an estimated street value of over $100 million was confiscated."

Juan Carlos Diego was livid. Again, he screamed obscenities as he heard the news. As if speaking directly to Rick Tolbert, Diego raised his fist defiantly and shouted, "At least the other third of my shipment will soon be safe in the U.S. underground!"

He had no sooner finished that outburst than the announcer resumed, "Since yesterday, Air Force AWAC reconnaissance has been tracking another ore shipment moving up the Caribbean. The freighter's manifest discloses that the shipment is bound for Galviston on the Texas Gulf coast. As soon as the freighter docks, it will be similarly checked for contraband.

Diego knew he was defeated. He was not accustomed to failure. $300 million was forever gone. He could not afford any more losses. His empire was crumbling. He must find another way to smuggle his drugs into the U.S.

The encrypted call from Wayne Clark could not have been timelier.

"Juan Carlos, did you hear the news?

"Of course, I heard. The BSDIA has devastated my entire smuggling operation. All this year's work is a total loss! Worse yet, each of my smuggling schemes into the U.S. has been detected."

"I too, Juan Carlos, am devastated. Without your supply, I have nothing to sell."

"I am sorry, Amigo, but even if I had another shipment, I could not risk its transport now." Diego remarked. The U.S. borders are under far too much surveillance to continue my smuggling operation."

"That is why I called you, Juan Carlos." Clark responded. "I have decided to move my base of operation. It's getting too risky even for me to work out of Miami. I have decided to look offshore for a foreign headquarters, and for a better way to smuggle your drugs in the U.S. I am certain that I have discovered a safe way to continue our smuggling partnership."

"I don't see how it could be done." Diego exclaimed incredulously. "I don't see how you could even smuggle a crack rock over the border on the back of a field mouse without it being detected! The American border seemingly has an impenetrable shield over it, Amigo."

"Yes, Diego. Over it, and all around it. But not beneath it."

"Beneath it?" Diego questioned.

"Yes, my friend. We need to meet and talk. Then I will tell you the details of my plan. I think you will be very interested."

"I am interested now. Where do you want to meet, Wayne?" Juan Carlos queried.

"I understand Belize is nice this time of year. Tomorrow I will send you a detailed encryption specifying the place and time to meet."

"Bueno. Adios, compadre."

"Buenos nochas."

Clark and Diego communicated primarily through an Onyxitron Encryptor. They had paid Onyxitron Industries, a Japanese electronics pioneer, $12 million for the Onyxitron Encryptor's production. There was no other communication device like it in the world. Its alphanumeric encryption codes were devised specifically to allow the user to pre-set a daily language code that would automatically change with the day and date.

If intercepted, messages were an unintelligible gibberish of letters and numbers that were virtually indecipherable without the use of another Onyxitron Encryptor. Its contrivance greatly reduced any chanced discovery of Clark and Diego's communications. Wayne Clark was confident no one could decipher their communiqués.

The FBI and Clark's own Central Intelligence Agency often detected the Encryptor's transmissions, but indeed, were unsuccessful in deciphering Clark and Diego's communications. Unbeknownst to Wayne Clark, the FBI was intent on identifying the source of the transmissions, even if they could not decipher the message.

Clark was still seething over the lost millions that he would have realized from distributing Diego's confiscated drugs. With the high costs of maintaining his elaborate distribution pipeline, his savings were rapidly dwindling.

In his CIA position, Clark was forced to show great pleasure and enthusiasm in the success of these BSDIA drug busts. Considering his personal misfortune, it was difficult to be a focused team player. Yet, it was necessary. He was Caribbean CIA Deputy Chief. He had Agency work that must be done.

CIA Director William Terry Fortson liked Wayne Clark. Clark was always prompt in completing his assigned reports. He always seems to take a keener interest in the drug smuggling entity of CIA intelligence investigation than did other sector Deputy Chiefs, Fortson though. He liked Clark's enthusiasm and included him as an inner-circle confidant.

Fortson needed intelligence information for a report to Congress. He had been asked to gather information on the benefits and complex use of offshore corporations to maximize investment profits and reduce U.S. taxable income. When the director had an important task assignment, Clark was usually his chosen man.

"I need someone to gather intelligence information on wire fraud and income tax evasion resulting from the use of corporate offshore tax shelters," the director said. "With your CIA duties and extra involvement with the BSDIA, I know you are busy. But I thought you might want this assignment anyway, since much of the investigation would be conducted in your territory."

Fortson added, "Since computerization and Internet access has greatly increased global communication and ready access to the economic and investment environment, more Americans, in an attempt to reduce U.S. taxable income, are partnering with foreign corporations in jurisdictions which have little or no income taxation."

"I need a complete report ready in two weeks, Clark" Fortson urged. "I know this is short notice, but I'd like for you to accept this project."

Wayne Clark was especially enthusiastic about undertaking this assignment. It would give him a diversion from his routine CIA activities and the time he needed to set up a drug smuggling régime in Belize.

"I'll do my best, sir." Clark responded. "Might this take temporary precedence over my BSDIA activities?" He prompted.

"Yes, it does. Until you complete this assignment, I will relieve you of those duties," Fortson replied emphatically.

"The Director is unwittingly throwing Brer Rabbit into the Briar Patch," Clark thought. "His investigation would relieve him of all direct BSDIA duty activities and allow him the unsupervised time he needed to move his operation offshore.

Oh, how Clark loved this job!

Intent on finalizing his intelligence report quickly so he could move on to the more important business at hand, Wayne Clark called on the one person he knew who could best provide him the information Fortson requested. He contacted his old friend, Romano Vicente, President and CEO of Cayman Island Capital Trust to arrange an interview.

More than 600 banks and trust companies located in the Cayman Islands shared more than $463 billion in assets. Vicente's Cayman Island Capital Trust attracted the biggest depositors. Not even the largest U.S. multi-billion dollar financial institution could boast of Vicente's deposit history. His old friend was pleased he could help Clark legitimize his CIA cover by providing him with the information the Director requested.

Two years earlier, Clark had conducted a private investigation for Vicente. The banker was still indebted to him for this service. After besting Cayman Island Capital Trust out of millions of dollars in transfer fees, Vicente's wire transfer manager, Garcia Blanco, had fled to Australia. Wayne Clark traced him to Queensland where he recovered most of the money from Caines International Guaranteed Trust. Clark made sure Blanco's body would never be recovered.

In gratitude, the trust company presented Clark with a nice financial reward. Vicente opened Clark his own personal numbered account with a $1 million deposit. Since that first deposit two years ago, Clark had added millions more in drug earnings. Vicente had realized a fortune in fees just from moving Clark and Diego's money safely around the world.

As Romano Vicente met Clark at the Owen Roberts Airport, they hugged liked brothers. "It is good to see again, Wayne Payton Clark." Vicente said, shaking hands warmly.

"You, too, Romano. It has been too long. I trust you have had no more employee embezzlements," Clark said.

"No, my friend. Hopefully, Mr. Blanco's was our last," Vicente replied, a note of amusement in his voice.

After Clark checked into the Hyatt Regency Grand Cayman Resort, Vicente drove him to the Cayman Island Capital Trust in George Town. Here Vicente would help Clark gather the offshore tax shelter information Fortson had requested.

"No one seems to be in a hurry." Vicente expressed, creeping along Seven-Mile Beach as they drove towards downtown. It was spring break week for many American colleges and universities, and the revelers cruised the beach in search of exotic temptation.

"Congestion in George Town is getting as bad as in America's largest cities," Vicente continued. "As many as seven cruise ships each day off-load their shore excursion passengers on our island of paradise."

Though traffic moved at a snail's pace, Wayne Clark was not bothered. He was in no hurry. He simply enjoyed the view as they idled along. He had so many plans to make and so little time in which to make them. This was a welcome, if only momentary break from reality.

Cayman Island Capital Trust, a palatial white, granite building, was located at the intersection of Fort Street and West Bay Road across from the Georgetown marine terminal. It was the cornerstone of the Duty Free

Centre and housed much of the great wealth of American entrepreneurs.

Upon arrival at Vicente's office, Clark specified the information Fortson requested. "I hate terribly to bother you with this, but I know you are a leading authority on the benefits of investing in offshore corporations."

"It is my life, Wayne. Sit and I will explain it to you as succinctly as possible. You can fill in the details for your report later."

Wayne Clark listened attentively and took careful notes.

Vicente began, "The benefits for Americans to use offshore corporations as a low-tax or no-tax shelter for their income is substantial. The corporations invest in or purchase such intangible assets as movie and book rights, patents, franchises, trademarks, copyrights, and computer software programs. These corporations then earn considerable royalties by licensing these assets to other individuals or corporations around the world. Income earned from the license of these assets is paid to the corporation rather than the individual who originally owned the asset."

"Corporations like Cayman Island Capital Trust structure the revenues from these license fees and royalties to be either minimally taxable or non-taxable. An obvious benefit from harboring asset profits in offshore trusts is the long-term tax deferral. When intangible asset revenue is left in an offshore corporation for at least ten years, profits can be paid out as dividends. When profits are eventually repatriated, the benefit from a ten year tax deferral and the reinvestment of untaxed profits during the deferral period, is a substantially less U.S. federal income tax assessment."

Vicente concluded, "Exploitation of corporate offshore institutions to reduce taxes, protect assets, and maximize profits in low-tax or no-tax countries allows the American taxpayer to legally redistribute tax responsibility over a period of 10 to 20 years. Comparatively, a substantial immediate tax liability would be assumed by the taxpayer were assets and revenue held principally within corporate America."

When Vicente had concluded his explanation, Clark stood and stretched. "You are most gracious, Romano, to spend your afternoon educating me on the economics of offshore investment," he said.

"You are most welcome, my old friend. To provide you with the detailed information you require to finish your report, I am giving you a copy of the 'Consumer Corporate Structure Guide to Offshore Investing' that we furnish to our potential investors."

"I am most appreciative of your help and information. Now, I should be able to complete my report in less than two days. That should leave me plenty of time to take care of some offshore business of my own." Clark chuckled.

"Now that you are educated on corporate offshore tax shelters, do not forget, my friend, that the best shelter for your 'acquired wealth' is still by 'direct deposit.' The Cayman Island Capital Trust always stands ready as your offshore shelter." Romano reminded laughingly.

"I promise, I will not forget." Clark replied. "Though I probably will not include that bit of information in my report."

Vicente, laughing with him said, "Come, let us go now and enjoy a few of the many exotic attractions of my island."

CHAPTER FIVE

With each passing day, the local, state, and national news media extolled a new BSDIA success in the accelerated war on drugs. From street drug dealers to major inner-city and urban distributors, the increase in detection methods and enforcement manpower was having a substantial impact on reducing drugs on the streets.

Never before in U.S. history had local law enforcement teamed with the military to defend the streets of American from illegal drug distribution. Arrests and drug confiscations were prominent headlines.

Americans once again felt safe living in their neighborhoods. They were pleased with their Republican President. He had promised to rid America of illegal drugs and return its streets back to its citizens. He was keeping his promise. Charles Douglas and Richard Tolbert were the nationally recognized leaders in this successful drug war. Neither A. Bixby Lane, Juan Carlos Diego, nor Wayne Clark was gratified with recent events. Each wore his own albatross.

A. Bixby Lane and the Democrats were desperately hoping for a chanced occurrence where they could get back into the national media forefront. The coming of summer and the national Memorial Day holiday would soon prove to be their vanguard.

Juan Carlos Diego and Wayne Clark knew they must move their operation offshore to avoid further disastrous consequences. With an ever-present risk of arrest, Clark knew Diego did not like to leave the safety of Colombia. Yet, the rendezvous would be necessary to finalize their offshore move. Clark made clandestine plans to meet with Diego at an isolated location where the FBI's most wanted would be least likely to be identified.

Ambergris Caye, isolated off mainland Belize would provide the perfect cover. As an extra measure of caution, Captain Morgan's Retreat on an even more isolated point on the northern tip of the island, far away from the usual tourist traffic was chosen for their rendezvous. The secluded resort would offer them perfect sanctuary. From the resort's private dock, Pepe could easily pick them up for their inspection of the mill site. From the resort, it would only be a short run up to Cerros.

Clark's voice mail encryption stated, "Must meet to discuss move. Have secured safe location. Plan to meet 17 April, 1700 hours, Buena Vista Restaurant, Captain Morgan's Retreat, Ambergris Caye, Belize. Am arriving Philip Goldson International 1230 hours. Maya Island Air to Caye. Will see you at restaurant."

Juan Carlos Diego responded, "Risky, but will meet you there."

Clark telephoned Tao Lopez to request that he contact Pepe to let him know he would need his services again. "I'll be coming in tomorrow, Papa, same time, but flying on to Ambergris Caye. See if Pepe can arrange to meet us at Captain Morgan's Retreat dock day after tomorrow. We'll be ready to leave by 10:00 AM. Ask him to bring clothes for two days. We may be away overnight. I'll pay all his expenses."

"Think you will have any trouble contacting him, Papa?" Clark asked.

"No, Wayne. He is easy to find. Always either at the Marine Terminal or running a charter. I will locate Pepe and let him know you need him. He will be glad to assist you."

"Tell Pepe I will have a friend or two along this time."

"That should pose no problem for Pepe. You know his boat. There is plenty of room."

"Is there anything else, Wayne?"

"Yes, two things really. Do you know a realtor who can be trusted to be discreet? My friends may want to buy some property."

"Yes, my brother-in-law. His work will be very confidential."

"Tell him then, that if there is a sale, after his commission, he will owe you a big referral fee!" Clark laughed.

"Arrange for him to come over with Pepe, if you will."

"Gladly. Perhaps I could bring you into town for lunch before your connecting flight leaves for Ambergris Caye."

"I'm not sure I will have time to come into Belize City for lunch. Thanks anyway. Perhaps next time."

"The other request I have, Papa, is to see if you can get a taxi to meet me around 1:30 PM and take me from Philip Goldson International to the Belize City Municipal Airport. I'm connecting with Maya Island Air out of Municipal to San Pedro at 2:00 in the afternoon. You know how hard it is to get a taxi sometimes at that time of the day."

"Nonsense, I will pick you up again, myself. See you at 12:30."

"Thanks Papa, you are a good friend. See you tomorrow."

His 'good friend' had no knowledge of what Clark intended to accomplish on this mission. Had he known, he would no longer consider Clark his friend.

Michael Miguel Thomas, Diego's First Lieutenant and most trusted employee arrived with Juan Carlos. Thomas managed Diego's shipping and contract work. In the event that Diego agreed to Clark's offshore relocation proposal, he would ask Thomas to remain in Belize to oversee the startup of the legitimate business that would front their smuggling operation.

Miguel Thomas was an American by birth. His Father was a U.S. Marine who had met Thomas' Panamanian Mother while on a peacekeeping mission in the Panama Canal Zone. They married and moved to South Carolina where Thomas was born. There, his Father continued his military service. Schooled at the University of South Carolina in chemistry and political science, Miguel spoke with a southern accent and could pass for a native southerner.

After his parents were killed in an auto accident, Miguel left the States to seek work in his Mother's native Panama. It was here that he met Juan Carlos Diego. Thomas was gratified when Diego offered him a job assisting in the management of his cocaine processing facilities.

In his employment offer, Diego promised, "Work with me, Miguel, and you will make more money than you could ever possibly hope to make in a legitimate trade."

In Juan Carlos's offer, Michael Miguel Thomas could not have found a more ideal job as a means to fulfill his long-term goals and personal objectives in life. He gladly accepted Diego's offer. Unknown even to the FBI, Thomas was Diego's perfect intermediary. Diego trusted him explicitly to look after his interests. With his American looks and accent, Clark knew Miguel Thomas would be the perfect accomplice for his plans to move Diego's drugs into the United States through Belize.

Wayne Clark was pleased with the progress he had made in revising his smuggling operation. He could finally visualize his long-devised plan becoming a reality.

Clark had requested an isolated backroom table at the Captain Morgan's Retreat restaurant. Here, he was certain Diego would feel less vulnerable to discovery. Even so, Diego passed furtive glances at everyone who entered the open-air restaurant. His precaution would be unnecessary. Only a few honeymooners and families were to be seen at this early dinner hour. Nonetheless, precaution was a critical element in their plans.

An opening round of margaritas lessened Diego's anxiety of discovery. After a second round, he soon became noticeably less anxious. Miguel Thomas had not shown even a hint of nervousness. Clark assessed, "This man must have ice water in his veins."

Diego was straightforward in his conversation. "I trust you have a good plan. I have many misgivings of our ability to resume a drug smuggling operation in America. This new drug agency and the President have devastated our smuggling efforts. Just exactly what is your proposal that will safely allow us to resume our partnership?"

"Let us order, then I will explain."

Later, Clark detailed his plan. "First, you might ask, why did I choose Belize to base our offshore smuggling operation? From my CIA background, I know the country is a democracy with a stable government. Belize is free of racial tension and there is no civil unrest. Their laws are unlikely to change with each new election. Belize has a long-standing tradition of protecting corporate and private property rights."

"During my visit here last week, I found an abandoned sugarcane factory on the coast near Cerros. The building was damaged in a recent hurricane. I believe it will serve as the perfect place to disguise our operation. Located in the Corozal district, not far from here, it is in an isolated location and will afford us the privacy we need. Tomorrow we will go there by boat for a close-up inspection."

"If you agree, we will purchase the property and building and turn it into a legitimate business that will front our smuggling operation."

"This is all good," commented Miguel Thomas, "but how do you plan to set up a smuggling operation in American? You know that every border entry into the U.S. is heavily guarded. The BSDIA confiscated our last three drug shipments and from our two best-disguised means of trafficking. And at our three best ports of entry!"

Diego added, "I cannot afford to loose another year's drug supply trying to find a successful way to smuggle my drugs into your pipeline. I tell you again, America has too tight a shield over its borders!"

"Yes," Clark agreed, "it does have a tight shield over its borders. But again, there is no shield beneath its borders!"

"Beneath its borders?" Thomas repeated.

"Yes, Amigos." Clark said emphatically. "We cannot smuggle our drugs across the U.S. borders, but I believe we can successfully smuggle them underwater - inside a submarine."

Diego and Thomas sat with a stunned look of bewilderment.

"In a submarine!" Diego asked skeptically. "But how do you plan to ship a drug cargo underwater without detection, and to where? Surely you don't propose that we can just dock unnoticed at any seaport and off-load our drugs, do you?"

"No, my friend. Let's finish eating and we'll sit down with a good Cuban cigar. I brought each of you a box of Partagas' Limited Edition Montecristo Robustos. You will enjoy your smoke and listen while I detail my plan."

They moved out onto the beach to the shelter of a secluded cabana. After each lit a Partagas, Clark continued.

"It is undeniable. The BSDIA has essentially closed all land portals into the United States. As best I can determine through CIA reports, there is little or no concern for submarine usage for drug trafficking. As you revealed, Diego, you simply can't cruise up to an American port or marina and unload a submarine without attracting considerable attention. I believe we can find a suitable place on the American coast where we can safely do that. We'll talk about a landing site later."

"First let's discuss how we can set up a submarine-based operation in Belize."

"The location we will look at tomorrow is a natural portal for submarine movement. There is a deepwater channel adjacent to the sugarcane factory that will easily disguise our entrance and exit from Belize."

Diego and Thomas smoked their Montecristo, listening with rapt attention.

"Juan Carlos, there is also sufficient flat land adjacent to the factory to build a runway where you can fly your drugs in from Colombia. As Corozal is the sugarcane district, we can legitimize our operation by restarting a legitimate sugar export business. With a few locals running the mill in the daytime, we can run the smuggling operation at night."

"What do you think of my plan so far?" Clark pressed.

"I am impressed. Despite my earlier misgivings, you just may have found a way to revive our operation." Diego answered.

Thomas added. "Your plan sounds feasible thus far. I do have a couple of questions though, that I'm sure you had already planned to answer. First, how do you propose to use a submarine without attracting a considerable amount of attention? What type of submarine would be small enough to avoid detection, yet large enough to economically transport several tons of cocaine? And where in America will you find a location that can safely harbor such a submarine that would likewise serve as the

U.S. distribution point?"

"I have the same questions." seconded Diego.

"All good questions. I will try to answer them for you, one at a time."

"Through my CIA files, I have found a Deep Submergence Rescue Vehicle submarine, or DSRV, that can be bought from the Russian navy. It is a smaller version of the American Lockheed's Mystic DSRV1 presently used by the U.S. Navy in its search and rescue operations."

"The DSRV's 28-foot length and 8-foot beam makes it an ideal size for our operational needs. I estimate that it can transport at least two tons of cocaine. Any larger sub would be difficult to maneuver along the U.S. coastline. Anything smaller would not have the range and transport capability our operation will require. Once we acquire this DSRV, we can have it equipped with the modern computerized navigational electronics and cloaking devices."

"To purchase and equip this submarine for our needs will not be cheap. But at $17 million, we can consider this as a necessary cost of doing business. I believe it is our only option for smuggling drugs undetected into the United States."

Diego remarked, "Aren't you concerned about the submarine being easily detectable by AWAC or heat-sensitive FLIR reconnaissance aircraft?"

"No Amigos." Clark responded. "This DSRV is powered by nickel/silver battery powered electric motors, and operates on one shrouded prop and four ducted thrusters. These give off virtually no heat. Compared to a gas, diesel, or nuclear-powered sub, battery-powered submersibles are essentially undetectable by infrared scanners."

"To make the sub less detectable to AWAC radar and submarine active and passive sonar detection devices, we will paint the exterior shell with the same radar-reflective coating that is used on the exterior surfaces of America's stealth fighters, the F-117 Nighthawk and the B-2 bomber. This should make the DSRV much less visible to above and below-surface radar and sonar reconnaissance craft. This radar-reflective coating is expensive, but again, is an expense that is necessary to the success of our operation."

"Additionally, we will contract with Matsujiyama Electronics of Japan to have the sub retrofitted with the most modern computerized navigational electronic guidance equipment. Matsujiyama recommends the MK-6 guidance system, the same that is employed on each U.S. Trident II missile submarine. They have a scaled-down version that will meet our needs."

"The MK-6's navigational program works on dual guidance principles. While on the surface, it utilizes a sophisticated global positioning system. When underwater, it uses both an electronic and mechanical inertial guidance system. Each system tracks the ships motion using gyroscopes that are constantly realigned by GPS, radio, radar, and satellite tracking and positioning systems. While submerged and underway, the MK-6 is accurate in its positioning to within 18 inches of any GPS waypoint."

"Likewise, Matsujiyama will install a carbon dioxide scrubber which replenishes oxygen and removes the CO_2 from the breathable air. Using a lithium hydroxide filter, expired air is cleaned of carbon dioxide and replenished with oxygen and water as a byproduct. Such an air cleaning system will allow the mini-sub to remained submerged for a prolonged 24 hour period with an assurance of breathable air."

"The DSRV can travel at a constant speed of 25 mph and transport a crew of four and a payload of 2 tons for a distance of 600 miles between battery charges. We would only need to find one stopover point between Belize and the United States to recharge the DSRV's batteries and change out the CO_2 scrubber."

Surveying a mental geographical map, Diego interjected, "Cuba, of course, would be our best stop-over port. I believe I could work out an arrangement with my old friend, General Hector Gomez, to allow us to land there."

"Fine. I, too, believe Cuba would provide a convenient stopover point." Clark responded. "You make the contact with Gomez. My research shows that the deepest water and least inhabited Cuban port would be Arroyos de Mantua just north of the Yucatan Channel. Tell the General he will, of course, be richly rewarded for his cooperation. Would a half million each roundtrip would be acceptable? If he wants more, offer him a million."

"It's just another cost of doing business, right?" Diego laughed. The pain of having lost $300 million last week was already beginning to wane.

"Tell him we would make his deposit to a numbered account at the bank of his choice. If he does not have one, let him know we would be glad to arrange one for him at Grand Cayman Capital Trust."

"I will call him tonight and get his answer," replied Diego.

"That would be best. We need to have all the details from the Belizean end worked out as soon as possible."

"That explains the submarine and plan for its use," Miguel remarked. "Now, what about selection of an American home port?"

"We will sit down again tomorrow night after our tour of Corozal and try to identify some areas which might be suitable and safe. I already have a few in mind," Clark responded.

"Tomorrow after we have looked at the factory property, if you approve, we will need to proceed with its purchase. I have asked my friend, the mayor of Belize City, to identify a realtor who could do this for us. The realtor will come over on the boat tomorrow with Pepe, the same skipper that I used last week."

"To hide your identities, Diego you will simply be introduced as Juan Carlos, a businessman from South America. Thomas will be Michael Miguel, a businessman from America. I will be Wayne Peyton."

"Is this agreeable, or would you prefer to use another name?"

Each responded affirmatively. Neither thought it would be necessary to use another alias.

"It will be easier to remember what to call each other if we use just our first and middle names," Diego agreed. "We certainly do not want to make either Pepe or the realtor suspicious of our real plans."

Clark added, "On the first trip out with Pepe, I explained to him that I was searching for a rather isolated location that was off the usual tourist path where I could enjoy an uninterrupted vacation. Told him I needed a quiet place to rest. It was his idea to search to the north in Corozal for such a place."

"All we discussed was finding a secluded vacation location. I did not disclose the fact that I was interested in looking at real estate, though I was constantly alert for an ideal site to relocate our offshore smuggling base. Tomorrow when I introduce you, I will tell Pepe and the realtor, that my original plans to find a secluded vacation hideaway have changed. I will inform them that you have decided to join me on vacation."

"I will announce that you are big businessmen in your countries, and that you are looking to expand your business opportunities. I will explain that you want to look at a property site Pepe showed me to see if it might offer a possibility for starting a business in Belize. Furthermore, if you determined that it did, you may want to buy it."

"I don't think that sounds suspicious, do you?" Clark asked.

"It certainly sounds believable to me," said Thomas.

"I do not think that explanation will cause any suspicion," Diego agreed. "I would expect that the realtor would be far too thankful for a possible sales opportunity, than to risk asking any probing questions that might cause him to lose a sale!"

Diego was right. Tao Lopez's brother-in-law, Marco Najera, was elated when Papa informed him an important American might possibly have some real estate work for him to do. The realty business in Belize City and in the Belizean districts could be described as slow at best. Though a capitalistic country, real estate sales in the inner cities were few. Most of the property sales were on the outer cayes where tourism was bustling. Many single-owner condominiums and time-shares were being sold, but only a few caye realtors benefited from these sales.

Najera was not one of them. He was hungry for a sale, literally. Tao informed him his American friend and some of his foreign business acquaintances might be interested in buying property in Belize. He was grateful to his brother-in-law for giving him this opportunity to accompany his American friend to look at real estate.

"If I make a sale, Tao, I will split the realty fee with you 50/50. Fair enough?"

"Fair enough, Marco." Lopez agreed. Papa told Marco that Pepe had taken Señor Clark north to Corozal. Najera contacted Pepe to ask if he had shown an interest in any particular property.

"Si, Marco." Pepe replied to his question. "Señor Clark seemed to have an interest in the old sugarcane mill south of Cerros."

Najera was exuberant. "Are you sure, Pepe? The old coast mill that was damaged by the hurricane?"

"That's the place, Marco."

He knew the mill property encompassed more than 1,000 acres. The mill was damaged beyond repair, but to the right buyer the property could still be valuable. The present owners, Belizean Sugar, Inc., had tried unsuccessfully to sell the property after the hurricane. Their asking price was $20,000 an acre, the going rate for sea-front acreage.

Were the location closer to Ambergris Caye or the Turneffe Islands, it had all the makings of an ideal resort. Its white sand beach and turquoise water were just too isolated and inaccessible from Belize City making the property unfit to develop for the tourist industry. Unless someone was interested in the property for sugarcane processing, there was little hope for its sale. No one prior to now had been interested.

Marco Najera knew the owners would more than likely take $10,000 an acre for the property. Marco did the math. At 6 % commission, he would make over $600,000! Even when split with his brother-in-law, that was more than he had made in his whole realty career! He could set up his own successful realty company in the cayes. He would be set for life.

Pepe Arilio Santos was very pleased to hear that his government Amigo would need his services again. His friend had paid him well. He would take Señor Clark anywhere he wanted to go.

Pepe and Najera left the Marine Terminal at 6:00 AM. Carrying a full passenger load, Pepe would not have room in his boat to carry the extra gas cans. They would need to stop at the San Pedro marina on Ambergris Caye to refuel. Departing at this early hour would allow sufficient time to refuel and eat breakfast before traveling on to the resort to pick up Clark and his friends by 10 o'clock sharp.

As Pepe refueled his boat, Marco walked along dockside looking about San Pedro. He was dreaming that soon he would be able to make this his new home. If he were able to close this deal, he would live out here among the country's rich. How he hoped this morning went well!

They docked at Captain Morgan's Retreat a few minutes before 10 AM. Pepe greeted Clark with an ardent handshake and introduced him to Marco Najera. After introductions all around, Clark told Pepe that they wanted to take a closer look at the sugarcane processing plant they had seen on their last outing.

Pepe gunned his motor and skippered his powerful Pursuit north-westward towards Sarteneja. Even at 10:00 AM, the temperature and humidity were high. The offshore breeze felt good as they cruised towards the Belizean coastline. It was difficult to carry on a conversation over the noise of the motor, so they settled back and enjoyed the tropical scenery.

Rounding the mangrove point as they approached the sugar mill, Diego and Thomas peered intently at the crystal clear water. They watched in amazement as the shallower water of the coral reefs plunged suddenly into the 450-foot ink black channel. Only Clark noticed their exchange of looks and wry smiles as they imagined that their submarine would soon navigate these same waters.

A canal, which served as a loading bay for the cargo ships that exported the mill's raw sugar, had been hewn into the coastline. Pepe moored to the rickety dock and they disembarked for a climb up an ever more treacherous flight of steps leading to the factory grounds.

Pepe cautioned, "Maybe we best go one at a time. Those stairs don't look sturdy enough to support all our weight at once." The others had thought the same thing.

The mill and its storage buildings had been destroyed by the hurricane. Only the steel support frame remained intact. The sides, roof, and contents of the mill had been ripped away and lay strewn across the expanse of the property.

Thomas made careful notes as they walked around and through the mill structure. They would later discuss how they might use this property to establish a new smuggling empire.

Next, they surveyed the surrounding acreage on the property. While the ground surrounding the sugarcane processing plant sloped slightly towards the Caribbean, a long flat stretch of land a quarter of mile inshore was almost perfectly flat. From the flat plain to the mill, rows of sugarcane had been grown to help supply the processing plant with cane.

Belize's tropical climate and fertile soil conditions allowed sugarcane to be grown year round. The district of Corozal, one of the largest sugarcane producers in all of Central America, produced sugarcane noted for its high sucrose content.

Because sugarcane stalks can dry out in a short period of time after cutting, processing plants must be located close to the cane fields. The sugarcane stalks are cut when they reach their maximum height of 10 feet, at which time the sugar content is highest. Stalks are crushed to extract their cane juice. The juice is then clarified, condensed, and boiled into raw sugar crystals. The raw, coarse brown sugar crystals are then shipped to refineries for processing into sugar.

This Cerros mill had once been a productive processing plant that exported one-tenth of the world's raw sugar needs. Clark, Diego, and Thomas were determined to return it to its former productivity, albeit, with a new principal export product.

With noontime already passed, Clark said to Pepe, "Why don't you two take the boat into Cerros and buy some Bar-B-Que sandwiches and drinks for lunch. While you are gone my friends will discuss whether or not they intend to buy this property."

Pepe agreed. "Si, Señor Clark, I, too, am getting hungry. Would you like colas or beer with your sandwiches?"

Diego replied for both he and Thomas, "Coronas would be nice."

Najera volunteered, "I'll buy lunch. You Amigos take your time and look over the property. Do you have any questions I might answer for you before we go?"

Diego asked, "What is the transportation system like around here? If we buy this place, we will need to totally rebuild it. To bring in supplies over water would be very expensive. Is there a road nearby?"

"Si, Señor Carlos." Just across the sugarcane fields is a paved road that connects directly with the Northern Highway. It travels through the Corozal and Orange Walk districts directly into Belize City."

"You know that Belize has few good paved roads, but fortunately one of the major ones connects here with this property."

Pepe said, "If no more questions now, we leave to get food."

As they left, Diego, Thomas, and Clark sat down in the shade to discuss their plans.

"Well, what do you think?" Clark asked.

Thomas let Diego respond first. "I don't think you could have found a better location. It's seems to be perfect. Fairly isolated. No immediate neighbors. No prying eyes. Good, flat ground to build an airstrip. Ideally suited to nautical shipping. I would say you have found the ideal base for our offshore relocation."

"I had thought you might say that." Clark said proudly.

"Thomas, what do you think?" Diego queried.

"Same as you, Juan Carlos. Excellent location to disguise a smuggling operation. The inland deep-water canal is an added bonus. And, if we construct a connecting building over the canal, the submarine could drive directly into the plant without detection."

"Do we all agree then that we buy the property, begin construction on a runway, reconstruction on the plant, and construction of a connecting bay over the canal?" Clark asked.

"Yes, as soon as possible." Diego agreed.

Clark continued, "I recommend that to finance this project, we set up a dummy corporation and corporate account through Romano Vicente and Cayman Island Capital Trust. Juan Carlos, I would propose that you and I each put up $50 million as start-up capital. All purchase and construction costs would be paid from this corporate account. This $100 million should be sufficient to purchase this property, buy and equip a submarine, and purchase port property in the U.S. If that is not enough, we will put in more."

"Agreed." Diego replied.

Diego asked Thomas if he could speak to him for a moment, in private. After their conversation, Diego reported to Clark, "Thomas has no ties in Columbia and I asked him if he would like to remain in Belize and oversee our reconstruction project. He has agreed. Additionally, I asked him if was willing to stay on and serve as our smuggling operations manager. He has agreed to do so for 25% of my profits."

"Miguel will be on my payroll. Not yours. You and I will split the costs of setting up our operation both here, in Cuba, and in the U.S. Once the entire operation is running smoothly, I will pay the Belizean and you will pay the U.S. costs of operation. Agreed?"

"Yes, Juan Carlos. Agreed. It's a deal." They shook hands all around. Soon they would salute their new partnership over cold Coronas and make Marco Najera a very rich and happy man.

Pepe and Najera returned with the sandwiches and beer. All during their food run, Najera had been worriedly excited. Worried that Carlos and Miguel would not want to buy the property, and excited that they would. He was too nervous to eat. Perhaps a beer or two would calm him down. It did.

Najera had done his homework. He would be glad that he done so. He had contacted Gaspar D. Jimenez, principle owner of Belizean Sugar, Inc., to apprise him that he may possibly have a buyer for his property.

Nonetheless excited, Jimenez had tried to appear calm. Najera, you know that our corporation is asking $20,000,000 for the 1,000 acres."

"Yes, and you have been asking that since the hurricane. Have you had any interest at all in the property?" He knew there was none.

"As a matter of fact, I am talking to a couple of interested buyers right now." Gomez exaggerated.

Najera did not refute him. "Perhaps you may be able to persuade them to pay that next week or next year, but I may have a buyer who would want to buy the property now. How would say, $10,000 an acre with a 6 % commission sound if they are interested?"

"Sounds like you would have a sale."

"Good, I'll call you as soon as I know something."

"Anytime, day or night!"

Marco Najera was overjoyed when Clark informed him that his friends had decided to purchase the property. He was already counting his commission.

"What price do you think the owner will ask for the property?" asked Diego.

"I must confess, Señor Carlos, when Pepe told me where he had taken Señor Clark, and that he seemed to show an interest in this property, I contacted the owner, Mr. Jimenez, to ask him. Just in case you were interested in buying it."

"What did he say?

"He said he was asking $20,000 per acre. I told him that was twice as much as I would recommend that my client pay."

"You were correct. And he said?"

"$10,000,000 total and it was a deal."

Diego finalized, "You call Mr. Jimenez and tell him we have a deal."

"Mr. Najera, there is only one obstacle to our purchase."

"What is that, Señor?" he asked reservedly.

"Privacy is very important to Señor Miguel and to me. As far as any-one is to know, you have never met the ones who purchased this property and do not know who they are. Your contact is with a Señor Romano Vicente, President and CEO of Grand Cayman Capital Trust in George Town. That is as much as you know."

"Is that a problem?"

"No, Señor Carlos. It is not a problem. I have already forgotten your names and what you look like." For over a half million dollars, he could forget a lot!

Diego, speaking to Pepe said, "Pepe, it is unfortunate that you will not receive any commission from the sale of this property as does Marco. In a gesture of our friendship and to reward you for showing Señor Clark this place, when we return to Captain Morgan's Retreat, I am going to send you home with a $100,000 charter bonus. But, you too, must forget all that you know."

"That is most generous, Señor Carlos. I don't know what to say."

"That's it, Pepe, you don't say anything!" For that much money, Pepe, too, had already forgotten their names.

It would be a fast trip back to Ambergris Caye.

As they departed, Marco Najera was profuse with his thanks. He said he would contact the property owner tonight to tell him the news. Tomor-row he would contact Vicente to begin purchase proceedings.

CHAPTER SIX

After dinner, the trio strolled back towards the secluded beachside cabana. They lit Montecristos and schemed to finalize their smuggling operation plans. "Juan Carlos," said Clark, "did you have a successful conversation with Gomez?"

"Yes, it went well. As you would expect, the General was quite pleased with our half-million dollar protection offer. He said there would be no problem using Cuba as a mid-point safe harbor. He, too, agreed that the Arroyos de Mantua Peninsula would provide the most accessible and isolated deepwater location for our venture, and agreed to construct a suitable docking facility on the peninsula where the submarine could rendezvous and recharge its batteries. He said he could easily disguise the facility as a port for his private fishing vessel."

"I emphasized the importance of secrecy in our use of Cuba as a waypoint into the Gulf of Mexico," Juan continued. "The General said that with a 24-hour advanced warning on the sub's arrival, he would make sure no military traffic would be in the area. Gomez guaranteed that we would not be bothered by any Cubans."

"When we discussed payment for his protection, he said that he did not have an offshore numbered account. Hector gladly accepted our offer to use Grand Cayman Capital Trust as his repository. He will contact Vicente tomorrow to establish an account. I told him that doing so would certainly make it much simpler for Romano to transfer his payoff from our account to his."

Clark remarked, "It seems that today we finalized the Belizean plans for our offshore relocation. Tonight we confirmed the Cuban component. Now we have only to discuss the American element of our plan. This will be the most difficult part to implement."

Diego agreed. "Choosing a location where we have minimal risk of detection and maximum disguise for our distribution operation is critical," he said.

Thomas looked at Clark. "Wayne, what are your American plans?

Have you chosen a location and what kind of business do you think will best camouflage our drug smuggling and distribution efforts?"

"I have studied U.S. Geological Survey maps of the Gulf of Mexico coastline from Brownsville, Texas eastward to Naples, Florida," said Clark. "Let's first talk about a location."

"Let us begin in Texas. Baffin Bay off the Madre Lagoon just south of Corpus Christi is a possibility. But I don't like the vast military presence in Texas. Much too risky, and the boat traffic on the Madre Lagoon is far too busy for my satisfaction. Same for Matagorda Bay and Galveston. There is simply too much of a military presence there. Too much risk for detection."

"Louisiana doesn't fare much better. The Bayou Delta provides perfect cover, but the water is too shallow. There are no isolated deepwater channels close to a major highway system. The New Orleans area is too well patrolled by naval vessels. Adequate port facilities and deep water, but again, just too much risk of detection for my comfort."

"Forget Mississippi - far too commercialized. No isolated ports."

"Mobile Bay in Alabama would be an option, but is seems half the U.S. Naval fleet maneuvers out of Mobile. Alabama, too, poses a high risk of detection."

"Forget the Florida panhandle, also. Pensacola, a huge Air Force base is located there. Fort Walton, Destin, and Panama City are all far too commercialized. Panama City also boasts an Air Force base. Too many sport fishermen in the area. Good, deep water, but again, far too risky."

Diego interrupted, "You seem to be running out of coastline, Wayne."

"Patience, my friend. I'm getting there."

"Apalachicola Bay gets better, but the coastal fishing villages are, again, far too commercialized. Rounding Alligator Point into the Big Bend area of Florida, the possibilities improve. West Apalachee Bay offers a number of isolated spring-fed creeks, but none deep enough at low tide for the DSRV. Panacea, Spring Creek, Shell Point, and Live Oak Island are possibilities, but none has the commercial facility we need to camouflage a smuggling operation."

"Next, we come to the St. Marks National Wildlife Refuge. Here, I believe is our best opportunity to establish our U.S. base. Going further eastward around the Big Bend area finds more of the same fishing villages as are located in West Apalachee Bay. Good deep harbors, but no commerce to disguise our operation."

"Gentlemen, I believe we have found a home at St. Marks. It is a rather isolated, coastal community, reliant upon the sea to support its economy. Everything there is dependent upon the marine environment, as is our operation."

Clark studied the faces of the other men. He could tell they were impressed by his thorough investigation of the possibilities for the U.S. base of operation. He continued to make his case.

"The town of St. Marks sits at the intersection of the St. Marks and Wakulla Rivers. At this point, the two rivers merge and become the commercially traveled St. Marks. The river has a 60-foot wide channel and a minimal 40-foot depth. It was once a destination for overseas oil tankers bringing crude oil into the storage depot at Newport, which is just three miles upriver."

"St. Marks was once a booming commercial fishing and navigation center for oil import. When the Newport facility lost many of its commercial contracts to the larger ports across the Gulf, St. Marks was left with only the fishing, crabbing, and shrimping industries as the base of its economy. There are a number of vacant commercial warehouses on the river that could serve as our base of operation."

Thomas questioned, "What business do you have in mind that we would operate there to front our smuggling operation?"

Clark answered, "It would make good sense to build a sugar refinery in St. Marks to refine the raw sugar that we process here in Belize, would it not? We could hire legitimate cargo ships to transport the raw sugar to the refinery. We would then have two well-disguised legitimate business fronts; the raw sugar processing plant in Belize and the sugar refinery in St. Marks. What do you think?"

"Sounds like we are getting into the powder business - powdered sugar and powdered cocaine," Thomas joked.

"Let's not get our loading backwards!" Diego added. "What is the risk of detection? What about area surveillance?"

"I believe we would have little risk of detection," Clark answered confidently. "There is only a negligible amount of surveillance in the area."

"In fact, only one Coast Guard station is located within the west Apalachee Bay area, and that is up the coast at Shell Island. There are no active duty Coast Guard or Navy personnel there, only volunteers who man the Coast Guard radio tower. There is virtually no underwater surveillance. The Navy and Coast Guard are centering their patrol and surveillance efforts on the larger ports like Tampa, New Orleans, Mobile, Pensacola, and Panama City. I don't think anyone would ever suspect that a submersible smuggling operation would be attempted, and especially not at a small fishing village like St. Marks."

"The Florida Marine Patrol is the only predominant law enforcement agency that patrols the bay area at all," said Clark, "and they primarily serve to enforce local hunting and fishing laws. When the sun goes down, they go to bed. And that is when we will begin our work!"

"Navigation of the submarine will be virtually unhindered. The commercial shipping lanes from the Tampa area westward to Panama City and New Orleans do not come within 50 miles of the Apalachee Bay. The only commercial craft that would be in the area is an occasional oil tanker and shrimp boat and the charter boats out of St. Marks."

Thomas, who was somewhat familiar with Florida coastal waters, remarked, "But Wayne, how would the sub navigate into the St. Marks River? It most certainly would have to surface to avoid running aground as it navigated to port. What would direct it to the coastline from offshore?" He paused briefly, then added, "Aren't you concerned that the sub might not safely find such a small river entrance among all the sand and oyster bars that front Florida's coastal waters?"

"Your questions and concerns are justified, Miguel," said Clark. "From Arroyos de Mantua, the submarine would navigate on an almost due north track into the Gulf of Mexico. It would remain submerged until it reached about two miles offshore of the Florida coast. Here, the water is still deep, 40 feet or more on low tide in the navigational channel. Using Global Positioning System navigation, it would be easy to traverse the Gulf to this point without fear of misdirection or running aground."

"You are correct that it would be best for the sub to make its approach at night. That would certainly lessen its chance of discovery as it approaches the coastline and the river entrance. That is another reason why I chose the St. Marks River system. The St. Marks is the only navigational river in the isolated Big Bend area of Florida that has a lighthouse serving to direct a safe entrance to port. The lighthouse also serves to warn the navigator of the myriad of sand and oyster bars that guard the river entrance. The presence of the St. Marks lighthouse effectively makes our plan possible."

"Your selection of locations both here in Belize, and in the U.S. have been meticulously planned," Diego exclaimed. "If everything checks out in Florida as it has here, we should soon have a successful restart to our smuggling partnership."

"I would like to ask that Miguel accompany you to America to help devise the plan to start up the U.S. operation. I too, would like to go, but you know that could be perilous. I would only risk going there if I had the chance to seek revenge on the Vice President or on Rick Tolbert for my $300 million drug loss. Perhaps one day I will get my chance."

Together, Thomas and Clark boarded an early morning Maya Island Air shuttle to Belize City. An American Airlines connection through Miami put them in Tallahassee by mid-afternoon. With daylight savings time in effect, over four hours of sunlight remained in the day. After renting a Chevy Tahoe, they decided to explore St. Marks for the remainder of the afternoon.

When they asked for directions, the friendly Avis rental clerk told them St. Marks was less than a 30-mile drive straight down 363 from the bypass. "Turn right out of the airport exit," she said. "Stay in the left lane and get onto the bypass. Keep heading south and 363 exits to the left midway round the loop. It's a short drive, but be careful to watch for all the fishin' traffic. It's bound to be a bit heavy this time of day."

Southbound traffic on the two-lane highway was indeed heavy. An array of pickup trucks and SUV's trailering boats to the area's coastal fishing villages clogged the highway. With the spring temperature in the mid-80s, Thomas and Clark lamented that they, too, would like to be headed out on the Gulf for a weekend of fishing. "But, regrettably, we know we must conduct business before pleasure," Clark noted.

Traffic slowed as it passed through the small communities of Lutterloh, Woodville, Vereen, and Wakulla. Soon they reached the intersection of U.S. 98. Clark informed Thomas that his map study had shown that 98 connected east with U.S. 19 and 27, then with Interstate 75 north and south. A short drive back up 363 to the Tallahassee bypass would connect with Interstate 10 and the western U.S.

"With St. Marks' nautical access, close airport proximity, and easy connection to the interstate highway system," Thomas said, "establishing a drug distribution conduit out of Florida would not pose the logistical problem I had feared it might."

Five miles further, they arrived in St Marks. Palm trees and palmetto bushes landscaped the highway as they entered town. On the left, huge oil depots stood as a testament to the former thriving oil transport industry. On the right was the remnant of a once busy motel. Time and the decline of the oil business had taken its toll. The motel was in desperate need of upkeep. A few scattered trucks and boat trailers were parked in front of its cabins. Fishermen milled around readying their craft and tackle in eager anticipation of tomorrow morning's outing.

The town of St. Marks was only seven streets in length. From the north edge of town, 363 became Port Leon Drive, which ended on the waterfront at First Street. It was on First Street that Clark and Thomas would begin their search for a suitable building from which to base their U.S. operation.

Crossing Sixth Street on the way in, they approached Two Rivers Restaurant, named for the two adjacent river systems. As they drove by, the fragrance of fried seafood wafted in the warm afternoon air. Hungry from their long flight, they knew where they would return for dinner.

Tired as well, they remembered they had made no prior motel reservations. Not wanting to return to Tallahassee for the night, they stopped by the restaurant to ask for local motel directions. With all the fishing traffic, they were concerned that there would be no place in St. Marks to stay the night. They needed to reconnoiter the town during the night as well as by day, and believed they would attract less attention if they were staying in town when they did so.

Opening the front door to the restaurant, they were greeted with the smell of seafood, the likes of which that had not found even in Belize. Though only 4:45 PM, the smell tempted them to stop and eat now rather than first seeking lodging. "May I help you, sirs?" the polite teenage hostess asked as they entered the restaurant.

"Yes, please. We just arrived in town. Before we return for dinner, we would like to know if you could recommend a nearby motel where we could spend the night?" Clark asked politely.

The sandy blond-haired girl responded, "Sir, the only motel we have is back up 363 on your left. We do have a fish camp though, which might have a room available. You could check, but it's the middle of speck season, and rooms usually stay filled this time of year. Especially on the weekend."

"It's worth investigating. Can you direct us there?" Clark asked.

"Out the parking lot, turn right back onto the highway. Turn left at the second street, that's Shell Island Drive, and just follow the signs to the fish camp. Road wanders around to the left through the slough before you get to the dry docks. Follow the gravel road pass the boat sheds, around the manager's office, and park anywhere in front of the marina. Just don't block the lift station. They get busy haulin' boats in and outta' the water this time of day. Check-in is inside the marina at the bait and tackle store. I sure do hope you get a room. Anyways, come back later and eat supper with us."

"Thank you very much." Clark said.

Thomas added, "We'll be back for, uh, supper, in a little while."

"Ya'll do that now, ya' hear!"

Thomas was chuckling as they returned to the Tahoe. He had forgotten that dinner in the South is commonly referred to as supper, and lunch is often referred to as dinner. It had been a while since he had heard these southern colloquialisms. They brought back fond memories of his youth in South Carolina.

He joked to Clark, "We must be careful if we're invited to dinner to ask, 'Would that be dinner at 12:00 PM or at 6:00 PM?'"

The girl was exact in her directions. The road did 'wander' a bit past mangrove swamps until it approached Shell Island. The fish camp was located on the Wakulla River about a half-mile upstream from where the Wakulla and St. Marks Rivers merged. Clark parked near the boat slips and away from the lift station. He was glad he had done so.

As they exited the Tahoe, they heard a loud roaring sound to their right. Rounding the corner between the dry docks was a 20-ton forklift carrying a 26-foot Twin Tower Stamus balanced on its outstretched forks.

Clark loved the sights, sounds, and smell of a marina. The outboard motor fumes mixed with the smells of salt air and the mangrove swamp conjured up warm childhood memories of happier times spent with his father. For a moment, he stood still, alive to everything surrounding him. Nostalgic, Clark thought back for a moment to the more civilized times in his life, back before he undertook a life of crime.

For a while, they watched the lift driver skillfully deposit the boat in the river alongside the boat dock. "Man, what a beautiful yatch!" Clark intoned.

"Must be a least a quarter mil," Thomas added. The two wished they had the opportunity to take a closer look inside the vessel.

The Shell Island Fish Camp dock rose and fell with the tide, giving mooring stability to the boats tied alongside. Once boats were tied to the dock, there was no concern for having to attend mooring lines during tide changes. Though rustic, the Shell Island Fish Camp offered the boating enthusiast and angler every modern convenience, including a vast assortment of bait and tackle. They hoped it would also offer them overnight shelter.

The outgoing tide pitched the gangplank leading dockside downward at a precariously steep angle. Clark and Thomas gingerly made their way onto the dock. Excited youthful voices could be heard even before they entered the bait and tackle shop. An older man stood behind the counter patiently attending three young preteens shopping for artificial lures for tomorrow's outing with their fathers.

Clark and Thomas overheard one boy excitedly exclaim to his friends, "Dad said these new chartreuse, curly-tail Salty Dog grubs are hot right now."

"Yeah, with the ¼ ounce red lead-head hooks," said a second.

"My Dad said to get a pack of Mercurochrome-colored curly-tails with the ¼ ounce yellow head hooks," another said enthusiastically.

"Mine wants two red-head with silver and black-spotted body Mirror Lures."

"Okay boys, I'll show you where they are in a minute. Ya'll look around for awhile longer whild'st I wait on these two gemmen here."

"How'dy folks. Wonna rent a boat for tomorrow?" he asked.

"Not this time, mister," Clark replied. "Thank you though, maybe another day. We're looking for a room for three nights. What's your regular room rate?"

"Fifty-five a night for a double, kids stay free."

"No kids. Just me and my partner."

"Do you have a room available?" Clark asked hopefully.

"Not right at the moment. Got one on hold 'til 5:00 PM though, but there's already a waitin' list. Two fishermen from up in Thomasville want the room. I'm s'posed to call 'um if it becomes available."

"It's about that time now, isn't it," Thomas noted.

"Yep, just a few minutes longer," the clerk replied.

"Think they'll show?" Clark asked.

"Nah, we're holdin' it for two good ol' boys from 'Bama. One of 'ums havin' an anniversary and his wife told him he danged shore better not even think about goin' fishin' this weekend. Told me his wife ain't gonna tell him what to do. Asked me to hold the room 'til five, then release it if they don't show. Appears they ain't comin' or they'd be here by now. Reck'n he had reconsideration for what his wife said he couldn't do!"

"Reck'n he did," Clark laughingly agreed.

"Well," the clerk continued, "it's five now, and they ain't here, so I guess the room's free."

"Think we might talk you into moving us up to the top of the waiting list?" Thomas goaded. "My friend, Ben Franklin, would really appreciate it."

"Huh!" Said the cashier.

Thomas pulled three hundred-dollar bills from his billfold and laid them on the counter. "You see, Ben surely was hoping he could get us a room here for three nights!"

The old man looked at the money, grinned, and said, "Now mister, I'm shore certain the owner wouldn't want me to disappoint yore friend, Ben. Room 112. Fill out this registration card if you don't mind."

"Now what kin I do fer ya, boys?" the cashier asked the three lads who had been waiting patiently.

Clark commented on the Southern slang with a chuckle as they left the marina, saying, "Thomas, welcome back to the country!"

"Yes," Thomas acknowledged, "it's been quite a while since I've heard this Southern drawl. It fondly reminds me of my childhood."

Their room was strictly 'no frills', but it was adequate and clean. Two doubles, AC, TV, and a bathroom. Indoor/outdoor carpet. Just what you would expect to find at a fishing village. Nothing comparable to last night's quarters at Captain Morgan's Retreat. But, then, neither was the price!

After a long, hot shower, they were ready for 'supper'. Exiting their room, they were greeted by the twilight 'no-see-ums' as the locals call them. "Ouch!" Clark cried as he swatted at the black swarm buzzing around his head. It was his first experience with the twilight plague.

Thomas laughed. He knew what they were, but had forgotten their omnipresence at dusk along the coast.

They were biting sand gnats, small as a pinhead, but whose bite causes intense itching. They hadn't been warned of these coastal residents. Tomorrow they would remember to replace their after shave with a splash of insect repellent!

When they pulled into the Two Rivers parking lot, it was almost full. The restaurant was famous throughout the Big Bend area of Florida for its seafood. On the weekend, tags from as far as three counties away could be found in the lot. Some had driven 80 miles to sample the seafood platters. With a waiting list and line already forming out the door, Clark and Thomas were afraid they would famish before they could be served.

As they went inside to register, the pretty hostess greeted them. "Right on time," she said. "Your table's ready. I guessed that you would be back around seven, so I made a reservation for you!" She smiled at the two.

Clark looked at the reservation's book as he passed the desk. Poking Thomas in the ribs, Clark smiled and pointed to one of the 7:00 PM time slots - Two 'out-of-towners' driving a Tahoe.

Clark sobered for a moment wondering why he ever got into the drug smuggling business, especially when nice people like this were often the victims of his trade.

It was but a fleeting thought.

The restaurant filled with laughter as tables of families and fishermen enjoyed both each other's company and the piles of seafood heaped on their plates. Looking at their menus, neither Thomas nor Clark could believe that a seafood platter comprised of a fish filet from your choice of grouper, snapper, or mullet, including shrimp, oysters, scallops, deviled crab cakes, hush puppies, and choice of salad or cole slaw was only $14.95.

Thomas grinned. "I hate to leave this good food," he said. Perhaps Diego could get another of his lieutenants to run the Belizean end of the business and let me work with you on this end."

Between mouthfuls of shrimp, Clark responded. "I know what you mean, Thomas. This seafood is the best I've ever eaten. If things go well here, perhaps we can persuade him to do so."

Despite the maddening pace at which the waitresses were required to serve their respective tables, they were nonetheless courteous and friendly. Just as importantly, they never let a tea glass get close to empty. Such food and service would rival that of even the most expensive resort. When the waitress presented their $32.54 bill, they tipped her a twenty.

As they left the restaurant, they also tipped the hostess $20.00. "Gee, thanks a lot, misters!" the bubbly hostess said. She expected no tip and was surprised when they acknowledged her at all.

"No, thank you for your thoughtfulness!" replied Thomas. "What is your name?"

"Cindy," she said.

"Well, Cindy, would you please make us a reservation again, for seven tomorrow night?"

"Sure Mr., uhh…"

"Clark and Thomas."

"Misters Clark and Thomas, 7:00 PM sharp. Gotcha down!"

Turning left out of the parking lot onto Port Leon Drive, they drove toward First Street in search of a market where they could buy some insect repellent. They wanted to walk around and smoke a cigar, but knew that without a dose of 'bug spray' it would be quite an unpleasant experience.

Since leaving Belize in the early hours of the morning, it had been a long day. By nine o'clock, they were ready for bed. Despite their meager furnishings, they slept soundly.

The marina showed signs of awakening at five the next morning. By six, boats were lined up and waiting their turn to be lifted into the water. Awakened by the busy sounds of the marina, Clark and Thomas dressed and walked to the bait and tackle shop to get coffee and doughnuts. Although it was just 7:00 AM, the marina was crowded.

CHAPTER SEVEN

T he three boys they had seen the previous evening had accompanied their fathers to the bait and tackle shop to buy live shrimp for the day's outing. The boys' exuberance was noticeably intoxicating to their fathers. All talked excitedly about the morning's fishing trip.

The boy's quizzed their guides as they readied the two vessels their fathers had rented for the day's excursion. One guide, Hank, was loading the two skiffs while his partner, 'Slim,' filled the auxiliary gas tanks.

"Where do you think we'll head out to this morning?" asked one boy excitedly.

"Good risin' tide this morning," Hank answered. "I thought we'd head west off the 'Klocknee Shoals 'til ebb. Whatcha' think, Slim?"

"Yep, drift the west flats this mornin', fingers, this afternoon." Clark and Thomas, still listening, learned that the fingers referred to the deep drop-offs running at right angles off the Live Oak Island channel which connected southeast with the St. Marks navigational lane. Some, 10-12 feet wide and as deep, were a hideaway for the crustaceans that came out of the channel on the rising tides to feed on the shallower water plankton.

While a fisherman's friend, these channels would prove disastrous for the submarine were it to veer only slightly off course as it approached the river entrance. The sub commander must remember to use caution here, Clark thought. One false turn would lodge the sub in the narrow channel, advertising its presence and effectively unraveling their smuggling operation.

The cashier from the previous evening who had been persuaded by a few Franklins to give them a room was working the loading dock this morning. "Mornin' fellas," he called as he spotted them walking along the dock. "Hope 'ya slept well."

"Fine," they responded.

"Sure you won't change yore mind about rentin' a boat?" he asked.

"Think we'll do just that." answered Clark.

"Fine, I'll gas this'un up fer ye. Just see the missus inside at the counter. She'll start ya a ticket."

"Ticket?" Thomas queried.

"Yup. We just run you an expense ticket. You don't have to pay daily. You just settle up the bill at the end of yore stay."

"Unbelievable," thought Thomas. "Anywhere else, you'd have to leave a credit card imprint before you even left the counter. Folks sure are trusting around here."

"We'd like to rent a boat, Miss." Clark stated as they walked inside.

"Not Miss, just Maggie." The clerk smiled. Suntanned and lean, somewhere around 45 years of age, Maggie looked as if she could wrestle alligators. These marina workers are hard working, hearty folks, Clark thought. He could tell Maggie had worked hard for most of her years.

Clark concluded that, if the other St. Marks area residents were as hard working as the marina staff, he would certainly have no problem hiring dedicated employees for the sugar refinery.

"How much for a boat, Maggie?"

"Whole or half day?"

"How much for each?"

"$100 half, $150 whole. You pay for gas, oil, ice, and bait separate."

"We'd like a rental for the whole day. Just gas and oil. No ice, nor bait."

"Ya' not fishin'?" she asked quizzically.

"Not today. We just want to take in the sights."

"It's your money, but the specks are bitin' real good right now. If you change your mind, you can rent tackle, too."

"Maybe tomorrow. We're in room 112. Gent outside said you'd start us a ticket?" Clark asked questionably.

"Gent!" Maggie laughed. "Bet ol' Cooter's never been called a gent before," she replied. "Sure, I'd be glad to start you a ticket."

"What time do we need to have the boat back?" Thomas asked. "We don't want to keep you working late."

Maggie smiled and said, "As they say 'round here, we work 'til dark-thirty. But, we'd like the boat back by five. We say five, 'cause if you're not in by then, we'll still have some daylight left to go out lookin' for ya'."

"Don't want you to have to do that now," said Clark. "We'll be back by five. Besides, we have a seven o'clock dinner reservation. Wouldn't want to be late for that!"

"You must have reservations at Two Rivers." Maggie said. "Best seafood anywhere!"

"You bet it is." Thomas replied.

After purchasing provisions, sunscreen, sunglasses, wide brimmed hats, and a navigational map, Clark asked Cooter for advice on navigating out to the Gulf.

"Easy navigating now while the tide is low." Cooter said. "You can see all the bars. Best be careful 'round ebb tide though, for some of the snags'll be just under water. Wouldn't want you to shear off the prop pin. It's a long paddle in! Just stay inside the triangles and cans and you won't run aground." Cooter explained that the 'triangles and cans' referred to the channel marker buoys that marked the outside edge of the deep-water river channel.

"Just keep the green cans on your right going down river and red triangles on the left. Just the reverse comin' in. Easiest way to remember is 'Keep the red on your right while returning.' Watch the 'No-Wake' zones and remember to slow to an idle speed when you're passin' an anchored or drifting fisherman. Courtesy rule of the water is, 'Don't rock the boat!' You'll hear plenty of cussin' if you do!"

"We'll be sure to remember," Thomas answered, chuckling. "Don't want to make any enemies around here on our first day out."

Clark cranked the outboard and Cooter gave them a shove off. Clark steered out into the clear water channel of the Wakulla and headed downstream. After a half-mile, the St. Marks merged from the left and the water became brackish. They were now officially in the St. Marks navigational lane. The depth gauge on the console read 38 feet. Sufficient depth for their sub, even at the lowest tide.

The eight-mile journey down the St. Marks passes through the St. Marks Natural Wildlife Refuge. There were no houses anywhere along the river. A single road a mile to the east managed by the Department of Natural Resources passed through the swamp and ended at the lighthouse. They could not have found a more isolated area as base for their U.S. operation. It seemed the perfect location. They were pleased with their good fortune thus far.

Upland swamps, fresh and brackish water tidal marshes, and a pristine salt-water estuary comprised this coastal ecosystem.

Traveling at a slow pace, they noticed a variety of birds alongside the river. Ospreys, egrets, and blue herons searching for a morning meal circled above the shallows along the marshland grass beds. Occasionally one would dive into the water with a resounding splash, only to emerge with a small pinfish or mullet in its beak. With one mid-flight flip of the bird's head, the fish was swallowed headfirst.

On nearly every marker buoy rested a brown pelican, some with wings outstretched as they sunned in the morning air. Everywhere there were sounds of black birds nesting in the sea grass. Flocks of sea gulls drifted by overhead searching for top-water minnow schools from which to feed.

An occasional gull would follow the boat close-by astern, squawking for a handout. Thomas would toss a Saltine Cracker into the air and watch the gull pluck it out of mid-air.

Despite the critical need to carefully survey and map the area, Clark and Thomas were enjoying this maritime adventure. They counted the buoys as they steered towards the mouth of the St. Marks. Red buoy stake number 62 marked the eastern turn into the St. Marks where the two rivers merged. Alternating with even numbers on the red buoys and odd numbers on the green, after 6 ½ miles, they came within first sight of the St. Marks lighthouse at buoy number 37.

On the previous night while waiting for dinner, Clark and Thomas had browsed the May/June issue of *Nature's Coastline*, the local magazine describing current events in the Big Bend area. In the magazine, they read with interest an article on the history of the lighthouse.

The article stated that the St. Marks lighthouse was first built in 1829 by Bostonian, Winslow Lewis, for a cost of $11,765.00. His finished product was found unacceptable because the walls were made hollow rather than solid. In 1831, Calvin Knowlton reconstructed the tower to assure stability. It was rebuilt again in 1842 when the soil beneath the foundation began eroding.

The white tower majestically rises 80 feet high and sits atop a 12-foot deep base. This solid foundation is made of limestone blocks taken from the ruins of old Fort San Marcos de Apalache that once guarded the ancient city of St. Marks. The walls of the tower are four feet thick at the base and taper to a solid 18 inches in thickness at the top.

The St. Marks light, originally a brass lamp, is now electrically powered. On a clear night, its 2,000 candlepower beacon can be seen for a distance of 15 miles. The original Fresnel reflector lens, made in Paris and installed in 1829, looks like a giant pineapple. A few noticeable scratches and chips in the lens are a result of the reflector being taken down by Confederate troops during the Civil War and hidden in the saltwater marsh.

The lighthouse, it seems, played a prominent role in Civil War history. In early March of 1865, a federal fleet of 16 warships anchored just offshore from the lighthouse. Here they began their attempt to capture Tallahassee. Retreating Confederate soldiers mined the lighthouse and its adjacent light-keeper's residence. Many of the advancing 1,000 Union troops were thus killed in their attempt to capture the lighthouse.

The citizens of nearby Woodville, many of them young teenagers, further thwarted the siege on Tallahassee as they pushed back advancing Union soldiers at Florida's historic 'Battle of Natural Bridge'.

During this attempted siege, the lighthouse sustained considerable cannon and shell shot damage. The lighthouse and tower were rebuilt to their present splendor in 1866. For over a century and a half, the St. Marks lighthouse has proudly stood sentinel, providing direction and warning to passing ships and barge traffic traveling up the St. Marks River.

Beginning at buoy marker 17 adjacent to the lighthouse, dozens of sand and oyster bars criss-crossed the perimeter of the channel. Built up by storms and changing tides over time, these bars stand as a solid barrier to navigation. Should a vessel steer out of the navigational channel, it would most assuredly become stranded.

"When we return with a GPS we must carefully chart these bars," Thomas remarked, "On a dark night, especially when these are invisible and only slightly submerged at high tide, one navigational miscalculation and our DSRV would run aground. Our operational disguise would then most assuredly be exposed."

As far on the horizon as they could see, from the east off the Gray Mare Rock Pile to the west off Live Oak Island, hundreds of boats glistened in the morning sunlight. "Perhaps we should rent tackle and try our luck at trout fishing in the morning," said Thomas. "Then tomorrow afternoon we can begin offshore at buoy number one, marking the GPS way points upriver into St. Marks."

As he watched joyous fishermen reel in fish after fish, Clark, too, was losing temporary interest in their task at hand. "Yes, we can at least take time in the morning to do some fishing of our own," he said. "Besides, a fishing outing will give us a reason to rent the boat again."

He mused out loud, "Miguel, do you ever wonder why you don't just take the money you have made and call it quits - just slip into anonymity somewhere like here?"

"Sometimes, like now I do, Wayne, when I see this slower pace of living. Then I remember that I am compelled to pursue a far greater goal

in my life. Continuing our drug smuggling venture is what keeps me motivated," Thomas said with a note of mystery in his voice. "It's my life-
blood."

"Me, too, I guess. But I'm getting tired of this almost constant cha-
rade."

Heading the skiff back upriver, they returned to the town of St.
Marks. "As we survey the depth of the river channel to make certain it is
deep enough for the mini-sub," Clark said, "we can search the riverfront
for a warehouse."

Soon the two reached buoy 62 and turned east, traveling up the St.
Marks towards the downtown riverfront. Boat traffic was heavy around
the beach area of the historical San Marco Fort, a sentinel that once
guarded early settlers from Seminole Indian attack. Reducing speed at the
'No Wake' zone allowed them to better survey the commercial property
that fronted the north side of the river.

The property on the south side was undeveloped marshland, lending
an extra degree of assurance that their covert operation had less a chance
of detection. Slowly trolling past the town's only fish house, workmen
were busy cleaning and packaging the day's catch of local fishermen.

The adjacent Shield's Marina was a bustle of activity. Fishermen re-
filled their fuel tanks for tomorrows' outing. Dockhands busily maneuvered boats out of the water and onto waiting trailers for their tow back to
the area motels and fish camps. Kids ran excitedly along the docks admiring each boat's catch.

Clark had learned that only during speck season was this much activity to be found in St. Marks. Much of the rest of the year's fishing was
relegated to the commercial shrimp and net fishermen. Their smuggling
operation would welcome the obscurity of these less busy times.

Continuing a slow pace along the riverfront, they reached Shield
Street. Here, the river made a sudden and sharp turn to the northeast as it
headed inland towards the Newport oil depots. At the turn, they noticed an
abandoned two-story warehouse that appeared to have once been a thriving commercial flourmill. A conveyor belt, long since rusted from the salt
air, ran from the loading dock to the bottom floor of the corrugated tin
building and disappeared through a loading gate.

The left side of the lower level appeared to be grain bins, while the
right half housed the office complex. The upper level, surrounded by large
glass windows, still contained milling equipment that had processed the
grain into flour. An inlet approximately 50 feet in length ran perpendicular

from the river alongside the east perimeter loading dock. A dilapidated, sagging tin roof that had once sheltered grain barges awaiting offloading, covered the inlet. A faded 'For Sale' sign was propped against the office door.

They had found the perfect place to front their U.S. smuggling operation. As Thomas watched the depth gauge, Clark carefully guided the skiff towards the sagging roof trusses. With the river at ebb tide, the depth read 38 feet. Even with an occasional low, negative tidal fall of 6 to 8 feet, sufficient depth would remain to commandeer the DSRV to port.

They shook hands, congratulating themselves on such a fortuitous find. Clark commented, "I expect we will have no trouble purchasing this property. There don't seem to be any other prospective buyers waiting to make an offer."

Thomas agreed. "I'd like to survey the area from shore." he added. "It's almost three o'clock now. Let's return the skiff and drive back to take a look around topside."

"Good idea," Clark agreed. "That's just what I was going to suggest."

Cooter was busy directing boat traffic around the Shell Island marina when they returned. "How'dy folks. Have a good outing?" Cooter hollered over the din of idling motors.

"Sure did, Cooter," Thomas answered. "Think we might rent the skiff again tomorrow?"

"Shore thang. Just tell Maggie and she'll put 'ya down. Just leave 'er here, boys, and I'll gas 'er up and have it waitin' fer 'ya in the mornin'."

"Thanks, Cooter," Clark replied. "Here's a twenty for your trouble."

"Much obliged, fellers!" Cooter shouted as they walked off.

Long lines of fishermen were waiting at the fish cleaning station for their turn to clean their catch. Clark and Thomas walked over to take a closer look at some of the huge fish on display. They peered into the ice chests at the fish waiting to be cleaned.

The three young boys they had seen earlier were now posing for pictures with their fathers and the day's catch. "Look-a-here, mister!" one of the boys exclaimed gleefully as he proudly held up a prized 5-pound speckled trout. "Took him with the red and silver spotted Mirror Lure. How'd ya'll do?"

"We didn't fish today. Just rode around getting our bearings," Clark answered. "We're considering going out tomorrow and trying our luck."

"You'll be missin' out on a great time if you don't!" another lad exclaimed. "This is more fun than Christmas!"

"Now you boys stop pestering these men," chided one of the fathers. "How do you do?" The man greeted Clark and Thomas. "My name's Jeff Thompson. These are my friends, Keith and John," he said as he introduced the other two fathers.

"I'm Wayne, and this is Michael." Clark responded as they all shook hands. "Looks like you had good luck today."

"We did. Hank and Slim, our guides really put us on 'um today. Fished west off the Panacea shoals this morning and drifted the drop offs near the river channel this afternoon. Overheard ya'll say you were going out tomorrow?"

"Looks like we'd be missing out on a good fishing opportunity if we don't," Thomas replied.

"Make sure you get an early start and head west-south-west off the light. Tide's low early, again, and it should be another good day for fishing." Thompson advised. "You guys aren't from around here, are you?" he asked.

"No," Clark answered. "We're here mainly to look at some downtown property. May want to invest in some real estate to start a local company."

His friend, Keith, quickly spoke up. "Again, I'm Keith Cason, a realtor from Tallahassee. I'd be glad to show you around if you'd like. I know just about every square foot of land in St. Marks."

"Alright," Clark responded. "What time do you think you'll be back in tomorrow?"

"Since it's Sunday, we usually fish the morning tide and head back to Tallahassee around mid-afternoon. I could send my son back with John and Jeff and stay to show you around. How's that sound?"

"It's set. We'll meet back here around three if that's alright with you."

"That's perfect. See you at three o'clock. Or maybe earlier if we cross paths in the morning!"

Keith Cason could hardly believe his good fortune. He might have chanced upon a sale in St. Marks. The real estate business had really been slow here. An occasional home sold, but not many commercial property sales were transacted.

He was excited at the prospect. As Clark and Thomas walked off, he said to his friends, "Dinner's on me tonight!"

Wayne and Miguel entered the tackle shop and arranged with Maggie to 'keep their ticket open'. "Thought we'd try our luck at trout fishing tomorrow, Maggie. Cooter is holding the boat for us. We'd like to rent some tackle. Could you get some gear ready for us to pick up tomorrow morning?" Clark asked. "We think you'd be better at selecting the rods, reels, and lures for us than we would."

"We'll be in around seven, if that's okay," Thomas added.

"That's fine. Be glad to. Room 112, wasn't it?" She asked.

"That's right. By the way, where can we purchase a GPS? We want to take some readings tomorrow while we're out."

"We sell 'um here. I'll have one charged and ready for you when you pick up your gear in the morning."

"Thanks, again," said Clark.

After a hot shower and a fresh change of clothes, Clark and Thomas doused themselves with insect repellant and headed towards Shield Street and Riverside Drive. From land, the abandoned building was even larger than it appeared from the water. They walked around the perimeter, peering into dirty windows.

The framing appeared structurally sound, though the perimeter and interior walls would require major renovation. The boat shed was too dilapidated to salvage. They had intended to demolish that anyway. They planned to construct a completely enclosed garage-type structure on a floating dock that would rise and fall with the changing tides. An electronic roll-up door riverside would create the appearance of a boat shed, serving as a façade to disguise the presence of the submarine when it was docked inside.

A hoist, concealed in the wall structure, would be used to lower the DSRV underwater once it had been unloaded. A surface vessel could then be moved into the enclosure and moored topside, hiding the presence of the submersible stowed underneath. It was a perfect plan.

True to her word, Cindy had their dinner reservation waiting when they arrived a little before seven that evening. The smell of seafood reminded them of their hunger. Despite the provisions they had taken with them on their day's reconnaissance, they had eaten little. After another succulent seafood dinner, they returned to the Shell Island Fish Camp and contacted Diego using the Onyxitron Encryptor.

Juan Carlos reported that the DSRV had been purchased from the Russians and was being retrofitted in Japan with the MK-6 computer guidance system. It would be ready for shipment in about four weeks. Allowing another two weeks for transportation, it should arrive in the early fall, around the same time as the Belize mill reconstruction was expected to be complete.

Diego was excited to learn of their success in locating a facility for their U.S. base of operation. "Complete the purchase as soon as possible," he urged. "Vicente now has our account established through Grand Cayman Capital Trust. You can have the realtor's financial institution contact Vicente directly to transfer purchase funds."

Juan Carlos continued, "Marco Najera has finalized the purchase of our Belizean property. Until you can return, Miguel, I have employed my brother, Ortega, to direct reconstruction of the sugarcane mill. He was only too happy to move his family out of Columbia to live in Belize. Ortega said that he would like to stay there and work with you on the shipping end. How much longer do you think it will take you to complete your business there in Florida?"

Miguel responded. "We will meet with the realtor tomorrow to initiate the purchase of the property. It will take more work to set up our operation here than it will in Belize. I would estimate at least three months. Hopefully, by the end of August or mid-September."

Juan Carlos asked Clark, "Wayne, who will direct the American distribution end of the operation?"

"I've thought about that, Juan Carlos. It would be easier to coordinate our smuggling activities if we have someone here who knows both ends of the operation. If you think Ortega can handle the Belizean shipment end, I believe it would be best to have Miguel stay here and take over distribution. That is, if he would like to and you have no objection."

"What are your thoughts, Miguel?" Juan Carlos asked.

"I, too, think it would be best. I would be glad to assume responsibility of the refinery end of the business if you have confidence in Ortega's ability to manage the sugarcane processing," Thomas replied.

"I do, and I concur with Wayne's reasoning. Because of your knowledge of our trafficking plans, you are the best choice to manage the refinery and receive the smuggled cocaine - that is if Wayne would like to hire you as his manager."

"I would."

"It's settled then." Diego said. "I will supervise the shipments out of Columbia to Belize. Ortega will manage the packaging and shipment out of Belize to the U.S. You, Miguel, will handle the repackaging for distribution out of Florida, and Wayne will manage U.S. distribution and collection of sales. All agreed?"

"Agreed," responded both Clark and Thomas.

"One other loose end, Wayne," said Diego. "Have you thought of a new way to launder the drug sales cash through a legitimate U.S. business?"

"No, I have not. When I return to my CIA office on Monday, I will work on a plan. I'll report back to both of you when everything is finalized."

Juan Carlos concluded, "Miguel, let me know when the St. Marks' property sale has been completed and, Wayne, get in touch when you have finalized your money laundering plans."

"I will," both replied.

Miguel Thomas was delighted at the chance to remain in America. Admittedly, he was glad to be back in the U.S. He liked Florida and was certain he could better accomplish his long-term goals in life from there.

Tired from the day's activities, they were asleep again by nine, as were most other resident fishermen. The croaking of frogs was the only noise that disturbed the serenity of the peaceful night. They slept soundly and awakened at six as the marina came to life. After a restful night's sleep, they were excited to combine a morning of trout fishing with the job of mapping a percise navigational course for the DSRV.

A breakfast of coffee, juice, and pastries at the marina fueled their eagerness to take to the Gulf. As promised, Maggie had their tackle assembled and Cooter stowed it in their skiff as they purchased fishing licenses and provisions for the day. After Maggie instructed them on the proper use of the displays and functions of the GPS, they motored away from the marina.

Despite the early morning hour, the heat and humidity were almost unbearable. There was no wind and the idle speed created little breeze to relieve the heat. They were glad when they passed the 'No-Wake' zone and could accelerate. The increased speed created a welcome breeze that helped to cool the humid air. Twenty minutes later they had entered the Gulf offshore of St. Marks Light.

Once safely past the sand and oyster bars that lined the navigational channel, they steered west-southwest toward the Ocklocknee shoal flats. It was easy to identify the fishing area where schools of speckled trout and Spanish mackerel were congregated. As many as a dozen boats were already drift-fishing in the area.

Maggie had advised them that fishing would be best in these shallow-water grass flats. Watching the depth gauge as they motored towards the boats, they noticed the depth fluctuated between six and eight feet. Suddenly the gauge changed to a steady four feet and the water became clearer. Long blades of sawgrass waved back and forth in the current.

Flashes of silver and gray could be seen darting through the grass.

They became excited. So this was what they had overheard all the fishemen discussing around the fish cleaning station. These were the 'flats', and the flashes of silver and gray were schooling specks and mackeral darting among among the blades of sawgrass as they fed on the smaller pinfish and shrimp.

So as not to cross other fishermen's cast lines, they idled their motor and observed the movement of the other boats as they drifted with the wind and the current. A light offshore breeze made the heat less noticable and served to propel the craft along on a steady drift. Several boats had cast out marker buoys which seemed to indicate the northern and southern boundries of the schooling fish.

As the boats reached the northernmost marker, the fishermen reeled in lines and speed back to the southern marker. Clark positioned his skiff outside of the southern marker and cut the motor. Soon they too, were drifting northwest in position where they would not interfere with other fishermen's casts.

Following the advice of the young boys in the tackle shop, from the artificial lures Maggie had selected for their tackle boxes, they chose a red-headed Mirror Lure with a red dorsal back and silver sides with black spots. They noticed that the lure seemed to most resemble the baitfish upon which the larger trout and mackeral were feeding. Quickly they tied a 20 pound leader wire onto their line and fastened a Mirror Lure to the swivel. They were ready to fish.

Casting downwind, they soon learned the technique for casting line from the open-faced reels without backlashing. They fished with a slow and steady retrieve but without any luck. All the boats in the drift but them were netting fish. Thomas commented, "We must be doing something wrong. Let's stop for a minute to observe how the others are fishing."

"Good idea." Clark agreed.

They had fished enthusiasticly but had not yet mastered the art of retrieve required to entice a strike. Miguel noted, "The locals hold their rod tip low to the water and perpendicular to their body as they reel. They often added a slight wrist twitch as they reel."

Smiling at having discovered the 'art' of trout fishing, they recast their lines.

"I seem to have hung up on the bottom," Thomas shouted. As his rod tip doubled, his line zinged across the bail as the boat continued its drift. Suddenly he felt a strong tug on the line and watched in amazement as it began to change direction under the waves. Fishing on the bow, he had hung a huge Spanish mackeral that was noticably peeling line off his reel while turning the boat sideways.

"Tighten your drag," cried Clark from the stern, as he too felt his rod bend from the strike of a large trout. Each battled his quarry as they bantered back and forth. Now they could see why the locals were so fervent about the springtime flats fishing. They, too, were hooked!

Their passion would grow with each passing retrieve and strike. Soon they began to perspire under the hot morning sun. "Let's stop for a cool drink before we make another drift," Thomas said.

They settled back in their seats, enjoying the excitement around them as fish after fish was netted from neighboring boats. "This certainly is great fun!" Clark commented. "I'm glad we decided to try our luck this morning."

"I am, too," Thomas agreed.

They had almost caught their limit of seven trout and four mackeral each and were readying to reposition the boat for another drift. Suddenly the air was rocked with vibration. They felt the vibrations before they heard the noise. Flying in low formation over the water, two blue Navy ensignia Sea Hawk helicopters approached from the east.

The whirling rotors vibrated the water as they slowly passed over-head. The reality of their presence suddenly lessened Clark and Thomas' passion for fishing. They watched as the helicopters veered southwestward along the coast, surveying the recreational craft and coastline for any sign of drug smuggling activity.

Having enjoyed their sport fishing respite, it was time to resume the primary task for which they had returned to the Gulf. A three-mile run to the east took them back to the navigational channel of the St. Marks River. At buoy marker one, two miles offshore of the lighthouse, they began mapping a course for the DSRV. As Clark steered the boat in the center of the navigational channel, Thomas began entering GPS waypoints.

Heading inshore, Thomas set a new waypoint every 50 feet. As they approached marker 11 and began navigating around the sand and oyster bars upriver, a directional point was set every 15 feet. When they reached marker 62 where the Wakulla and St. Marks Rivers divided from the main channel, Thomas set a directional point every 10 feet. As they approached the downtown riverside docks, a waypoint was set every five feet until Clark steered the skiff into the inlet alongside the old grain mill.

They congratulated themselves on having successfully plotted a precise navigational course that would guide the mini-sub through the maze of perilous bars that threatened navigation upriver. Clark would transfer these satellite directional readings onto a computer disk that would then be encoded into the DSRV's computer guidance system. They were confident that with this precise guidance information, the autopilot could safely navigate the sub from offshore to the security of its anchorage in port without running aground.

With their GPS mapping task completed, Clark guided the skiff back to the Shell Island Fish Camp where they returned the boat and tackle to Cooter. "Ya'll back early." Cooter commented. "Did'ja have any luck?"

"Quite a bit," Thomas professed, opening the ice chest for Cooter's inspection.

"Whew! That's a mighty nice mess o' fish! Should make ya' some good eatin,'" Cooter expressed admirably.

"We don't have time to clean them, Cooter. Think you might know someone who would like to have them?" Clark prompted.

"Shore do." Cooter answered, rubbing his chin wryly. "Reckon' I might have time to clean 'um myself, that is if yore certain ya' don't want 'um." He added.

"They're yours, then. Hope you enjoy them for supper," Thomas replied.

"'Preciate it," he said thankfully.

Clark spoke up. "You're certainly welcome, Cooter. Thanks for all your help this weekend." Pulling a twenty from his billfold, he handed it to Cooter saying, "Here's a little tip for all your troubles."

"Much obliged, fellers, but it warn't no trouble at all. Glad to be o' service. Ya'll come back again real soon now, won't 'ya?"

As they walked into the marina to pay their bill, Cooter acknowledged aloud, "Mighty fine gemmen, them two are!"

Clark asked, "Maggie, do you mind if we settle our account today? We'll be leaving early tomorrow morning."

"Glad to," Maggie replied. "Enjoyed havin' 'ya with us. Ya'll come back again now, 'ya hear!"

"We'll be back. I promise," Thomas said graciously.

CHAPTER EIGHT

At precisely 3:00 PM, after a shower and change of clothes, Thomas and Clark returned to meet Keith Cason at the marina. "Hope ya'll had a good outing," Keith expressed as they shook hands.

"We did," Thomas answered. "Nine trout and six Spanish before we quit. Thanks for advising us where to go."

Sportingly Clark asked, "How did you and the boys do?"

"We limited out on the morning rise. As usual, the boys had a great time. They're still busy over at the fish cleaning station. They'll probably be there awhile. Thanks for getting me out of the cleaning chores!"

"Now where did you say you wanted to look at some property?" Cason prompted, steering the conversation around to the business at hand. "Why don't we hop into my Suburban and I'll drive us there."

"Know where Riverside Drive and Shield Street are?" Clark questioned.

"Certainly."

"We thought we might be interested in the old grain mill."

"Have us there in a moment." Cason assured. They reached the mill site in less than five minutes. "Come on, and I'll show you around. As we walk along, I'll tell you the history of the property."

"This once was a productive flour mill," Keith Cason explained. "The property last belonged to the Matson brothers. Both are dead now and the property is in trust with the Apalachee Coastal Savings and Loan in Tallahassee. Relatives in New Jersey inherited it."

"They ran the mill unsuccessfully for a while from out of state and finally decided to close it. They had no desire to relocate here in hopes of turning a profit. They've had no luck selling the property. Paying the real estate taxes is putting a tremendous financial burden on the heirs. I expect it could be bought for a fraction of its estimated property value. I'm quite certain they would be eager to sell!"

"As a result of the slow down in oil imports, the entire coastal economy is in a recession," Cason said. "A couple of former mill supervisors tried to borrow the money to restart the mill. It would have been a real boost to the local economy if they could have done so, but they were unable to raise the investment capital."

"What do you intend to do with the property, if you don't mind me asking?" quizzed Cason of his two potential buyers.

"We have interests in a sugarcane processing plant in Belize," Clark answered. "We are interested in building a sugar refinery in the United States where we would import the raw sugar from Belize. From here, we would then wholesale the refined sugar. I believe that with a little capital investment, we could easily convert the grain mill into a sugar refinery."

"I would certainly think you could!" exclaimed Keith Cason, enthusiastic for a sale.

Thomas asked, "What should we expect of this area's workforce potential? I anticipate we would need to hire up to three dozen refinery workers."

"I know there is a good and available workforce. The locals are hardworking people. Certainly, they would need to be specially trained, but I'm sure you would be pleased with those you hire. They pride themselves in a willingness to work 'from can 'til can't!' as they say around here."

"I know," agreed Thomas. "I've noticed that same quality in the people working at the Shell Island Fish Camp. They work long, hard hours, seemingly without complaint."

Clark seconded Thomas' observations. "I have no doubt we will be able to find a sufficient number of reliable workers. Now, let's discuss purchase of the property. What's the market price?"

"There are 14.4 acres here. The trust is asking $360,000, or $25,000 an acre. I would expect it could easily be bought for $200,000, less than $15,000 an acre." Clark smiled in agreement, and Thomas winked at him in acknowledgement.

Clark explained that he was leaving for Miami in the morning, but Michael would remain to close the deal. "If the trust company will agree to sell the property for $200,000, Mr. Cason, then we have a deal."

Thomas continued, "I'll drop Wayne off at the airport and meet you at your office at say, 1:00 PM tomorrow, if that's agreeable."

"Wonderful!" Cason exclaimed. "I will begin negotiations with Apalachee Coastal's trust department first thing in the morning. Perhaps by the afternoon, we can finalize the sale. My real estate office is located at the intersection of Capitol Bypass NE and Miccosukee Road, adjacent to the

Savings and Loan. You will pass right by my office tomorrow."

"I'll be on the lookout for it as I drive Wayne to the airport." remarked Thomas. "I'll meet you there at 1:00 PM."

"If you're ready to go now," Cason offered, "I'd like to take you to dinner. Would Two Rivers be okay? After dinner I'll drive you back to the fish camp."

"That's fine with me," Clark replied as Thomas too, agreed.

During dinner, Cason made mental calculations of his realtor's fee. He figured that at his usual 6% fee, he would make a quick $12,000.00! Not too bad a catch for a weekend fishing retreat!"

Next morning before 6:30, Clark and Thomas were headed to Tallahassee. Clark had a 9:30 AM flight back to Miami where he had to finish his report for CIA Director Terry Fortson. Just before he departed, Clark stated to Thomas, "Miguel, call me as soon as the property deal has been made. You know all transactions should be made through Vicente."

"I know. I'll call as soon as possible," he promised. "So long, Wayne. I expect I will be talking to you soon. Keep the Onyxitron charged!"

"I will. So long."

Miguel stopped by Avis to extend rental of the Tahoe for another week. Four hours remained before his appointment with Cason. As he planned on staying in the area a while longer, he needed to shop for some more clothes. On their way to the airport, he had noticed Kevin's Outdoor World off the Capitol Circle Bypass, not far from Cason's office. He decided to stop and look around.

The store was literally what it advertised. There was a section devoted to almost every imaginable outdoor recreational sport. The entire back half of the store was devoted to hunting and fishing supplies and clothing. Thomas grinned; he would have no trouble idling the time here until his appointment.

He was amazed at the variety of artificial baits and lures. In assorted sizes, shapes, and colors, there were lures designed from the smallest pan fish to those made for the larger sailfish and marlin. He investigated row after row of displays. When he came to the Mirror Lure section, he noticed that most of the red head with silver body and black dots were sold. Smiling, he now understood why!

He chose several pair of khaki shorts and cotton pullovers, a pair of boots, a Gortex waterproof rain suit, and more insect repellent. As he paid for his purchases, he realized he had only an hour remaining to eat lunch. He had perused the store for three hours. It only seemed like one. With his newfound hobby, he had enjoyed just 'lookin' around,' as the young boys at Shell Island would have said.

After a hasty Italian meal, he drove to the realty office. Cason greeted him warmly, extending his hand before Thomas had entered the building. "I have good news!" Cason exclaimed. "They have accepted your offer. All that is left to do is make financial arrangements, sign the papers, and transfer the title. Isn't that splendid news?"

"Yes, quite," Thomas replied.

Cason didn't tell him he could have saved him $100,000 on the purchase. The trust would have taken half the $200,000 he and Clark had agreed to pay. When Cason called the trust officer, he didn't even negotiate a price. He simply said, "I know the trust is asking $360,000. My clients are willing to pay $200,000. Take it or leave it!"

"Take it," the trust officer said without hesitation. "But the owners are willing to accept half that amount just to get rid of it."

Not wanting to loose a $6,000 commission, Cason replied, "My clients have offered two hundred. Just take it and close the deal! He hesitated a moment, then prompted, "You could up my commission to 10 % for being so generous with my client's money."

"Deal," said the loan officer David Langley.

A $20,000 commission! Cason was ecstatic. Now he could afford that nice Center Console boat he and his friends had been admiring. It was perfect for trout fishing. He welcomed his luck. "Just a matter of being in the right place at the right time, and taking advantage of what's offered to you," he postulated.

Cason searched Thomas' face for a hint of suspicion of his deception, but found none. Thomas was secretly pleased with the acceptance of their offer. Cason couldn't possibly have known that without blinking an eye, Clark and Diego would have paid a half-million for the property.

Thomas advised, "I want all transactions handled through Romano Vicente, President and CEO of Grand Cayman Capital Trust on Grand Cayman Island. Here is Vicente's phone number. Do you think Apalachee Coastal Savings and Loan can handle that transaction for us?"

"I'm sure they can. Let me call my friend, David Langley in trust."

When Cason repeated the question, Langley responded, "Of course. I'll call you as soon as a transfer of payment has been received."

Ten minutes later, the funds were transferred. When the trust officer called with the news, Cason put him on speakerphone. Langley advised, "I will have our institution's attorney complete a title search and draw up the necessary papers for transfer of title."

"Under what name shall I place the title of new ownership?" Langley asked. "Caribbean Sugar Export Partners, Limited." Thomas responded as an extemporaneous thought. Clark and Diego had forgotten to discuss this small detail. Thomas listed the partner's first and middle names as principle owners.

Langley continued, "This transaction should be complete by noon tomorrow. Would it be convenient for you to come here around two in the afternoon to sign the papers?"

Keith Cason looked quizzically at Thomas who nodded affirmatively. "We'll be there," he responded.

Precisely on time to sign the transfer papers, Miguel and Keith Cason were ushered into the Savings and Loan Company's conference room. An array of papers lay before them on the conference table. All financial transactions had been completed with the exception of Thomas' signature. He signed, Michael. M. Thomas, d.b.a. 'St. Marks Sugar Refinery', 'For the Partnership' And with that, the sale was complete.

David Langley thanked Thomas and added, "I hope you will consider allowing our institution to continue to serve your banking needs. We could have checks available for your use within 24 hours notice."

"That is a kind offer. I will discuss it with the partners and let you know."

As they left the Savings and Loan, Keith Cason was profuse with his thanks and offered the obligatory, "If ever I may be of service to you, again, please do not hesitate to call. We'll have to get together and go fishing soon. I'd love to take you out in my boat."

As soon as Thomas drove away, Cason planned to go directly to Capitol Circle Marine and make its purchase.

"Perhaps." Thomas replied. Fishing was now not foremost on his mind. He was focused on getting the U.S. base of operation completed as soon as possible.

"By the way," Thomas added as they walked to the parking lot, "Can you recommend an architect who could assist me in my remodeling plans?"

Despite his anxiousness to depart to purchase his new fishing rig, Cason replied. "Yes, I can. In fact, two brothers, Alton and Albert Roberts, are friends of mine and should be able to help you. One brother does the architectural design and the other the construction. They are very reputable and specialize in large government projects. I will be glad to call their office on my car phone and get you an appointment."

"Thank you." Thomas replied.

Reaching his vehicle, Cason dialed. "Hello, Fran. This is Keith Cason. May I please speak to Alton?"

"Certainly, one moment, please."

Alton's voice came on the line. "Hello, Keith. How are you? How's the family?"

"We're all fine." Cason replied. "How's your family?"

"We're all fine, too," Alton responded.

With the pleasantries out of the way, Roberts asked, "What may I do for you, Keith?" He knew Cason would not call him at work unless it was business related.

"Listen, Alton, I would like to refer a client to you. I have you on my car speakerphone with a Mr. Michael Thomas. We're just leaving Apalachee Coastal Savings and Loan. His offshore partnership has just bought the old Matson brother's grain mill in St. Marks. They plan to remodel the mill into a sugar refinery. I told Mr. Thomas you could manage such a project."

"Thank you, Keith, and good afternoon, Mr. Thomas. I would be very interested in talking with you concerning your renovation plans," Roberts responded.

"Good afternoon to you, too," Miguel replied. "When do you think we might get together and talk?"

"Today, if that's convenient with you. Is the rest of your afternoon free?" Alton inquired. "I'm available to stay as late today as you need."

"Yes, this afternoon is convenient for me." Thomas answered.

"Good. Keith can give you directions. We're only two blocks west on Miccosukee Road."

"I'll be there in less than five minutes."

"Fine, I'll be waiting. And, thanks again, Keith."

"You're welcome, Alton. Bye now, and thanks for taking care of my client."

Keith Cason was excited again. The Roberts brothers always gave him a hefty fee whenever they signed a referral client. "Of course," Cason reasoned, "Thomas need not know that, either."

Cason was certain the Roberts brothers could provide the services Thomas needed.

Miguel arrived promptly. Impressed with the modern architectural design of the building, he had a positive feeling about this meeting. After formal greetings, Alton showed him representative display models and pictures of their past architectural and construction projects. Sensing Thomas was ready to talk, Alton said, "Come. Why don't we sit down and discuss the general details of your project? I am familiar with the old grain mill, and I'll take notes as you discuss your plans."

"Of course, you are under no obligation to contract with us. After our initial discussion today, if you think we can be of service to you, I would certainly welcome the opportunity." Miguel immediately liked Alton Robert's forthright professionalism.

Thomas told Roberts of their plan to transform the plant into a sugar refinery. "We will purchase all necessary equipment. To help in a draft of the blueprints, we would provide you with an equipment list, its relative location within the facility, and the equipment's physical dimensions."

Roberts asked, "Other than utilizing the first floor for milling operation, what other plans do you have for remodeling and construction?"

"The second floor will become a state-of-the-art laboratory for conducting chemical analysis and product quality assurance testing," Thomas answered. "We will purchase that equipment and assure its installation." Equipment that would serve as a façade for repackaging powdered cocaine and for producing crack cocaine, Miguel thought.

Continuing, he said, "We also plan to build a connecting boat storage facility over the adjacent canal. It will be completely enclosed, much like a car garage. We would have you design and construct a mooring facility within, whose interior dock will rise and fall with the changing tides. The riverside entrance must have an electronic door that would automatically roll up and down much like a garage door. Could you design such a boat housing?"

Alton Roberts answered, "Design and construction would be no problem. Cost, though, might be a concern to you. All metal parts must necessarily be fabricated using stainless steel. In the salt air, even galvanized steel and zinc-plated metals will eventually deteriorate."

"Cost will not be a concern," Thomas answered candidly.

"There is one more construction plan relative to the dock facility that must be kept secret. For security purposes, we do not want its design even detailed in the overall construction plans. It will require its own separate set of blueprints."

Mystified, Alton thought to himself. To what could he be referring? He could understand a request for perhaps, an underground storage tunnel or room. But not at sea level. What could they possibly construct in an enclosed boathouse that would require such secrecy? He was intrigued.

Miguel, sensing his perplexity, continued, "We need you to design and construct a special hoist system. Constructed of the type of 'belly-band' strap system that marina's use to lift a boat on or off a trailer."

Roberts was puzzled. Quite baffled in fact, at the request for secrecy for such a common marine structure, he interjected, "That is not a problem. It is quite common to see these suspension lifts at marinas and private boat bocks throughout the Gulf Coast. They provide a very effective dry-docking mechanism. By fastening an electric winch to the ceiling above the water and lowering straps under the bow and stern of the boat, the winch simply lifts the boat free of the water.

"Again, these lift systems employ a very common hoist mechanism that is used extensively throughout the Gulf coast and other marine environments."

Thomas patiently allowed him to finish his assertion. "We do need a dry docking winch lift installed in the boathouse. We will use this mechanism to dock the fishing vessel we intend to purchase. Using a dry-docking hoist rather than mooring certainly better protects the vessel in high wind and wave conditions. Even when a boat is moored to an enclosed, floating dock, as ours will be."

Miguel continued, "Our operation will require a rather special type of hoist assembly to be constructed in the boathouse in addition to the overhead wench - an unusual system that will operate underwater. Rather than serve as a mechanism to lift a boat up and out of the water, this hoist system would function principally to lower objects from the surface of the water down to the bottom of the inlet."

He went on. "Its hoist assembly will operate similarly to the winch mechanism. The system would employ strap-bands upon which an object would rest as it is lowered underwater. Like the above water structure of the boathouse, the underwater configuration must have an egress to the river. Rather than a roll-up door, the submersible cavity would utilize an underwater riverside door that would swing outwards beneath the surface of the river."

"What are you designing, an underwater safe-harbor for a submersible craft?" Roberts jokingly asked.

"Thomas had anticipated this question, and answered with feigned laughter. "No, this part of our operation is the most secretive. We will conduct scientific tests on the stability of both raw and refined sugar when sealed in airtight containers and stored at varying atmospheric pressures.

My partners have hypothesized that the raw sugar will retain a more stable molecular structure, and thus retain its sweetness longer, when it is exposed to a colder temperature and greater external pressure, than it does when it is stored at ambient temperature and atmospheric pressure."

"Similar principle to food remaining preserved for a much longer period of time when frozen in depressurized airtight containers, than when frozen in a zippered-closure container. Makes sense doesn't it?" Thomas asked. He was hoping the architect's scientific knowledge was limited to algebra and trigonometry, rather than physics and biochemistry.

"I guess," a perplexed Roberts answered.

"Building an apparatus that can be lowed underwater, thus subjecting its contents to a colder, greater external pressure, will be less expensive that constructing a hyperbaric chamber for the same purpose."

"All that I have told you, of course, is to be kept confidential. Please repeat this to no one, other than Albert, of course, as you must. If our hypothesis is proven true, this could revolutionize the sugar processing industry. We would have an edge on the world market with a processed sugar product possessing a superior sweetness. Sort of like a concentrated powdered sweetener, if you will."

Lost in this hypothesis, Roberts considered Thomas' completely ludicrous explanation and his biochemical absurdity. After only a short period of contemplation, Alton scratched his head, and laughingly responded, "We'll just design and build it. You do the experimenting."

Looking less perplexed, Roberts appeared either to have bought Thomas' explanation or he recognized that it was technically beyond his comprehension. Either way, it was their money, thought Alton. If his clients were willing to pay for it, he and Albert were willing to design and construct it.

Assured that Roberts was satisfied with his explanation, Thomas continued, "To test this hypothesis we need you to design a hoist system that would allow pallets of sealed containers to be lowered to various depths within the inlet."

Then to ease the conversation back toward Roberts' architectural specialty, Miguel asked, "Do you think you can handle such a challenging request?"

Knowledgeable in architectural mechanics, Roberts contemplated the request then knowingly responded, "Your underwater hoist system will definitely be a design challenge, but not an insurmountable construction project."

"I sense you already have some thoughts on a design plan?" Thomas asked questionably. "Am I right?"

"I do have a few thoughts," Alton responded. "I believe the whole carriage assembly could be constructed at a metal fabrication plant that specializes in stainless steel construction. Built in two or three sections, these could easily be shipped by truck to the mill site. There they would be offloaded by crane, then welded together into a single piece mechanism."

"Once assembled," Alton said, "the crane would lower the unit into place in an underwater concrete frame. After the carriage system has been put in place, the motor system would be built and hidden within a concrete floor frame. Next, the hoist assembly would be constructed and concealed in the block wall structure."

Roberts concluded, "I'm positive I could design, and my brother could construct such an assembly that would be completely concealed from view."

"None but our crew would know what we were constructing, and they wouldn't have enough interest to even ask questions. They know from past government projects, that construction confidentiality is essential to their job security."

Continuing Roberts noted, "Until the hoist assembly is constructed and concealed, to provide maximum site security we would surround the property with a chain link fence topped with barbed-wire. Additionally, we could impose a 'Dangerous Construction – No Trespassing' restriction on the property."

Miguel responded, "That should certainly be sufficient to secure the construction site. We would appreciate it if you could do that."

Continuing, he remarked, "Time is essential to our operation. We would like to be operational by the end of August if possible. Do you think it is a realistic expectation to hope construction could be completed in 14 to 16 weeks?"

"My brother, Albert, will finish a project at Florida State University in two weeks. His demolition crew should be available now to begin razing all but the existing framework. If I can complete your blueprints in two weeks, his framing crew could start by the second week in May."

Roberts continued, "Depending on the availability of milling equipment and how soon it could be available for on-site instillation, I see no problem with construction completion by the end of August, first week in September tops. That is, if you are willing to pay for overtime and any extra crew that would be necessary to complete your project by your target date."

Thomas responded, "We are."

Miguel continued resolvedly, "Alton, I like what you have said, and so will my partners. I will contact them tonight and discuss signing a contract with your firm. The contract will be contingent, of course, on design approval and your brother's construction timetable."

Alton said, "I will talk with Albert tonight to see when he can start his demolition team. Can you come back tomorrow after lunch where we can talk further? Say, 1:00 PM?"

"Yes, I can."

"Good, I'll see you tomorrow," answered Roberts. He could envision a big profit from this project. Experience had proven that any request for a rapid construction completion always brought a willingness to pay handsomely for the expedience.

Miguel ate a late dinner. When he returned to his hotel, it was almost midnight. He was tired but knew he must call Clark. Their conversation was short but gratifying. Clark was pleased with his choice of partnership and business names. He was amused at Miguel's deceptive explanation of their reason for needing an underwater hoist. "That was good thinking!" he laughed complimentarily. "Diego, too, will be pleased."

"You have done a fine job for us, Miguel. Thanks for your hard work. Your responsibilities to process cocaine shipments for distribution and to manage the mill's legitimate sugar refinery are paramount to the success of our smuggling operation. I feel it only right to give you as well as Ortega a share of the profits. I will talk with Juan Carlos about making both of you an equal partner. I'll call you soon."

"Many thanks, Amigo!"

CHAPTER NINE

Though well over fourteen months remained before the Presidential primaries, the campaign rhetoric was becoming as heated as were the late spring temperatures. This would be a high-stakes election year. Control of the House and Senate, as well at the presidency was up for grabs. With the possible retirement of three U.S. Supreme Count Justices, the next President would additionally have the opportunity to appoint persons who could reshape America's justice system.

Even state legislative parties were preparing for a hard fought election. Census results would redraw and realign both congressional and legislative districts.

This election would have a tremendous impact on American politics. From those aspiring for local city councils, up to the state House, and on to the White House, politicians were beginning to expound their political principles. A. Bixby Lane was not the least of them.

Those of the Republican persuasion promoted their generally moderate political views. Principally conservative in their viewpoints and proposed legislative agenda, conservatives supported free-market economic principles and lower taxes. In general, they supported a stronger local and state government and favored less federal bureaucracy. Conservatives tended to distrust the media and its often-obvious attempts to promote a more liberal governmental agenda.

Conversely, those of the Democratic Party promoted their mostly liberal political views. Liberals tended to favor a stronger federal government and believed that Congress was responsible for remedying social injustices. Generally, they supported a woman's right to choose when and if to give birth and supported similar freedoms of personal choice.

Overall, the media seemed to favor liberal viewpoints. There were certain of the media who strongly favored A. Bixby Lane as the Democratic Presidential candidate. Never shy about granting an interview, Lane had thus received considerable free campaign press coverage.

Despite the media's focused attention on the early campaign, the

American electorate wasn't paying much attention. With the economy doing exceptionally well, there was little public interest in the election at this early date. Though the press has an obligation to cover the campaign from the first political announcement until the election, the populace never seemed to show much interest until primary election time. On the campaign trail, Americans easily became bored hearing the same canned campaign speeches and promises.

With the incumbent President announcing that he would not seek reelection, Charles Douglas became the front-runner for the Republican Party. Though not assured of the nomination, few Republicans could effectively challenge the Vice President.

Throughout history, many Vice Presidents have sought the office of the presidency, but few have been successful. However, with the national economy remaining strong and stable, and due to his newfound national exposure for his oversight responsibility of the BSDIA, Douglas was virtually unbeatable as the Republican nominee.

Despite Douglas's position as leading party nominee, history had proven that few incumbent Vice Presidents were elected to serve as President. Douglas knew he must campaign hard, with a sense of purpose, and not with the usual campaign rhetoric and idle promises made by most candidates.

A man of principle, Charles Douglas was determined to campaign on his merits and on a platform whose issues were of importance to America. He would have goals that were purposeful and obtainable. The media would be less interested in reporting on a political campaign of such non-controversy. They liked A. Bixby Lane's flamboyancy. He kept their job interesting.

For another 10 months, at least until Super Tuesday the following March, the Democrats would fight among themselves to decide on a nominee for their party. Their leading candidate was always Bixby Lane. Believed by many of his party to be the only Democratic who could retake the White House, Lane campaigned as if he already was the party nominee. The hard-money corporate contributions to his campaign far outdistanced his closest competitor. He received numerous invitations to speak as if he was the Democratic nominee.

Lane was invited by the Democratic National Committee to be the keynote speaker at a Democratic rally to be held on the Washington Monument mall on Memorial Day. Quite naturally, Lane was proud to represent his party on such an occasion.

Lane's team of strategists worked a full week writing his speech for the Memorial Day event. Through this speech, they proposed to propel him into the national forefront as the leading Democratic Party Presidential nominee, and keep him there.

It was a pleasantly cool Memorial Day morning in Washington, D.C. The Democratic Party had wisely used $9.4 million dollars to plan and implement this extravaganza. Their strategy was to exhibit their chosen Presidential nominee, A. Bixby Lane, to the nation using Democratic Party soft-money contributions that can only be used to promote Party activities. It was a prudent strategy.

From positive phone responses, event planners had estimated that with cooperative weather and the promise of free food and entertainment over a half-million Independent and Democratic supporters would be prompted to participate in the holiday festivities. The national press corps was covering the full day's activities, and the networks were transmitting live feeds to cover Lane's speech. The Democratic National Committee (DNC) billed the event as A. Bixby's finest hour - the official kick-off for his national campaign.

By 8:00 AM, traffic congestion was seen as far out as the I-495 and 95 perimeters. TV 5 Alive!'s Eye-in-the-Sky helicopter reported traffic jams along the 66, 395, and 295 interstate routes into the city. Democrats from around the country flocked to the event. By 10:00 that morning, Constitution and Independence Avenues paralleling the mall were blocked off to pedestrian traffic only.

By noon, well over a half-million people stretched from the Lincoln Memorial to the Washington Monument. The Mall's reflection pool highlighted the carefully placed assembly of American flags flying in bipartisan symbolic respect over the crowd. The media would later report on this "most patriotic event." The Democrats were jubilant in this outpouring of support for their chosen candidate. The size of the crowd far exceeded their expectations.

The impact this televised event would have on the American voter would be incalculable. Lane was cautioned that he must be prepared to rise to the occasion. It was 'make it or break it day' for his campaign, the DNC advised. His speech prepared and rehearsed, A. Bixby was confident he was up to the challenge.

The speaker's platform was constructed on the foreground of the Lincoln Memorial. Loudspeakers were placed every 50 yards along the Mall. Beginning at the west-end of the reflection pool, continuing around Ellipse

Road and the Washington Monument perimeter to 15th Street, the speakers were strategically placed so that not a word of Lane's remarks would go unheard by the crowd of Democratic faithful and undecided voters.

For dramatic effect, organizers had planned a grand approach to the podium fronting the Lincoln Memorial. To promote a Presidential appearance, A. Bixby would arrive by motorcade along a circuitous route beginning at Union Station and ending at the Lincoln Memorial. The Washington D.C. Police Department had cooperated with assurances of crowd and traffic control and participation in the parade.

At precisely 2:00 PM, an escort of 20 motorcycles, five-pair abreast ahead and behind, would begin Lane's limousine ride from Union Station. With sirens blaring, the motorcade would slowly circle the U.S. Capitol building, then head west on Independence Avenue. At 15th Street, the parade route would turn north in front of the Washington Monument.

At the turn, the introductory theme song to "2001, A Space Odyssey," would sound from the strategically placed speakers. Immortalized as the introductory music that welcomed 'The King,' Elvis Presley, on stage, event planners chose this same grand intro to pronounce A. Bixby Lane's arrival.

The music was timed to conclude at the precise moment the motorcade drew adjacent to the White House. Over the loud speakers, an announcer would implore the crowd with the introduction, "Ladies and Gentlemen, allow me to introduce to you, the next President of the United States, A. Bixby Lane."

Perched high on the back seat of his limousine convertible, Lane would stand to accept the accolades of the masses. Continuing along Constitution Avenue, the motorcade would turn south on Henry Bacon Drive, then deposit Lane beside the Lincoln Memorial.

It was time for the DNC plan to become a reality. The parade started on time and proceeded flawlessly to the Lincoln Memorial. The crowds extolled their perceived new leader. Lane was gloriously introduced to the world. Now he must support this pomp and circumstance with a worthy speech.

Amid boisterous cheers from the crowd, Lane ascended to the podium. With great confidence, he began speaking. A hushed silence befell the crowd.

"This Memorial Day, we gather here in the symbolic shadows of America's greatness. We stand among the monuments dedicated to those who have fought and to those who have died to preserve the freedom that we enjoy today. Their unselfish valor represents all that is good in the American people, and all that is great in America.

"On this Memorial Day, I am reminded of the immortal words spoken by our great American President, Abraham Lincoln, in his Gettysburg Address. His words then as now, stand as a testament to those who have struggled to keep American free.

"We too shall resolve that these brave men and women who have fought, and often have died for our American freedom and heritage, shall not have died in vain. On this Memorial Day, we reaffirm our resolve to give our nation a new birth of freedom where all men shall be able to proclaim this a sweet land of liberty.

"From America's mountains to its plains, from sea to shining sea, America's flag held high memorializes a united symbol of freedom. This is as it should be. This is what our forefathers and our loved ones have fought to preserve.

"The architects of our American republic drafted a magnificent Constitution and Declaration of Independence. Its framework is the arbiter of our American democracy. For over two centuries, these documents have stood as a testament to our political sovereignty. In this democracy, we, the people united, enjoy the freedom of a society strengthened by a common goal of ensuring liberty and justice for all.

"Our liberty, though, has not come without sacrifice. On this Memorial Day, we pause to remember that America is the land of the free because it is the home of the brave. Today we celebrate our freedom and America's greatness because of those who have fought to keep it great and free.

"Today let us recognize and honor our men and women in military service who are prepared and willing to fight and die if necessary to protect and defend our freedom and America's principles.

"On this Memorial Day, let us resolve to protect our liberty, to strengthen the American society, and to rekindle optimism and opportunity for every American. Let us pray also that others around the world can enjoy the same principles of democracy, justice, and freedom that we enjoy today.

"As I close, I ask that you look around you at the memorials dedicated to those great Americans who have sacrificed their lives and pledged their sacred honor to this great nation to allow you and me to enjoy this freedom. Let us give thanks to all who have served and are serving to assure that our government, of the people, by the people, and for the people, shall never perish.

"I most humbly thank you for allowing me the privilege today to honor America on this our celebration of Memorial Day. May God bless America, and God bless these United States."

As the crowd erupted in thunderous applause, the announcer asked that everyone join him in saluting 'our next President of the United States, A. Bixby Lane.'" The roar of the crowd grew louder. Not since the "I Have A Dream" speech of Dr. Martin Luther King, Jr. on August 28, 1963, had such a crowd responded so receptively to a Washington oratory.

As far as one could see along the Mall, people were cheering, hand-held flags were waving, and veterans in their military caps adorned with ribbons and metals cried openly. This outpouring of emotion and display of patriotic celebration was captured by the throngs of media covering the event.

Sound bites and images from the event were televised around the world. Cable news network anchors gave A. Bixby Lane instant credibility as the Democratic Party's leading Presidential contender and proclaimed it Lane's finest hour.

Earlier in the day, President Edward Walters had delivered an address for the Armed Forces Memorial Day Ceremony held at Arlington National Cemetery. Despite media coverage, his homage paid to America's patriots was dwarfed by the spectacle of the Democratic Party's celebration.

A. Bixby walked the length of the reflection pool, greeting his admirers and well-wishers. "Mr. President!" shouted one young voter as she pleaded with him to please stop where she could have her picture taken with him.

He grinned and replied, "I'll be glad to little lady. Never to busy to accommodate the public." Her plea was unnecessary. She didn't know Lane would do most anything to pose for a picture. The television cameras focused on a smiling Lane and his young admirer as he struck a stately pose.

"Oh, thank you, sir," she exclaimed, hugging him.

"Always my pleasure to meet and greet the youth of America," Lane responded with a fatherly smile.

From within her apartment in Jamaica, Simone Mariquez watched news coverage of the Memorial Day's event in America. She listened intently to the report as the announcer hyped Lane's marvelously patriotic

Memorial Day eulogy and his love of America's youth.

Only too well, she knew Lane's love for youth was not limited to the shores of America. To her fourteen-year old son, she commented, "Look Santiago, there is your father!"

Santiago knew the truth about his single mother and his father who lived in the United States. As he grew older, he asked fewer questions about him. He stared intently at the smiling face on television. It was obvious Lane was his father. They looked identical. Looks separated only by the years, by the Caribbean, and by Lane's choice.

Had America known that at this very moment, Lane was being introduced to his illegitimate son, albeit, through the medium of TV, A. Bixby would have chosen to beat a hasty retreat to the sanctity of obscurity.

Another reveler cried, "Mr. Lane, may I please have your autograph?"

"Of course," he replied. Jokingly he added, "That is, of course, if you promise to vote for me!" The crowd roared with laughter.

"Oh, I do," came the response.

"Me, too," echoed the shouts of the throng.

A. Bixby Lane enthusiastically responded to all requests. His walk to the Washington Monument took an additional three hours. Proud and Presidential, he milked the media coverage and public acclaim for all it was worth. It had been a successful day. The Democratic National Committee's plan came off without a hitch - even better than they had hoped.Not one penny of Lane's hard-money campaign contributions had been used in this momentous effort. The DNC had outwitted the campaign finance reform laws Congress had recently imposed upon itself. The following morning, Lane would personally realize his largest single day's receipt of campaign contributions.

Following Lane's self-imposed coronation, America's labor unions, considered the 'cash-cow' for the Democratic Party, rapidly began unloading its coffers to the proposed-to-be front-runner. Many in the entertainment world did likewise. By the end of the first week in June, A. Bixby had amassed an incredible $22 million dollars in campaign contributions. It was money that would be needed to wage a political battle against the Republican's likely Presidential candidate, incumbent Vice President Charles K. Douglas.

As early summer temperatures and the Presidential campaign began to heat up, so did the activity of the Border Surveillance and Drug Interdiction Agency. With U.S. military personnel serving to beef up security and surveillance and with the additional funding of technologically advanced surveillance and detection equipment, America's borders were fast becoming impenetrable to even the most ingenious drug smugglers.

Using helicopters with their infrared night vision capabilities to patrol the Mexican border, nighttime over-land border crossings became much riskier and far less successful. Military personnel assisted Border Patrol agents with all-terrain-vehicle and mounted horse patrols. Land motion sensor detectors were planted and constantly monitored along the border in areas where past crossings had been prevalent.

With these ever-present surveillance and detection devices in place, drug smugglers went to great lengths to disguise their efforts to move contraband across the border. Where State Route 89 in Nogales, Arizona, intersects with the Mexican border at West International Street, for example, federal agents discovered an elaborate tunnel system designed to smuggle drugs under the Mexican border and into a car wash on the U.S. side.

Through an elaborately constructed and electrically lighted 48-inch wide plywood tunnel, drugs were smuggled into the Los Amigos Car Wash from a business across the border in Mexico. Once inside the car wash, a second tunnel channeled the drugs into an adjacent home in Nogales. Once secreted across the border, the drugs were repackaged for distribution throughout a well-established drug pipeline in Arizona and New Mexico.

The 7:00 PM national news telecast began with this White House announcement. "This just in on the Associated Press news wire: BSDIA federal officials report that they have broken up a major cocaine smuggling ring in Nogales, Arizona. When a traffic accident ruptured a city fire hydrant, local water system utility workers became suspicious when the cascading water disappeared into the sewer system only to reappear a block away flowing from the doors and windows of a local residence. BSDIA agents were called to the scene when packets of cocaine were found floating among debris exiting the home. Agents seized an estimated 1,200 pounds of cocaine having a street value of some $20 million."

The media interviewed BSDIA Director Rick Tolbert by phone. When asked to comment on the chanced discovery and sophistication of the smuggling scheme, Tolbert remarked, "BSDIA agents were quite surprised at the engineering technology employed in construction of this elaborate tunnel system. It was a fortuitous discovery. Were it not for the traffic accident that ruptured the fire hydrant, and for the alertness of the Nogales utility workers, this underground drug trafficking scheme might have gone undetected for a long time."

Tolbert continued, "We have long suspected that an underground tunnel system was a possible entranceway into the U.S. from across the border. This discovery substantiates our suspicions. Agents will now begin a methodical search for tunnel systems in all U.S. towns that border Mexico. Using the Orca Wave Sonar, agents will search all streets within a two-block area of the Mexican border for the presence of similar underground passages."

"We are certain we will discover other sophisticated labyrinths that drug smugglers have been using for years. This new sonar technology recently made available to the BSDIA has proven a tremendous asset in closing the American borders to drug smugglers."

Another reporter queried, "Mr. Tolbert, would you care to comment on the ongoing litigation by some environmentalists to stop construction of anti-drug smuggling construction projects? And do you support the President on his position in answer to their concerns?"

In the rural areas of certain U.S. cities that bordered Mexico, the military had begun construction of helicopter landing pads and other staging sites designed for use in border surveillance and interdiction efforts. Without completion of another lengthy environmental impact study, environmental advocates were certain such construction projects would forever ruin the desert ecosystem and desecrate possible undiscovered ancient Indian ancestral sites. They had threatened to sue the federal government if another impact study was not done. As a preliminary move, they had already filed an injunction to have the staging project halted until a federal judge could rule on the necessity to proceed with another 12-month study.

When these environmentalists demanded that the President immediately cease construction and stop earth moving and land leveling efforts until the federal court could rule on their injunction, President Walters responded, "Hogwash. We are not halting this project to undertake another lengthy impact study of the desert environment."

"For over 200 years we have investigated and identified possible historical sites. You must remember that this is federal land. Not one acre of our staging area is even close to an Indian reservation or any other area suspected of intrinsic historical value. We are not excavating the land for goodness sakes, we're only leveling certain small areas sufficient in size to land helicopters and make an encampment."

Standing firm, he concluded, "Sue us if you must, but I will not postpone this project for one moment. To do so would be detrimental to our surveillance and detection efforts. Delaying the establishment of these rapid deployment bases would severely affect our long-term drug interdiction efforts. The BSDIA program would be placed at far too much risk of failure to achieve its goals. And that is something that I will not tolerate."

To Vice President Douglas and Rick Tolbert, Walters privately commented, "I think these environmentalist extremists would rather have the streets run white with cocaine than permit this virtual no-risk to the environment drug interdiction project to continue. They are more concerned with a self-perceived environmental endangerment, which exists only in their imagination, than they are with the consequences of allowing tons of illegal drugs onto the streets of America. Where are their priorities? I say, 'Nuts to them. Let them sue!'"

To the media's request for comment on the ongoing litigation and of his position on support of the President, Tolbert diplomatically responded, "Thank you very much for the opportunity to comment. I wholeheartedly support the President's position on continuing staging area construction. Unlike the environmentalists, I know and understand the consequences of halting construction. To do so would be detrimental to America and would undermine our efforts to stop cross-border drug smuggling."

"We need these staging areas," Tolbert explained, "to allow our agents quicker access to the more remote areas within the Southwest. Whenever infrared imaging detects illegal smuggling activity, or when smugglers activate underground sensors while attempting a border crossing, a closer proximity to the smuggling activity will allow for a faster response and interdiction. These rapid deployment staging areas are most critical to the success of our drug interdiction efforts."

"I am personally very irritated at certain environmental activists who seemingly strive to prevent this project's success. Their concerns of environmental degradation are completely unfounded. We are extremely sensitive to both the environment and to the region's historical value. If the environmentalist's efforts to stop construction and land preparation are successful, most assuredly, this will result in more illegal drugs on the streets of America. More drugs to tempt America's youth. That is not what America needs, and I don't think that is what America wants."

True to Tolbert's conjecture, the next day a federal judge ruled in favor of the BSDIA construction project. In her ruling, U. S. Federal Judge Nina Baldwin disclosed, "I find no substantiation to the claim by the plaintiffs, the Environmental Freedom Protectionists of America, Inc., that the construction underway in Arizona, Texas, and New Mexico is either illegal or detrimental to the environment of the Southwest. Therefore, I will issue no preliminary injunction to halt this project."

"Furthermore, the President has chosen to intensify efforts to interrupt drug smuggling activity and has instructed the Border Surveillance and Drug Interdiction Agency to do whatever is reasonable and necessary to carry out this directive. I have determined that construction of these staging areas for a more rapid deployment of men and equipment in the surveillance, detection, and interdiction of illegal drug activity is both reasonable and necessary."

"In further finding of fact, I conclude that allowing construction to continue so as to provide for such surveillance and detection activity is in the best interest of the citizens of the United States. Therefore, I will issue no restraining order and am ruling in favor of the U.S. Government. With these conclusions I pronounce this case closed."

This was good news to Rick Tolbert. This ruling gave authority for his agency to continue its interdiction efforts in the Southwest. It also came as welcome news for Clark, Diego, and Thomas. More surveillance along the Mexican border meant less concentrated time that the BSDIA would spend in surveillance and detection activities along the Gulf coast.

CHAPTER TEN

I mmediately following lunch the day after their initial meeting, Miguel Thomas returned to Alton Robert's office to meet with him and his brother. Both brothers were eager to sign Thomas to a construction contract. After Albert and Thomas were formally introduced, Alton began, "I have discussed your project with Albert, and we feel that we can provide you both the quality draft and design, and construction services your project will require."

"I have no doubt that you can," Thomas replied. "Do you think an early fall completion date is a realistic expectation?"

Albert replied, "Baring any unforeseen weather problems or material shortages, Alton and I feel reasonably sure that we can meet a construction completion deadline by the end of August or first of September at the latest."

"Well, that's certainly a good report." Thomas stated.

"Incidentally, I checked on the current zoning status of the mill site," Alton Roberts reported, "and was pleased to discover that the property is still zoned for commercial construction. I was afraid that if we had to make an appeal to the zoning commission for an ordinance change, we might be delayed a couple of weeks before we could begin construction."

"That is good news," said Thomas. "I hadn't even thought about a zoning ordinance problem."

"That's just part of our job," Alton replied smilingly. "I am certain that I can have your blueprints drafted within two weeks," he reported. "That would allow Albert to begin construction by the middle of May."

Albert Roberts assured Thomas, "If you decide to contract for our services, my demolition crew could immediately begin dismantling the old mill. I anticipate that it will take about two weeks to complete demolition. My expectations would be to begin construction around the third week in May, as soon as Alton's design plans receive approval."

In response, Thomas conveyed the news the brothers had anticipated. "My partners have given me the authority to sign a partnership contract,"

Miguel Thomas said. "I appreciate your honesty. You are not just telling me what I want to hear in order to get our business; you are telling me what I must know in order for us to have a successful business partnership. I like your forthrightness and I trust your integrity. I am ready to sign a contract, provisional of course, of approval of your design plan."

Alton responded, "That is what we had hoped you would say. We have prepared a contract for your consideration. Please feel free to take it home, look it over, and let us know your decision."

"It's not necessary to take it home," Miguel said. "Just give me a few moments, if you will, to look over the details."

"Certainly," Alton said.

"Take as long as you need," added Albert as he and Alton quietly left the conference room to allow Thomas to study the contract. In less than fifteen minutes, Thomas was ready to sign. "There is one addition to my original plan proposal that I would like to have you add to the second floor design," he noted.

"Anything," Alton responded. "What do you need?"

"I had almost forgotten that I need a permanent residence. Over the boathouse, I would like you to design an apartment suite with four accompanying guest bedrooms with private baths, and a kitchen, dining room, and den - basically, a four-bedroom condominium. Also, please construct a three-car garage alongside the boathouse. And, of course, add these extra design plan and construction costs to the contract. I will pre-sign the contract with a provisional note for their inclusion."

Alton responded, "That will certainly be no problem with design, though it may delay my completion of your blueprints by up to a week."

"That is understandable."

Albert likewise noted, "These construction additions would necessarily delay project completion too, of course."

"That also, is understandable. How long do you think it would add to the completion of the project?" Thomas asked.

"Four to six weeks minimum, I would expect. Perhaps less, if I can get extra crews in to help with construction."

"Do so, if possible. If not, the delay is reasonable and expected, and we are prepared to pay for your additional inconvenience and the added expense."

Thomas signed the contract and prepared to leave. "I'll be staying at the Tallahassee Hilton in case you need to reach me," he said. "Though I may be out of the country for a while, I will keep in touch. Please leave any messages for me at the hotel. And thanks for your willingness to work with us to bring our project to completion."

Alton replied for them both, "The pleasure is all ours."

By Memorial Day, all appearance of the old mill was gone. Except for the structural support, the dilapidated mill had been demolished. Plans were drawn and approved, and construction had begun.

The partners were hopeful the entire facility would be completed and the sugar refinery fully operational by early fall. By late summer, a new crop of Colombian coca plants would be ready for harvesting and processing. By October, it would be time to resume cocaine trafficking. The refinery must be operational by mid-fall or their entire smuggling operation would be delayed.

Before then, much unfinished work remained to be done. Sugar refinery equipment had to be purchased and transported to the St. Marks mill site. Thomas himself had to learn the intricate details of the refinery process. He needed to become proficient in refinery management. The employees he would recruit must, likewise, be specially trained.

Juan Carlos would call on his friend, Batista Herra Demarquez, manager of the Mecosta Paulo Sugar Refinery outside of Sao Paulo, Brazil, for his help in this specialty training. At the Mecosta Paulo, Miguel would learn the refinery trade and determine what processing equipment must be purchased to mechanize their facility. A phone call from Diego to Demarquez arranged for Thomas to visit the Brazilian mill and learn the intricacies of sugarcane refinery.

In preparation for his departure from St. Marks, Miguel contacted Albert Roberts at the construction site. "Albert, I will be out of the country for about two weeks to purchase our refinery equipment." he informed him. "Arrangements for your construction draws have been made with Apalachee Coastal Savings and Loan. Before I leave, besides furnishing you with equipment dimensions and their physical location within the plant, do you have any concerns we need to discuss that might delay construction?"

"No, Michael, none that I can think of. Construction is proceeding according to schedule. We'll be working on exterior framing for about 10 more days before we begin pouring the foundation. As soon as you fax Alton those equipment dimension and location specs, he can complete a draft of the floor plans. We'll need those to lay in the plumbing and electrical conduits before we can pour the foundation."

Thomas responded, "As soon as possible, I'll make arrangements to purchase our milling equipment. As I do, I will ask the manufacturer to fax Alton the specifications. I'll also take a copy of our blueprints along with me and ask for advice for the equipment's best location within the mill. I'll have this specific information marked on the plans and will return them by UPS to Alton."

Roberts stated, "I know completing construction by mid-September is imperative to your anticipated start-up date. If you can get this information to Alton within the week, we should experience no construction delays."

"That is good news. Tell Alton he should expect this information to arrive within the week."

Early the next morning, Thomas boarded an American Airlines flight out of Tallahassee bound for Miami. From Miami, he connected to Brazil. It was a hot, humid afternoon when Miguel landed in Sao Paulo. A bumpy hour-long ride in an un-air-conditioned taxi brought him to the front gate of the Mecosta Paulo Sugar Refinery. The eight-foot tall barbed-wire fence surrounding the refinery complex served to announce the refinery's tight security efforts.

It was a rare occasion when Demarquez welcomed visitors to tour his facility, particularly those in competition for his refined sugar product. Demarquez's mill was running at full capacity, and when his old child-hood friend, Juan Carlos Diego called with his request, he could not deny his friend this favor.

Demarquez reasoned that with the mill operating at full capacity, and with Diego's explanation of the purpose of his request, his sharing of knowledge with his compadre's partner would not jeopardize either the refinery's processing quotas or its sales.

"Besides," Demarquez said aloud to himself, "Diego has offered a substantial cash payment for providing education and training to his part-ner." Batista was to be paid handsomely for training Thomas in refinery management, and for offering his advice on the interior design plan and location for equipment within the St. Marks' mill. Certain that he would not be hurting his refinery sales to do so, Batista considered there was no good reason to turn down Diego's $100,000 'educational services' offer.

The gate guard directed the taxi to the plant manager's office. Batista Demarquez greeted Miguel warmly. "Miguel Thomas, welcome to the Mecosta Paulo, Amigo. I am Batista Herra Demarquez. Please call me Ba-tista."

Demarquez continued, "For my friendship with Juan Carlos, I am glad to welcome you to Brazil and to teach you about the sugar refining process."

"Thank you," replied Thomas. "It is very kind of you to offer to teach me the information I will need to know to manage our refinery. Along with this payment envelope, Juan Carlos sends his greetings and also his thanks for allowing me to come."

"Gracias," said Batista, carefully pocketing the envelope in his jacket pocket. "It would be hard to deny the request of my Amigo, Juan Carlos. How is my old friend?" He asked.

"Fine and working hard to increase the yields of his crop production, if you know what I mean!" Thomas retorted.

They both laughed. Batista knew.

Demarquez had wondered why Diego was getting into the sugar refinery business, but knew better than to ask. He countered, "I am glad to see my Amigo get into the legitimate 'white powder' business. I will do what I can to teach you well."

"Thanks, Batista." Thomas replied.

"I know you must be tired from your flight. After a good meal and a good night's sleep, you will feel better. I hope you will find our accommodations acceptable. Come; let us get you settled in. Then we will eat dinner. Tomorrow we will begin your intensive education and training."

Thomas awoke refreshed, but apprehensive of the tasks ahead. He knew nothing of the sugarcane refinery business, and had much to learn in a relatively short period of time.

Batista greeted Thomas at breakfast and laid out his plans for the first day. "I thought we would spend the morning touring the mill to acquaint you with the different pieces of equipment used in sugarcane refinery. I think this would be the best way to give you a good overview of sugarcane processing. I know your mill will primarily function to refine raw sugar, but I think it will be beneficial for you to see and learn the whole refinery process from the cane field to the finished product."

"Then we would spend the afternoon looking over your mill plans. From the morning tour you will be somewhat familiar with the various pieces of milling equipment you will need, and I will offer my advice on where to best locate this equipment within your mill."

Thomas agreed that this was a good schedule. He was ready to begin his education but confessed to Demarquez, "I am somewhat apprehensive about my mission to learn the sugar refining industry and become proficient at managing our mill. Since I know relatively nothing now, it seems a daunting task, but I will try to be a good learner. I know that you will teach me well. So, where do we start?"

Batista responded, "Before we begin our tour, let me give you some background information on sugar cane processing that will help you to better understand the refinery business. The cane plant is a member of the grass family. Sugarcane has a coarse, pulpy inner core. Its sweet juice and crystallized sugar content have been dated in China and India as far back as 2,500 years ago. Understandably, the cane juice is high in sugar or sucrose content."

"Amazingly, the sugar content is highest in times of drought when the cane plant receives less moisture. In an effort to minimize dehydration, the plant concentrates its water as a viscous juice that is less likely to evaporate from the plant. This is why the sweetest sugarcane is best grown in dry, temperate climates like those found in Central and South America."

"When the cane stalk reaches about 10 feet in height, it is at its peak of sugar production and content, and is ready for harvest. This sugar content, commonly called cane sugar, is rather a compound sugar consisting of glucose and fructose."

"In the field the cane is cut as a single stalk and loaded on trailers for transport to the mill. Cranes load the cane onto conveyors that take the stalks into a wash station to remove insects and debris. Next, conveyors resume transport into the mill where the stalks are hammered and pulverized. The juice is extracted and collected while the stalks are conserved and used to feed the steam boilers. After the juice has been treated with lime to neutralize acids, it is heated to a low temperature. The juice becomes concentrated and is vacuumed and re-heated until it becomes a thicker, heavier syrupy concentrate. As this concentrate is reheated, it becomes caramel-colored and slowly begins to crystallize."

"If a white sugar is desired as the final product, after crystallization, the powder is washed with water to remove the brown color. If a brown sugar is the desired end product, the crystals are heated a little longer and left unwashed as a caramel color." Demarquez continued, "The crystals are then treated to a slow and extensive drying. In giant tumblers the crystals are heated consistently until they become the granular dry powder you see packaged for consumer sale. If powdered sugar is the desired end product, the dried granules are crushed under giant rollers into a finely ground residue."

Demarquez concluded his introduction, "This is the entire sugar refinery process in a nutshell. Perhaps with this brief overview, you will better understand the function of the machines you will see this morning."

"Thank you, Batista." Thomas remarked. "I am already feeling less overwhelmed by what I have to learn. Now I am ready to observe each intricate step in the milling process."

"Before we go into the mill," Batista responded, "let me give you some basic information on another process in our mill operation. Ethyl alcohol is an easily fermented by-product that is often produced at cane processing facilities. We process an industrial grade ethanol that is sold to the petroleum industry and is used as an addictive in the manufacture of gasohol. This is a very profitable part of our business. You may also want to consider doing this. "

"There is one major drawback to its production, though. As you know, ethanol is very flammable. That is one reason we have such an elaborate fence and security system in place. If you choose to install a vat to manufacture ethanol, you must take precaution to isolate your mill, particularly from persons and external sources that might spark an explosion."

For the little income that would be generated from ethanol sales compared to the damage to the mill an explosion might cause, Thomas had already discounted recommending that Ortega consider an ethanol by-product production in Belize. Unlike Batista's operation, the Belizean processing plant was only a façade for their more profitable white powder commercial enterprise.

"Likewise, there is another reason for concern to secure your mill from outside personnel. Each step in the refining process is dependent upon the previous. With one inadvertent malfunction brought about by an accident caused by a curious onlooker, the entire mill would suffer tremendous downtime."

Thomas inwardly smiled gleefully. This last reason was a legitimate and qualified explanation of why they would secure their mill from prying eyes and the curious public. Their drug smuggling venture would have far less risk of discovery under such guarded protection.

Batista continued, "We meticulously recycle everything possible and make wise use of all aspects of byproduct processing. You will better understand what I mean as you tour the mill. We try to become as energy-efficient as possible. Our mill uses both steam power and electrical power, both of which we generate on-site. By burning the cane debris in the steam generator, we relieve ourselves of a tremendous amount of waste that would have to be disposed of elsewhere. This is an environmentally sound practice."

After the morning tour, Miguel indeed felt less overwhelmed. That afternoon, Batista scrutinized the St. Marks' mill plans. He made specific recommendations on where to best locate the mill equipment to assure maximum use of refinery space. With his recommendations, Thomas was satisfied the equipment placement would provide for an orderly process in their step-by-step refinery efforts.

The next morning, Thomas had the plans shipped by UPS to Alton Roberts. That afternoon, again with Batista's recommendations, Miguel contacted various manufacturers to purchase refinery-processing equipment. After each purchase, Thomas requested that the manufacturer fax the technical schematics to Roberts where he could complete the foundation plans. By the end of the day, this task had been completed.

After two weeks of careful observation, meticulous note-taking, and practice with the skills necessary to operate the machines involved in each step of the sugar refining process, Miguel felt sufficiently prepared to assume the managerial role at the St. Marks Mill.

Having completed this vital task, Thomas flew to Columbia to meet with Diego and discuss their progress. From there, both partners flew on to Belize to talk with Diego's brother, Ortega, and check on the progress of the Corozal Mill construction.

After touring the construction site, Juan Carlos noted, "It appears that the Belize mill essentially needs more reconstruction than primary construction work. I expect Ortega's project will be completed more rapidly than will yours, Miguel. Bringing this mill into operation first is critical in meeting our target date for resuming our smuggling operation. Ortega can then begin to produce the raw sugar you will need to start up the St. Marks refinery."

Thomas replied, "Yes, I agree. Ortego and I have discussed this. We feel that the anticipated construction completion dates will be timely for both mills. Completion of the Belize mill first, should allow Ortega sufficient time to process and provide me with both an initial raw sugar and cocaine supply. Hopefully, by the time he finishes his first production and it is shipped to St. Marks, we should be ready to start up the refinery."

Juan Carlos asked his brother, "How soon do you think the processing mill and 'quality control laboratory' will be completed, Ortega, and do you think you will be able to start on schedule?"

Ortega replied, "Barring any major tropical storms, it appears that construction we will be completed and we will be fully operational by the first of August, exactly as we had planned. The cane crop is developing well and we should have no shortage of available sugarcane. Juan Carlos, if you can transport the raw coca and your chemists by the time the mill begins production, I see no reason why we would be delayed at all."

Diego responded, "Excellent, Ortega. I promise you will have your men and my first coca shipment by the time the sugarcane mill is up and running. Just keep me informed of the construction progress and let me know when you are ready to receive the initial shipment to process and repackage for delivery to Miguel."

Juan Carlos added, "I am pleased to report that I have employed my Russian friend, Comrade Vladimir Kerchenkov to command the DSRV that we purchased from the Russian Navy. All the electronic guidance equipment and radar cloaking modifications have been installed according to our specifications."

"Matsujiyama reports that the submarine will be ready for delivery by the end of June. This delivery date will give Kerchenkov sufficient time to train his crew and plot the best travel route from Belize to St. Marks."

"This is good news," said Thomas. "As soon as I return to Florida, I will contact Wayne and bring him up to date on the construction progress of the two mills and of our conversation today. It seems we are right on schedule to begin our October drug shipments."

By the end of June, the DSRV was ready for delivery. Its 28-foot length and 8-foot beam made it an ideal size to be shipped overseas by Oceanic Cargo Transworld Container Corporation. In readiness for transportation, a special roller assembly was built inside one of Oceanic's 15 by 15 by 50-foot cargo containers. The DSRV was rolled into its container berth and carefully secured for its ocean going voyage. The submarine began its two-week journey across the Pacific, through the Panama Canal, into the Caribbean, and on to Belize City.

Arriving at Deep-Water Cargo Terminal Number 3 in Belize City, the cargo container was off-loaded onto a semi-tractor trailer rig and driven overland to the Corozal mill site. Here it was stored alongside the various other cargo containers that housed the newly purchased raw sugar processing equipment.

When ready for deployment, the mini-sub would be rolled out of the cargo container, removed by crane, and lowered into the canal running adjacent to sugar processing mill. Here it would remain hidden inside its newly constructed docking berth.

The $20 million price tag to purchase and equip the DSRV for their needs was a small price to pay considering the profits that would be realized from their smuggling operation. With its 2-ton cargo capacity, each delivery would gross a street-sales profit of around $18 million. Estimating 20 deliveries per year, this $360 million in annual drug sales would more than pay the cost of their offshore relocation.

Diego contacted Cuban General Hector Gomez to check on the progress of setting up the Arroyos de Mantua mid-point safe harbor.

"Amigo, the boathouse is completed," Gomez responded when asked of the construction progress. "It is waiting on your need to use it."

"Gracias, Hector." Diego replied. "What was the construction cost?"

"Almost $125,000, Amigo."

"Were you able to set up an account with Vicente?" Diego asked.

"Si, Juan Carlos."

"Good. I will transfer $225,000 into your account tomorrow. $125,000 to cover your costs and another $100,000 for your trouble."

"Gracious, Juan Carlos. It was no trouble."

Diego continued, "I have hired Vladimir Kerchenkov as the sub's commander. I will give him your phone number. Either Ortega or I will contact you 24 hours in advance of each arrival at Arroyos de Mantua. Soon, Kerchenkov will be ready to make his first test run from Belize."

"I will listen for the call."

Now that Thomas had acquired a level of expertise and the confidence that he could start up the St. Marks refinery, it was time to begin the interview process to hire mill workers. It was imperative these workers also be competently trained in the special skills that would be required to perform the step-by-step processes in sugar refinery.

Unless the mill was successful in its refinery business, the disguise of the drug smuggling operation would be in jeopardy. Unskilled workers would require too much of Thomas' direct supervision, drawing him away from the real purpose of the mill's operation.

Thomas contacted the Tallahassee Area Employment Agency to seek advice on attracting and hiring area workers for the refinery. Selina Jacobs, managing director recommended that Thomas run a newspaper advertisement announcing the upcoming job availability at the refinery.

She stated, "If you prefer, our agency can serve to handle all applicant processing and coordinate the appointments for the interview process."

Thomas agreed and signed a contract for her to initiate the hiring process and begin scheduling applicants for interview.

Next, Thomas placed a full-page ad in the Sunday edition of the 'Tallahassee Democrat'. He was hopeful he would have a sufficient number of high-quality applicants to fill the needed positions.

> The St. Marks Sugar Refinery is seeking applicants for specialty work in the processes of sugar refinery. No prior experience is necessary. All applicants hired will receive an extensive two-week training at an overseas refinery. The St. Marks Sugar Refinery will pay all expenses for this training.
>
> The refinery is seeking dedicated applicants with a reliable work record. This is an equal opportunity for employment. Any interested party should contact the Tallahassee Area Employment Agency for details on seeking application. Interviews will begin July 5. Only hard working, dedicated workers need apply. For more information, call 850-555-WORK (9675).

By Monday noon, the switchboard at the employment agency was inundated with requests for information. By the end of the week, 82 applicants had been scheduled for an interview.

The Big Bend area of the Gulf did not offer many opportunities for workers to realize a high paying job. Most worked in the fishing industry or at unskilled jobs paying only a minimal salary. Thomas and Clark had decided on a starting salary of $18.00 per hour for lesser skill-required assembly workers, plus benefits equal to those offered by any union. Workers specially trained to supervise and manage a specific step in the refinery process would make much more.

Wayne Clark was determined that no worker's union would be allowed to represent the workers at the St. Marks refinery. "There would be no need for snoopy union representatives to be involved in their daily work process," Clark stated emphatically. He and Thomas would take care of their workers with both a higher-than-average area salary structure, and with benefits equal to or better than those offered in unionized plants. Thomas intended to keep his workers happy, productive workers. Both Thomas and Clark knew the success of their smuggling operation was dependent upon the capability of the refinery to disguise their covert drug smuggling activity.

Ortego Diego was going through the same hiring process for the sugarcane-processing mill in Belize. His job though, would be much easier. Many of the locals in Corozal had worked at the mill prior to its destruction by the hurricane. Most were unemployed or working in menial jobs just to make a living. All would be glad for the opportunity for re-employment. As soon as the mill was rebuilt, his workers would already be trained and ready to begin work on the processing of sugarcane into raw sugar.

Thomas, on the other hand, would have to get all his employees trained in the art of sugar refinery. For a $500,000 'training fee', Demarquez had agreed to let his mill staff train Thomas' workers on the intricate processing steps required in sugar refinery. The fee would include this specialized training, two weeks lodging for the trainees at the mill's residence housing facility, and all meals at the refinery's cafeteria.

All things considered, Thomas surmised that it was not, in fact, a bad price to pay to give his employees instant proficiency in the process of sugar refining – proficiency that was paramount to the success of their drug smuggling operation.

Thomas was concerned that his ad might not attract a sufficient number of quality applicants to enable him to meet his staffing needs. He need not have worried.

82 persons made application. Thomas personally held the applicant interviews. Allowing a half-hour for each, he methodically interviewed the 82 applicants over a 5-day period. He easily found the 36 employees he needed. Mostly unskilled in other than marine-related jobs, those hired were eager for a chance to make a better living.

Most had families, and would now be better able to provide for them. Most scrimped from paycheck to paycheck, barely able to buy essential necessities. They had longed for a few of the finer things in life. Now, they would be able to afford them. They were grateful to Miguel for hiring them. He would not have to worry about their work ethics. These folks would work as long and as hard as necessary to perform the duties that would be required of them.

Two of the applicants hired were cousins, Cletus and Dewey Tanner - Southern rednecks personified. Their schoolmates often joked that if someone searched the Encyclopedia Britannica for 'redneck,' they would be sure to find Dewey's and Cletus' photo as pictured examples."

The cousins preferred to call themselves 'countrified.' They lived in a dilapidated mobile home, drove an old Chevy 4 x 4 so dirty that it was hard to determine its original color, chewed Red Man, drank only long-neck Budweiser, believed that WWF wrestling was real, and thought the moonwalk was a staged Hollywood event.

At age 29, they were not known for their work prowess. Thomas hired them essentially for their forklift skills and for their long-distance, big-rig driving experience. Each held a Class 5 CDL (Commercial Drivers License), though they hadn't used it since 'the accident.'

Since high school graduation, the cousins had driven oil tankers cross-country for the Big Bend Oil Refinery. When not on the road, they drove forklifts in the refinery yard loading pallets of 55-gallon drums of diesel fuel onto flat bed trailers for transport to area lumberyards. It was a boring and monotonous job. They soon grew to hate the work, but couldn't quit because they were unskilled in any other trade where they could make a living, albeit, a meager one.

On the weekends, they worked as deck hands on various charter boats working out of the St. Marks marinas. The extra money they made there was their weekend beer money, which they usually drank up long before midnight each Saturday. They never made enough money to buy a new truck, or enough to pick up one of the local girls who frequented the Front Street Tiki Bar on the weekends. They were determined that one day they would have so much money that girls would flock to them for attention.

Today, though, was not that day.

Locally, the girls considered them 'plain white trash.' They pretty much lived up to their reputation. They worked. Got drunk. Sexually harassed any female over 16. Drank even more. Got arrested. It was their way of life.

Tired of long-haul trucking and forklift driving, of not having enough money to get a girl, of cutting fish bait and scrubbing down boats they couldn't even afford to charter for a half-day fishing trip, Cletus and Dewey concocted a scheme to solve their financial woes.

"If our plan is successful," Cletus conjectured. "I reckon we'll no longer have to work."

"We'll be living on 'easy street.'" Dewey likewise reckoned.

It was a risky scheme. If unsuccessful, they would be jailed for attempted fraud. The cousins decided to fake an on-the-job accident from which they would claim irrevocable back damage. The accident would appear to result from negligence in 'failing to maintain safe working conditions.' They knew the right legal terms that would be used to fault the Big Bend Oil Refinery for the accident.

"After the dust settles," Cletus boasted, "we can live off our insurance settlement."

They had never worked harder any one single day as they did to set up their 'accident.' Their scheme was to create the appearance that an accident occurred while they were off-loading pallets of diesel fuel from an adjacent railroad freight car into the oil refinery's warehouse. Carefully they loosened several bolts that held the loading platform together, rubbing dirt and grease into the threads to give an appearance of long-term neglect. The platform served as the forklift ramp leading from the warehouse into the freight car.

As the other refinery yard workers broke for lunch, Cletus and Dewey put their scheme into action.

"You guys go ahead," Dewey hollered to the others as they called for the cousins to join them. "We just want to unload this one last pallet before we break for lunch." Their co-workers waved in acknowledgement and disappeared into the warehouse in the direction of the dining tables.

With bolts sufficiently loosened, the cousins knew the ramp would give way under the thousands of pounds of forklift and fuel oil weight. In the railroad car, they loaded the forklift with a pallet of oil drums. From the safety of the freight car, the cousins carefully steered the forklift down the ramp with long 1 x 4 boards. Dewey guided the steering wheel while Cletus pressed the accelerator. Four feet from the entrance to the freight car, the ramp suddenly gave way.

With a loud crashing noise, fuel oil drums cascaded across the loading ramp spilling diesel fuel everywhere. At the same time, the forklift tilted forward, rolled over onto its side, and crashed six feet down to the ground.

Hurriedly, the Tanner cousins discarded their 1 x 4's and jumped down, wedging themselves between the sprawling oil barrels. Both began to scream as if in unmerciful pain.

Attracted to the noise and screams, curious co-workers and the shift supervisor ran from the warehouse. A quick ambulance ride brought Cletus and Dewey to Tallahassee Memorial Hospital.

After four days of hospitalization and numerous CAT scans, MRI's and X-Rays, their doctors could find no physical cause for their intractable back pain. By experience, they knew these types of injuries often did not show a definitive physical cause.

It was difficult to determine the extent of damage such an accident could have caused to their skeletal muscles. Pain management specialists were certain the cousin's pain was real. Cletus and Dewey's constant moans and complaints of pain would not let them believe otherwise.

Their orthopedist discussed the possible causes of the cousins' injuries and excruciating back pain with an anxious Big Bend Oil Refinery CEO and his accident insurance representative. "These types of back injuries often don't evidence any definitive physical manifestations. Considering the type of accident Cletus and Dewey experienced, there must be considerable muscular trauma precipitating their pain. These types of muscular stains and contusions often don't exhibit either an observable physical injury or a conclusive radiological confirmation."

The CEO asked, "Do you have any idea if their injuries will be permanent?"

"Gentlemen," the physician asserted, "from the circumstances surrounding this accident and the fall that these two men experienced, I have little reason to doubt that their injuries could be permanent. Their pain could just as easily subside as it might remain. No one knows."

With this conclusion, the insurance representative determined it would be in everyone's best interest if they could quickly settle a claim with the Tanner cousins. Especially since the physical evidence at the accident scene showed that several bolts holding the ramp together had been allowed to work loose without repair. In a court trial, the oil refinery would most likely be found negligent in its duty to meet federal Occupational Safety and Health Administration standards to provide a safe work place.

Though several '800-CALL-ME' personal injury attorneys tried to sign the cousins to a contract, they knew a lawyer would not be necessary in order for them to receive the claim settlement they knew would be forthcoming. They were correct in their assumption. Cletus and Dewey settled for a half-million tax-free dollars each, plus medical expenses.

Their ruse had been successful. They were now rich beyond their wildest imaginations. They would soon have the local females flocking to their door to try to help them spend their money. Or so they thought. Yet, despite their huge settlement, the cousins' social status never rose higher than 'rich white trash.'

Nevertheless, they enjoyed their newfound wealth. Their first purchase was a 10-acre woodland tract of land that fronted a tributary of the St. Marks River on the eastern edge of town. Next, they purchased a new deluxe doublewide mobile home, complete with all the modern conveniences. At Circuit City in Tallahassee, they filled the trailer with every conceivable electronic gadget that was available for purchase. They even bought a computer, thought they had no idea of how to use it.

Two new Chevrolet Z-71 crew cab pickup trucks adorned their pine needle lined dirt drive. An array of gaudy new clothes lined their closets.

They lavished money on their redneck friends who now looked at them with renewed respect. Especially when they routinely ordered drinks for everyone at the local watering holes. The Tanners were certainly now more that just plain old Saturday night drunks.

They were every night drunks. They could afford to drink seven days a week. And so they did.

At the Tiki Bar, two local blondes who had previously spurned Cletus and Dewey's repeated attempts to pick them up, immediately rose and draped themselves across the cousins' arms as they entered the bar.

Rickie Gail Malloy, a buxom bleached blond, was Cletus' favorite of the two. She wore skin-tight jeans and a deep-V tee shirt advertising all her surgically augmented charms. "Oh, man! This girl is so hot, and she's coming on to me, for a change!" Cletus thought.

Dewey's flame, Brenda Sue Higgins, likewise, wore tight jeans and an even tighter tee shirt advertising 'Big Bubba's Oyster Bar'. On the front was the face of a smiling oyster 'on the half-shell'. The back read, 'Like Big Bubba's Oysters, I'm Not Real Easy to Shuck, But After Six Beers I Loosen Right Up!' "Now, that's my kinda girl!" Dewey mused.

Admiring their new snakeskin cowboy boots, belts, and hats, this bevy of beauties had finally decided to help the cousins spend they newly acquired wealth. "Cletus and Dewey, ya'll really lookin' good tonight." Rickie Gail exclaimed as she guided Cletus across the bar room.

"What ya'll up to anyway?" Brenda Sue asked suggestively, pulling Dewey by the arm.

"We're up to havin' a little fun with you two, if you're interested!" Dewey replied wistfully.

"Why now, I'll just bet you are," Rickie Gail said flirtatiously, as she let them to a corner table.

"Why don't ya'll buy us dinner and drinks while we talk about it," Brenda Sue urged.

After dinner and several longnecks Buds each, Rickie Gail said seductively, "Heard ya'll got a nice new double-wide with a big hot tub."

"Shore do," Cletus answered proudly. "Big enough for four, too! Think you might wonna take a dip in a little later on?" he asked hopefully.

"I reckon' we might," Brenda Sue answered. "Take a skinny dip, that is! Think you might wonna join us?"

It was Cletus and Dewey's lucky night!

Their lucky nights would last less than a year. In nine months, they had squandered most of their settlement money.

"Typical southern rednecks," the respectable townspeople would say.

"Money that's here today is gone tomorrow. That's their philosophy. No plans for the future. Fools, just living for today."

As soon as their money was gone, so was the admiration of their friends and the company of Rickie Gail and Brenda Sue. With their cash reserves nearly depleted, it was necessary for them to find a job.

Dressed in their best jeans and Polo shirts, the Tanners convinced Thomas to hire them. They assured him that with their experience, they could manage the loading dock duties at the mill. They also pointed out that their trucking experience would prove valuable in helping Thomas manage the mill's wholesale distribution of its refined sugar products.

Convinced, Miguel gave them a job. Juan Carlos Diego and Wayne Clark would one day regret that Thomas had ever met the Tanner cousins, and even more so, that he had hired them to work in the refinery.

CHAPTER ELEVEN

Despite the oppressive mid-July heat, A. Bixby Lane stumped his political campaign on the street corners across America. He was still reveling in the media attention and national exposure he received from his Memorial Day speech. At every campaign stop, huge crowds gathered to see and hear the man proposed to retake the White House from the Republicans.

Though the national party conventions were more than a year away, Lane campaigned as though he had already won the Democratic nomination, and Douglas the Republican. Bolstered by the media's declaration that he was the 'principal Democratic Presidential candidate,' Lane declared open political war on the Vice President.

Before his Memorial Day speech, the Zogby and Harris polls showed Lane held a 42 percent favor ability rating among Democrats. After his speech, the percentages more than doubled to 86 percent.

From this latest poll, Lane was firmly convinced he would emerge as the Democratic Party's nominee. Rather than focusing his campaign on defeating another Democrat for his Party's nomination, Lane ran a purposeful campaign to defeat the Vice President, who was by far, the leading Republican Presidential candidate.

Vice President Charles Douglas' favor ability percentages among Republicans showed a strong 91 percent. Even among Democrats, Douglas rated at 11 percent. Despite the positive national publicity he and the Republican Party had received from the successful BSDIA cross-border drug detections and interventions, Douglas was not complacent in his efforts to continue a rigorous campaign for the presidency.

Meeting with his political strategists, Douglas was determined to reverse some of Lane's recent popularity. They revised the Vice President's campaign platform to appeal more to moderate Republican and conservative Democratic voters. Charles Douglas was perceived as the traditional family man whose moral values promoted a high standard of ethics, principles, and character. His strategists intended to play upon this strong family moral values perception.

They advised the Vice President to continue his campaign strategy to promote a continued BSDIA stepped-up detection and intervention effort to reduce America's illicit drug supply. As an additional strategy, Douglas would confirm his support for promoting a stronger lifestyle of family moral values, which he believed, if adopted by America's families, would discourage both illicit drug use and prescription drug abuse.

Douglas would now advocate that a strong national detection and intervention program, coupled with encouraging a strong core system of family moral values, would serve to reduce the available drug supply, while diminishing the demand for those drugs. It would become a winning platform in Douglas' campaign.

Lane's campaign strategy remained singularly focused on his assertion that promoting a strong family system of values would do more to reduce drug use and abuse than would the present administration's efforts to strengthen cross-border detection and intervention.

While Lane could not openly advocate his support for the BSDIA deterrent program, neither could he deny its overwhelming success. Conversely, the Vice President did gain considerable recognition for his promotion of family values as an added deterrent to illegal drug use.

As this was Lane's sole response to deterring drug use in America, its intrinsic value and appeal to the American voter became noticeably diluted when Douglas revealed it as part of his campaign platform. Douglas had succeeded in his quest to reverse some of Lane's earlier voter appeal.

The polls at the end of July showed Lane's favor ability had dropped a significant 7 percentage points among Democrats. The Vice President continued his strong appeal ratings.

Lane became frustrated. He knew that to regain his percentage of appeal, he must refocus his campaign on other issues where he and Douglas differed decidedly. Lane's strategists proposed that he focus on issues that were of economic importance to consumers. Lane carefully crafted his strategy. If successful, he was certain that with the considerable knowledge he had gained serving in the House of Representatives, on any economic issue of debate, he would have an edge over Douglas. He was certain he would soon regain his percentage of appeal.

The dog days of August presented Lane his opportunity to refocus his campaign. Oppressive heat and humidity were stressing power companies' ability to meet the ever-increasing demand for electricity. The west coast experienced frequent rolling blackout periods where electricity had to be rationed within certain cities and rural areas. The citizenry was frustrated with America's apparent inability to manage this annual crisis.

Summer utility rates had increased as much as 80 to 100 % in some states in the Northeast and Midwest, and, particularly, in California. With summer vacations at their peak and with a higher travel demand for gasoline, all Americans felt the squeeze on their paycheck from the traditional rise in summer gas prices.

High gasoline prices coupled with outrageously higher utility bills, often hundreds of dollars a month more than usual, brought these economic issues to the campaign trail. Lane and Douglas had decidedly different opinions of how to resolve these economic issues.

A. Bixby was stumping at Venice Beach in Los Angeles, walking among a crowd of thousands of mostly young liberal Democrats. The temperature was 98 degrees in the shade and the tempers were as hot as the afternoon sum.

L.A. was one of the California cities hardest hit by an inadequate electricity supply and experienced constant rolling blackouts. NBC correspondent, Steve Shaffer, asked Lane, "Congressman Lane, we are on a live national feed. Would you please comment on what you consider to be the cause of the national energy crisis, and what you, as President, would do or promote to resolve this problem? How does your strategy differ from the Vice President's?"

Bixby Lane welcomed the opportunity to comment. He was prepared for this question. He had rehearsed his answer for days. Lane would purposefully tell them what he knew they wanted to hear, rather than what they needed to hear.

"Like yeah, dude," shouted one from he crowd, "what are you going to do about this energy crisis? It's a bummer, man. I can't keep my beer cold with the electricity going off every day!" The crowd roared with laughter.

Bixby Lane, too, laughed heartily.

"Now that is a problem," Lane cajoled. "For the past three and a half years, in an effort to solve America's energy crisis, President Walters and Vice President Douglas have promoted an energy policy fraught with unrealistic goals and expectations. Mr. Shaffer, let me answer your questions by stating what I perceive to be the problem and how Mr. Douglas and I differ in our approach to resolve this problem."

"California, and all of America, is indeed facing an energy crisis. Americans struggle to pay their utility bills, to fuel the family car at the gas pump, and to buy the winter fuel oil they need to heat their homes. Without a change in administration and a different approach to resolving these problems, I'm afraid America's energy situation will continue in crisis, crisis that will impact not only individual families but could threaten the entire U.S. economy."

The crowd vigorously nodded their approval of Lane's perception and his criticism of the Walters' administration to resolve this energy problem.

"I believe the present energy crisis exists because of two simple reasons. First, there are an inadequate number of power plants to supply our electricity needs. America needs to build more generating plants to meet our increased demand for electricity. Secondly, America lacks the necessary alternative means to generate electricity to meet any spot shortages where and when there is an increased demand."

"To resolve these two issues, I would propose that the federal government commit the funds necessary to invest in alternative energy production sources such as geothermal, hydroelectric, solar power, wind turbine, and geological reclamation projects that are environmentally safe sources for producing electricity. These alternative energy sources would be more than sufficient to meet our peak demands for electricity."

Lane watched the crowd intently as heads continued to nod enthusiastically at his proposals.

"Americans deserve a cheaper, more environmentally friendly energy source for our trains, planes, and automobiles and to heat our homes," he said. "My administration will commit the capital necessary to develop alternative energy sources and lessen the financial burden on American families for the costs of family transportation and home comfort."

Lane knew these were not the reasons for California's present energy crisis, but knew Californians were clamoring for more power sources to meet their immediate need for more electricity. Likewise, he knew Californians were generally ecologically and environmentally conservative, and would approve of his proposal for more geothermal, hydroelectric, solar, wind, and reclamation alternative sources for energy production.

He was correct in his assertion. The crowd cheered boisterously for his proposal.

"Well, you've heard it, folks, and Californians here obviously heartily approve," Steve Shaffer exclaimed. "Democratic Presidential hopeful, A. Bixby Lane has unveiled his national energy platform–a stark contrast to Vice President Douglas' proposal of keeping energy production in the hands of private enterprise."

Lane's interview was carried lived on the six o'clock news on the East Coast. President Walters watched intently as Lane proclaimed the foundation for his energy platform.

When he finished, Walters exclaimed, "Claire, for once you'd think the man could tell the truth. He knows my national energy policy is not fraught with unrealistic goals and expectations. It's the Democratic liberals in the House who have fought our every effort to promote a fiscally sound and ecologically responsible energy policy."

"These liberals believe that the federal government should be the principle fund and management source for America's energy production. Erroneously, they claim that the free market production and sale of energy has failed, and they call for the federal government to take over regulation of America's public and private utility services and power plants."

"Now that, my dear, is an unrealistic idea rooted in disaster. Could you imagine the federal government managing all U.S. utility services? Energy, like the U.S. Post Office's postal delivery charges, would likely increase exponentially each year. Other than maintaining a strong military force and a national criminal investigative and intelligence operation, I can think of no program the federal government can operate as efficiently and cost-effectively as can private enterprise."

"That's the premise upon which I was elected and upon which we must build the Vice President's energy platform," he said, now talking more to himself than his wife. "The federal government is obligated to help with regulations, funding, and tax incentives when it can, but it must allow the free enterprise system to manage America's energy program. To do otherwise would be irresponsible."

Likewise, Charles Douglas listened with rapt interest as Lane exposed his energy platform. "What a sham," Douglas said to his wife, Margie. "While there may be some who support Lane's federal takeover of U.S. utilities and power plants, I can't believe the American public as a whole would support such an obviously foolish proposal. The less the federal government intrudes into the private sector economy, the better off the consumer is. America was founded on a free enterprise system, and to propose that America adopt a socialistic approach to managing the energy crisis is unsound politics."

From his private living quarters in the White House, the President phoned Douglas just as he was finishing his thoughts. "Yes, Eddie," he said, "I heard his speech. I, too, think it's ludicrous, but the American voter may just be sufficiently incensed with the present energy crisis to believe that Lane has the answer to the nation's energy problem."

"Let's meet first thing in the morning to plan a televised response to Lane's press conference," the President prompted.

"My thoughts exactly. I don't think the public understands why we are having an energy crisis or what can best be done to address it," Douglas said.

"I agree," replied the President. "It's time America knew the truth. We will use the bully pulpit of the Oval Office to see that they do."

By noon they and their political advisors had written a platform response that the Vice President was scheduled to deliver in a prime time telecast that evening. Throughout the day, the news networks referred to the Vice President's upcoming telecast as "the Republican response to the Democratic Party's energy platform."

"Good evening, America," Douglas began. "Yesterday, I listened with interest as Mr. Lane unveiled his national energy platform. I would like to thank you for allowing me this opportunity to present my and the Republican Party's energy plan and proposal.

"America, indeed, is in the midst of a national energy crisis. But, I take exception with Mr. Lane's assertion that the President's national energy policy is fraught with unrealistic goals and expectations. This administration has made every effort to promote a fiscally sound and ecologically responsible energy policy. There are certain Democratic liberals in the House who have fought against us at every turn in our efforts to resolve our energy problems.

"Tonight I will tell you the truth about the present energy crisis and how I would propose that America resolve this emergency. The problem with Mr. Lane and the Democratic Party's energy platform is that they do not address the real issues which have created our energy crisis, nor do they offer any specific plans in their energy platform that address how they will resolve these energy issues.

"In general, I would describe their platform as a focus on illusion and a presentation of delusion. The only part of the platform with which I agree is their proposal to develop alternative energy sources to lessen the financial burden on American families for transportation and home comfort costs. That is laudable. Yet, Lane offers no specific suggestions of how he would propose to do so.

"Furthermore, he offers no insight into the specific causes of the energy crisis. Neither does he provide you with the information you need to know in order for you to become a better-informed taxpayer, consumer, and voter. Lane and the Democrats just offer you the solution they think you want to hear and give you a band-aid approach at resolution.

"Let me state unequivocally that the high cost of gasoline and electricity you are now paying did not result from a failure of President Walters' energy policy as Mr. Lane proposed. Today's high prices and shortages of electricity are, in part, the result of a failed energy policy proposed by the past Democratic administration and of Congress to enact our present policy objectives.

"Former President Clanton and certain liberal politicians in Congress share duplicity in their failure to understand the economic principles of the petroleum industry to produce gasoline, natural gas, and fuel oil, and those of utility companies and power plants for generating electricity.

"To develop a long-term plan to deal with our long-neglected energy problems will be a challenge," admitted Douglas. "There is no quick-fix resolution to the energy crisis. All Americans must make sacrifices to help resolve this issue. Likewise, those you have elected to represent you in Congress must work in a bipartisan comprehensive effort to remove the barriers that have prevented this administration from adequately dealing with this crisis. I would further propose that those who do not work in such a concerted, bipartisan manner should not be re-elected to return to Washington!

"Over the next several months, as Congress addresses these energy problems, I invite you to take careful note of how your Senator and Representative votes on specific energy issues. If they do not vote in your best interest to resolve this energy crisis, you may want to vote them out of office next election!

"We have too many self-serving members of Congress who feel they are elected as a career politician, not as a legislative and regulatory servant to you the people they represent. From their vote, you will discover the true measure of character and integrity of those you have elected to represent you.

"Our administration's energy policy will focus on increasing our energy supply as we begin an era of greater energy conservation. As we increase our energy reserves, we will not make environmental trade-offs to do so. In our renewed energy conservation efforts, we will focus on means to reduce both our personal and industrial energy usage.

"In an effort to reduce our dependence on foreign oil, we will place a high priority on increasing America's production of oil, natural gas, coal, and nuclear energy. Additionally, we will adopt new strategies to develop renewable energy sources such as solar, geothermal, wind, hydroelectric, and reclaimed landfill gas as sources of energy.

"A first step Congress must take in addressing the current energy crisis is to remove the barriers that prohibit the most prudent use of the fossil fuels we excavate within the United States. The Trans-Alaskan Pipeline Authorization Act must be revised to repeal the requirement that all Alaskan oil produced must be consumed domestically in the U.S. while none may be exported. This single export restriction imposes significant profit restraints on the petroleum industry operating both within the Alaskan North Slope and offshore of the western states.

"While the TAP Authorization Act opened vast oil reserves in Prudhoe Bay, because of these restrictions on its foreign sales, producers do not realize sufficient profit to reinvest in future oil exploration and production. The transportation costs for moving North Slope oil are expensive. The oil must be transported through the trans-Alaskan pipeline to the port of Valdez then transported by oil tanker to refineries within the U.S. This transportation cost alone increases the wellhead production cost of oil about $5.00 per barrel.

"The most natural market for Alaskan oil is in Korea, Japan, and in northeast Asia," Douglas explained. "To this export market, shipment costs would be reduced to around 50 cents per barrel. Allowing the export sale of Alaskan oil would insure a higher netback profit for producers, which in turn would provide a sufficient income for reinvestment in future oil exploration and production.

"Because the only current sales option for North Slope oil developers is within the U.S., West coast oil depots have become glutted with Alaskan oil. With an oversupply and the high cost of transportation, the netback profit for Alaskan oil has accordingly fallen to the point where further drilling and production becomes unprofitable in both Alaska and California.

"If Alaskan oil was permitted to be exported and sold worldwide, a greater world oil supply would necessarily lessen the demand for OPEC oil. In the economic laws of supply and demand, a lesser demand for OPEC oil translates into a drop in OPEC's price of oil per barrel. Any drop in OPEC's oil price dictates that the petroleum industry would see a paradigm shift in the oil market from a seller's to a buyer's market. A buyer's market would result in lower energy prices for gasoline, home heating oil, and natural gas.

"The U.S. energy program is caught up in a senseless system of cross-transportation of American produced and foreign produced oil. Revising the TAP Authorization Act to allow export of Alaskan oil would result in a natural balance of oil import and export.

"Alaskan crude oil is considered a heavy-grade crude, high in residual oil and particularly preferred in the Far East for use as ship fuel. As a heavy grade crude, Alaskan oil is not as well suited for the production of gasoline as is OPEC oil. Though North Slope oil is lower weighted than California crude, it does not contain the octane-enhancing additives necessary to produce the higher-octane gasoline required by automobiles manufactured in America. Conversely, OPEC produces a lighter grade crude oil that is higher in additives and better suited for the production of America's gasoline and home heating oil.

"Considering these facts I think it would be wise to repeal the Trans-Alaskan Pipeline export restrictions. To permit Alaskan oil exportation would effectively result in lower gasoline and home heating oil prices, would provide for a more efficient use of our world's natural supply of oil, and would insure a more abundant supply of oil, natural gas, and fuel oil for our domestic use.

"Additionally, I call upon Congress to repeal the Mandatory Oil Import Program - a program which restricts crude oil imports in order to maintain a domestic price level that is higher than foreign crude oil import prices. This program erroneously removes all incentives for oil companies to export domestically produced oil at an often lesser world market price.

"The next step to address the national energy crisis is to have Congress work to cut the federal income tax for petroleum companies by offering tax incentives for future reinvestment in exploration and oil production. The state of Alaska could similarly be offered incentives to reduce the state royalty tax of up to 20% per barrel on the cost of production that oil companies are presently charged for the exploration rights to use the Alaskan state land fields.

"Understanding the economics of the petroleum industry, we find that in a world market of fluctuating oil prices, selling oil at less than a $2.00 per barrel net profit is often insufficient for an oil company to reclaim its production capital investment. By revising the TAP Authorization Act and providing these tax incentives I have described, we could assure a sufficient profit margin for the oil companies to insure that there is a future for oil exploration and production.

"The next step my administration would take in resolution of the en-

ergy crisis would be to encourage the building of more oil and gas refineries and power plants to meet our gasoline, natural gas, fuel oil, and electricity demands. In proposing these construction investments, let me state
emphatically that neither in oil exploration, production, refinery construction, nor in plant operation, do I, for one moment, propose that we relax
our federal environmental quality standards. For my entire political life, I
always have and always will continue to strongly support our federal efforts to safeguard the environment.

"To meet present and future energy demands, America must explore
each of its available domestic oil reserve sites. We must consider tapping
California's oil reserves in the Santa Maria Basin and Santa Ynez on the
federal outer continental shelf and off the coast of Santa Barbara; those
prospective oil reserves in the Gulf of Mexico off Louisiana and Florida;
and the known reserves in Alaska at West Sak and in the Artic National
Wildlife Reserve.

"In our efforts to relieve the oil crisis, it is prudent that we move forward with these exploration projects to increase our domestic oil and natural gas supplies. Both West Sak and ANWR are estimated to be super-
giant North Slope oil reserves containing oil deposits at least equal to the
Sadlerochit reservoir of Prudhoe Bay. American has the technology to extract this oil from the Alaskan National Wildlife Reserve and that off the
California, Louisiana, and Florida coasts without endangering the environment to do so.

"In an effort to relieve the natural gas crisis I would propose that the
federal government invest in constructing a new natural gas pipeline that
would be used to bring billions of tons of natural gas from Alaska to the
lower 48 states. After construction, the pipeline would be leased to those
natural gas exporting companies who use it, and who would be responsible
for its operation and maintenance."

"Now," said Douglas, "let us focus on the electrical energy crisis.
Many of America's power plants have antiquated electric generating
equipment whose constant use does not meet the federal environmental
protection standards that were proposed to protect the nation's air, soil,
and water. If elected, my administration will promote a bipartisan effort to
offer tax incentives for these generating plants to upgrade their equipment
and increase their generating capacities. This effort will increase our energy supply, yet also continue to protect the environment.

"In the draft of these tax credits, I pledge to work diligently to protect
both the environment and the U.S. taxpayer from legislation that might be

fraught with industrial greed and any self-serving interests of Congress. For far too long, pork barrel politics have stymied both energy production and legislative conservation efforts. In our efforts to produce legislation that would increase energy production and serve to protect the environment, the American people have been held hostage at the expense of individual Congressional pork barrel projects.

"In our efforts to resolve the energy crisis," he added, "I would propose that America invest in more efficient electricity transmission lines and storage depots. These too, could be leased to the power and utility companies who use these lines for the intrastate and interstate distribution and storage of electricity.

"America must also focus on the need for more investment in alternative means to generate electricity. Again, we can offer tax incentives for the development and implementation of alternative means for electricity production. I would propose that the federal government invest in further research for, and offer tax incentives to those companies that generate electricity utilizing solar technology, geothermal, fuel cell power, wind, hydro, and landfill gas renewable energy projects.

"There are also significant ways that America can reduce the demand for and improve our efficiency in energy use and consumption," Douglas continued. "The automobile industry must advance the technology to increase the Corporate Average Fuel Economy of America's cars, trucks, minivans and SUVs. If Detroit could just double the CAFE of these vehicles, in only 10 years time this increase in fuel efficiency could make America virtually independent of a need for OPEC oil. We must also renew our efforts to explore and investigate new technologies like solar energy fuel cells, which could be used as alternative energy sources for transportation other than the use of fossil fuels.

"And finally, we as American citizens have a co-responsibility to do our part in conserving energy. As consumers what can we do? We can purchase more energy efficient home appliances, turn off lights when not in use, and learn to moderate our home heating and cooling thermostats. We can conserve fuel and gasoline in efforts to make more prudent use of our non-renewable natural resources. Every ounce of gasoline and each single watt of electricity saved is important in reducing the current energy crisis.

"In conclusion, I propose that my energy platform is a balanced focus on conservation of energy for the present and an investment in energy production for the future. If Congress works with my administration like it should to accomplish the steps I have outlined for you tonight, and if you the American consumer will do your part at energy conservation, I have faith that we can resolve of our present energy crisis and move forward to provide an adequate energy supply for our future.

"It is altogether prudent that we do so as an investment in the future for our children and for our children's children. On this, I would hope that you agree.

"Thank you for allowing me to speak with you this evening, and may God bless each of you and these United States of America. Good night."

It was difficult for even the most liberal news commentators to conclude that Douglas' speech was nothing less than a superb diagnostic commentary on the underlying causes of the energy crisis, and a logical proposal for its resolution.

The next day, the Harris and Zogby polls showed that Douglas had increased his approval rating among the usually ultra-conservative Democrats above the 30 percent favor ability rate. Walters, Douglas, and his team of advisors were pleased with these figures and with Douglas' well-received press conference.

The mid-August heat and humidity did not deter the citizens of the Corozal district from attending the reopening ceremonies of the Cerros Sugarcane Processing Mill. At the moment, Ortega Diego was the most popular man in Corozal. He had rehired 36 of the former mill workers and hired an additional 14 workers skilled in the sugarcane farming industry. The entire Corozal community was enthusiastic about the restart of the mill.

The long-awaited reopening of the sugarcane-processing mill would fill a much-needed employment void in the depressed Corozal economy. Had they known the true purpose in reopening the mill, the government officials in attendance might perhaps have been less enthusiastic about its restart. The local citizenry could not have cared less why Diego and Clark had rebuilt the mill. All they knew was that Cerros and the surrounding community would again flourish with economic activity and prosperity.

Most of the workers rehired had been unemployed since the hurricane destroyed the mill. Those who had been fortunate to find work found no more than menially paying jobs. The people of Corozal knew the economic benefits that would be realized from the mill's payroll. Each dollar spent in the local community by the mill's salaried employees generated approximately twelve additional dollars in the local Corozal economy.

The mill proposed to pay an average of $8 per hour for each salaried employee. With an annual payroll of $665,600, the local economy would expect to grow annually by an estimated $8 million. Not an insignificant amount of money in an otherwise depressed local economy.

For every worker employed in the mill's processing plant, six more workers benefited from employment outside the plant in the related sugarcane industry. An additional six area jobs unrelated to the sugarcane industry, would be expected to benefit from the mill's re-opening.

Jobs for workers in the local food establishment and movie and entertainment facilities would benefit now that this additional money would be available for circulation in the local economy. People would now have more money to enjoy those extra things in life that they could not previously afford. The local grocery and dry goods stores, clothing and hardware stores, electronics outlets, private citizen's retail crafts trade, and, in fact, every aspect of the business economy would benefit. The people of Corozal were excited. Life would once again return to a semblance of economic normalcy.

Ortega Diego had planned a lavish Bar-B-Que for the mill's re-opening ceremonies. The entire population of Corozal had been invited to attend the day's festivities. Dignitaries from as far away as the State House in Belmopan participated in the formal ceremonies. Diego was pleased with the outpouring of enthusiasm for the mill's reopening and at the turnout of the Corozal citizens.

Perched high on the Lowry's Bight peninsula, the mill shined in polished splendor in the mid-morning sunlight, offering a spectacular panoramic view of Chetumal Bay. The building's outer shell, festooned in the local colors of coral-pink and trimmed in turquoise, blended perfectly with the spectacular white sand beach, mangrove trees, and turquoise-blue water below. A new mile-long runway, purported to ease the transport of supplies to and from the processing plant, occupied a portion of the upper level of the property adjacent to the plant's sugarcane fields.

The outward beauty of the mill and the community's excitement in its reopening served to disguise the real purpose for the plant's operation. The excitement for this long-awaited day would likewise work to dispel any suspicion that the plant would operate primarily as the clandestine hub for an international narcotic trafficking and drug smuggling venture.

Diego was confident that the expressions of support from the state government and local community would further serve to remove any suspicion from Belizean narcotics inspectors that his mill could be involved in such a nefarious business enterprise. Ortega Diego was confident the drug trafficking business would go undetected.

At noon on the first day of mill operation, Ortega greeted the DC-10 from Bogotá as it landed at the Cerros Mill's runway. As guaranteed, Juan Carlos delivered on his promise that he would provide the principals chosen to run the cocaine processing and shipment end of the Belizean operation. In addition to the transport of the Colombians, included on the flight were the Russian Vladimir Kerchenkov and his hand-picked crew of three former Russian naval submariners hired to command and navigate the DSRV.

After a warm welcome, Ortega drove the men into Cerros to sign the housing contracts he had prearranged for their arrival. The Colombians' wives and families would join them the next week. The start of the school year was scheduled to begin in two weeks. Each of their families was excited to begin a new life in Belize, away from the often-authoritarian rule of local government officials in Colombia.

Neither Vladimir Kerchenkov nor his crew had a wife or immediate family. Just as Wayne Clark was married to the CIA, they had been married to the Russian Navy. With promises of riches and wealth they could never hope to realize from employment in their Motherland, they had been lured away by Juan Carlos Diego.

They were tired of the Russian winters and disgusted with the low military pay and post-Cold War promises by the Russian government that better times and greater economic prosperity lay ahead. The better times and prosperity never seemed to come. They were glad for a chance to flee Russia and live in the tropical climate of Belize.

"Besides," Kerchenkov shared with his sub crew after they had contracted with Juan Carlos, "piloting the sub for Diego would not be work; it would be recreation. Just think," he continued, "we will be getting paid handsomely for doing something we enjoy. This will be quite a change from the severe Russian winters, from the low pay of the military, and from the drudgery of life in Russia."

Each was excited about the possibility of a new life outside of the former Soviet Union. They understood the risks they would be taking in leaving their Russian homeland and becoming involved in an international drug smuggling operation. For the chance of a new life and the lure of wealth beyond their previous comprehension, it was a risk they were more than willing to take.

That night, under cover of darkness, Ortega, the Colombians, and

Vladimir Kerchenkov and his submersible crew of three unlocked the cargo container storing the DSRV. The submarine was slowly rolled out of hiding. From its roller bed, the mill's cargo crane carefully deposited the mini-sub into the canal adjacent to the mill.

With much jubilation, the DSRV was secured inside the newly constructed docking berth that was specially built to conceal its presence. The Russian crew spent hours studying the guidance system and navigational controls of the refurbished mini-sub. They were eager to take it out for a trial run.

Diego and his team of narco-traffickers celebrated the night with a cooler of Coronas and Cuban cigars. They toasted their raison d'être. They were finally ready to begin their cocaine smuggling operation.

The sugarcane processing workers had been told that these newly arrived employees were scientists who were brought in do research for the sugarcane industry. Ortega further explained that the scientists would be working independently of the plant's sugarcane processing personnel. With this explanation, Diego hoped to dispel any suspicions for their presence and for their work role at the processing plant.

Mill workers were told that the scientist's work on the second floor of the mill was secret. For security reasons, the second floor would be off limits to them and to the public. Ortega need not have feared any questions of concern for the Colombians presence or for what they were doing at the processing plant. He would hear no complaints or concerns from the Cerros mill workers. They were simply too appreciative for their return to work to say or do anything that would jeopardize their jobs.

With Corozal sugarcane production at its peak, the Cerros mill began the immediate harvest of its cane crop. From harvest to processing into raw sugar, the first shipment was expected to be ready for transport to the St. Marks refinery in three weeks. During these weeks, much work remained to be done to ensure their readiness for the restart of the smuggling operation.

Vladimir Kerchenkov and his submersible crew would use this time to plot their transport route from Belize to Cuba and onward to St. Marks. The St. Marks refinery workers would require intensive education and proficiency training to gain the skills required in the sugar refinery processes. Miguel Thomas would use this time to take his 36 newly hired employees to Brazil to the Mecosta Paulo Sugar Refinery to receive their intense training.

It would be a busy three weeks.

CHAPTER TWELVE

Thomas gathered his employees at Two Rivers Restaurant to inform them of his upcoming plans to fly them to Sao Paulo. "There," he explained, "you will receive intensive training to operate the machinery used in the various steps in sugar refinery." Thomas had reserved the private south wing banquet room at Two Rivers for his meeting. The mill's new hires got their first chance to meet their fellow employees and learn from Miguel the expectations of their job.

Several in the group were local Wakulla countians who knew one another by sight, if not by name. Some, chosen from the Apalachee Bay area's fishing industry, had plied their trade either as deck hands or first mates on local charter fishing boats. Others were hired from the local logging industry. All were glad for the opportunity for a well-paying job that offered benefits essentially unavailable to them in their previous employment.

Not unlike the Corozal mill workers, those hired for the St. Marks refinery eagerly anticipated the start of their new jobs. Though it was a precondition for employment, no one voiced concern about the international travel required for his or her training. Few, if any, had ever been out the Southeastern United States, much less out of the country, and there was a buzz of excitement about the upcoming travel.

Smiling faces greeted Thomas as he welcomed them to 'the refinery family.' Wide grins replaced their smiles as Thomas called them one by one to the front table and handed them their first month's paycheck - in advance. The workers were astounded; it was mid-August and Thomas was paying them a full month's pay even though they had not yet done a day's work!

With his generosity, Thomas ensured loyalty from his workers. He had no doubt that now, without complaint, they would work whatever hours were required to meet the wholesale obligations of the refinery. With tearful eyes, several of the female employees expressed their gratitude that their children would now be able to start the school year with new clothes and new school supplies. In years past, many of the families represented could little afford such luxuries. Their children, who could not afford the latest designer clothes, often faced ridicule from insensitive classmates. They welcomed this beginning to a new life.

A giant of a man, the Italian Ralph Fiacincio was a transplant from New York who had been lured to the South by the promise of work in the pulpwood industry. Fiacincio had been hired specifically to oversee the off-loading of the raw sugar imported into St. Marks. Additionally, he would supervise the overland transport of the mill's refined sugar products to wholesale and retail centers throughout America.

Previously a crane operator and log-hauler dispatcher for the St. Joe Paper Company, the Italian had been responsible for supervising the loading and transport of pulpwood and saw-timber from the tens of thousands of acres of pine forest owned and managed by St. Joe throughout north and central Florida and south Georgia.

Cletus and Dewey Tanner would work directly under the supervision of Ralph Fiacincio. Fiacincio would have his hands full with the Tanner cousins.

During his interview, Fiacincio recommended that Thomas consider hiring his good friend Bill Knox as head of security. Knox was chief of security for St. Joe's forestry property and for the company's pulp and paper mills.

Thomas knew the importance of securing the St. Marks plant from inquisitive outsiders. Fiacincio's friend met the criteria for his security needs.

Bill Knox had graduated from Florida State University with a degree in business administration. An outstanding offensive lineman for the Seminoles, Knox followed his college career with a stint in the pros, playing with the Miami Dolphins. After a career ending knee injury, his college degree and football fame brought him the well paying job as head of security with the St. Joe Paper Company headquartered in Port St. Joe, Florida.

Knox, who had not applied for a position at the St. Marks refinery, nonetheless complied when his friend requested that he at least speak with Thomas about the position. Bill Knox had liked Miguel, who recruited him with the offer of a substantial pay raise, a matching retirement plan, no overnight travel, and the promise of time off to pursue his twin passions - hunting and fishing.

Unbeknownst to Miguel Thomas, Bill Knox was the younger brother of Lincoln Knox, Richard A. Tolbert's lifelong best friend. At least once each year, Lincoln, Rick, and Bill spent a weekend trout fishing offshore of St. Marks. In fact, Rick Tolbert had been Bill's childhood idol and mentor. Bill Knox considered Rick a second brother, and though they seldom had time for other than their fishing retreats, the two talked several times each year.

Had Juan Carlos Diego and Wayne Clark known that Thomas had just hired the one person who each year would bring the head of the BSDIA to the Shell Island Fish Camp, situated less than a half-mile from their U.S. smuggling base of operation, they likely would have had many nights of restless sleep.

It was Sunday, the end of the first week following the opening of the Cerros Mill. The sugarcane processing plant remained closed on Sunday - an important day of religious celebration for the Corozalians. They would not work on Sunday. Their religious belief and worship activities were the cornerstone of their society.

Sunday then, became the perfect day for Ortega to accomplish the drug smuggling tasks that had to be performed outside of the tight security on the mill's second floor. With the property vacated for the day, Ortega remained secure in the knowledge that their chance of discovery was unlikely. Wayne Clark had seemingly happened upon not only the perfect location, but also the ideal societal cover for their smuggling operation.

Ortega Diego and Vladimir Kerchenkov used this first Sunday to launch the submersible and test its underwater capabilities. At Vladimir's request, the nose of the DSRV had been retrofitted with a Plexiglas bubbled window and pressure tested to a depth of 3,000 feet. Through this window, the pilot could closely monitor the forward movement of the sub, allowing less reliance on global positioning and sonar for guidance during close quarter docking maneuvers.

Kerchenkov assured Diego that the bow window would provide for better navigation into and out of the sub's berthing dock at Arroyos de Mantua in Cuba, and particularly at St. Marks. Considering the mini-sub's confined quarters, Vladimir noted the added luxury the window would provide for observing undersea life as the DSRV traversed the Caribbean Sea and the Gulf of Mexico; this, said Vladimir, would make for a less stressful journey. Though a significant added expense, Juan Carlos was glad to comply with Kerchenkov's request. He knew their smuggling venture was reliant in part, upon a successful submarine transport. Diego was willing to do almost anything to keep his sub commanders happy.

The bow bubble was added as the Japanese engineers installed the navigational and communication equipment. Vladimir Kerchenkov and his crew enthusiastically awaited their first chance to test the sub's navigational and guidance capabilities. Though much smaller than the Russian Navy submarines they were accustomed to commanding, the sub used similar guidance principles. The captains were certain they would have no trouble navigating the mini-sub through the labyrinth of undersea coral formations that led from the Chetumal Bay into the open Caribbean.

The DSRV was unberthed at 7:00 that morning as a brilliant Belizean sun was beginning its steady climb overhead. The bright mid-morning to mid-afternoon rays would give excellent illumination to the subterranean waters below. The low-tide depth in the mill's canal read 99 feet as Vladimir and his crew of three navigated out into Chetumal Bay. Nicholas Krasnaya, the eldest and most experienced of Kerchenkov's first mates, was at the helm. Peter Segonyva and Vedonosti Novostey, each with 20 years or more experience at the console of Soviet nuclear submarines, rounded out Kerchenkov's most capable submariner crew.

Less than a half-mile offshore at a depth of 138 feet, the sub suddenly came upon the ruins of what appeared to be an underwater city. Not familiar with Belizean culture and history, Kerchenkov did not know they were passing ancient Cerros Maya, a once thriving port city that served as the principle Belizean coastal trade center for the ancient Mayan Empire of the third century B.C.

The Mayan trade center of Cerros Maya had come to an abrupt end in the Early Classic Period of history when the waters of the Chetumal Bay suddenly inundated the Corozal seacoast. Eventually, the rising tide swelled to a height of 68 feet above sea level and the entire city was enveloped by the rising floodwaters. Over the centuries, the bay waters only deepened, and the city was never rebuilt.

In its place, the surviving Mayans built a ceremonial temple mound aptly named Cerros Maya, in reverence to their ancestral home. The temple mound, built on the bluff of the Lowry's Bight Peninsula overlooking the Chetumal Bay, still proudly stands as a testament to the once-thriving seaport.

Kerchenkov circled the sub in awe of the sunken city. Built more than two thousand years ago, the ruins appeared as if they had just recently been deposited into the bay. Treasure hunters and recreational scuba divers had long since removed the once prevalent artifacts, but the architecture of the buildings remained a fascinating observation. Had they not remembered that the purpose of this excursion was to map a navigational egress out into the Caribbean, the crew might have spent the entire afternoon traversing the impressive ruins.

Kerchenkov turned towards Quintana Roo, Mexico's southernmost State. Here, he handed control of the helm to Nicholas. This direction would take them past Sarteneja on the Belizean coast, then northeast toward Santa Cecilia on the southeastern most tip of Quintana Roo and the Mexican coastline.

Their route passed through the Chetamul Bay Straights along the Bacalar Chico National Marine Reserve separating Mexico from the barrier islands of Belize. In traversing the straights, they had to navigate around the coral outcroppings lining the bottom of the 400-foot deep channel. To come any closer to the surface might attract the unwanted attention of the commercial fishermen, recreational scuba divers, and pleasure boaters who plied these waters off Ambergris Caye.

As they approached the Chetumal Channel barrier islands, Nicholas skillfully navigated the sub on a steep downward glide towards the channel bottom. "Ten degrees down bubble." Kerchenkov instructed his helmsman as he watched the depth gauge quickly fall past 200 feet. Kerchenkov kept a watchful eye on both the radar and side sonar readings on the instrument panel.

"Port thruster one-half full," he commanded. The sub sharply turned 30 degrees to the right without listing. The captain carefully scrutinized the instrument panel while glancing out the forward porthole for assurance they were experiencing no pitch or yaw from the aft and side thrusters.

"Fifteen degrees down bubble, all ahead full aft-thruster, full starboard thruster." Nicholas calmly and skillfully followed his orders. Kerchenkov was testing the sub's ability to avert any forward obstruction that might suddenly appear on the radar screen. The sub nosed smartly downward at a 15 degree angle while vectoring at an almost 45 degree angle to port. The complete maneuver was accomplished in less than a 50-foot track.

Vladimir had successfully tested the DSRV's capability to respond to the close quarter maneuvering required to navigate the numerous coral heads they would undoubtedly encounter. Having successfully completed this exercise, Vladimir was confident they could likewise easily maneuver the sub to berth within the close confines of the Arroyos de Mantua and

St. Marks' docking enclosures.

Now off the Belizean coastline, Vladimir navigated north-northeast into the Caribbean. Once safely past the Punta Calentura and Islote Cayo Lobos atolls of Quintana Roo's Banco Chinchoro barrier islands, the direct route to Arroyos de Mantua on the southwesternmost point of the Cuban coastline would be unimpeded.

Because Kerchenkov did not intend to travel into Cuban national waters, he had not contacted Hector Gomez. Their navigational position was still some distance from Cuba, so there was no concern for detection from any Cuban naval vessels on maneuver.

His goal this day was not to dock in Cuba. Rather, Kerchenkov's mission was to set a navigational course from Belize for an approach to Cuba. Having done so, he and the first mate headed back to Cerros. The outbound trip had taken almost 7 ½ hours, and they had navigated over halfway to Cuba. Vladimir carefully monitored the battery and O_2 gauges. The instrumentation determined that on a journey of less than 24 hours, they would have battery power and oxygen generating capacity to spare.

As they returned to port, Kerchenkov allowed Peter and Vedonosti a turn at the helm so they could become familiar with the intricacies of handling the mini-sub. After putting the DSRV through a similar series of vertical and horizontal maneuvers, each felt competent at the helm.

It was almost 10:00 PM before they finally reached port. Despite the late hour, Ortega and his chemists were waiting for them. Vladimir reported that the phase one testing of the sub's maneuverability, battery, oxygen generating capacity, and guidance system operation had proven both successful and uneventful. Ortega hurried to the Onyxitron Encryptor to convey the good news to his brother and to Wayne Clark. Juan Carlos would share the success of their mission with Thomas upon his return from Brazil.

As Ortega made his calls, Vladimir excitedly told the Colombians of their chanced discovery of the underwater city. The crew described what they called 'the Belizean Atlantis.' The Colombians as well, knew nothing of Belizean history, but expressed their eager desire to see the underwater city. "One day soon," Kerchenkov promised, "I will take you to see it."

Ortega returned and reported to the group that the final phase testing of the sub's ability to compete a successful roundtrip to Florida would soon follow. A trial run to St. Marks with a mid-way stop over at Arroyos de Mantua on each leg of the voyage must be tested for operational readiness. There must be no weak links in the navigational chain else the entire smuggling operation would fail. Because the St. Marks refinery remained under construction, their work in Belize remained on hold.

Meanwhile, Juan Carlos suggested to Ortega that he give the Colombians and the sub crew a week's vacation to explore their new country. He instructed Ortega to give them $5,000.00 each to help them enjoy their vacation. Juan Carlos intended to keep these men happy; he knew they were the key to the success of the Belizean end of their smuggling activity.

The Colombians were sure their families would enjoy touring Belize before the start of the school year. Vladimir and his men talked excitedly about relaxing at a tropical resort on Ambergris Caye. Though they missed their Russian Vodka, the crew joked that they were sure they could learn to appreciate Jamaican Rum just as well. While on vacation, they were determined to sample every tropical rum drink possible. Tenacious workers, they were equally dedicated to celebrating their leisure time just as resolutely whenever possible. The Russians were clearly excited at the opportunity to explore and enjoy the tropical beauty of Belize. The Motherland seemed but a faraway memory.

Like fine wine, Diego knew faithful employees had to be cultivated over time. Giving his key smuggling employees a week's paid vacation before they had even worked a full week on the job was a giant step towards securing their loyalty. Despite his caustic demeanor, Juan Carlos possessed considerable managerial skills.

Construction equipment towered over the downtown streets of St. Marks, giving the small town the appearance of a major metropolis. In an effort to complete final construction blueprints, Alton Roberts had worked diligently with the equipment specifications. By mid-August, Albert Roberts' construction crews were working in eight-hour shifts around-the-clock to meet a final construction completion goal of mid-September.

By the end of the first week in September only the basic finish work remained. The trim, painting, carpeting and flooring installation, security system, and landscaping would take less than two weeks to complete. Soon, the St. Marks Sugar Refinery would be ready for operation. Miguel Thomas was pleased with the construction progress.

He was equally pleased with the readiness of his workers to begin the refinery process. Overall, they were more than adequately prepared to take over independent operation of the newly installed refinery equipment. Batista Demarquez and his staff at the Mecosta Paulo had trained them well. They had returned from Brazil at the end of August as a close-knit family of workers, eager to join together to accomplish the production goals of the mill. A close camaraderie would ensure the smooth operation of the refinery, Thomas thought.

Thomas was determined to see that they retained their cohesiveness. Upon their return, he gave each of his newly trained workers a check for $2,000 and announced that, as a reward for their hard work the past two weeks, he had made reservations for them and their families to enjoy the long Labor Day weekend at Walt Disney World. Chartered buses, he reported, would pick them up on Thursday, and transport them to Orlando.

Some of the workers had lived their entire life in St. Marks, less than a five-hour drive from Orlando, but never had the money to take their family there on vacation. Each was excited for this chance for a paid vacation - a vacation given even though they had not yet done a day's work at the refinery. Most felt fortunate to have their new jobs and would work diligently to keep their boss happy.

These workers had been properly trained to run the mill virtually independent of his constant supervision, and Thomas was pleased with this. A credible, independent workforce would leave him more time to devote to supervision of the drug smuggling operation. In less than two weeks, they should be ready to receive their first shipment of raw sugar and cocaine.

That night, Thomas signaled Juan Carlos, Wayne Clark, and Ortega Diego with his news. Their well-conceived plans were finally becoming a reality. In less than a month, they would be ready to launch full-scale cocaine distribution throughout the United States.

Before that time Clark needed to assess whether his drug pipeline was ready for delivery. The sophisticated pipeline used a pyramid-stepped approach for distribution. Clark had divided the U.S. into a north, east, south and west region. A regional lieutenant, or 'drug kingpin' as they were referred to on the street, managed each region. Working under them were the individual 'state drug lords.' These state distributors divided their shipments among the 'local drug lords,' who managed local cocaine sales on America's urban city streets and in its suburban neighborhoods.

Clark had devised an elaborate inventory system for sales accountability. He scrupulously monitored reports. Through meticulously kept records, Clark knew to the kilo, ounce, and gram how much cocaine each distributor along the pipeline received and how much profit each was expected to return in cocaine sales. Those holding back on cash collections would be dealt with swiftly and finitely.

The word on the street spread quickly. You did not double-cross 'The Commander'. To do so would result in horrible consequences. Clark employed a half-dozen henchmen strategically located across the United States who meted out his 'discipline.' With a single communiqué, one of the enforcers would be sent to 'sanction' anyone who Clark determined had shorted reported sales.

Most often, the sanction would be delivered in the form of an unmerciful beating, given as a lesson to the offender as well as to others in the cocaine pipeline. More severe incidents of missing cocaine or stolen money resulted in murder. These professional homicides usually went unsolved and were most often written off as a local gang hit. Those in Clark's ever-efficient pipeline knew better.

Sanctions were seldom necessary. The Commander gave everyone a fair cut of the profits. Only a few greedy individuals needed to be taught a lesson. The lessons left a lasting impression on all who worked for Clark. As a result, he had little trouble with his distributors or his street-level sellers.

Clark's principal regional distribution cities were Atlanta, Los Angeles, Chicago, and New York City with smaller distribution hubs in Houston, Miami, Philadelphia, and San Francisco. From the principal regional distributors to the street-level dealers, Clark's network operated through a sophisticated cellular telephone calling system. To thwart law enforcement's interception of calls and to identify shipment delivery points, Clark purchased cell phones in bulk quantities, discarded them, and then changed phone numbers at least monthly. In higher interdiction effort areas, the phones were exchanged more frequently.

Clark's street-level traffickers were a tight group of thugs whose gang was difficult to penetrate. Depending upon the geographical area of the country, the structure of these gangs referred to by Clark as 'local cells,' was built upon familial, ethnic, or tribal relationships.

Cells in the North and along the West Coast involved either the Crips, Bloods, or Chicanos street gangs, while cells throughout the South and along the East Coast were comprised primarily of Jamaicans, Haitians, and Dominicans or of Mexican, Cuban, or African-American street gangs. When local authorities were successful in a street-level interdiction, cocaine traffic was only temporarily affected.

Over the course of a year, Clark's retail-level distribution of cocaine employed imaginative methods of concealment. One such imaginative scheme worked well for more than a year, during which Clark's pipeline participants distributed close to a half-ton of crack cocaine and realized sales of almost a $100 million.

The ingenious plan incorporated hiding up to 50 grams of 87 percent pure crack cocaine in hand-made pottery sold from a craft booth at a Los Angeles flea market. A secret password identified users who paid $2,100 for each 50-gram packaged craft item. The scheme worked well until an off-duty K-9 drug squad commander and his drug-sniffing canine, 'Challenger', wandered by the display one Saturday afternoon.

As they approached the craft booth, the dog struck his drug detection posture, signaling a presence of narcotics. When the officer unleashed the dog, he bounded the counter, tearing into the craft selections concealing the contraband. In the afternoon drug bust, law enforcement officers confiscated 2 kilos of crack cocaine and more than $55,000 in cash netted from the day's drug sales.

It had not been a good day for Clark. He had just lost one of his West Coast's most profitable sales markets. Ultimately, the drug bust proved only a temporary inconvenience. In less than a month, the operation resumed at an open-air fish market on the Embarcadero in San Francisco.

With a new cocaine harvest forthcoming, Clark began a reassessment of his pipeline's readiness to restart cocaine trafficking. Unbeknownst to each other, Clark had summoned his four regional lieutenants and 48 contiguous state drug lords to the Venetian Hotel in Las Vegas. Though assembled at the same hotel, none could identity other members of the network from outside his territory.

Clark would never address them in a group. His penchant for anonymity carefully guarded the identity of each distributor from others outside their distribution region. Such secrecy denied anyone caught by the authorities the opportunity to snitch on fellow drug traffickers for the promise of a lighter sentence.

Over the phone, Clark spoke with each lieutenant and drug lord individually. After concluding his interviews, he determined each key player in the pipeline was ready to restart their network of distribution. From the regional level, down through the state level, and on to the street level, Clark was pleased with the readiness of his drug trafficking network.

In addition to gathering them to assess their distribution readiness, Clark had brought them to Las Vegas to show his appreciation for their key role in his distribution network. At the conclusion of each interview, Clark expressed his thanks and informed his pipeline players that he was giving them a gaming credit of $5,000 in addition to this all-expense-paid weekend of food and entertainment. Clark considered this outlay of money a good investment; it would help to ensure continued loyalty in the 'family'.

No one in the drug distribution network knew Clark's identity. He worked persistently at keeping that a closely guarded secret. Wayne Clark's only method of communication with his cocaine distributors was over the telephone. To disguise his voice Clark utilized an electronic voice scrambler that converted his own vocalizations into an electronic computer-generated speech pattern. This robotic voice imitation was all that was known of Clark's identity.

Using such cryptic methods had proven a wise move in the past. Several attempts had been made over the years to uncover Clark's identity. In past years, three of his state drug lords were caught and confronted with long jail sentences. When offered a reduced sentence if they could identify the ringleader, Clark's penchant for carefully disguising his identity had proven to be a vanguard of defense. All three attempts at disclosure had failed.

Clark's network traffickers could only contact him through a pager number. To avoid detection, he changed numbers weekly. Not even the pager company from whom he rented the paging system could identify him. Thus far, his disguise scheme had been foolproof. Attempts to trick him into returning a page or to keep him on the phone for a prolonged period in an attempt to trace the call had likewise proven unsuccessful.

Clark talked for no more than 60 seconds. Regardless of the purpose of the call, he hung up after one minute. His plan for maintaining anonymity had never failed, even when phone calls were taped and a trace was attempted. His rituals of ringing off after 60 seconds and use of a voice scrambler made for a failsafe method of anonymity.

Late that Friday evening, Clark had encrypted a communication to Juan Carlos, Ortega, and Miguel updating them on his drug trafficking network's preparedness status. "The pipeline is ready to begin distribution as soon as we receive Ortega's first delivery," Clark reported.

"Thomas," he asked, "how much longer before construction completion at the St. Marks refinery?"

Thomas responded, "Albert Roberts assures me that construction work will be complete in less than 10 days. In fact, tomorrow I will begin moving into the living quarters over the boathouse. All that remains to be done is a small amount of trim work, the finishing touches of painting, and the exterior landscaping. I am pleased with the quality of the construction work and with the diligence at which Roberts' men have worked around-the-clock to finish this project."

Thomas, obviously elated over the progress at St. Marks, continued. "The underwater lift works flawlessly. It is completely hidden within the block wall of the boathouse, and the noise of the motor wench is almost imperceptible. You will be pleased with the outcome of its design plan and construction. It's a masterful work of mechanics."

"Excellent!" Clark and Ortega exclaimed.

Juan Carlos joined the conversation. "I am eager to launch the final test phase in determining the DSRV's capability to navigate a roundtrip run from Belize to St. Marks. We must test the vessel with a full trial run including each navigational leg of the trip and the planned stopovers in Cuba."

"I agree," Clark responded. "We must have assurance that the navigational route, the guidance coordinates, and the readiness of the crew have all been fully proven. We all know that a successful underwater transportation system is the key to our smuggling venture."

"It appears then," Juan Carlos said, "that about the time Ortega's men return from their Belizean vacation, the St. Marks refinery will be completed and ready for us to conduct a trial run. Thomas, keep us informed on the progress. Ortega, you call General Gomez and alert him to stand ready for our call. Meanwhile, I will be preparing for the transport of my cocaine to Belize."

There were congratulations all around. Having once thought the BSDIA initiative would end their smuggling partnership, they were now more confident they could restart their operation without fear of interdiction from U.S. federal authorities. It had been a good summer for the malevolent quartet.

The Colombians and their families returned from their paid vacation having spent the week learning more about their new country. They visited the ancient Mayan historical sites of Lamanai and Xunantunich. At the Shipstern Nature Reserve near Sarteneja, they were introduced to the native plants and wildlife indigenous to Belize.

They shopped at the craft market in Belize City and took the usual tourist day trips to the outer barrier islands of Half Moon Caye and Caye Caulker off the Placentia district. Coming from the poor economic rural countryside of the Andes, when they visited Ambergris Caye, they were awestruck by the rich lifestyles enjoyed by the tourists and privileged few wealthy Belizeans who lived in San Pedro City.

The children particularly enjoyed the glass-bottom boat ride over Belize's famous Blue Hole, where they reveled in the opportunity to peer into the crystal clear waters of the Caribbean. It was their first glimpse at the underwater life of the coral reefs. On their last day of vacation, while the women and children sunbathed at the beach on Ambergris Caye, the men spent the day bill fishing off Turneffe Atoll enjoying cold Coronas, Red Stripes, and fine Cuban cigars.

The wives relished the opportunity to dine in fine restaurants and to be pampered by the wait staff of the hotels and restaurants they patronized. They were not accustomed to such luxury; now that their husbands would be earning a good salary at the sugarcane-processing mill, they promised each other that they would enjoy this pampering more often.

The wives returned with a greater appreciation of their new country - especially the beauty and charm of the nearby resorts of Ambergris Caye. Their husbands returned refreshed and ready to begin work for Diego. His kind gesture of a paid vacation had endeared them to work hard for their new boss. Like their wives, they had learned to love this new lifestyle.

The Russians returned sunburned and relaxed from their week spent at Captain Morgan's Retreat on Ambergris Caye. Having a voracious appetite for Russian vodka, they nonetheless learned to appreciate a variety of Jamaican tropical rum drinks during their week of leisure.

They spent their days fishing the barrier islands, while roaming the beachfront bars at night. They quickly learned to appreciate the beauty and activities to be enjoyed in Belize. They, too, had adopted their new homeland and would work hard to please their new boss.

Except for the few family members they had left behind in the former Soviet Union, they had no reservations about having left Russia. With the money they would make this year, they had promised those family members left behind that next year they would bring them to Belize.

Returning with a renewed energy, these career submarine commanders were ready to begin their navigational duties. The undersea world was their life, and they eagerly anticipated another opportunity to operate the mini-sub. That opportunity would come as soon as they returned to Cerros.

On Monday morning, Ortega Diego alerted General Gomez that tomorrow they would initiate their trial run to Florida. Gomez promised to move the military traffic out of their navigational route and await them at the base in Arroyos de Mantua.

"What time should I expect Vladimir to arrive?" Gomez asked.

"They will depart at 12:00 AM. According to navigational charts, it is a journey of 362 statute miles from Cerros to Arroyos de Mantua. A 25 mile per hour forward speed should put them in port at approximately 3:00 in the afternoon," Ortega replied.

"Bueno. I will have a supply of sandwiches and drinks awaiting their arrival," Gomez replied.

"Gracias, Hector. I'm sure the sub's crew will appreciate that. Just make sure the drinks are all sodas now. No Coronas!" Ortega chuckled. Despite the Russian's fondness for alcohol, he knew neither Kerchenkov nor his crew would drink while they were on duty.

Gomez laughed, too. "I promise. No cold Coronas while on duty. But, on their return trip to Cerros, I will give them a case to ice down in celebration of their successful journey."

"I'm sure they would appreciate that, too." Ortega laughed knowingly.

Turning his attention to the objective for this expedition, Gomez said, "Until we can fully assess the ability of the sub to navigate underwater into the safe confines of the boathouse, I will redirect all military traffic. And I'll restrict all commercial boating from the area."

Knowing that ordering Cuban vessels away from the area around Arroyos de Mantua would greatly lessen the likelihood of the sub's chanced discovery, Ortega nonetheless cautioned, "Restricting military traffic would be to our advantage, but I am concerned that you might arouse suspicion if you intervene in restricting commercial traffic lanes also. How do you intend to do that?" Diego asked.

"As military commander of the Cuban Navy, the commercial fishermen and transport vessels will not second-guess my directive. I will announce that we are holding secret military exercises and the area is restricted for today only. No one in the military or the commercial industry will be the wiser."

"You will have an unrestricted run of the waters off the Southwest Cuban Peninsula de Guanahacabibes coast. Instruct Kerchenkov to first set guidance for the Cabo de San Antorrio peninsula point on Latitude 21.819 N and Longitude 84.998 W. These headings will navigate the sub directly into the cove of Arroyos de Mantua."

Gomez continued, "Tell Kerchenkov it will be safe to surface as soon as he enters the Yucatan Straights and sights the peninsula on sonar. It will be much easier for Vladimir to plot accurate GPS waypoints while he is running on the surface. Then, without fear of detection, they can navigate directly underwater into the boathouse on return voyages."

"I thank you for your help, Hector." Ortega responded. "So do Wayne Clark and my brother. Even though this is a trial run, Juan Carlos said to tell you, that in appreciation of your cooperation, he will transfer fifty thousand dollars into your account at Cayman Island Capital Trust."

"Thank you, Amigo, and tell Juan Carlos, "Muchos Gracias," also. I did not expect that. On Kerchenkov's return trip, I will send you all a generous supply of our finest Cuban cigars."

"Gracias, to you, Hector. That would be nice. We will enjoy them in celebration of our first successful roundtrip into St. Marks. With a more serious tone, Ortega reflected, "We need everything to go smoothly on this trial run. We must assess our capability to move cocaine into the U.S. without detection. Again, Hector, thank you for your help. Much of the success of our smuggling operation depends on you and your preparation."

"You are welcome, Amigo. Tomorrow at 3:00 PM, I'll be waiting for the crew's arrival. Before they depart for St. Marks, we will set up a time to meet on their return trip."

"Gracias, again, Hector."

CHAPTER THIRTEEN

Vladimir Kerchenkov and his crew arrived at the Cerros mill before midnight. Though it was still seven hours before the day shift was due to arrive, they were apprehensive about discovery as they began their first complete roundtrip exploit in the DSRV. Departing at this late hour would lessen the likelihood that they would be noticed by anyone from the Corozal district.

A bright half-moon night gave partial illumination to the dark waters of the Chetumal Bay. Though apprehensive, the submariners were eager to begin their journey. Peter Segonyva and Vedonosti Novostey untied the DSRV from its secluded berth and stowed their gear in the aft storage section. On this inaugural trip, the crew brought along a supply of replacement carbon dioxide scrubbers and the equipment needed to recharge the silver/nickel electrical batteries. On each stopover at the Arroyos de Mantua base and in St. Marks, it would be necessary to replace a scrubber and recharge the batteries.

Vladimir Kerchenkov and Nicholas Krasnaya ran the checklist for the navigational and guidance instruments. They checked both the functional integrity of the CO_2 scrubbers to recycle oxygen and the power level of the onboard electrical batteries. With the checklist complete and supplies stowed away, Novostey closed the hatch. Kerchenkov began the sub's vertical descent to the bottom of the inlet.

Turning on the bow lights, Vladimir carefully steered the sub out of the inlet and into the Chetamul Bay. Once they reached the open waters of the bay, Kerchenkov turned off the bow lights to avoid detection. Even in the half-moon light, he was able to easily guide the sub through the crystal clear waters.

To check the accuracy of the GPS waypoints integrated into the sub's computer guidance system, Kerchenkov set the DSRV on autopilot and thrusters to half-throttle. The sub descended to 128 feet, holding steady 10 feet off the bottom.

The fore, aft, and side-thrusters worked synchronously to accurately maneuver the sub around the Cerros Maya ruins and the coral outcroppings of Chetamul Bay. Entering the deeper water of the Chetamul Channel, the DSRV plunged and held steady at a depth of 390 feet as it headed northeast toward Santa Cecilia on the Mexico peninsula of Quintana Roo.

Kerchenkov and his crew watched in relief as the guidance system navigated the sub with precision around the coral heads of the Bacalar Chico barrier islands in the Chetamul Straits. Once past the southeastern-most tip of Quintana Roo, the autopilot turned abruptly to Latitude 18.171 N and Longitude 87.837 W, and navigated north-northeast toward the Banco Chinchoro barrier islands off Quintana Roo's east coast.

Once past the island atolls, Vladimir took the sub off autopilot, and Vedonosti Novostey took over the helm. Holding a constant 22-knot speed, the sub descended to 500 feet, holding its north-northeast heading past the Punta Calentura and Islote Cayo Lobos atolls off Banco Chinchoro. Only a seven-hour voyage remained before they reached Cuba.

The MK-6 navigational and guidance system worked flawlessly. The CO_2 scrubber kept a constant re-supply of oxygen circulating in the sub. In another six hours, the bottom-reading gauge rose quickly from the 14,360-foot depth of the Mexico Basin to a depth of 762 feet. Their on-board navigational map showed that they had reached the eastern edge of the Campeche Bay in the Yucatan Channel.

Their sonar showed the western tip of Cabo de San Antorrio, Cuba, to be less than 8 nautical miles from their present location. More importantly, the sonar displayed no surface traffic. Cautious nevertheless, Vedonosti slowly surfaced, and Vladimir scanned the horizon with binoculars to confirm that they were alone. Seeing no ships in the area, they knew that General Gomez had been successful in keeping their navigational lane into Arroyos de Mantua clear of all military and commercial vessels.

Kerchenkov used a cell phone to signal Hector Gomez on his pager. A pre-arranged numerical code signaled that they were now within sight of land and would be docking in one hour. Vladimir reduced mid and aft thruster speed to half. As they approached the Cuban coastline and their safe harbor at Arroyos de Mantua, Peter Segonyva sat aloft the hatch cover. He dutifully entered their navigational waypoints on the GPS. Once safely inside the boathouse, Kerchenkov would feed these same coordinates into the computer guidance system. Their next arrival at Arroyos de Mantua could be made completely underwater.

In less than 60 minutes, they were safely secluded in Gomez's newly constructed boathouse. The first of four legs of their voyage had been completed flawlessly and without consequence. As they glided to a stop, the general greeted them as if they were his long, lost brothers.

"Welcome, welcome," Gomez shouted as they berthed the sub.

"I am Generalissimo Hector Gomez. Please call me Hector," the general said as he shook hands warmly with the crew.

Vladimir introduced himself and the members of his crew.

"Are you hungry?" Gomez queried.

"Starving," they replied. "Our boxed food has long since been gone."

"Good! I have brought you a supply of sandwiches and sodas."

"Gracias, Hector." Vladimir replied for all. He and his crew downed their sandwiches and cold drinks then attended to offloading their supplies into the boathouse storage room.

"Are you sure the boathouse is secure?" asked Kerchenkov. "We must store our carbon dioxide replacement scrubbers here. Nothing must happen to them. They are invaluable to a successful operation; without a replacement filter, we could only navigate on the surface."

"Do not worry, comrades," Gomez responded. "The few area residents know this is my personal boathouse. No one would dare to come onto this property. I will assure you of that."

"This is what I wanted to hear. Incidentally, Juan Carlos sends word that your bank account has been significantly increased," Vladimir remarked with a grin.

"Bueno!" Gomez responded, rubbing his hands gleefully. "In turn I have something for you, Juan Carlos, and Diego to enjoy. On your return trip, for each of you, I have a case of both Montecristo Robustos and Coronas to enjoy in celebration of your first successful round-trip voyage. Do not forget to take these with you on your return departure."

"Do not worry," Vladimir replied. "We will not forget," he said with a laugh. Shaking hands all around, the crew readied for 12 hours of rest before their journey to Florida. Before his departure, Gomez promised to return and bring them a late night dinner. He asked, "When do you think you will make your return stopover? I want to make sure I am here to meet you. What are your return plans?"

Kerchenkov answered. "It's about 4:00 PM now. We will rest overnight and wait to depart around 4:00 AM. By navigational charts, it is 574 miles to the mouth of the St. Marks River. I expect a journey of around 22 hours to reach the St. Marks lighthouse, then another hour upriver until we are safely inside the refinery boathouse. We need to be docked at least two hours before daybreak, somewhere around 4:00 AM before the early morning charter boats leave port."

"After sleeping most of the morning and afternoon, we will spend a few hours with Miguel, and depart around eleven tomorrow night. That should put us back at Arroyos de Mantua sometime around 10:00 PM day after tomorrow, I would think. It is about a 15-hour voyage back to Cerros. We will rest and be underway again by daybreak, returning to Cerros an hour or so after dark, somewhere around 10:00 PM. That is our plan now. If anything does change, we will have Thomas encrypt a call to Ortega and he will let you know."

"Good," Gomez remarked. "I will have a late snack awaiting you."

Waving goodbye, Gomez departed for home. Three of the crew stretched out on cots to rest. Each would stand guard for a two-hour rotation while the others sleep. For their protection, they carried a 30-round 9 mm Uzi and a 40-caliber Glock with a 15-round clip. If anyone inadvertently walked in on them, the intruder would not leave to divulge the crew's presence. No member of the crew would hesitate to use his firearm if necessary. They had been instructed to shoot first. No questions would be asked later.

At 4:00 AM, before the faint gray of dawn slowly began to illuminate the Yucatan Channel, Vladimir lowered the sub to within 10 feet of the bottom of the cove channel and then backed away from the coastline. In less than 150 yards, the water dropped to a depth of over 700 feet.

They had yet to make this voyage from Cuba to Florida, but the crew had meticulously planned their journey. In choosing their route, they had studied the navigational chart of the Gulf of Mexico designed by NOAA, the National Oceanic and Atmospheric Administration.

Drafted using satellite imaging technology, NOAA's maps were the benchmark for worldwide navigation. Drawn to international standards, these electronic navigational charts, or 'smart charts' as they were referred to by naval and ship captains, incorporated navigational data with GPS satellite and other sensory imaging. NOAA's smart charts were a reliable tool used extensively by sailors to vector navigational directions.

Kerchenkov and his crew knew they could trust their NOAA map to guide them across the Gulf. The mouth of the St. Marks River system was charted at latitude 30.081 and a longitude of 84.195 W. They determined that a compass heading of 9 degrees north-northeast from Cabo de San Antorrio would take them the 572 miles into the Apalachee Bay, then directly into the river basin two miles offshore of the St. Marks lighthouse.

They descended to 500 feet and set the autopilot on 9 degrees north-

northeast for their journey toward the Florida coastline. Less than a mile beyond the Yucatan Channel, they crossed the Yucatan Wall. Here, the bottom gauge dropped suddenly from 768 feet to 4,580. They had just crossed the steepest of the continental slopes in the United States, steeper even than the slopes off the Hawaiian Islands or the 'Bimini Wall' off the Bahamas and Puerto Rico. The wall gently sloped to a depth of 12,884 at the bottom of the eastern edge of the Mexico Basin. The sub descended to 2,500 feet.

Unaccustomed for the opportunity to peer out through windows on their submarine, each crewmember starred in amazement at the eerie darkness of the depth below. The powerful halogen headlamps on the mini-sub illuminated their forward course outwards to 25 feet. Spellbound, they watched as translucent fish, colorless sea worms, and other phosphorescent invertebrates rose from the depths below and crossed in front of the bow lights.

Occasionally they would pass through what appeared to be opaque water currents. From their study of marine biology, they identified this opacity as a thermocline layer produced when cold water currents were interspersed with circulating warm water currents. They knew that the bottom of the Gulf of Mexico consisted of layers of sheets of salt, rather than mud and silt sediment. As these salt sheets bent, broke, and folded over upon other salt layers, they create a rugged topography of domes, faults, and fissures. From these fissures, the rich oil and gas deposits in the Mexico Basin leaked out causing these layers of thermoclines.

Midway across the Mexico Basin, with Peter Segonyva and Vedonosti Novostey at the helm, the port sonar alarm sounded, alerting the crew to the sudden presence of massive objects coming up from the aft port side of the sub. As suddenly as the alarm sounded, the sub lurched violently to starboard.

Each crewmember was bounced around the fore cabin. Looking anxiously out the bow window, they laughed with a sigh of relief when they saw what had collided with their vessel.

From early to mid fall, pods of sperm whales and dolphins traverse the Florida Straights and settle into the depths of the Mexico Basin. Here, they feed off long strands of floating Sargassum Weed algae and the large schools of baitfish that congregate in the warm waters of the Gulf. Concentrated in those areas where warm eddies break off from the Gulf loop current, the algae and baitfish are favorite food of the sperm whale and dolphin.

In crossing one of these eddies, they had steered through the path of a pod of sperm whales. Apparently annoyed with the intrusion, one of the whales had brushed the DSRV with its tail fluke. After determining that the fore, aft, and side thrusters were not damaged, Kerchenkov decided to reset the side sonars to maximum sensitivity where they would be alerted sooner to any possible future collisions.

Other than their brush with the sperm whale, it was an uneventful journey across the Gulf of Mexico. At 2:30 AM., they crossed the Aucilla Ridge and began their ascent along the rising Gulf floor. The slope gradually inclined, taking them to a steady depth of 40 feet. Just 30 minutes later, they reached buoy number one marking the entrance to the navigational channel of the St. Marks River. Their on-board guidance system had been precisely accurate in their navigation to the offshore marker.

Kerchenkov brought the sub to a complete stop, hugging the bottom of the 40-foot deep channel. Noting no nearby movement on the radar or sonar, he slowing surfaced and opened the hatch. At this early morning hour, no navigational lights on either the Gulf or in the St. Marks River were visible.

The only evident light was the steadily blinking navigational lantern of the St. Marks lighthouse. Its rhythmic signal directed vessels to the mouth of the St. Marks River, while it warned of the nearby sand banks, oyster bars, and land outcroppings that sheltered the entrance to port.

Until they approached the downtown area, Kerchenkov decided to navigate upriver on the surface where they could get a better visual perspective of the river contours and of the adjacent sand and oyster bars. He paged Thomas to alert him that they were beginning their trip upriver. The GPS waypoints previously set by Clark and Thomas had been incorporated into the computer's electronic guidance system. Vladimir set the navigation on autopilot and the aft thruster to 15 mph. Steadily the on-board guidance system navigated the sub from offshore towards the mouth of the river.

Entering the river on a medium high tide, Vladimir reduced speed to 10 mph. He was glad that the guidance system had been pre-set with navigational headings. Many of the oyster bars were practically imperceptible in the light of the half-moon until the sub was almost upon them. Only when the guidance system made a course correction away from the obstruction did the sand or oyster bar become clearly visible.

Without internal guidance, Kerchenkov was certain he could not have safely navigated the channel without running aground. Never had he been more thankful for an autopilot guidance system. For seven-and-a-half miles, the autopilot took the sub safely through the twists and turns of the St. Marks. On their journey upriver, they encountered no approaching vessels that would have forced them back under water.

Rounding marker 62, Vladimir submerged and slowed the sub's forward speed. In less than 10 minutes, the console beeped a signal that the pre-set guidance coordinates were ending. As Vladimir reduced speed to an idle, the DSRV made a sharp 90-degree left-hand turn and glided through the underwater riverside doors of the boathouse.

The boathouse doors closed quickly behind them. Vladimir switched on the bow lights to illuminate the interior walls of the boathouse. With a short reverse burst of the aft thruster, the sub came to an abrupt halt.

Through the bow window, the crew could see the interior lights of the boathouse deck above. Slowly the sub rose to the surface. Vladimir opened the hatch. Waiting on the port-side deck was a smiling Miguel Thomas. "Welcome to St. Marks, Florida, Comrades." Thomas greeted the crew with excitement.

Amidst fervent handshakes, introductions were made. Cheers of congratulations for a job well done bounced off the boathouse walls. All were glad that the journey had finally ended. They noted that the time was precisely 4:00 AM. It had been a long day, and all were tired.

Despite their exhaustion, the crew unloaded a supply of their precious carbon dioxide scrubbers and stowed them in the boathouse storage shed. After unloading the supplies, the sub was lowered by the submersible hoist to the bottom of the canal where it completely disappeared in the dark waters below. Thomas was pleased with this ingenious concept and design.

Miguel adjourned with the crew to his new upper living quarters. As crew members took well-deserved, long, hot showers, Thomas cooked them a Southern breakfast of grits, scrambled eggs, fried ham, toast, and biscuits served with blackberry jelly, hot coffee, and orange juice. The mariners ate with a ferocious appetite, enjoying seconds on everything but the grits. This was their first taste of genuine southern cuisine.

On behalf of his crew, Kerchenkov thanked Thomas for the breakfast. "It will probably take some time for us to learn to like those grits, though!" he admitted with a chuckle

"What didn't you like about them?" Thomas asked those gathered for the welcoming meal.

"I think I prefer oatmeal or cream of wheat. It tastes better with sugar and milk than the grits do," Peter responded.

Miguel laughed, "Amigos, you are not supposed to put sugar in grits! It should be eaten with salt and pepper! Forgive me, I should have told you. Next time try them that way. I'm sure you will learn to like them," he said promisingly.

"We will try," Vladimir responded, half-heartedly.

It was now 6:30 in the morning, and the crew was exhausted. They retired to their comfortable sleeping quarters for a much-needed rest. While they slept, Thomas called Wayne Clark, Juan Carlos, and Ortega Diego to update them on the success of the journey.

The partners were excited. This voyage had proven unequivocally that their smuggling operation could be accomplished by means of an underwater route beneath the U.S. border. By the end of September, the three were certain they could restart their smuggling venture.

Three loose ends remained undone, however, which needed to be accomplished before they could be fully operational. Clark needed to disclose his plan for laundering the millions of dollars of cash they expected to take in from their cocaine sales. Ortega needed to make final arrangements to transport the first shipment of cocaine to St. Marks. Finally, Juan Carlos needed to supply Thomas with the cocaine experts he would need to manage the packaging and shipping of the St. Marks refinery's cocaine through the U.S. distribution pipeline.

When Juan Carlos prompted an answer to the laundering question, Clark responded, "I have pondered this one unresolved issue for months. There is constant scrutiny of cash bank deposits by the Federal Banking Commission, the FBI, and the CIA. I am positive that it would prove to be our downfall if we tried to deposit our immense cash collections in a legitimate business enterprise and later wire the money offshore."

"This usual method of laundering cash seems to be a far too risky method for us to consider," Clark offered. "The records of the millions each month we would wire offshore would be certain to attract attention to our operation. I have given this much thought. Rather than deposit our cash in the U.S. banking industry, I would recommend that we transport our cash directly offshore for deposit at Cayman Island Capital Trust."

"Interesting idea," Juan Carlos noted, "but how do you suggest that we do that?"

"I would propose we use the submarine to rendezvous with a transport ship sent out by Romano Vicente to return the cash to George Town," Clark answered.

"It sounds risky," Ortega said. "I would much prefer to turn over our cash to an institution where we control our deposits and wire transfers."

"I agree, that would be the best option," Clark said, "but again, I'm fearful of the intense federal scrutiny of wire transfers. I too, hate to trust someone else to handle our money. But, considering the risk of detection by the feds, I believe we have little choice but to consider this alternative and trust Romano to manage the transfer and deposit."

Juan Carlos added his thoughts to the debate. "I too, would prefer a direct deposit into a U.S. banking institution. But if Wayne believes our operation will be at greater risk of detection if we do, I suggest we consider his proposal. I think it would work, especially if we pay Romano say, a $1 million transfer fee and make him personally responsible for each shipment once the money is transferred to his transport team."

Clark added, "I am not concerned about having to pay out additional money to get our cash deposited at Cayman Island Capital Trust. If we used banking institutions to wire our money offshore, we would be paying up to a 10 % wire transfer fee anyway. Paying Romano a deposit fee would not be any larger than the transfer fee we would pay. My concern is for the money actually reaching Vicente in George Town."

"Yes," Thomas agreed. "That is the highest risk. But, if Romano is willing to accept responsibility for the maritime transfer of the money, it does seem to be our best option."

Clark then asked, "Well, is this plan agreeable, or does anyone have a better idea?"

"I see we have little choice," Thomas replied.

"Me, either," said Ortega.

"It doesn't seem we have a better alternative," Juan Carlos concluded. "I can certainly think of no better transfer method. I will call Romano and make the arrangements to set the plan into motion. We will just have to have faith that Vicente will choose a team he can trust. Romano needs to let them know that if they double-cross us and run off with our money, the world will not be a large enough place for them to hide!"

Tired from having traversed the northern Caribbean and entire width of the Gulf of Mexico on their 946-mile voyage, the sub crew did not awaken until late afternoon. As this was their first visit to America, they considered staying an extra day to look around the Gulf area. But since General Gomez was expecting them the next evening, they did not postpone their return trip.

They spent the afternoon in seclusion in Miguel's condominium, pouring over NOAA navigational maps while keeping a close watch on the Weather Channel. The Gulf and Caribbean weather map showed no marine disturbances that might hinder their 11:00 PM departure.

At eight o'clock, Kerchenkov signaled Hector Gomez notifying him that they would depart at eleven, as planned. He could then expect them to arrive at Arroyos de Mantua in approximately 23 hours, at around 10:00 the next evening. The crew ate the tasty Two Rivers Restaurant seafood buffet take-out order that Miguel had brought them. After a short nap, it was time to ready the sub for departure.

With the silver/nickel batteries recharged and the CO_2 scrubber replaced, they thanked Miguel for his hospitality and entered the sub. As Nicholas and Vedonosti checked the instrumentation, Vladimir showed Thomas the interior of the sub. He marveled at the internal guidance system, the helm seating, and aft storage area where they would transport bundles of cocaine into and take bundles of cash out of St. Marks. As soon as Miguel exited the sub, Peter closed the hatch cover.

Thomas untied the mooring ropes and opened the underwater door into the river. The crew waved their goodbyes as the DSRV slowly descended to the bottom of the channel. Hovering just five feet off the bottom, Nicholas slowly reversed the sub through the boathouse doors into the traffic lanes of the St. Marks.

Vedonosti set the autopilot and eased the aft thruster forward to 5 mph. Confident in the accuracy of their computer guidance system, they did not turn on the forward running lights. At this time of night, there was no boat traffic on the river. In addition, they feared the lights might attract the attention of one the revelers who frequented the Front Street honky-tonk.

It was an erroneous fear.

Considering the amount of alcohol anyone hanging around the marina juke-joint would have consumed by this time of night; observing the underwater bow lights traversing downriver might lead an inebriated soul to claim that he had seen 'the glowing eyes of a sea creature swimming up the river'.

"Just another of your hallucinations," those listening would chide. "Why don't you go home and sleep it off."

Thomas and the submariners felt secure in the belief that their movement, especially at night would not be discovered. They were seemingly right in their assertion. No one except Thomas had witnessed their departure.

The trip upriver was uneventful. The on-board guidance system automatically maneuvered the mini-sub without consequence through the twists and turns of the navigational channel and around the dangerous sand and oyster bars. The sub responded immediately to each digital navigational signal. In less than 45 minutes, they reached the lighthouse and open waters of the bay. A radar scan showed no vessels in the immediate vicinity.

Surfacing, they opened the hatch, glassing the bay waters to corroborate the radar findings. The sub slowly took them further out into the Apalachee Bay. They sat topside around the hatch breathing in the warm salty air. For a few moments, they enjoyed the tranquility that one finds in the peaceful solitude of drifting quietly alone on the calm Gulf waters with a gentle breeze blowing in from offshore.

Once they reached the two-mile offshore marker of buoy number 1, they re-entered the sub, closed the hatch, and began their slow descent to 900 feet. Setting the aft and side thrusters at full speed, they quickly made their way across the interior of the Gulf of Mexico basin. At 9:00 PM, after an uneventful journey, they slowly surfaced, surveying the surrounding area with their radar and side-sonars for boat traffic. Finding none, they paged Gomez with the signal that they would arrive at Arroyos de Mantua on schedule.

In less than an hour, the autopilot accurately navigated them into the seclusion of the boathouse. Once inside, they turned on the bow lights and slowly ascended. Through the clear Caribbean waters, they could see a smiling Hector Gomez waiting for them as they rose towards the surface.

"Good evening, Amigos," Gomez said in greeting. "I trust you had a safe and uneventful trip."

"We did on the return trip, Hector, but we had a quite an experience with a sperm whale on our journey to St. Marks," Vladimir answered. He then explained their encounter with the annoyed whale pod.

Laughing, Gomez said, "It is not unusual to hear local fishermen describe similar encounters with the whales in the fall season. If they are surface feeding, they will not veer away from any fishing vessel which happens to navigate into their feeding area. You have to keep a watchful eye for them during September, October, and November. I'm sure they're just as possessive of their undersea feeding grounds as they are of their surface territory. I'm sorry; I should have warned you about them."

Nicholas replied, "We did experience a sudden fright, not knowing what had collided with us. We were lucky that the whale's heavy tail fluke did no damage to the outboard thrusters."

"We will forever be more vigilant for their presence," Vedonosti stated.

"I will guarantee that," Vladimir interjected. "We had to increase the side-scan sonar's sensitivity readings even though it means we have to endure constant false alarm alerts from schools of bait fish and floating algae in our navigational path."

"Well, I'm glad that's the only close call you had. No contact with BSDIA surface or air surveillance?" Gomez queried.

"None that was indicated on either radar or sonar," Kerchenkov answered.

"Excellent. I hope that is a good omen for future voyages!" Gomez remarked. "I know you must be hungry. Please come, sit, and eat the dinner meal I brought. I'm afraid its just sandwiches, potato salad, fruit, chips, milk, colas, and coffee. I haven't as yet devised a plan to provide you with a warm meal, but I'm working on that," he said.

"That is not a problem, Amigo," Remarked Vladimir. "Your provisions are more than adequate. After a few hours rest, we plan to depart for Cerros again around daybreak. Will you return with more food or should we divide some of this dinner breakfast for our morning breakfast?"

"I will be back, Amigo, to bring you breakfast if you would like."

"We would like that very much," Vladimir answered for his crew, "if it is not a lot of trouble."

"No trouble at all," said Gomez. "I must return anyway to bring you the cases of Coronas and cigars I promised. I will leave you now, and return in about six hours. You'll not be disturbed."

"Bueno," Kerchenkov remarked. "We will see you early in the morning."

As promised, Gomez returned a few minutes before five with a box of ham, egg, and cheese biscuits, juice, milk, and coffee. After eating breakfast, the crew and Gomez moved outside and sat on the rocky shore. Under an awakening dawn sky, the submariners enjoyed one of their Montecristo Robustos cigars and watched the sun rise over the Caribbean.

They talked of the similarities and differences of life in communist Cuba compared with life in the former communist Soviet Union. As a general in the Cuban military, Gomez said he did not lead a bad life, but that he longed for retirement and the chance to live his remaining years somewhere other than Cuba. At six, the crew returned to the boathouse. Vedonosti changed the CO_2 scrubber while the others loaded the beer and cigars into the cargo hold.

After exchanging hearty handshakes, the crew climbed into the DSRV and Vladimir closed the hatch. Gomez opened the boathouse doors and watched as the sub descended beneath the water and backed away. Despite the clarity of the water and a calm sea, the sub quickly disappeared from view as it descended towards the 780-foot depth of the Yucatan Channel.

At 500 feet, Peter set the autopilot and the fore, aft, and side thrusters to full throttle. In relief, they watched the autopilot correct their compass heading to southwest. In seven hours, they reached the Banco Chinchoro barrier islands off Quintana Roo's east coast

With another course correction to the west-southwest, the sub navigated towards the Chetamul Channel and Santa Cecelia. Ascending to 390 feet as they entered the Chetamul Straits, Peter cut the fore thruster power and reduced speed to one-fourth throttle in the aft and side thrusters. The DSRV's guidance system maneuvered around the coral outcroppings as if steered by hand. Once through the strait, the sub corrected its course to southwest. Slowly it began a gradual ascent and leveled off at a depth of 128 feet when they reached the Cerros Maya ruins.

Nicholas took the helm and reduced the speed to one-fourth aft thruster. Passing the ruins on the south side, the sub ascended to 90 feet holding steady at 10 feet off the bottom. Within 20 minutes, they had maneuvered through the adjacent mill channel and ascended into the security of the boathouse.

Vedonosti and Peter exited the hatch and secured the DSRV to its berth. It was after 10:00 PM by the time the crew replaced the air filtration mechanism and finished offloading the beer and cigars. Suddenly they realized the significance of this moment. They had proven their navigational proficiency and successfully tested the capability of the mini-sub to smuggle drugs undetected across the U.S. border.

The tired submariners headed towards Cerros and a well-deserved night's sleep, content in the knowledge that soon they would all become very rich men. After lunch the next day, they gathered with Ortega at his mill office for a complete debriefing of their journey.

They scrutinized their trip in fine detail. From Belize to Cuba to St. Marks and return, each of the four legs of the voyage was analyzed to identify potential vulnerabilities and to determine if any changes could be made to improve upon the effectiveness of the operation.

The crew disclosed that during their arrival and departure at the Arroyos de Mantua stopover in Cuba, they felt they were at their greatest vulnerability for detection. Kerchenkov noted, "We are solely at the mercy of General Gomez to keep the waters off the Cabo de San Antorrio peninsula clear of military traffic."

"True," Ortega concluded, "That is one intangible over which we have no control. We will just have to trust the General to do his part where the smuggling operation can proceed unobtrusively."

Continuing, he added reassuringly, "With the money Gomez is getting paid to perform that task, I am sure he will not let us down. To do so would most certainly jeopardize our operation. I do not like this single reliance on Gomez to do his job any more than you. Nonetheless, it is his country, and, quite simply, there seems to be no other option."

Kerchenkov discussed a change the crew knew must be made in order to improve the effectiveness of the operation. Vladimir noted, "On our Cuban stopovers, we have relied principally on Gomez to provide our primary food and drink rations."

He acknowledged, "A hot meal is a nice alternative to packaged food if it can be provided. But we are practical naval officers. I feel it would be wise to take along a large store of military MREs on each voyage. As insurance, of course, in the event that Gomez is unable to furnish us with provisions on each of our Cuban layovers."

Vedonosti added, "Meals-Ready-to-Eat are certainly not our preference over a hot meal, but, if something happens and Gomez cannot provide us with food, at least we would have something of sustenance until our return."

Their logic convinced Ortega that the crew must be better prepared in the future. "MREs it is then," he said. The crew laughed in feigned anticipation.

"I'll have Juan Carlos include them on his next flight to Belize," Ortega promised.

With the debriefing over, Ortega encrypted a call to Juan Carlos, Thomas, and Clark to fill them in on the outcome of the inaugural journey. Exuberant over the success of their trial run, they discussed the remaining preparations that must be completed before they could set their smuggling operation into motion.

Juan Carlos asked his brother, "Ortega, when do you think the sugarcane processing plant will be ready to deliver its first shipment of raw sugar?"

Ortega replied, "Two weeks ago we began processing the sugarcane we cut from our own cane fields. In another week, we should have 400 tons of raw sugar ready for shipment to the St. Marks refinery. Four hundred tons will fill one Trans-Caribbean Transport barge. Traveling at a 5-knot speed, we have been told it will take about seven days for the barge to make the approximate 1,000-mile journey from Cerros to St. Marks. "

Ortega asked his brother, "Juan Carlos, when will you transport your first shipment of cocaine to me for processing and how much will you initially send?"

Juan Carlos replied. "I will have my first two tons of raw coca ready to fly to Cerros in three days."

Mentally calculating, Ortega remarked, "That is good. The Colombians can process about two tons in one week. That would leave seven days to transport the cocaine into St. Marks before the raw sugar is expected to arrive."

Clark asked Thomas, "Miguel, can you estimate how much time will be required to refine the 400 tons of raw sugar and have a supply ready for wholesale distribution?"

Delivery of the raw sugar to St. Marks and its refinement to processed powdered sugar was paramount to Clark's plan to distribute the cocaine through his pipeline. Clark had a special delivery system designed to smuggle the cocaine to his regional drug kingpins. Until the refinery was geared up to refine the processed sugar, the distribution operation could not get underway.

"Running the mill at full capacity, we can process about 200 tons of raw sugar each five-day work week. I would expect that we would be ready to ship at least a half dozen semi-truckloads within the first two days of beginning the refinery process," Thomas answered.

"Excellent!" Clark exclaimed. "That will time perfectly with getting my overland freight system ready to transport the cocaine. It seems the one loose end we need to tie up before beginning our operation is for Juan Carlos to staff the St. Marks refinery with his Colombian cocaine chemists."

Fundamental to the success of the distribution system, these men would be responsible for repackaging the cocaine into street level sale quantities. Additionally they would be responsible to process a certain portion of the cocaine powder into crack cocaine.

Clark asked, "Juan Carlos, is everything in place to send your men to Florida?"

"Yes." he answered. "Plans are finalized, and the men are ready to begin their journey to Florida as soon as Thomas is ready to receive them."

"You may send them any time then," Thomas said. "Everything is in place for their move to St. Marks."

"How will you get them settled into the community, Thomas?" Clark asked. "Where will you house them?"

Thomas detailed his plan for receiving the Colombians. "Until they can construct a home on a lot of their choice within the St. Marks vicinity, I plan to settle them into temporary mobile homes set up on a lot adjacent to the refinery. They will be quite comfortable there until they can build their own home."

Juan Carlos stated, "That is good news. I will then make final arrangements for their immediate departure."

"Let me know the details of their flight arrival, Juan Carlos, where I can meet them at the Tallahassee airport." Thomas requested.

"I will call you tomorrow, Amigo, with all the details," Juan Carlos promised. "I have hand-picked these men for you, Miguel," Diego continued. "They are the best of all the chemists in my processing labs in the Andes. They look forward to their new job in America, and I know you will appreciate their commitment to our smuggling operation."

Diego continued, "Their identification papers were prepared by the best forgers in St. Petersburg, Russia. Their new identification is complete with a birth certificate, a Florida driver's license, social security number, and passport. I trust you will find all their papers in order."

"It will be necessary for them to be put on your plant's payroll, Miguel," Diego added. "Please make arrangements with the bank to open an account for each of them. "Their employment records will show that they are moving to St. Marks from the Napa Valley wine country of California."

"I have devised a simple plan to disguise their true identities," Juan Carlos continued. "First, under their Colombian identities, they will fly a commercial airline from Colombia to Buenos Aires, then on to Los Angeles. After an overnight layover, their Colombian identities will just disappear into the California sunset."

"Under their new identities they will fly on to Florida. Miguel, please make them feel welcome. They have no families and are excited to be moving to America. They are committed to the success of our smuggling operation. I am certain you will find them more than adequately competent to process the cocaine for transportation. They are also expert in converting powdered cocaine into crack. I am confident they will serve you well."

"I look forward to meeting and working with them, Juan Carlos. I will make sure they feel a part of the community. As soon as I receive your call, I'll be ready to pick them up in Tallahassee." Thomas replied.

Ortega remarked, "Miguel, I will notify you as soon as the first shipment of cocaine is packaged and ready for transport."

"That is the one call I eagerly wait to receive!" Thomas answered jovially.

With these final arrangements complete, Clark said, "Gentlemen, after almost six months it appears we are almost ready to restart our operation. Here's hoping for a long successful partnership!"

CHAPTER FOURTEEN

As promised, within three days of their conference call Juan Carlos delivered 4,000 pounds of raw powdered cocaine to Cerros. In finalizing his shipment plans, Diego discovered that smuggling his drugs into Belize would not be as easy as his efforts to smuggle drugs into La Palma, Panama.

The ever-present Colombian military kept a vigilant eye out for fixed-wing aircraft exiting their country. This was Diego's usual means of moving cocaine, heroin, and marijuana out of Colombia's interior and across the border northward. He determined he had to employ a different transport method or risk interdiction.

After some thought, Juan Carlos devised a safer ground route to move his cocaine from the Andes coca fields to the coast. To disguise his movements, Diego sacrificed the quicker aerial route from the coca fields for the less suspicious, cross-country journey through the Colombian countryside. Though a much slower means of transport, he was certain it would provide less risk of interdiction.

He planned to move the raw coca by mule train across the Andes Mountains to Curumani, situated on the foothills of the western mountain ridge. Produce trucks moved the coca along country roads past San Rogue to San Cristobal. Here the load was hidden in overland wholesale food delivery trucks.

Traveling north through Learndra, El Copay, and Fundacion, the drugs reached Cienaga where they were transferred to grain barges. Hidden in grain bags, the drugs traversed the Cienaga Grande Santa Marta Lake system and were then transported the short distance overland to Barranquilla on the northern Caribbean coast of Colombia.

On a heading of 310 degrees west-northwest, it was a 1047-mile flight from the north Colombia coast to Cerros, Belize. Juan Carlos' Boeing 737, which could maintain a steady speed of 545 miles per hour, could make the trip in less than three hours. Diego built an airstrip in the remote countryside of Barranquilla. Local authorities were paid well to ignore the arrivals to and departures from his private airport.

Diego's pilots were well-paid risk-takers, daredevils paid handsomely to avoid detection. These pilots actually preferred travel in inclement weather. Shortly after take-off, the pilot would descend sharply to less than 100 yards above the water's surface, flying just under the detection capabilities of land-based radar.

Diego's pilots flew with no navigational lights. Caught flying without navigational lights and below an air traffic controller's authorized hard deck was the least of their concerns. Fearless, they knew their route to the mile.

The navigators had designed a flight plan with no fixed land obstacles along their path. When an occasional ship showed up on radar, they simply skirted it, leaving anyone on deck wandering what had screamed by amidships.

After midnight, Diego's 737 lifted off on a northerly heading across the Caribbean. Sighting the bright lights of Ambergris Caye at 2:30 AM, the captain quickly ascended northwestward to 2,000 feet to align with the runway lights of the Cerros mill. The mile-long runway was more than adequate to provide a safe landing. At 3:05, the pilot taxied to the safety of the mill's hanger and cut the engines.

A sleepy, but smiling Ortega welcomed the crew to Cerros. In less than an hour, the raw coca had been safely transferred to the second floor laboratory of the mill. After turning over the security of the drug stash to the Colombian chemists, Ortega remarked to the pilot and crew, "Come, let us drive to Cerros for some well-deserved sleep."

The next afternoon, the crew would fly south to the Philip Goldson International Airport, where the captain would file a legitimate flight plan back to Colombia.

Included in Diego's delivery were cases of assorted MREs. Having sampled a variety of the packaged food choices, Juan Carlos determined he would have to be very hungry to even consider opening one of these meals. He admired the submariner's request that MREs be supplied on each undersea voyage. Their resolve was certainly greater than was his.

For seven days, the Colombian's worked to process the two tons of raw coca into 3,600 pounds of pure, powdered cocaine. Packed in one square-foot blocks weighing 25 pounds each, the packages occupied a volume of 144 square feet. At midnight, the crew began storing the packages in the DSRV.

With the four pilots, supplies, and cargo, the sub would be filled to maximum capacity. Before sunrise, the shipment had been readied for transport. At 9:00 AM, Ortega notified General Gomez that the crew would depart a little before midnight the following day.

"That should put them here around three o'clock in the afternoon, then," Gomez said. "Let them know I will be waiting with an early dinner."

"I am certain they will appreciate that," said Diego. "Thank you for your help."

Ortega's next call was to Miguel Thomas. He informed his partner that the first cocaine shipment would be underway the next morning.

"That's good news, Ortega," Thomas said. "If Kerchenkov's travel schedule follows the timetable of the trial run, I'll expect them to arrive here around 4:00 AM of the second day. Isn't that right?"

"Yes, Miguel. Kerchenkov stated that they do intend to follow the same timetable," Ortega reported. "You should expect them to arrive 4:00 AM, just as before."

At precisely 12:00 PM, Kerchenkov and his crew of three departed the Cerros mill and entered the Chetamul Bay. The voyage to Arroyos de Mantua was uneventful. After an early dinner, Vladimir and his comrades sat outside the boathouse enjoying one of Gomez's fine Cuban cigars and the warmth of the afternoon sun.

Tired from their 15-hour voyage across the Caribbean, the men half-dozed as they savored the flavor of their Montecristo. They welcomed the serenity and solitude they found on this peaceful stretch of the Cuban coastline. Without warning, their relaxation was interrupted. The crew sat up abruptly as three huge American naval vessels rounded the Peninsula de Guanahacabibes.

They stared in disbelief as an American battleship flanked by two destroyers cruised slowly southward, less than a quarter-mile offshore. In their apparently isolated location, the Russians had felt secure. They had become complacent knowing that Gomez would protect them from discovery by the Cuban military and the commercial fishing vessels that routinely navigated the waters of the Southwest Yucatan Channel.

The sudden realization that Gomez could not control American military vessels on route to the Guantanamo Bay Naval Station on the southeast coast of Cuba raised doubts about their mission's success. Their maiden voyage from Belize to St. Marks had been made without consequence. They had neither seen nor detected any American military craft. As they returned to the boathouse to get some sleep before their next 23-

hour voyage, they wondered about the success of future journeys through these waters.

Sleep came sporadically. They were still tired when their 4:00 AM departure hour came. Kerchenkov waited an additional half-hour to begin their departure. As Hector Gomez rolled open the doors of the boathouse, they scanned the horizon for military traffic. Seeing none, Peter Segonyva submerged the DSRV, set the autopilot, and watched as the sub headed to nine degrees north-northeast from the Cabo de San Antorrio coastline. It would be a long 574-mile journey.

Still shaken from the unexpected appearance of America naval vessels, Kerchenkov decided to navigate at an additional 400-foot depth. With Peter Segonyva and Vedonosti Novostey at the helm, the crew watched as the sub nosed down at a sharp 45-degree angle until it leveled off at 2,900 feet, close to the maximum depth at which the bow window was pressure tested for stability.

Even though the DSRV's outer shell was coated with its radar deflective coating, they felt the additional 400-foot depth would give them extra insurance and a decreased possibility of detection. They need not have feared; only one American submarine was on patrol in the Gulf of Mexico, and it was situated off the coast of Galveston, Texas, more than 800 miles away.

Though the crew was tense, the voyage proved uneventful. They relaxed somewhat when they crossed the Aucilla Ridge and began to approach the shallower waters of the Apalachee Bay. Their sonar showed two surface vessels 1,600 yards and 15 degrees to starboard. Upon reaching navigational buoy number 1 offshore of the lighthouse, the sub slowly ascended to the surface. They were relieved when their binoculars showed two shrimp boats at anchor eastward of Gray Mare, vessels whose presence posed no threat.

The crew had departed Cuba a half-hour later than planned. They knew that several of the offshore charter boats would head downriver to the Gulf in less than hour. Electing extra caution, the crew decided to make the journey into St. Marks completely underwater. Submerged, there would be less chance for detection.

Kerchenkov took control of the helm. Setting the thrusters at 15 miles per hour, he submerged the vessel, which now hugged the bottom of the channel. The sub's guidance system responded perfectly as it maneuvered around the sand and oyster bars and the curves and bends of the river channel. At 4:50 AM, they signaled Miguel Thomas of their approach to the refinery.

The underwater boathouse doors swung noiselessly outward into the river. With one final 90-degree guidance to port, the sub coasted to a stop. The boathouse doors closed quietly behind them. The first 1.8 tons of pure cocaine had arrived safely on U.S. soil.

Thomas called Juan Carlos, Wayne Clark, and Ortega to notify them that their first shipment had made it safely to St Marks. It was not the 10-ton delivery of which Juan Carlos and Wayne Clark were accustomed, but, nonetheless, it was a beginning. As overland and sea-surface smuggling operations had virtually come to a halt, their submarine transport scheme was their only option. The small but successful underwater operation did have its advantages.

Anticipating two deliveries each week, Clark thought that it would not take long at all to build up the supply of cocaine that America's addicts and recreational users demanded. "By the end of November," Clark quipped, "the streets of America will again be 'snowed under' with cocaine. Until that time, we will slowly begin to fulfill America's addictive death wish."

When Juan Carlos asked Wayne to estimate the street value of each delivery, Clark made some quick calculations. On the street, cocaine sold for $10 per gram - in street slang a 'dime' bag. With one kilogram equal to 1,000 grams, each kilogram would sell for $10,000. To calculate the total value of the shipment, Clark converted the shipment from pounds into kilograms. With one kilogram equal to 2.2 pounds, the 3,600-pound shipment weighed 1,636.36 kilos. This kilogram weight multiplied by the street sale value of $10,000 per kilo gave Clark his answer.

"Juan Carlos, the present American street price for cocaine is $10 per gram. Each 3,600 pound shipment should expect to bring sales of over $16,300,000," Clark concluded.

Diego smiled at the news. "With the associated deposit fees we will have to pay, I'd estimate our expenses to be about one-third of our sales. It looks like we'll net around $10 million for each shipment. Two shipments each week will realize about $80 million a month. Split four ways, $20 million each. Is that about what you calculated?"

"Exactly," Clark replied.

"I guess I can live on twenty mil a month!" Juan Carlos said with another laugh. With Clark, Ortega, and Miguel's hearty agreement, the conversation ended.

The second floor cocaine lab would be kept busy throughout the next week. The Colombian chemists worked tirelessly repackaging the cocaine into street-salable gram bags. These were further packaged into one-pound boxes. Each box contained 454 one-gram bags of pure coke. Clark determined that he could keep better accountability of distribution through the pipeline with the cocaine divided into these smaller packages.

It was a great day of celebration at the Cerros sugarcane processing plant - a day all had eagerly awaited. In the early pre-dawn hours of Saturday, October 1$^{st.}$, the 580-foot Caribbe Sea II eased its way into the canal adjacent to the loading dock. Today the first shipment of raw sugar from the Caribbean Sugar Export Partners, Limited, was ready for transport.

The Corozalians had worked overtime to process the plant's first crop of sugarcane into 400 tons of raw sugar. For their efforts to reach the tight deadline, Ortega had promised each worker a bonus of $5,000. The bonus was more than most had made in any single year since the plant last closed. They worked without complaint.

A cookout had been planned in celebration of this day. The workers and their families gathered on the mill grounds to enjoy a Bar-B-Que lunch and to watch as the crane loaded the raw sugar into the belly of the Caribbe Sea II. The men drank iced Corollas. "In recognition of a job well done," toasted Ortega. He personally presented each worker with the generous bonus check.

In less than 24 hours, with a blast of its horn, the transport barge eased away from the loading dock and out into the Chetumal Bay. With the fore, aft, and mid-ships tower lights illuminating the deck, the Caribbe Sea II steered northeast toward Quintana Roo. In the darkness of night, the massive structure resembled a small floating island.

Ortega Diego watched until the lights of the ship disappeared over the horizon. As he watched the barge fade into the early-morning darkness, Ortega smiled, knowing that its departure from Belize initiated their nascent offshore smuggling operation.

America would soon fall prey to the renaissance of the largest successful drug smuggling ring ever operated on American soil. American streets would soon experience the resurgence of the white scourge of cocaine.

The Caribbe Sea II experienced clear weather and calm seas on its maiden voyage. Seven days and four hours from its time of departure, the barge maneuvered around marker 62 and made its turn upriver in the direction of the St. Marks wharf. With great fanfare, local pleasure boaters escorted the barge toward the refinery with their signal horns blaring.

Many of the townspeople turned out to welcome the barge to St. Marks. Its arrival meant prosperity for the community. Other than the occasional oil tanker that traversed the St. Marks on its way upriver to the oil depots in Newport, this was the first commercial barge to dock in the town of St. Marks in more than a decade.

Young children watched in fascination as the captain skillfully maneuvered the barge alongside the refinery dock. Eager dockhands looped the vessel's six-inch tie down ropes to the huge stanchions lining the wharf. A blast of the barge's foghorn drowned out the diesel engines. The first load of raw sugar had officially reached St. Marks.

"This is a great day of celebration," Stephen Mainor, mayor of St. Marks, began. He officially welcomed the refinery to the community.

"Thank you, Mr. Mayor, for your gracious welcome on this day," Thomas said. "The official opening of the St. Marks Sugar Refinery is indeed a great day for me, the partners of this joint venture, our refinery workers, and this fine community. We look forward to many productive years in St. Marks."

Following the ceremony, the captain of the Caribbe Sea II allowed those interested to come aboard for a tour of the impressive vessel. The townspeople were astonished at the size of the cargo hold that recessed the 400 tons of raw sugar. Children were fascinated with their tour of the wheelhouse, perched high atop the stern. The captain let each sit behind the helm and give one blast on the foghorn. It was a day none of these youngsters would soon forget.

For 24 hours, Ralph Fiacincio and his team were kept busy offloading the raw sugar at St. Marks. From the belly of the barge, the sugar was loaded onto conveyor belts and deposited into the adjacent dockside stainless steel storage bins.

Eager to test the refinery skills they had acquired in Brazil, Thomas's staff was abuzz with activity that afternoon and again the next morning. With absolute certainty, Bill Knox carefully identified the workers and cleared them through security. Thomas had wanted to eliminate the risk that anyone other than mill workers would be admitted to the refinery. He would chance no surreptitious discovery of their smuggling operation.

The St. Marks Refinery was responsible for the final steps in the processing of sugarcane into marketable sugar products. The raw sugar transported from Belize would go through a five-step refining process before it would be ready for market.

The first step involved re-dissolving and reheating the raw sugar under successively higher degrees of vacuum pressure. Reheating the sugar under pressure would remove non-sugar colloidal impurities and protect the sucrose molecule from further hydrolysis and conversion into the less marketable reduced sugars, D-sucrose and D-fructose.

The second step in the refinery process involved de-coloring and purifying the raw sugar. By passing the sugar slurry through carbon filters, a clear, colorless syrupy liquid was formed. This syrup was further heated and tested with a hydrometer until it reached the desired density. At this point, if brown sugar was the desired final product, a batch was sent back to the cooking vat and heated until it caramelized.

In the third step, the colorless or caramelized syrup was crystallized and dried in a huge centrifuge. Here, wet sugar was spun under centrifugal force until the moisture was effectively removed from the syrupy sludge.

The damp sugar was then dumped from the centrifuge onto a vibrating conveyor belt. As the belt moved the sugar along towards the final step in the refinery process, the constant vibration served to break up and layer the damp clumps of sugar into packed flat plates. This marked the fourth step in the complicated refinery process.

From the conveyor, the moist flats of sugar moved into the fifth and final step of the refinery process. The thin plates fell into a giant, heated tumbler where the sugar was slowly tumbled under a constant warm temperature. After drying, the sugar granules were conveyed into large bins and held until transfer to the packaging machines.

At this final point in the process, if powdered sugar was the desired product, a portion was conveyed through a series of large steel rollers that pulverized the granules into finely ground, powdered sugar. The powdered sugar was then vacuumed into separate holding bins.

The packaging of the granular and powdered sugar was accomplished through sophisticated computerized automation. From the holding bins, sugar was siphoned into a machine that weighed and packaged the sugar into individual one-, five-, ten-, twenty- or fifty-pound bags, depending upon the desired fill weight. A portion was packed into individual sized serving packets and boxed for wholesale distribution to the restaurant and food service market.

As quickly as the sugar was packaged, Ralph Fiacincio and his crew loaded the bags and boxes onto pallets. Once loaded, Cletus and Dewey Tanner moved each pallet by forklift into the warehouse. With expert driving skill and precision, the cousins maneuvered the forklift within the close confines of the warehouse.

On their first day, working in three, 8-hour shifts, the mill workers processed over four tons of raw sugar into refined sugar. The St. Marks refinery yielded 96 pounds of refined sugar per 100 pound of raw sugar. With current wholesale sugar prices of 23 cents per pound, the mill would expect to generate over $17,000 a day in sales - a nice daily profit in addition to the millions they would make in cocaine sales.

After the first week, Thomas reduced the shift work to two 8-hour shifts each day. Eliminating the midnight-to-dawn shift allowed Thomas' chemists the unimpeded time necessary to manage the cocaine smuggling activity. Using plain brown, unlabeled bags, the Colombians packaged the cocaine for distribution. Sealed in cardboard packing cartons, only a K-9's acute olfactory sensors could detect its presence, and Clark had a specially devised plan to lessen that probability.

By the end of the first week in October, all 3,600 pounds of cocaine had been packaged for shipment and distribution. Wayne Clark used a simple plan to transport the cocaine to his four regional distribution sites. The uncomplicated, yet very effective plan used rented Ryder trucks to transport the contraband to key sites across America. Clark had decided that the use of rental trucks to move the cocaine up through his distribution pipeline would better allow him to avoid interdiction.

Clark had employed his own team of cross-country drivers who followed a meticulously planned smuggling route. Each team was comprised of a young male and female posing as a married couple moving their personal belongings cross-country. Clark knew that many drug interventions were made on America's highways due to nervous, careless couriers speeding toward their destination and thus attracting the attention of law enforcement. Clarks' drivers were cautious and always obeyed the speed limit.

In another effort to evade detection, Clark wisely required his couriers to rent their Ryder truck from various cities across the United States. In the event that a truck was intercepted, the rental location would be far removed from their St. Marks base of operation.

Unless the courier talked, it would be difficult to connect a single confiscated shipment to the cartel. Clark had little fear that his couriers would betray the smuggling operation if ever caught. They knew that to betray the Commander would be suicide. Facing a prison term would be far safer than striking a plea bargain with a prosecutor in exchange for a reduced sentence. Cooperating with authorities, they knew, would mean living in constant fear of retaliation. Constantly looking over their shoulders for the inevitable hit man sent by Clark to find and murder them would not be worth the shorter prison sentence.

Thomas prepared the first cocaine shipment for the principal regional distribution sites in Atlanta, Los Angeles, Chicago, and New York City. At 3:30 AM that Sunday, four Ryder trucks loaded with used furniture, kitchenware, clothes, and miscellaneous personal items pulled through the gate of the St. Marks Refinery. Thomas had informed the on-duty security guard to expect them. Told that the trucks were to be loaded to deliver items from the plant's research laboratory, the guard was none the wiser. He would not question his employer.

Nine hundred pounds of cocaine were to be shipped to each of the four regional lieutenants. While not a large initial delivery, it was nonetheless, a long awaited beginning. The cocaine-laden cardboard packing cartons were quickly loaded and hidden in the truck's front-end cargo compartment. The convoy was underway in less than an hour.

Two trucks headed east on U.S. 98 on route to Atlanta and New York City on the east coast. Heading eastbound, 98 intersected with U.S. 19 at Perry. Here, the two drivers headed north through Thomasville, Georgia, and on to Albany, where 19 intersected with GA 300 North to Cordele. At this point, the trucks entered the interstate highway system.

Interstate 75 North took them to Atlanta. Traveling together for as long as possible provided an extra measure of security should one of the vehicles encounter mechanical problems along the route. Later that afternoon, the truck bound for New York City headed north as the Atlanta team made its delivery.

Upon their departure from St. Marks, the other two trucks headed north to Tallahassee where they connected with Interstate 10 West. Traveling until early morning, the drivers stopped in Mobile, Alabama, to sleep. Later that afternoon, they separated. One team headed north on Interstate 55 toward Chicago; the second continued west to Los Angeles.

Eight hours later, westbound on the I-10 bypass in Houston, the 'husband and wife' team of 'Rob and Elizabeth Summers' of Tallahassee, Florida, encountered a military roadblock. A row of Humvees displaying BSDIA insignias, lined both the eastbound and westbound lanes of the interstate. The two looked on apprehensively as each vehicle in line was meticulously searched.

When their turn came, Rob Summers had calmed his breathing to an almost normal rate. He could not, however, control his perspiration. He was sweating profusely. Thankfully, he thought, the temperature this day in early October was still warm. Traveling with the windows open gave him a legitimate reason to perspire.

"Howdy, officers," Summers said heartily as he slowed to a stop.

"Good afternoon, sir," said the soldier unsmilingly. He was all business. "Mind if I check your truck?" It was more a request than a question.

"Heck no, officer. Help yourself," Summers stated boldly. "Just moving our belongings to California. Here's the key to the loading door lock, sir." As the soldier moved towards the rear of the truck, the search dog of a K-9 team barked incessantly and suddenly bounded towards the rear of the van immediately in front of them. With guns drawn, officers ordered everyone out of the van with instructions to "put your hands on the hood; place your feet back and spread 'em!"

The soldier returned Summers' padlock key and ordered him to "Go ahead and move on out."

"Sure, officer," Summers answered, pocketing the key as he eased his truck around the arrest scene enfolding in front of them.

"Whew!" the driver announced to his partner as they pulled off. "Even though the cocaine is hidden in the front of the van and surrounded by other boxes, clothes, and furniture, I'm glad the van was protected with the 'cover up' just in case we were inspected.

"Me, too!" Elizabeth said. "Despite assurances of the cover up, I'm glad we didn't have to go through a thorough K-9 search."

"That makes two of us!" Donald replied.

Clark always prepared his truck's cargo hole with a homemade cocaine scent masking 'cover up.' Earlier in his career, he had read DEA top secret reports on the agency's efforts to test the nation's best-trained dogs for their ability to detect illegal narcotic contraband under extremely scented conditions.

The DEA tests showed that two chemical agents in particular effectively interfered with a K-9er's drug detection ability. Kept a closely guarded secret, the report disclosed that even open packets of cocaine went undetected in the presence of either sprinkled Cayenne pepper or, Tinks 69 Buck Lure.

When discussing this report with Miguel, Clark had said, "We'll use this information to our advantage. Tinks 69 is a commercially available concentration of natural doe-estrus urine used by deer hunters during the rutting season to attract bucks. To humans, the product has a putrid odor, but to a rutting buck, the 'Doe-In-Estrus' urine imitates its favorite 'female cologne'. Only a few drops placed in the vicinity of cocaine will mask the scent of the drug."

"I see," Miguel said. "So, when Tinks is mixed with a trace of Cayenne pepper, the concoction is certain to overpower the smell of cocaine, effectively neutralizing a search dog's ability to discern even large deposits of hidden contraband."

"Exactly."

Before their departure, Clark had instructed his drivers to sprinkle a few milliliters of this mixture in the bed of each transport vehicle. To legitimize the smell, a broken bottle of Tinks 69 would be placed on the floor of the truck's cargo hold as if it had been accidentally broken during transport.

If stopped for inspection, the driver would feign surprise as the cargo door was opened, exclaiming "Oh man that smells awful. I should've been more careful packing that bottle!"

"Any inspector would certainly agree," Clark stated unequivocally. "The smell is simply nauseating, especially in hot weather; bad enough to gag a buzzard!"

Though Clark's transport trucks were seldom inspected, the ruse had always worked. He knew that if ever a scented truck was intervened upon, he would have to change his transport scheme. From that point on, the BSDIA would be put on alert to carefully check every Ryder truck, particularly those scented with deer attractant.

Less than 72 hours after the trucks departed St. Marks, the four shipments had been safely delivered to their destinations. The driver teams dropped off the Ryder trucks and were taken to hotels adjacent to the local airport. The following morning, each couple flew back to their respective hometown. After a careful de-scenting, the trucks were returned to a Ryder rental location.

In Clark's network, his street sale strategy was meticulously planned. As the cocaine moved through the pipeline, his orders were followed to the letter. Cocaine addicts and recreational users alike welcomed this new supply of 'nose dust.' Within the week, all that had been delivered had been sold. Over $16,000,000 in cash had been collected and packaged for return to St. Marks. Clark had achieved his initial objective to prime cocaine users and abuser's desire for the drug. Sales were brisk, and the money came easily.

Such high-volume cash collections posed a unique problem for the smuggling enterprise. Selling the illicit drug was easy; disposing of the cash proposed a challenge. Somehow, Clark had to hide, transport, and deposit the cash.

Generally collected in five, ten, and twenty-dollar bills, the bulk weight of the street cash amounted to around six times the original weight of cocaine sold. In their smuggling operation, every DSRV shipment of 4,000 pounds of raw cocaine produced 3,600 pounds of pure cocaine. With over $16 million generated in cash sales from each shipment, about 21,000 pounds of cash that would have to be laundered.

Federal, state, and local banking regulators and federal anti-money laundering special investigators were known to be meticulous in their efforts to expose huge cash deposits and deter overseas wire transfers. Once in American banks, such cash deposits would point directly to domestic drug traffickers. International money launderers would face strong undercover operations to track and intercept the natural flow of money out of U.S. banks to offshore accounts.

Romano Vicente quickly accepted Juan Carlos Diego's offer to launder cash through Cayman Island Capital Trust for a $1 million per shipment 'deposit fee'. "Certainly, my friend," Vicente said with pleasure. "I will be glad to offer my services."

"We were hoping you would," Diego remarked. "Clark convinced us our best option would be to load our cash onto the submarine and transport it out of the U.S. Once in international waters, we could transfer the cash to a surface vessel that would transport it to you on Grand Cayman. It is best that the transfers take place in the dark of night and at a secluded location, far away from the normal shipping and fishing lanes. Do you think you can devise a plan to transfer the cash to Grand Cayman?"

"I am positive I can work out a scheme to accomplish that," Vicente replied. "I have no doubt we can safely transfer the cash from your submarine to Grand Cayman Island. I will purchase a fishing vessel and hire a captain and crew I can trust to rendezvous with the submarine and transfer the cash onboard. How does that sound?"

"Exactly what we were hoping you would say," remarked Juan Carlos. "Call me when you have everything in place."

"I will call you soon," Vicente promised.

Vicente's plan to intercept and transfer the cash was simple. The authorities would not be suspicious of a private fishing vessel's frequent departure from George Town for recreational sport fishing. Grand Cayman Island was well known for its world-class bill fishing. The 18,300-foot deep Cayman Trench was less than 20 miles south of George Town and was something of a Mecca for the sailfish and marlin sport fishing industry.

For $1,200,000, Romano Vicente purchased a 67-foot Bertram sport fishing yacht. Fittingly, he named his expensive vessel the 'Capital Investment'. The yacht's wide 19-foot beam, ample fishing deck, large triple decked cockpit area, and lavishly appointed interior design provided a smooth riding fishing vessel, ideally suited for the long offshore round trip that would be required to transfer the cartel's cash to Grand Cayman.

Marine Yachting magazine had described recreational sport fishing on the magnificently designed vessel as "fishing from your living room." Its sub-deck engine room boasted 124 square feet of storage capacity - more than sufficient to conceal the cash and camouflage the money laundering operation. While considered the Cadillac of recreational bill fishing, the Bertram 67 would provide the perfect cover for their clandestine money-laundering scheme.

Vicente hired a captain and a crew of three. He trusted the four implicitly. For each "fishing junket," Vicente would pay the captain a hefty $100,000 fee; each of the three crewmembers would receive $50,000. With at least two fishing expeditions slated for each week, the captain and crew would soon become very wealthy men.

A 2,008-gallon fuel tank fed twin CAT 3412-powered diesel engines, each producing 1,420 horsepower. The Bertram could cruise at 31 knots, steadily covering over 600 miles of the open sea in less than 18 hours. The range capability of this 'six-seventy' model provided the requirements of speed and stability that would be necessary to rendezvous with the submarine and transfer the cash to George Town.

Vladimir Kerchenkov chose a point midway on the DSRV's direct travel route from Cuba back to its home base in Belize. The location was well within the nautical range of the 'Capital Investment'. From the NOAA map, a fixed location of latitude 18.743 N and longitude of 84.947 W was chosen.

Isolated from the usual commercial navigational and sport fishing lanes, the meeting point was 219 miles due south of Cabo de San Antonio and 196 miles east of the Chetamul channel in the shallow waters of the Greater Antilles and Rosario Banks. Kerchenkov knew commercial traffic would skirt these shallow shoals and recreational fishermen would be found more than a hundred miles to the northeast, trolling the Cayman Trench for marlin and sailfish.

It was a well-planned scheme. The carefully chosen, isolated rendezvous point provided for an orderly transfer of the millions of dollars the cartel would collect from its illicit drug sales. Once safely in the vaults of Cayman Island Capital Trust, these millions would be free from detection by U.S. federal agents and from confiscation by BSDIA federal interdiction agents.

The money-laundering plan completed the drug smuggling puzzle. It had been the final piece. Now the Belizean Cartel of the Diego brothers, Clark, and Thomas could begin a full-scale, uninterrupted operation.

CHAPTER FIFTEEN

T he first week's street sales of $16 million was ready for transport to St. Marks. Each lieutenant knew he would be held personally accountable for accurately reporting his sales. Other than their percentage cut, not one extra dollar was withheld. The money was packaged in cash bundles of $10,000 and boxed in $60,000 increments. Each box weighed around 40 pounds.

Thomas rented four Ryder trucks and returned the four 'husband and wife' teams to retrieve the cash. In the unlikely event that there was a discrepancy in the cash totals, Clark had devised a plan to identify the source of the discrepancy. In the presence of the transport team, the regional lieutenant electronically recounted the cash. Each signed a packing slip verifying the cash content. The box was then sealed with a tamper-evident seal. If the box returned without the security seal intact and the money was short, only the transport team could be blamed. If the box arrived with the seal intact and money was missing, both the lieutenant and the courier would be held accountable. All knew that a lack of accountability would prove an unpleasant experience. To date, Clark had never experienced a cash loss during shipment.

To offload the 21,000 pounds of cash from the Ryder trucks into the refinery would take considerably more time than did the loading of the 3,600 pounds of cocaine. To assure that the offloading went undeterred, Thomas gave the nightshift security guard the night off. Each transport team timed their arrival for 3:00 AM Sunday morning. At this early hour, any late-night revelers would be too drunk to take notice, and the hour was too early for local citizens and fishermen to be about.

By 4:30 in the morning, the boxes of cash had been unloaded and transported by elevator to Thomas' private quarters. By midmorning, Thomas had electronically recounted and reconciled all the cash. He then placed an encrypted call to the partners to report his receipt of the cash.

"Miguel, I have been anxiously waiting to hear from you," Clark said.

"Likewise, Wayne, I have anxiously awaited this moment," Thomas replied. "I have good news. I have just counted our first cash receipts. All total, $16,280,210. After our payoff to Gomez and Vicente, we'll clear a profit of almost $15 million."

"Excellent," exclaimed Clark.

"Not too bad considering everything that could have gone wrong," Thomas added.

"If we can achieve these results twice a week, even after paying Diego's pilots, the Belizean and St. Marks chemists, the sub crew, Gomez and Vicente, our monthly income should be around $20 million each, just as we surmised," Clark reflected. "By the way, Miguel, what has Kerchenkov and his crew been doing for the last week while waiting on the cash to be delivered?"

Thomas laughed, "Learning to enjoy Southern cooking and doing a lot of fishing on my new boat. I think they really like saltwater fishing. I had planned on buying a fishing boat anyway, just in case anyone should ask why I had such a big boathouse and no boat!"

"What kind of boat did you buy?" Clark asked.

"Not boat, but boats!" Thomas replied. "I bought a 21-foot Pursuit Center Console for trout fishing and a 36-foot Stamus for offshore trolling."

"Sounds like you really got bit by the fishing bug," Clark said laughingly.

"Yeah, kinda," Miguel confessed. "I thought that since I needed to purchase a larger boat to moor in the boathouse, I might as well buy a vessel that could easily accommodate six people for a three- or four-day offshore trip during the mackerel and billfish runs."

"Sounds like a great idea to me."

"Remember the Stamus we saw at Shell Island on our first morning there?" Thomas asked.

"Yeah, I sure do."

"Well, this one is bigger, and complete with all the bell and whistles," Thomas said. "It's a thing of beauty. I don't think I will be able to get Vladimir and his men away from it. They have it out almost every day. On the days they aren't out in the Stamus, they are out in the Pursuit. By now, I believe they know these waters as well as any local fisherman. You ought to see them at night pouring over nautical maps and planning their next fishing trip. Just like a bunch of kids."

"I'll bet you're sitting right there along with them, just as enthusiastic as they," Clark chided.

"You're right," Thomas said. "There's just something about St. Marks that gets in your blood. It's the whole nautical atmosphere. I love it here."

"I'm glad you do. Save me a fishing trip, will you?" Clark said. "I hope to find time to get back that way again soon."

"Like they say at Motel 6," Thomas replied, "'we'll leave the light on'. Hope to see you soon."

The following day Thomas contacted Hector Gomez and Romano Vicente to alert them that the sub would depart St. Marks at 11:00 PM.

"I will expect them around 10 PM, then, day after tomorrow," Gomez replied. "Please let them know that a late dinner will await them."

"Thank you, Hector. I will let them know. They don't expect you to provide that, but the crew always welcomes and appreciates you bringing them a meal when you can."

"What are the plans for the 'Capital Investment' to rendezvous with the sub?" Romano asked.

"Despite the isolated location, I know Wayne and Juan Carlos want the transfer to take place after dark," Thomas replied.

"How long does their trip take from Cuba to Belize and when do they usually depart for Cerros?" Romano asked.

"The voyage usually takes them about fifteen hours as best I know, right Hector?" said Thomas.

"That's right, Miguel. They usually depart Arroyos de Mantua around 6:00 AM, arriving in Cerros around ten at night." Gomez answered.

"What time should I tell the captain of the 'Capital Investment' to plan on a rendezvous with the sub?" Vicente asked.

"Let's say 9:00 PM," Thomas replied. "Since the rendezvous must be at night, the crew can rest all morning and leave a little after noon. Vladimir will not be late. He will study their navigational charts and leave in plenty of time to meet your crew at nine o'clock."

"How long do you expect it will take to offload the cash from the DSRV to the yacht?" Vicente questioned.

"With all eight men moving the 40-pound boxes, I expect it will take about an hour to transfer the 21,000 pounds of cash onboard." Thomas surmised.

"If Kerchenkov could be underway again by 10:00 PM, they should arrive at the Cerros mill between five and five-thirty in the morning. That would leave them about an hour to berth the sub before the mill crew arrives for work. Yes," Thomas reflected, "I believe a 9:00 PM rendezvous would be a workable timetable."

"Does that sound about right to you, Hector?"

"Yes, knowing the sub's navigational capabilities, Vladimir should be able to meet that timetable without any problem." Gomez responded corroboratively."

With plans set, Thomas changed the subject. "I'm just curious, Romano, how do you plan to move the cash from your yacht to the bank?" he asked.

"I have given that much thought," Vicente replied. "After offloading the cash from the sub, the yacht captain will cruise the 268 miles back to the Cayman Trench, 20 miles south of George Town. The next day they will join the other private and commercial fishermen, troll for billfish until mid-afternoon, then return to the boathouse around 5:00 in the afternoon. I don't believe this agenda will attract undue suspicion. All local fishing excursions usually return to port around the five o'clock hour."

"Miguel, you know my home is located not far from George Town on the northwest coast. To house the 'Capital Investment', I have built a boathouse adjacent to my dock on my private deep-water canal. My plan is to bring the cash directly to my home, then transport it to the bank."

"The cash will be transferred to my Suburban a load at a time under cover of darkness. No one will question my comings and goings from the bank's private parking garage. Using transport carts, the cash can easily be moved from the garage into the bank vault. Once deposited, I will transfer the cash into the Diego brother's, Clark's, and your account, Miguel. The transfers will be easy and will attract no undue attention."

"Sounds like a simple plan," Thomas said, "but I would ask that you not forget to make two additional account transfers."

"Would that perhaps be my fee and compensation for Hector?" Romano asked smilingly.

"Yes, Amigo," Thomas said jovially. "Don't forget to take your cut before you deposit ours."

"Those are two deposits I most certainly will not forget to make!" Vicente promised Hector Gomez.

"Gracias, Amigo!" Gomez replied.

The rendezvous of the mini-sub with the Capital Investment proved uneventful. In less than an hour, the cash was safely offloaded. Despite their relative isolation, both crews were apprehensive about transferring the cash. Their fears were unfounded. Radar scans showed no surface traffic closer than 55 miles.

Vicente received the cash less than 42 hours after its transfer. After a careful recount, he deposited each smuggler's share into their account at Cayman Island Capital Trust. The Diego brothers, Clark, and Thomas each received $3,695,000. Gomez received his $500,000. From his $1,000,000 deposit, Romano paid his crew a total of $250,000. If future cocaine shipments, pipeline distribution, street sales, and money laundering efforts were as financially successful as were those of this first shipment, all the players in the cartel's smuggling venture would indeed soon become very wealthy. Their plan had worked flawlessly.

Now that all phases of the smuggling operation had been tested and proven successful, the Belizean operation could move ahead at full speed. Though the fall cocaine-growing season was rapidly coming to an end, Juan Carlos anticipated he could process at least 80,000 additional pounds of coca from his Andes fields. The cartel would be busy moving another twenty shipments under the U.S. border during the winter months to come. Juan Carlos began to make special plans for his last 4,000-pound cocaine shipment.

Seven months had passed since the President had first disclosed his illness. Despite a slight loss in motor function, Walters displayed little inability to accomplish his daily schedule of activities. Though his agenda had been modified to include fewer public appearances, Edward Walters did not change the routine performance of his presidential duties.

At precisely 7:00 each morning, Walters walked the stairway from his upstairs residency in the White House to the Oval Office. Jim Atwood encouraged him to proceed with a normal routine of physical activity, though he warned Walters to expect limited ability in the future due to the progression of ALS. At present, Atwood saw no reason for the President to place limitations on himself. He was told to listen to his body and to challenge himself with any physical activity he desired. His body would tell him when and what were his limitations, Atwood had advised.

In his daily activities within the White House, Walters stayed as physically active as possible. Only when he was placed in a position within public view did he pace himself and limit the extent of his physical activity. He was careful not to be perceived by either the media or the public as weak and incapable of accomplishing the duties required of him as President.

Walters spent his first half-hour in the Oval Office in uninterrupted reflection. He cherished this half-hour of solitude, a time for meditation and reflection. As devoutly religious as he was patriotic, Walters prayed for the country and for peace in the world. His fervent prayer was that throughout the course of his disease, he would remain mentally strong, if not physically. He prayed for strength to lead the nation and the wisdom to recognize when he was incapable of continuing to do so.

He closed his morning prayer with the hope that America would be a stronger place because of his leadership, and that his leadership would be an inspiration to all those around him. He need not have worried. Edward Walters was already an inspiration to those around him, particularly to Charles Douglas, his vice president, best friend, and political ally.

At precisely 7:30 AM each weekday morning, the vice president entered the Oval Office. Walters had asked that Douglas enter without any formal knock of invitation. It was unnecessary. Walters would be expecting him at this time and the president looked forward to this half-hour visit with his friend.

Should his health fail before his term of office was over, Walters was grooming Douglas to make a smooth transition to the presidency. Walters did not make a presidential decision that was not discussed with his trusted vice president; he shared his every action with Douglas. The President greeted Douglas each morning.

"Good morning, Charles."

"Good morning, Mr. President." Douglas responded effusively. Though Walters had requested that he not address him formerly as 'Mr. President' in private, out of respect for the man and the office, Douglas could not help but do so in his first greeting of the day. "How are you feeling this morning, Eddie?" he asked out of genuine concern.

"Fine, Charles. I'm having a good morning."

With that response the President informed Douglas that he was capable of attending to the duties of the presidency that were required of him that day. They had openly agreed that only when the President responded differently should there be cause for further conversation about his disease. They did not openly discuss Walter's ALS nor its progression.

The president elected not to dwell on the disease that was slowly taking his life. He chose to look forward with a positive attitude focused on serving as CEO of the United States, rather than looking back with decadent self-pity on what might have been his future had he not become afflicted with ALS. In characteristic leadership, he took little introspective reflection. He focused on the broader scope of serving as President.

Walters' dogged determination to educate his vice president for his opportunity to claim the presidency, either by constitutional ascension or as an electorate of the people was not lost on Charles Douglas. He listened attentively and learned by example.

It was a cool, crisp mid-October morning in Washington, D.C. Only five months remained until March's Super Tuesday primaries. The cool temperatures of the approaching winter were reflected in A. Bixby Lane's drop in approval ratings. The Democrats were at a strategic crossroads. The direction of Lane's campaign hung in the balance.

Even at this early date in the campaign process, A. Bixby realized he was running a distant second place to the Vice President. He and his political advisors knew they must revise his campaign strategy if he was to have any hope of defeating Charles Douglas.

They were unconcerned about the Democratic primaries. Lane was far ahead of the next closest challenger, Senator Hiram J. Dority, Chairman of the Senate Finance Committee. Though a powerful force in the U.S. Senate, Hiram Dority was well known by few outside the hallowed halls of the U.S. Capitol, and then not well enough to consider voting for him for president. The Democrat faithful were pinning their hopes on the front-runner, A. Bixby Lane.

The Vice President's August prime-time telecast on the nation's looming energy crisis had polarized many moderate voters. The DNC had underestimated the former academian's political knowledge and his ability to communicate with the American people. Douglas' increase in approval ratings reflected in the Harris and Zogby polls temporarily tempered the Democrat's rhetoric to promote their anointed one. Lane's press conference had paled in comparison with Douglas'.

Charles Douglas already had many devout followers outside of the Republican Party, and the strength of A. Bixby's Memorial Day speech was slowly waning in the minds of the politically undecided voters. Lane knew he must secure the 270 electoral votes that would be required to defeat Charles Douglas.

Article II of the U.S. Constitution and the 12th Amendment stated that the winner of the majority of the 538-vote total of the Electoral College would be elected to serve as President. Each state was assigned a number of Electoral College votes equal to their state's representative number of the 435 U.S. House of Representative members. The balance of the Electoral College was comprised of two votes for each state's two members of the U. S. Senate, and three individual votes for the District of Columbia.

Lane's strategists determined that 133 of the 538 Electoral College votes were represented by a number of the state's undecided voters.

Lane's campaign strategy for the winter would be to attract these un-decided and moderate voters - voters who A. Bixby knew were easily in-fluenced to vote for the candidate supported by the often-biased liberal media. Lane was certain he could swing the media's support back to his campaign.

He could not, however, hope to reclaim their support and win the presidency if he continued his single campaign strategy of simply extol-ling his own self-professed virtues. His candidacy had lost much of its previous luster. Of equal concern to Lane was the knowledge that no new Democratic platform issues were under proposal that would recreate an immediate public attraction.

In an effort to refocus attention to his campaign, A. Bixby and com-pany decided to adopt a negative campaign strategy designed to convince the national media and the American public that Douglas was the wrong person to serve as President. Lane was an expert at aspersion. Negative campaigning was his specialty. The liberal media would love the bloodlet-ting.

Lane's negative attack ads were intended to discredit the Vice Presi-dent and malign the Republican platform. Though negative campaigning did not appeal to most Americans, Lane would seek every opportunity to focus the media's attention away from the credibility of the Vice Presi-dent. Once the darling of the media, A. Bixby was confident he could re-focus the Presidential campaign back on himself. He would use the media to his advantage. They liked controversy. More importantly, they often incited it.

At one of his early morning conferences with the Vice President, Ed-ward Walters began his plan to launch Charles Douglas' national cam-paign. The Vice President's August address to the nation on his proposed resolution to the energy crisis had been a good beginning.

With his considerable campaign experience, the President advised, "Charles, we know Lane can't be trusted to run a campaign strictly on the issues. Before we concentrate on your campaign platform, I feel we should first develop a well-planned defensive strategy to deal with any negative campaign issues. Lane will surely dissect my administration in an attempt to disclose any issues that the Democrats might perceive as Republican weaknesses."

"Charles, we know that in my first State of the Union address to Con-gress I introduced my four-year plan to reduce drug smuggling by 75%. I'm afraid that with the obvious success of the BSDIA, Lane will certainly propose that anything less than a proposed 75% reduction will be perceived as a Republican Party failure. How are we doing on meeting those expectations?"

Douglas responded, "Yesterday afternoon, I attended Rick Tolbert's staff briefing where he detailed the first six month's progress report. His report indicated that, based on sting operations, border interdiction, and street arrests, illegal drug use is down at least a measurable 55%."

"He reported that, particularly in the first three months of operation, the combined efforts of the BSDIA surveillance teams intercepted 43 tons of cocaine, 47 tons of marijuana, and 18 tons of heroin. Total street value of these confiscations was over $2.7 billion dollars!"

"These are certainly laudable figures, particularly considering the BSDIA initiative is still in its infancy. I am still concerned, nonetheless," Walters said, "that reducing drug smuggling by any less than my stated goal might be perceived as a failure of this administration. Likewise, I'm worried that such a perceived failure will be used by the media and the Democrats to negatively impact your campaign."

Douglas responded, "The amount of illegal drugs that do make it past our surveillance efforts continue to have a devastating effect on America's youth. This fact, though, should be perceived simply as the personal choice of certain Americans to simply 'just say no.'"

"That is true, Charles, but we must be mindful that despite the success of the BSDIA and the quantities of drugs that have been kept off America's streets, the Democrats will propose that anything less than a 100% success is a weakness of you and the Republican Party to protect America from this scourge on society."

"While that is true, Mr. President," Douglas countered, "one positive aspect of our drug interdiction efforts can be seen in the decrease of the approximately 17,500 drug-related deaths America experiences each year, principally among its youth. Just in the first six months that the BSDIA has been in operation, we have seen these death rates cut in half. That fact alone speaks to the credibility of your initiative."

"Believe me, Mr. President," Douglas continued, "you need not worry about anything you do or have done that might negatively effect my bid for the presidency. If a 75 % reduction was the targeted goal, certain of the liberal media and the Democratic leaders would use even a 70% reduction as our failure to meet expectations. Don't give it a second thought, Eddie. The American people are wise and will see through this façade."

Douglas continued, "If need be, I am certain we will be successful in dispelling any of Lane's or the media's assertions to the American people. The public is far more perceptive than either Lane or the media give them credit."

"Eddie, you should be proud of your drug interdiction efforts. There are far fewer illegal drugs on America's streets now than there were just six months ago. This is a tribute to your foresight in enacting the BSDIA. I concur with Rick's excellent assessment of the agency's accomplishments in its first half-year of operation. We would be well served to remember his wise words should we have to counter any negative Democratic suppositions of the BSDIA's ineffectiveness."

Tolbert had motivated his staff by concluding his earlier staff meeting with these encouraging words. "In just six short months, we have made considerable headway in reducing the amount of illegal drugs that invade America's streets and neighborhoods. Unfortunately, despite our best efforts to interdict these drugs and to discourage illegal drug use, America's youth are still attracted to the mind-numbing effects of cocaine."

Tolbert had continued, "Cocaine's occasional recreational use quickly leads to hard core drug addiction and abuse. We simply cannot stop America's drug problem until there is no longer a demand for its use. Despite our best efforts, despite repeated attempts to encourage America's youth to 'just say no,' the street pushers will continue to have an illegal drug market; and the U.S. will continue to have an ever present drug problem until Americans make the personal decision to abstain from illegal drug use and abuse."

"Until there is no longer a desire to use these addictive and often deadly drugs or until there is no longer a supply source, moral America and the BSDIA still have a job to do. Let us continue to stay vigilant in our efforts to stop illegal drugs outside America's borders."

Walters concluded. "Tolbert's assessments and our effective percentages in drug interdiction will then be our defense to any negative campaign tactics Lane may employ to disparage our efforts. We will, we must continue to protect America against the scourge of illegal drugs."

During the last two weeks of October and throughout November and December, the cartel was kept busy delivering the cocaine, collecting the cash, and making their offshore deposits. By the first of January, all members of the smuggling operation had become very wealthy men. Once again, cocaine was prevalently available in America. Over the last two and a half months, Clark's pipeline had saturated the streets with 76,400 pounds of the addictive drug.

The last 3,600-pound shipment of cocaine was saved for the St. Marks chemist's special processing skills. Clark and Diego sold a gram of their powdered cocaine on the street for $10. To turn the cocaine powder into crack cocaine would increase the value to $100 per gram.

Diego saved his last shipment to test the organization's ability to manufacture and market crack. As no more cocaine would be shipped until the spring crop was harvested, the St. Marks chemists would have plenty of time to convert this 3,600-pound shipment into crack.

Thomas read several scientific articles that discussed cocaine addiction, its physiological and pharmacological properties, and the chemical methods of converting cocaine powder in crack.

"Powdered cocaine is the powerfully addictive recreational drug most often misused by America's wealthy, favored by its white collar professionals, and by the easily influenced college crowd." Thomas read. "Recreational cocaine users who snort powdered cocaine experience a rapid, intense central nervous system stimulant effect as the drug is absorbed through the nasal membranes into the blood stream."

Additionally, one article provided information on cocaine physiology. "Crack cocaine is the abusive drug of choice of America's hard core cocaine addicts. As this solid form of cocaine is smoked, the inhaled vapor is as rapidly absorbed into the bloodstream, as it would be by injection. As cocaine crosses the blood brain barrier, dopamine, the chemical messenger for the brain that causes the euphoric feelings of hyper-stimulation, focused mental acuity, and reduced fatigue, is rapidly released."

Thomas read an article's on the inhaled drug's physical effect on the body. "Pharmacologically, crack addicts experience a much faster absorption of cocaine and a more intense euphoric high than do those who snort cocaine. But with the faster, more intense high, comes a shorter duration of euphoric effects. The high produced from snorting cocaine usually lasts from 15 to 30 minutes, while the high from inhaling vaporized crack lasts a brief 5 to 10 minutes. The physical and psychological addiction to crack occurs extremely rapidly, often after the first use."

The article noted that, "Increased usage promotes an addiction that requires smoking hundreds of dollars of crack each day to curb the physical cravings. These hundreds of dollars were commonly derived from criminal activities."

Juan Carlos and Clark were unconcerned about the increase in crime that accompanies crack addiction. Likewise, they were unconcerned about the lives destroyed either directly or indirectly from addiction. Their only concern was accumulating wealth. The quicker they could saturate the streets with powdered cocaine and crack, the quicker their bank accounts would grow.

Another article discussed the chemical processes involved in converting powdered cocaine into an inhaled product. "'Crack,' is the common street name for the solid form of cocaine that is processed from raw powdered cocaine hydrochloride."

"In its solid 'free base' form, crack is smoked for its rapid euphoria." The article continued informatively. "To smoke raw cocaine powder would ultimately be lethal. If smoked, the inhaled vapors contain not only aerosolized stimulant cocaine, but also vaporized hydrochloric acid that is immediately corrosive to the lungs."

"To 'free base' cocaine, the corrosive acid must first be removed from the base cocaine. Two chemical processes are employed to reduce the cocaine powder into a solid form that is free of hydrochloride."

"The more volatile and most dangerous chemical process used to extract the cocaine base from the inorganic acid requires dissolving cocaine powder in ether. The volatile ether and hydrochloric acid are then boiled off to produce crack or "rock" cocaine as the free-base product is known on the streets."

Additionally, Thomas learned that the less volatile and least dangerous process for purifying cocaine powder involved combining the powder either with sodium bicarbonate and water, or with ammonia, and heating the suspension until the hydrochloride is volatilized and removed. This method produces a solid product of bicarbonate and cocaine that makes a unique 'crack'ling sound that is heard as the solid mixture is smoked. The free base product obtained from ether extraction makes no sound as it is smoked. The euphoric high produced from either crack or rock cocaine is the same."

With his chemists, Thomas discussed the pros and cons of each method of converting powdered cocaine into the inhaled form. The chemists advised Thomas to employ the bicarbonate method of extracting the free base. They determined that there was less risk of an explosion in the lab using this method. The ether extraction method would produce highly volatile ether vapors that could easily be ignited by the machinery used in the sugar refinery process.

During the three weeks following the New Year, the chemists had refined the 3,600 pounds of cocaine powder into 5,800 pounds of free base crack cocaine. The primary markets for their crack were California, the north-central states, and the Northeast. Clark shipped 2,500 pounds to the California market. Another 1,500 pounds went to Chicago. New York received 1,000 pounds, and Atlanta, 800 pounds.

The crack shipment would realize almost $160 million, as much money as had the past six weeks' sales of powdered cocaine combined. By the end of winter, each of the already wealthy smugglers would become enormously wealthier.

CHAPTER SIXTEEN

Deep powdery snow blanketed the ski resorts of Colorado. Already measuring a 156-inch packed base, 28 inches of fresh powdered snow had fallen on the ski runs in Vail during the past four days. It would be a perfect weekend for snow skiing. The upcoming long Martin Luther King, Jr. holiday weekend enticed many college ski faithful to the slopes of Vail.

"Come here, Corey," said his twin brother, Casey, reclining in their den as he took a break from his studies. "Look at this Weather Channel ski report."

As a Christmas gift, the sons of U.S. Congressman, C. Terrell Sheffield had been given a four-day ski vacation to Vail for the upcoming King holiday. Several of their fraternity brothers planned to join them.

"Look at all that new snow!" said Casey excitedly as he joined Corey to watch the ski report. "Only two more days. I can't wait to get there."

"Me, either," seconded Corey. "We'll need a break after this week's exams."

They were first year law students. Because their Father was Chairman of the House Appropriations Committee and likely to be tapped by A. Bixby Lane as his running mate, the twins felt considerable pressure to excel in their studies and not embarrass their Father academically.

"You bet we'll need a break. I don't know about you, but I'm about burned out," said Casey.

"Yeah, me too," Corey said. "Staying up half the night studying every day for the past three days and running on little sleep has about wasted me, too."

"We'll make up for our missed play time when we get to Vail," Casey said.

"Definitely!"

The Thursday morning preceding the King Holiday weekend finally arrived. At 11:00 AM, the private jet transporting the Sheffields and three of their fraternity brothers landed at Denver International Airport. The boys rented a Suburban, stowed away their ski equipment and luggage and headed westward on Interstate 70 towards the Rocky Mountains and the ski resort of Vail.

"Man, just look at this snow!" exclaimed Corey as he slowly drove toward the foothills of the Rockies. "It's been a long week. I didn't think this day would ever get here!"

"I hope the girls are as beautiful as this scenery, and as plentiful as this new fallen snow," Casey said. The others laughed.

"I thought you came here to ski," said one of the fraternity brothers.

"I did, in the daytime. But the nighttime is reserved for ski bunnies!"

"Better cool it, brother," chided Corey. "As tired as you are, you had better save your energy. You'll be exhausted just thinking about all those tight ski pants!"

"You're right brother. You drive while I sleep and recharge my batteries."

Three and a half hours and 101 miles later, Corey exited I-70.

With only an hour of daylight remaining, the sun was beginning to set over Vail Mountain. The golden glow of twilight painted the fresh fallen snow with an illusion of warmth. Despite the cold temperature and their exhaustion, the boys felt rejuvenated. They gazed up at the lighted runs of the ski slopes on Front Side and watched lines of skiers zigzag their way down the mountain.

On the short drive westward on South Frontage Drive, they passed resort after resort of ski lodges and condominiums. Skiers crowded the sidewalks and shopping malls. Some were no doubt on their way to Happy Hour or hurrying to make dinner reservations.

Less than five minutes from the Vail town center, Corey turned left into the Vail Cascade Lodge and Conference Center complex. Children scurried playfully on the lodge grounds, throwing snowballs and building snowmen. Their exuberance further rallied the boy's energy.

A large stone fireplace and a roaring fire greeted them as they entered the hotel lobby. While their bags were unloaded by the bellmen, the boys were offered a cup of hot cocoa. The registration clerk, a cute co-ed, greeted them with a warm smile. Her nametag identified her as Sarah.

"Glad you made it in safely before the next snow storm," she said. "We're supposed to get another 10 - 12 inches tonight."

"How's the skiing, Sarah?" Casey asked, more to prompt further conversation than glean information.

"It's been great!" she exclaimed. "Last night I skied Front Side from after dinner until almost midnight. The slopes are in fantastic shape. The new powder is about a foot deep on the lower and mid-slopes. The black diamonds are super fast. You guys surely came at a good time."

"Sounds great," Casey replied. "This is our first time in Vail. Can you recommend a good Italian restaurant for dinner?"

"Sure, the best in town is Gambetta's just up the road at the intersection of Frontage and Vail Road. It's my favorite. Would you like me to call and make you a dinner reservation?"

"Sure! That would be great." Replied Casey.

"Would it just be for you five? Or are you entertaining dates this evening?" Sarah asked quizzically.

"Uh, we just came stag." Corey replied.

"You could make our reservation for six if you would care to join us," Casey added quickly.

"That would be great. I get off at seven," Sarah replied. "If you would like, I could call four of my sorority sisters and see if they are free for dinner."

"We would like that very much!" Corey said. The others grinned and echoed his sentiments.

"Let's get you checked in, and you'll have an hour or so to freshen up and relax. Well," she said, checking their registration cards against their reservations, "it seems you are on our VIP list. I'm impressed!"

"Oh, Dad's secretary must have made our reservations," Casey responded modestly.

"Let's see, yes, your reservations were made by U.S. Congressman Terrell Sheffield's office. He's your dad?"

"Yes," Casey and Corey responded in unison.

"Could you please wait just a moment? The manager would personally like to greet you and escort you to your suite."

A call was quickly made to the manager's office. "Mr. Becker, a group of VIP registrants have arrived. I knew you would want to greet them personally."

"Yes, of course I would, Sarah. Who are they?"

"Congressman Sheffield's sons and a few of their friends."

"Okay. I'll be right out. You do know who their father is, don't you, Sarah?"

"Sure, a U.S. Representative."

"Yes, a U.S. Representative who will probably be the next Vice President of the United States!"

"Goodness," said Sarah. She had thought the twins were cute; now she had an even greater interest in escorting them around town.

"Hello, gentlemen. Welcome to the Vail Cascade!" Becker said in warm greeting. "It's a pleasure to have you join us for the weekend."

"Sarah," he continued, "have these young men's suites already been assigned?"

"Yes, sir. In the north wing, double room suite 1505 and triple 1509."

"Excellent, Sarah."

To the twins and their friends Becker remarked that these rooms were reserved for special guests. "The north wing suites offer our best, unrestricted view of Vail Mountain and the slopes. I trust our accommodations will meet your needs," he said. "Your wing is adjacent to our private ski lift station and overlooks Gore Creek. The view is spectacular, and your in-room and outdoor patio fireplaces will offer you a warm, comfortable place to end your day. Come; let me escort you to your rooms."

"That isn't necessary, sir," Casey said.

"Nonsense. I want to make sure you are settled in okay. Sarah, call the bell stand and have the porters bring their luggage around."

"Yes, sir."

"By the way, have you made dinner reservations for this evening? If not, I would be glad to ask the concierge to make them for you."

"That's kind of you, sir, but Sarah has already offered to make our dinner reservations and has also offered for her and her friends to be our escorts for the evening."

"Wonderful," said Becker. "Sarah, you're scheduled to be off this weekend, aren't you?

"Yes, sir, I am."

"Good. Then, why don't you take tomorrow off as well, so you can escort our guests around Vail and show them the slopes?"

"Thank you, sir. I'd love to," Sarah replied happily.

"Excellent," the brothers said in unison. Casey and Corey laughed at this. Since childhood, they had thought along similar tracks, and speaking the same words at the same time was a common occurrence.

"Great," said Sarah. "While you get settled in. I'll call my friends and invite them to dinner. Why don't you come back, around say, 6:45 and we'll all meet in the lounge before we take the shuttle to dinner."

"Sounds like a good plan," Casey said.

When Becker escorted the boys to their suites, he advised them to read the complimentary Cascade Hotel newsletter provided in each suite.

"It will give you some insight into Vail, the ski slopes, and current activities in Vail Village."

"Thank you, sir. We will." Corey replied as Becker turned to leave.

"Boy, this is great! Casey exclaimed to Corey as he looked about the cedar-paneled suite. "Two private bedrooms and a large sitting room."

"You said it," Corey replied. "Look at that huge stone fireplace. I'll get the gas logs lit while you take a shower."

"Deal," Casey said. "How about unpacking, too?"

"You're pushing it, brother, but okay. Get a move on. I can't wait to meet the other girls. If they're as pretty as Sarah, we are in for a great weekend."

"Don't you know it!" Casey agreed.

The brothers showered and changed for dinner. They opened the curtains to enjoy the view of the nighttime slopes and settled in the large comfortable armchairs to read the newsletter.

"It says here that Vail is the nation's largest resort community, boasts the largest ski mountain in North America, and some of the best snow skiing in the world," Corey said excitedly.

"Did you read this, Corey?" Casey said, looking over his shoulder. "The *Vail Cascade* reports that Vail Mountain has over 5,000 acres of skiable terrain and is surrounded by 14,000 peaks and an unparalleled blue sky."

"Boy, I'll say!" Corey agreed.

Casey continued to read. "The Mountain has 193 trails and allows skiers from the beginner to the experienced to enjoy the mountain's white powdery snow. I can hardly wait until tomorrow."

"Me, either! And how about the activities we can enjoy after leaving the slopes?" Corey read aloud from one of the brochures. "It says here that Vail Village's charismatic neighborhood provides extraordinary dining, unique shopping, and non-stop nightlife."

"Yeah," Casey joked, "the nightlife, that's what I'm waiting for!"

"Me too! I can't wait to walk around Vail Village. And how about the complimentary shuttle service? We don't have to worry about drinking and driving."

"Speaking of which, it's 6:35. Time to go meet the girls," Casey prompted.

"Let's go get the others and head downstairs, then," Corey replied.

When they walked into the lounge, they found Sarah sitting at the corner table by the large stone fireplace. Four other beautiful co-eds turned their heads to smile at them as they approached the table.

"Hi, Sarah," Casey said. As the other girls rose for introductions, the five friends greeted Sarah as well.

"Hi, guys." Sarah said. "I've ordered a pitcher of Margaritas. Drag up a chair and join us. I'll introduce my friends and you can introduce yours."

"This is Jenny, Beth, Dawn, and Karen."

"Hello, ladies," they responded in unison. "It's nice to meet you," Casey took the lead and introduced himself and the others. "I'm Casey, and this is my twin brother, Corey, and our friends, Dan, Ben and Will."

The girls shook hands with the boys and invited them to sit down and have a drink before dinner. Casey was glad when Sarah grabbed his arm and settled him down beside her.

"I made reservations for 8:00 PM at Gambetta's. We have about a half hour before we need to take the shuttle to the village. Mr. Becker said drinks were on the house tonight. When you finish your Margarita, order whatever you want from the bar."

"Thanks. That was nice of him," Casey replied.

"He wanted to make sure you had a good time this evening," Sarah said with a warm smile.

"I think we're certainly off to a good start," Corey replied as he toasted their new friendships.

After dinner, they walked along historic Bridge Street peering into the quaint art shops. At the Lion's Head lounge, they drank pitchers of Miller Genuine Draft beer - "the preferred drink of collegiate beer drinking champions," as it was known in their fraternity.

Having had little rest and an excessive amount of alcohol, by 11:00 PM they excused themselves and headed back to the Cascade to get some sleep.

"We'll ride back with you, just to make sure you get back okay," Sarah said. "You don't think you're going to get rid of us that easily, do you?" teased Dawn who had attached herself to Corey.

"Oh, believe me, we're not trying to get rid of you," Corey responded. "We're just dog tired. We've had little sleep this week because of exams, and we're just exhausted."

"Besides," Dan added, "Don't you want to spend the day on the slopes tomorrow? If we don't get some shut-eye, we won't even have enough energy to ski the bunny slope!"

"Okay, okay." Sarah replied laughingly as they entered the Cascade lobby. "We know you're not trying to dump us. We'll see you bright and early in the morning in the lobby for breakfast. Say at 7:30?"

"Oh man. That's early!" Casey groaned teasingly. "But, it's a date." he replied as he hugged her goodnight. "See you in the morning."

The morning sun was just beginning to peak over the ridge of the eastern mountains as the brother's alarm clock rang at 6:30 AM.

"Throw that darn thing out the window," Corey pleaded from his room.

"I'm too tired to get up and throw it, or I would," said Casey.

Remembering his beautiful blonde date who would soon be waiting for him downstairs, Casey forced himself out of bed. "Come on sleepy head," he said as he went into Corey's room and swatted him on the back with a pillow. "The girls await."

Just the thought of the voluptuous brunette Dawn in her tight ski pants roused Corey out of bed. "Yeah, we wouldn't want to keep the girls waiting, would we?"

In the early morning light, the boys thought the girls looked even more beautiful than they had the night before. After a hot breakfast, the shuttle took them to Vail Village where they bought a three-day lift ticket and ski pass. Then they boarded the Vista Bahn Express Lift and rode the Eagle Bahn Gondola to Adventure Ridge.

The 10-minute ascent gave them an unrestricted view of Vail Village and the 127 trails on the front side of Vail Mountain. The 50-foot evergreens were blanketed with fresh fallen snow. More than 16 feet of the winter's packed snow covered the trunks and lower limbs of the mountainside evergreens.

"This certainly is a skier's paradise," Sarah said excitedly to Casey as the gondola climbed its way up Vail Mountain. They held hands, mesmerized by the vista of the valley floor below.

The unspoiled vastness of the pale blue sky, the panoramic view of the slopes and valley, and the beautiful girl beside him rejuvenated Casey. He barely remembered his early morning fatigue.

"Isn't the view just beautiful?" Sarah exclaimed.

"Yes. It is," Casey said. He turned and stared directly into her bright blue eyes. "But it's not only the view that is awe inspiring." Casey leaned in to kiss her lightly on the lips.

Sarah held his hand tightly and returned his kiss. "Even if this is only temporary affection," she thought, "it makes me feel so good to be with him."

"The feeling is mutual," she replied to his earlier compliment.

Casey's glance around the gondola found the other couples experiencing similar moments. All were holding hands and quietly reflecting upon the beauty of the morning.

At Adventure Ridge, they transferred to the Mountaintop Express Lift that ascended to Vail Mountain's Summit. For three hours, they skied the black diamond Prima slope and its 3-mile Riva Ridge run to the valley floor. Returning to Summit at mid-afternoon, they paused to nourish their voracious appetites.

At the Summit Restaurant, the group picnicked at outdoor tables, enjoying the beauty of the pristine slopes on the back side of Vail Mountain, including the mountain's famous Back Bowls and Blue Sky Basin ski runs.

"We've got to return tomorrow and ski Blue Sky Basin," Casey remarked. "It doesn't look like there are many ski tracks on the slopes. We certainly wouldn't encounter nearly as many skiers on Back Side's slopes as we have on the front."

"Sounds good to me," said Sarah. "But the Ski Patrol recommends that we get a knowledgeable local ski guide. The trails are well marked, but it's easy to get disoriented on the twists and turns as the ski slope falls over 11,000 feet to the Basin Valley."

Despite everyone's confidence in his or her own skiing ability, the group agreed to hire a guide.

"After lunch, let's make one more run down Prima," Sarah proposed, "then head back to change for the evening. I think this will be a very special night." She took Casey's hand, smiling coquetly.

"That's a good idea," Casey said sheepishly. "After all, we do need to hire a guide for tomorrow."

They met Justin Hardison while waiting to be seated for their dinner reservation. He appeared to be around 30 years old. His chiseled face was suntanned except around the eyes where ski goggles were worn. He must have spent a great deal of time on the slopes, Sarah thought to herself.

Hardison had overheard their animated conversation about skiing and their need to hire a local guide to lead them down Blue Sky Basin the next day.

He approached the group in the restaurant lobby. "Hello, I'm Justin Hardison. I couldn't help but overhear that you needed to hire a guide for tomorrow. Look no further. I'm your man. I've been skiing Back Side since I was in high school."

"Sounds like we've found our guide," Corey concluded. "How much do you charge for the day?"

"A hundred bucks," Replied Hardison. "I love skiing, and I'd guide you for free if I didn't have to make a living," he added.

"You've got yourself a deal," said Casey. The two men shook hands. "What time do you guys want to head out?"

"How about nine?" Corey suggested.

"Fine. I'll meet you at the Vista Bahn at nine."

After a long night of wining, dining, and dancing, the couples headed back to the Cascade for hot chocolate. Around 1:00 AM, the group finally decided to call it a night.

"I guess its time to bid you goodnight," Casey said to Sarah as he kissed her. "I'll see you early in the morning." he added, holding her close.

Prolonging the embrace, Sarah stared into his eyes and remarked, "Yes, you will. When we wake up," she said pulling him by the hand. "Let's go to your room."

Sarah's light stroking of his hair roused Casey from a deep sleep. He had drunk too much alcohol and they had not fallen asleep until almost dawn. He smiled as he looked at her beautiful blue eyes and tousled hair.

"Time to get up, sweetie," she prompted.

"Go back to sleep," Casey grumbled. "We haven't even had two hours of sleep."

"You weren't complaining last night," Sarah said laughingly as she prodded him under the covers.

"Who said I was complaining." Casey replied as he hugged her. "I just meant that I'm exhausted. Very happy, but exhausted! I'll probably feel better when we get out on the slopes."

"Of course you will. Let's get ready for breakfast. I'm starved. I'll go see if Corey and Dawn are up yet."

"You do that," Casey replied. "But don't be surprised if you get a pillow tossed at you. Corey isn't easy to wake up."

"I'll let Dawn take care of that," she laughed. "Just getting you up and going will be chore enough for me."

Despite a hot breakfast, three cups of coffee, and the cold morning air, Casey could hardly drag himself off the shuttle bus.

"Just take it easy," Sarah said comfortingly. "You'll feel better when we get to Summit and you see the beautiful white slopes of Back Side."

"I hope so. I'm really dragging now. Let's stop at the Lion's Head and get some aspirin. Maybe that will pick me up."

On the ascent to the summit, Casey's head pounded with each heart-beat. If I don't begin to feel better soon, Casey thought, I don't think I will be able to ski. I certainly wouldn't want to disappoint Sarah and the others, though.

Relieved when they arrived at the lift station, Casey desperately needed some fresh air. He hoped it would clear his head. He tried vainly to act as excited as did his friends as they prepared to make their first run. With great effort, he donned his ski gloves and goggles and fastened his boots into the ski bindings.

"Everyone all ready?" Justin queried.

Casey was too embarrassed to say that he would rather sit this run out.

With an "Okay then, let's go!" Hardison pushed off and the five couples followed in pairs.

Exuberant shouts could be heard throughout the adjacent slopes as the 11 skied their way down the run. Twenty minutes later, they had reached the valley floor at the foot of the lift station. Casey could not have been happier to see the run end. He didn't think he could make another. Despite his reluctance to disappoint Sarah, he was determined to skip out on the rest of the morning's skiing. Maybe he would feel better in the afternoon, after he had rested awhile at Summit's indoor restaurant. His lack of energy did not go unnoticed by his friends.

He leaned on his skis to catch his breath. "Whew," he exclaimed. "I'm tired."

"Sarah, will you please excuse me for a moment. I need to talk to Justin."

"Sure, sweetie," she replied with a worried look.

"Hey Justin. Can I talk with you a minute?" Casey asked as they prepared to get on the lift for their return to the top of Vail Mountain.

"Sure, Casey. What's up? You don't look so hot."

"I'm not feeling very well. My head is splitting and I'm really dragging. I hardly have enough energy to put one foot in front of the other. I'm afraid I won't be able to ski anymore this morning."

"Yeah, man, I know what you mean. After a hard night of partying, I occasionally get bummed out, too. I have a quick fix for your hangover, though, that will really pick you up. It'll give you an incredible burst of energy that will let you ski like an Olympic downhiller. Trust me, it works. Game to try it?"

"I feel so bad, I'll try most anything right now. I sure don't want to give up skiing with Sarah."

"Here, man, go into the men's room and sniff a little of this," Hardison said as he extracted a small vial of white powder from his ski jacket. "In just a minute you'll feel like you're on the top of the world."

"Is that cocaine? You mean you want me to snort coke?" Casey remarked astonishingly. "I don't do that. I really should just sit the rest of this morning out."

"Whatever, man. You mean you're going to leave that ski bunny alone on the slopes for the rest of the morning? Don't be such a wimp. Just try it. I promise it will make you feel like a new person by the time you come out of the restroom."

"I don't know. I've never used any illegal drugs before. I'm really concerned about doing this!" Casey confessed.

"What you should be concerned about is cutting out on you girlfriend. I'm sure she will really be impressed."

"Alright. Give it to me."

"Sarah, I need to run to the restroom. I'll be back in a minute."

"Okay, we'll be waiting right here. Hurry back now." She flashed that contagious smile.

"What am I doing?" Casey asked himself as he stared at his haggard reflection in the restroom mirror.

Quickly, he reconciled his first use of any illegal drug. "I'm just trying to keep up with my friends. That's all I'm doing. After this morning, I won't ever do this again. Besides, no one else will ever know."

In movies and on television, Casey had seen others snort cocaine. He knew what to do. Tearing off a piece of paper towel, he rolled it into the shape of a small straw. Onto the palm of his hand, he sprinkled out a three-inch line of powder about an eighth of an inch in width.

Putting the paper straw into his left nostril, he slowly leaned forwards and moved his hand upwards. He exhaled deeply, then quickly inhaled the powder. He repeated the process for his right nostril.

Even before he had even capped the vial of powder, Casey felt a numbing of his throbbing headache. In seconds, it was completely gone. Within a minute, he experienced an acute level of energy, the likes of which he had never felt before.

"Incredible. I feel completely energized," he said aloud. Rejuvenated, he bounded out the restroom door and ran towards his friends.

"Let's go slow pokes," he shouted as he picked up his skis. "What are you waiting for? Come on, Sarah. Get a move on. Let's go skiing."

"Well, isn't someone feeling better now!" Sarah stated astonishingly.

"Yeah," Corey remarked apprehensively. "What's gotten into you, brother? A few minutes ago, you could hardly take a step."

"Don't worry about it, Corey. I feel great now. Let's get going."

"Okay. I'm right behind you."

On the 10-minute ride back up the mountain, Casey chattered incessantly to Sarah about the beautiful day, the beautiful scenery, and how much he enjoyed being with her.

"Your aspirin certainly must have given you some remarkable relief," Sarah commented in amazement. She marveled at his sudden change in temperament.

"Must have," Casey lied. "I can't wait to make the next run."

The sun shimmered off the open slopes in stark contrast to the darker curves and drop-offs where the evergreen and spruce trees shaded the trail. Their second run was an incredible adventure. Casey skied with the authority of a professional. He whooped and hollered with every twist and turn as he and Sarah zigzagged their way down the mountain.

By the time they reached the valley, 30 minutes had elapsed since Casey had first inhaled the cocaine. The euphoric effect was rapidly wearing off. "I need to make another pit stop, Sarah. I'll be right back."

Aware that he abusing an illegal stimulant and out of fear that he might want more and more to keep that great feeling of exuberant energy, Casey decided to snort only one line of coke this second time.

"Can't hurt to take just a little bit more," he rationalized. "After all, it's our last run of the morning, and after lunch and a little rest, I shouldn't need any more."

Within seconds, he felt revised again, re-energized, and ready for another run. Hurrying back out to his friends, he furtively passed the vial of cocaine back to Justin. "Thanks!" he whispered as he skied towards Sarah and his friends.

On their ride back up the ski lift, Casey again talked incessantly. Sarah surmised he was making up for his unusually quite ride up from Vail Village earlier that morning.

The sun was now directly overhead, casting a blinding white glare over the mountain. Without polarized ski goggles it would have been impossible to see well. Even with goggles, at times, it might be difficult to clearly focus on the sunlit trails.

Once at Summit, Casey chided his friends. "Hurry up and get ready. Let's go, times a wasting," he said.

Soon, all had their boots locked in their bindings and were ready to push off. It had been less than 15 minutes since Casey's last snort of cocaine. Still euphoric from the stimulant effect, he pulled Sarah by the arm and guided her down the slope.

Ten minutes into their 20-minute run, Casey suddenly felt his energy level begin to fade. It was as if someone had turned off his power switch. His exuberance quickly waning, Casey suddenly grew very quite. He stopped his shouts of exhilaration as he tried desperately to focus on the steep downhill slopes ahead.

"What's wrong, Casey?" Sarah shouted above the roar of the wind.

"Nothing, Sarah," he struggled to reply. "I'm just getting tired again."

"Then we'd better slow down," she cautioned.

"No, it's okay. Let's keep ahead of the others."

At a point mid-way in the run, they approached the steepest downhill curves on the trail. They rapidly sped in and out of the shadows and into the blinding light of the open slopes.

Unexpectedly, Casey could not focus his eyesight nor command his legs to guide his skis. As the cocaine wore off, his visual perception and mental alertness had become seriously impaired. Casey and Sarah gathered speed as they flew down the open trail. Suddenly, the run ahead cornered sharply to the right as it rapidly dropped downhill.

As Sarah approached the curve, she maneuvered her skis into tight S-turns to slow her speed. She watched in horror as Casey simply leaned into the turn and flew off the downhill slope. She screamed as he lost his balance and landed headfirst into a large aspen.

"Oh, my God," she shouted. Quickly, she signaled to the others trailing behind to stop.

"Casey!" Corey cried as he watched his brother crash. He knew Casey would be injured. He only hoped his brother would not be hurt badly. They watched in horror as Casey bounced off the snow and tumbled downhill. His free fall did not stop until he reached the flat plane of the next turn. There, he lay motionless.

Corey flew downhill and plowed to a stop beside his brother. Blood trickled from Casey's mouth and ears. He had a deep laceration on his forehead. Worse, he was not breathing.

"Casey!" he screamed again. "Wake up and talk to me."

Justin Hardison arrived at almost the same moment Corey did. "Move aside Corey. Let me check for a heart beat."

Finding none, he lit a smoke-signal flare. Pulling his walkie-talkie from his backpack, Hardison quickly alerted the ski patrol that they had a skier down. "Better send the rescue chopper," he informed the dispatcher. "The victim has no pulse and no respiration."

For the seven minutes that it took for the helicopter to transit the mountain and land beside the crowd of skiers, Justin and Corey performed CPR. Sarah and the girls cried hysterically while the brother's friends watched in horror.

Corey kept shouting, "Come on Casey. Wake up." The limp, prone body had not moved since coming to a stop in a crumpled heap.

Corey felt a momentary sense of relief when the helicopter arrived. Moving quickly, the rescue workers continued CPR while carefully strapping Casey's lifeless body to a backboard. Noting that one of the skiers who had been performing CPR was a twin of the victim, they asked Corey if he'd like to fly back to the hospital with them.

In less than 10 minutes, the life-flight rescue helicopter landed at Vail's community hospital. The emergency room staff had been alerted that they were inbound with a ski victim who had crashed headlong into a tree. "The patient is non-responsive, with no signs of pulse or respiration," the attending emergency medical technician reported. "We are administering CPR."

Corey was escorted into the ER waiting room while Casey was rushed into the emergency trauma center. In less than 20 minutes, the trauma team's chief physician, Dr. Tom Richards, walked in and sat beside Corey. He felt great trepidation for the news he must deliver to the obviously distraught young man.

"I'm sorry to have to tell you this, but your brother did not survive. We did all we could to resuscitate him, but our best efforts were unsuccessful. I expect your brother died instantly upon impact with the tree. I will assure you, he did not suffer. I'm very sorry. If you'll come with me, we can contact your parents."

Corey was in a state of shock. Just 24 hours earlier, life had been great. The twins had met two beautiful girls and were enjoying a great vacation. What could have happened to Casey? He was an expert skier."

"Mom and Dad." Corey said aloud. "This is going to kill them, too." He cried.

"What is your brother's and your name, son?" the physician asked quietly.

"My brother's name is Casey. My name is Corey Sheffield, sir. My father is Congressman Terrell Sheffield. Will you please call him for me? I can't do it. I just can't do it."

"Certainly Corey. Would you like to come with me?"

"Yes, sir," he said.

Retiring to his private office, Richards was quickly connected to Sheffield's office in the House Office Building. "This is Dr. Richards from Vail, Colorado. I need to talk with Representative Sheffield immediately, please.

"I'm sorry doctor, but the Representative is in the middle of an appropriations committee meeting. May I have him return your call after committee?" asked his Chief of Staff.

"I'm sorry but you need to interrupt the Representative now. I have a message of utmost personally urgency for Representative Sheffield. It's about his son, Casey. Please get him immediately for me."

"Yes, sir. I will. Would you like to hold, or may I have the Congressman call you back?"

"I'll wait while you get Mr. Sheffield."

As chairman of the House Appropriations Committee, C. Terrell Sheffield was in the midst of conducting a budget and finance meeting when his aide rushed in to advise him of the phone call. "Sorry to bother you, sir, but the caller said it was a matter of extreme personal urgency."

"Please excuse me for a moment ladies and gentlemen, for I must leave for an urgent phone call. "Vice Chairman Anderson, would you please take charge of the meeting in my absence?"

"Certainly, Mr. Chairman."

Sheffield hurried to his office suite where he noted his staff awaiting him with apprehension. Retiring to his private office, he pushed the blinking light on his phone. "This is Terrell Sheffield. How may I help you?"

"Representative Sheffield, this is Dr. Richards of Vail Community Hospital. I am sorry to have to tell you this. Your son, Casey, has been involved in a tragic skiing accident. I'm afraid that he did not survive."

"Oh no! This can't be true. Oh my God. No. Not my son. Not my son," Sheffield cried. He slumped into his office chair.

"I'm very sorry, sir. I have Corey here with me now. He's quite shaken, I'm afraid. I am going to give him a sedative and let him rest here in the hospital until you arrive. I'll fill you in on the details when you get here."

"Thank you, doctor. My wife and I will be there as soon as possible. May I please speak to Corey?"

"Dad," Corey began. He could find no other words and started to cry.

"Oh, Corey. This is so terrible. Are you okay?"

"I'm not hurt, Dad," Corey managed to say. "I guess I'm just in shock. I'm so sorry. I should have watched Casey closer."

"I'm not sure what you mean, Corey. But whatever happened, don't blame yourself. We'll talk about it when we get there. May I please speak with the doctor again?"

"Congressman Sheffield. How can I help you?"

"Just take care of Corey until we arrive. And, please, can you arrange for a local mortuary to prepare Casey? I don't want his Mother to have to see him in the morgue."

"I will do both. We will watch Corey closely. He is in shock, but otherwise physically okay. His friends are in the waiting room. They have insisted on staying with him until you arrive."

"Please thank them for me."

"I certainly will. I know I don't need to remind you that Colorado state law requires that an autopsy be performed for any accidental skiing death. I promise that I will insist on expediency so that Casey's release will not be delayed."

"I would appreciate that very much. Oh, my poor Casey. I just can't believe this has happened," Sheffield exclaimed in tears.

"Again, I am very sorry to have to convey this news to you."

"Thank you, doctor. Now I have the sad task of informing my wife. We'll be there as soon as we can."

A private jet was waiting for the Sheffields at Reagan National Airport. His wife had been heavily sedated and had to be helped onto the plane. Word of the tragic accident had quickly spread throughout the Capitol. Many of his fellow Congressmen, Democrats and Republicans alike, worked rapidly to arrange the Sheffield's journey to Colorado. In Sheffield's time of adversity, congressional partisanship was placed on hold.

As promised, the autopsy was competed well before the Sheffield's arrival. The coroner arranged for a local mortuary to hastily prepare the body for viewing, burial, and transport. The hospital prepared a private suite for the family.

Word that a skiing accident had claimed the life of a son of U.S. Representative Terrell Sheffield quickly reached the Colorado news media. The major wire services and television networks rushed coverage to Vail. Out of respect for the Congressman, and out of courtesy for the bereaved family, the hospital's administration banned cameras from the hospital.

After landing in Denver, the private Bell helicopter of the Colorado Realty Company stood ready to transport the family to Vail. The hospital had arranged for the courtesy shuttle to meet them at the local heliport. Within six hours of the Doctor's call, they were at Corey's side.

Congressman and Mrs. Sheffield spent a half hour in grief-stricken seclusion with Corey learning the details of the skiing accident. Afterwards, they and Corey's friends spent an hour in mournful solitude surrounding Casey's body. After Sheffield had thanked Dr. Richards and the administrator for their courtesies, the group was ushered through the back entrance of the hospital where they received a police escort to the Vail Cascade.

Manager Becker greeted the family with heartfelt sadness and personally guided the family to their room. "We took the liberty of packing the boys luggage. We've had it transferred it to your suite."

"Thank you, Mr. Becker. You are very kind."

"We at the Cascade were deeply saddened to learn of Casey's death. He was such a nice young man."

Out of respect for the family, Corey's friends remained in the lobby. After giving them a half hour alone, Dawn called and asked to speak with Corey.

"Corey, if you feel up to it, we would all like to be with you tonight. We are in the lobby, if you would like to come down."

"Yes, I would. Let me ask my parents."

"Dad," Corey asked, "if you and Mom don't mind, I would like to spend some time with my friends tonight. They are downstairs waiting in the lounge."

"Certainly, son," he replied. "I think that would be a good idea."

"Corey, when you get downstairs, please have Dan call me to make arrangements for his, Ben, and Will's early return home." Terrell Sheffield requested.

"Sure, Dad. I will."

Early the next morning, just as the Sheffield's were finishing their room service breakfast, Dr. Richards phoned. "Representative Sheffield, we have the autopsy results available. May I please come over to your hotel and speak with you about them?"

"Certainly, Dr. Richards," Sheffield responded apprehensively.

They met in the lobby, and Mr. Becker ushered the two men into a private conference room. Richards got straight to the point.

"Congressman Sheffield, I'm afraid that Casey's toxicology screen noted a trace of cocaine. Skiing while under the influence of cocaine could certainly have attributed to his accident."

"That's ridiculous! My sons don't use drugs. There must be an error in your toxicology screening," Sheffield said incredulously.

"We tested both blood, urine, and tissue samples. I'm sorry, but the report is accurate."

"I beg you, until I can talk with Corey and his friends, please don't let this report leak to the news media. After an investigation brings forth the facts, I promise you that I will personally inform the news media myself."

"I will assure you, Congressman, no one except those required will receive the autopsy results. Only the Secretary of State's office, the local authorities, and your insurance company, when you decide to file Casey's death benefit claim, will have any knowledge about the toxicology results. These agencies are bound by strict confidentiality laws not to disclose any information about either a death certificate or autopsy report."

"Thank you, doctor. Until all the facts have been disclosed, I don't want my wife to have to be subjected to hearing my son's reputation slandered in the media."

Sheffield asked Mr. Becker if he could arrange for his administrative staff to contact all the college friends who were skiing with Casey at the time of his accident and ask them to meet with him, Corey, and Chief of Police Lee Gorham, in the conference room at noon.

"I will be glad to do that, Representative Sheffield." Becker replied.

By noon, all of Casey and Corey's friends had gathered for the meeting. As introductions were made, Sarah cried as she hugged Sheffield's neck. "I'm so sorry for you and Mrs. Sheffield. Casey was so very special. During the past two days, Casey and I had become very close. I'll do anything I can to help you."

"Thank you, Sarah, for offering. Chief Gorham would like to tape our conversation today to have an official report of Casey's accident. We would like for each of you to describe the events of yesterday morning and as much about Casey's actions as you can recall. Corey, will you please begin?"

"Well, when we woke up, we were both still very tired. It was hard to get Casey up and ready for the morning's ski trip." He did not volunteer the fact that Sarah and Dawn had stayed the night with them.

Sarah intervened. "As we rode the lift, Casey kept saying how extremely tired he was. He kept hoping that the aspirin he took before we rode to Summit would make him feel better. At the end of our first run, Casey just leaned on his skis, exclaiming that he was totally exhausted. I wasn't sure that he would be able to ski any more that morning."

"That's right," Corey added. "He asked our guide, Justin Hardison if he could talk with him for a moment. They walked away from the group to have their conversation. I suspected that Casey was telling Justin that he didn't feel like skiing any more that morning and was too embarrassed to let the rest of us hear him say it. I just thought that he was begging out of the rest of the morning's runs and wanted Justin to inform the rest of us."

Sarah continued, "After he and Justin finished their conversation, Casey excused himself to go to the restroom. He was gone only a few minutes. When he exited the restroom, he bounded back to our group with renewed energy. He had an amazingly high energy level. All the way back up the lift, he talked incessantly about the beauty of Vail and the mountains, how much fun he was having on vacation, and how he was looking forward to another run down Blue Sky Basin with me."

"That's right," Ben volunteered. "Casey raced us to the ski run and was the first to put on his skis. I couldn't believe the difference in his energy level. It was as if a new Casey had reappeared from the restroom."

"I asked him about his renewed energy," Sarah remarked. "He said that his aspirin must have kicked in. Some powerful aspirin, I remember thinking."

Corey added to Sarah's comments. "On our second run, Casey skied the slopes like an Olympic downhill racer. I have never seen him ski better. It was a thing of beauty to see him take the curves and drops at mid-ridge. He was awesome."

"When we reached the bottom," Sarah continued, "Casey seemed to have run out of gas again. He excused himself again to go to the restroom. When he returned, it seemed as if he had received a transfusion of energy. Casey again talked excitedly as we rode the lift up."

"Back on the slope for the third run, Casey again hollered and shouted excitedly as we traversed the run. About a minute before the accident, he became very quiet. I saw him struggle a bit to keep his balance. He said he was suddenly tired again. He seemed to struggle, as if he couldn't regain his focus."

Sarah began crying uncontrollably. Nevertheless, she continued valiantly. "As we approached mid-ridge, instead of snowplowing to slow his speed, Corey just flew over the precipice and crashed into the aspen. It was the most awful thing to see."

Having been asked to re-experience the traumatic events that lead to Casey's death, Corey and his friends were brought to tears. After learning the tragic details of his son's death, Sheffield, too, sobbed in anguish. Now that he knew how the accident had occurred, the Congressman was faced with the painful chore of informing the group that Casey had probably died because of cocaine use.

It took a few moments for all to regain their composure. The Representative then told the group that Chief Gorham had something to share with them about Casey's accident.

The Chief stated quietly, "I'm sorry to have to tell you this, but Casey's autopsy report determined that he had been under the influence of cocaine at the time of his accident."

"I can't believe it," Corey exclaimed in disbelief. "Chief, Casey had never used any illegal drugs. We often talked about how stupid it was using them. We both knew we would be kicked out of law school if we were ever caught using any illegal substance. I can assure you, Chief, Casey did not have any cocaine in his possession before we went skiing that morning."

"I believe you, Corey." Chief Gorham stated sympathetically. "Now I would like to ask you to try to help us determine where Casey might have gotten the cocaine. I know it won't be easy for you to relive the morning's experience again, but I'm certain it will be helpful if you try to remember any unusual occurrence or situation where Casey might have obtained the drug."

Corey's lip began to quiver as he thought of his brother's tragic accident and what probably had precipitated it. Pausing to regain his composure, Corey continued, "I still can't believe that Casey used cocaine. It is so out of character for him. He would never have used the drug unless it was offered to him and he was enticed to do so."

Sarah added, "I remember Casey had complained of an awful headache and that he was so tired. I agree with Corey. I am certain that he must have been persuaded to try the cocaine to make him feel better. That would certainly explain Casey's sudden burst of energy, his incessant talking, and his hyper-excitement."

Her voice began to tremble, "I wish I had had some idea that Casey had taken cocaine to try to keep up with the rest of us. I would have insisted that both of us sit down until he felt better." Again, she began crying uncontrollably.

"It's not your fault, Sarah," Terrell Sheffield said. "Listening to your impassioned words, I know you would have done that. It's easy to tell you liked Casey very much. I'm so sorry that you and the others have to relive this tragic event in order to help us determine where Casey might have obtained the cocaine."

Corey again stated emphatically, "I know Casey didn't have any cocaine with him before we left that morning. I'm sure he must have gotten it sometime after we started skiing. The only time Casey was separated from the group was when he took Justin aside to talk to him. It seems Justin is the only one who could have given him the cocaine."

"That's right!" echoed several of the others.

Sheffield asked, "Chief Gorham, do you know Justin Hardison?"

Gorham answered, "Yes, I know Justin Hardison well. He's had several run-ins with the law. No steady job. He just does odd jobs around town and contracts his services as a ski guide for Vail Mountain's Back Side slopes. He has been arrested twice for possession of cocaine, but never for distribution. Considering his past, I have little doubt Hardison could be involved. If prompted, I'm certain he would have proposed that Casey try the drug to boost his energy level."

"With his background and this group's description of Casey's energy level and demeanor both before and after he and Hardison talked, I have no doubt Justin persuaded Casey to try cocaine to enhance his energy level," Gorham said. "I am certain we have disclosed Casey's supplier."

"Chief," Mr. Sheffield asked, "do you think you have sufficient evidence to bring him in for questioning?"

"Yes, sir, essentially circumstantial, but more than sufficient. I now have enough evidence to arrest him on suspicion. And that I will do as soon as I leave here. I will assure you, Representative Sheffield, that the District Attorney and I will get the truth out of him. I am confident that Hardison will fail a lie detector test. Don't worry, sir, if he is guilty, we will get him to confess. I promise you. And, when we do get him to confess, I will charge him with second-degree murder."

"Thank you, Chief. It seems my son made a terrible error in judgment that cost him his life. Unfortunately, like so many youth, he was a vulnerable victim of persuasion. Casey obviously used cocaine with the assurance it would give him the temporary energy lift he needed to enable him to keep up with his friends."

"It would certainly seem that way," Gorham stated. "I know that I speak for the citizens of Vail as I extend our heartfelt sorrow to you and your family on this sad occasion."

"Thank you again, Chief. Please let me know the outcome of your interrogation of Hardison."

"I assure you, Congressman, you will be among the first to know."

CHAPTER SEVENTEEN

Unfortunately, the allure of cocaine had left its blight on yet another American family; and this time a quite prominent one. Sheffield received many letters of condolence, including personal notes from the President, the Vice President, and Rick Tolbert. Each letter conveyed a personal message of sorrow for the tragic loss of the Representative's son. Rick Tolbert's letter provided the most personal and introspective revelation into Casey's tragic accident and its purported cause.

Richard A. Tolbert, Director
Border Surveillance and Drug Interdiction Agency
United States Federal Office Building
Washington, D.C.

The Honorable C. Terrell Sheffield
United States House of Representatives
U.S. Capitol
Washington, D.C.

Dear Congressman Sheffield,

With my deepest sympathy, I offer my sincere condolences to you, Mrs. Sheffield, and Corey upon this sad occasion in your life. Casey's tragic death and the circumstances surrounding his accident were as much a shock to me as I'm sure they were to you and your family.

Though I did not know Casey personally, I do know you and the example of high moral standards you exemplify in both your political and personal life. Those demonstrable values assure me that in no way can you or Mrs. Sheffield accept any personal blame for this unfortunate tragedy. There are always those accusers who will attempt to assign blame to every parent whose child's death can be attributed to drug use.

Out of respect for you and your family, I hope they will not. Invariably though, there will be those in the national media and even certain within your Democratic Party who will seek to accuse you of not having taught Casey the proper ethical and moral values that would have persuaded him not to use cocaine.

I sincerely hope that you will pay them no attention. Please believe that those who really know you best, know better. Likewise, ignore any innuendoes or accusations of persons who may try to use the tragic loss of your son for their own political advantage. Such implications would persuade no reasonable person.

I will assure you that my agency will redouble its efforts to keep illegal drugs out of America so that unfortunate and tragic accidents like Casey's can be avoided. Again, to you and your family, I offer my deepest sympathy and sincerest condolence in the loss of your son.

It is my earnest hope that this letter may, in some small way, help to deflect any detractor's condemnation or blame towards you for the circumstances that led to Casey's accident.

If ever I, or the BSDIA, may be of service to you or your family in any way, please do not hesitate to let me know.

Sincerely,

Rick Tolbert
Richard A. Tolbert

Sheffield was heartened that Rick had conveyed to him such an intimate message of sympathy. As he and Tolbert were members of opposing political parties, a short note of condolence would have been more than respectable. Sheffield was touched with Rick Tolbert's message.

Wiser counsel could not have been spoken. Though his political career was not foremost on his mind, Sheffield saved Tolbert's letter as a reference of moral support.

Despite these words of condolence and the support of their closest friends, the Congressman, his wife, and Corey were not coping well with Casey's death. The loss of their son and brother was having a devastating effect on their family.

In the weeks that followed, Congressman Sheffield navigated as best he could through a difficult time both personally and politically. He made every effort to perform his duties as Chairman of the House Appropriations Committee, yet, knowing he was doing an ineffective job, he temporarily turned the duties over to the Vice Chair.

Corey tried vainly to return to law school, but was unable to concentrate on his studies. The death of his twin brother had taken a drastic toll on his mental health. Despondent to the point that it was unsafe for him to stay alone, the Law School Dean recommended to Sheffield that Corey take medical leave for at least the remainder of the semester.

Given assurance that his place in school would be saved until he wished to re-enroll, Corey returned home to spend time with his family. His return was as important to his mental recovery as it was to his mother's.

Mrs. Sheffield, too, was taking Casey's death extremely hard. The fact that her husband had to disclose to the media that Casey's death was attributable to cocaine use practically destroyed both her mental and physical health. Though the media used restraint in reporting the cause of Casey's death, the stigma that would always be associated with the death of her otherwise fine son brought considerable despair to the family.

Under Chief Gorham's and Vail District Attorney Fred Lowery's intensive interrogation, Justin Hardison eventually admitted to supplying Casey with cocaine. Though the evidence was primarily circumstantial, they informed Hardison that he was facing a possible second-degree murder charge. If convicted, the charge carried a maximum 25-year prison sentence with no eligibility for parole.

When Hardison's attorney informed him that Casey was the son of a U.S. Congressman, he knew it would be futile to continue to deny the charges. Justin was advised that the D.A. would be relentless in his pursuit of a guilty plea. His attorney convinced him it would be best to admit his guilt and plea-bargain to a reduced charge of involuntary manslaughter. Hardison agreed. Ultimately, he was sentenced to 12 years in prison; he would be eligible for parole in four years.

Satisfied with Justin Hardison's conviction, Terrell Sheffield expressed his appreciation to Chief Gorham and D.A. Lowery for their efforts to help bring closure to Casey's tragic death. With Justin Hardison's arrest and conviction confirmed, Sheffield was certain that he, his wife, and Corey would begin to regain some normalcy in their lives.

In exchange for a reduced charge, Hardison additionally agreed to divulge the name of his cocaine supplier. Upon this disclosure, Rick Tolbert immediately moved a complement of BSDIA agents into Colorado in an attempt to track the cocaine backwards through the supply pipeline to the source.

Despite an inward urgency to re-involve his choice of running mate in the Democratic Party's race for the presidential and vice presidential nominations, Bixby Lane displayed extreme empathy to Sheffield. He would not push Sheffield to reenter the campaign. His empathy did not go unnoticed by the media. As Bixby Lane and Sheffield embraced after Casey's funeral, he remarked with feigned compassion, "Don't even think about politics now, Terrell. Just take care of yourself and the family and call me when you feel like sitting down to discuss your future in my campaign."

"Will do. Thanks, Bixby, for your patience and understanding." Terrell answered with some reserve. Sheffield searched Lane's expression carefully for any hint that Casey's death and its association with cocaine use might have lost him an opportunity to continue as Lane's proposed vice presidential ticket mate.

Seeing none, he relaxed considerably and added, "I hope to call you soon."

"Fine, take as long as you need."

The press was quick to report Lane's extreme display of compassion and empathy for his friend and probable running mate.

Network correspondent Stephanie Neyland reported, "Despite the urgency to involve his proposed vice presidential running mate in his ongoing bid for the White House, an intense A. Bixby Lane showed that he truly is a kind and compassionate individual. Even in the midst of waging a hard fought Democratic campaign for his Party's nomination, Congressman Lane willingly put his campaign on hold until his strongest political ally and friend could overcome his personal grief."

Neyland continued her supposedly unbiased news reporting. "This heartwarming expression of compassion demonstrates the strong resolve and leadership qualities of Bixby Lane, qualities necessary to get him elected to the highest office in the land."

Oh, how the media loved A. Bixby Lane.

Despite Lanes' declared support of his purported running mate, the incidence of cocaine use that led to Casey's death was embarrassing to many influential Democratic Party supporters. Those prominent party leaders encouraged Lane to reconsider Terrell Sheffield as his running mate. They preferred that Lane choose another Democrat with a less inauspicious family character blemish.

"How can you keep Sheffield and promote family moral values as the Democrat's premise to discourage drug use and abuse? Wouldn't allowing him to continue as your proposed ticket mate be the antithesis of this premise?"

Exactly the juxtaposition Rick Tolbert had predicted. However unfortunate the death of Sheffield's son and the stigma that certain Democrats perceived would follow C. Terrell as a result, Lane did not want to consider another running mate.

"Don't you realize that Sheffield will garner an appreciable number of sympathy votes because of his son's death and the tragic way in which it happened? Besides," said Lane, ever the consummate strategist, "perhaps we can turn his personal tragedy into a positive campaign statement."

"After all, are not Republicans touting their drug interdiction efforts as having a profound effect on America's street level of illegal drugs? It obviously wasn't very effective in Colorado, was it?"

Even at the expense of Terrell Sheffield's misfortune and pain, Lane had no reservation about using the tragedy to his political advantage. In doing so, he would try to find some way to blame Walters, Douglas, and the entire Republican Party for Casey's temptation with cocaine.

Tolbert knew that as the BSDIA's surveillance net was tightened around the U.S. borders, the initial interdictions of cocaine, marijuana, and heroin shipments had greatly reduced street levels of the drugs. Despite his agency's best efforts, Tolbert also knew it was unrealistic for anyone to think that the BSDIA could remove all illegal drugs from the streets of America.

Yet, the Democrats and national media liberals would no doubt exploit Casey Sheffield's death as a failure of the BSDIA to protect America against illegal drug smuggling. Because of Charles Douglas' administrative oversight of the BSDIA, these pundits would accuse the Vice President and particularly the Walters' administration of failing to live up to their campaign promise to essentially rid America's streets of cocaine and other illegal drugs.

Tolbert was resolved not to let Bixby Lane denigrate either the President or the Vice President. These men had trusted him with the responsibility of reducing cross-border drug smuggling into the U.S. This was the foundation of the Republican's campaign against illegal drugs and the primary project of the President's administration. "If any blame was assigned because of a partial failure to do so, it would be he who would accept it, not the President or Vice President," Tolbert asserted. He was resolute in his efforts to uncover the cocaine trail that lead to Casey Sheffield's tragic death.

BSDIA agents worked relentlessly to identify the distributors along the pipeline. They initiated their quest by executing intense raids on the street vendors in Vail. In less than three weeks, their investigation had advanced through the mid-level Colorado distributors and moved westward to the regional lieutenant's headquarters in California.

Under the threat of a possible charge of accessory to murder, each cocaine distributor from the street seller in Vail back through the pipeline to the Los Angeles kingpin was identified and arrested.

Even when faced with a long-term prison sentence, Chei Tsai Phat, Clark's west coast distribution lieutenant, refused to disclose any details of how he received the cocaine from his supply source. He had not forgotten Clark's promise to punish anyone who did so. Phat was offered a reduced sentence if he could provide any information that would lead to the arrest and conviction of his supplier.

"I swear I do not know his name," Chei Tsai exclaimed truthfully. Under the personal and inexorable interrogation of Rick Tolbert, Phat could only claim that, "I know him only as 'The Commander'. All his voice communications are scrambled and disguised. You know, like a robot voice. I couldn't identify him if my life depended upon it."

Phat surmised it would not in his best interest to disclose the one fact that would aid the BSDIA in their efforts to identify the cocaine source.

"Come on, Chei Tsai, make it easier on yourself. You're facing 25 to 30 with no chance of parole if you don't talk. Tell us what you know," Tolbert prompted in an attempt to draw additional information out of Phat.

Chei Tsai agonized on whether to tell Tolbert that the Commander's cocaine was always delivered in Ryder trucks. This one tip would probably be beneficial to Tolbert, but it would also seal his fate while in prison. Phat remembered that the Commander's promise: "Not even prison walls would provide a safe haven from his retribution should anyone ever snitch on his distribution network."

Chei Tsai agonized on whether to turn state's evidence and reduce his prison sentence or to just keep quite and ensure his existence. Phat decided that a few extra years in prison would be far better than having to constantly fear someone walking up to him somewhere within the prison walls and shoving a shiv into his back.

"That's all I know," he replied to a relentless Tolbert. "I can't tell you anything else." He lied, desperately wanting to tell everything he knew. Still, the threat of death from one of the Commander's enforcers was sufficient to silence him.

Tolbert knew Chei Tsai had additional information he could divulge; he also knew he was afraid to do so. Tolbert had uncovered a major distribution network operating throughout America. With the arrest of Phat and his distributors, Tolbert had been successful in cutting off one of the network's main distribution tentacles. He was determined to uncover the remaining.

With these arrests, Rick Tolbert and the BSDIA had put a serious dent into Wayne Clark's west coast distribution network. Tolbert quickly flew back to Washington to meet with the President and Vice President and report the full details of this latest arrest event.

President Walters informed the networks that he would address the nation that evening at 7:00 PM. He intended to discuss the discovery and arrest of a large west coast cocaine supply and distribution network and speak to America's youth. He wanted to discourage them from that first temptation to try cocaine and other illegal street drugs. He had received Terrell Sheffield's permission to use Casey's death as a tragic example of what could result with even the first use of an illegal mind-altering drug.

The President requested that all department and agency heads, their assistant directors, and the Joint Chiefs join him for this important announcement. As a CIA Deputy Director, Wayne Peyton Clark was expected to attend.

"Good evening my fellow Americans," Walters began. "I would like to share with you publicly tonight, information that I shared privately with the Honorable Terrell Sheffield this afternoon. Because of the tragic death of Representative Sheffield's son, Casey, the Border Surveillance and

Drug Interdiction Agency began an intensive investigation into identifying cocaine supply sources within Colorado."

"I am pleased to inform you that the BSDIA's persistent investigation and interrogation has uncovered a significant cocaine distribution network operating out of Los Angeles, California. Likewise, I am happy to report that the west coast drug kingpin, Chei Tsai Phat, and his drug distributors have all been arrested, and his entire cocaine distribution network has been dismantled. Director Tolbert reports that the BSDIA is employing every method possible to reveal their supply source."

Hearing this, Clark took a sharp intake of breath. The color drained from his face. Quickly calming himself, he rose in applause with the other attendees. As they sat down, Clark glanced around to determine if his exclamation of surprise had attracted attention. Thankful that his outburst and ashen appearance had gone unnoticed, he sat motionless in silent disbelief. All but he were exuberant with the President's announcement.

Not until this moment when the President disclosed to the nation that the BSDIA had been successful in the discovery of his west coast network, did Clark know that one-forth of his distribution pipeline had been dismantled.

At this particular moment in time, Wayne Clark could picture his smuggling and distribution empire crumbling even as the President spoke. Beginning tomorrow, it would not be business as usual for the Belizean Cartel. Clark knew the distribution operation must undergo significant changes or risk further discovery. He would call Juan Carlos and Thomas immediately after the President's address to propose changes.

It was the first Tuesday in February, less than three weeks since Casey's funeral. The previous day, President Walters had invited Terrell Sheffield to the White House for a private meeting. It was Terrell's first private audience with the President. He had felt anxious when a White House messenger delivered the invitation, hand-written by the President.

The next morning, Edward Walters greeted Terrell Sheffield warmly as if they were long-lost friends. Having seated himself on one of the plush armchairs that served as a less formal seating area in the Oval Office, Walters invited Sheffield to sit beside him. He could tell that the Representative was somewhat apprehensive in being there.

Intending that this meeting not have a presidential atmosphere, Walters chose not to sit at his desk. This would be an informal conversation, far removed from the regality of most meetings held in the Oval Office.

Walters began the conversation by again offering his condolences on the tragic loss of Sheffield's son. "I would like to tell you again, Terrell, how saddened Claire and I were to hear of Casey's tragic accident. I cannot begin to understand the anguish that you, Mrs. Sheffield, and Corey must be going through. I do hope that in some small way that what I have to share with you today will help to heal some of your pain."

An otherwise slightly surprised Sheffield responded, "Thank you for your concern Mr. President. It has been very difficult on all of us, especially considering the circumstances that led to Casey's accident."

"I'm certain that it has been difficult, Terrell, and more so under those circumstances. When you addressed the press to report that cocaine was a contributing factor to Casey's accident, my heart went out to you. Claire and I sensed that you were feeling a considerable amount of discomfort in having to report Casey's cocaine use, especially since your fellow Democrats are proposing, that in any young person's drug related death, seemingly little or no system of family moral values exists."

"Yes, sir. It was, and is especially difficult given my place as the leading Democratic Vice Presidential candidate. My wife and I are being unfairly accused of not having properly taught our boys the perils of illegal drug use. Essentially, such accusers have asserted to the American public that my family has little or no morals, ethical values, or personal character."

"I thought you might say that," Walters remarked. "Charles Douglas and I discussed your situation at some length and thought this issue might be causing you a considerable amount of mental anguish," Walters said sympathetically. That's one reason I asked you here today, Terrell."

"Tonight," the President continued, "I will deliver an address to the nation to discuss a major drug bust whose investigation was initiated because of Casey's tragedy. I would like to have your permission to use Casey's accident as an example to the youth of America why it is dangerous to become involved with illegal drugs."

"Likewise, I would like you to know that I will stress that a lack of family moral values had nothing to do with the accident. I will propose that Casey's accident was attributable only to personal choice, and not to any breakdown in your character, ethics, or principles."

"Thank you, sir, for saying that. You have my permission to use Casey's accident as an example to America's youth of how even a first drug use can lead to tragedy, and I appreciate your disassociation of Casey's death with a breakdown in my family's personal moral values and character."

"You're welcome, Terrell. That, I am glad to do. Its pronouncement is no less that what you and your family deserve. Additionally, Terrell, before I address and inform the nation, I wanted to tell you personally that the primary distributors of the cocaine that lead to Casey's death have been identified and arrested."

A misty eyed Terrell Sheffield declared appreciably, "Thank you, Mr. President for your efforts to bring these suppliers to swift justice."

In support of the President's proposal, Sheffield encouraged the President to use Casey's accident as an incentive for America's youth to make the personal choice not to use drugs. Sheffield remembered Rick Tolbert's comments that certain of the media and his own party might try to use the tragedy as a political ploy. He knew that by allowing the President to allude to the accident, disassociate the tragedy from any breakdown in the Sheffield's family values system, and encourage the youth of America not to make the same mistake, he was taking the politics out of the tragedy.

Walter's address to the nation did just that.

After the President's address, Terrell Sheffield was convinced that this sad chapter in his family's life was closed. Should anyone ever revisit the incident in hopes of gaining a political advantage, he knew they would be perceived as callous and insensitive. No political gain would be realized by anyone who tried to exploit Casey's accident.

After the President's address, all of America now knew that Casey's death was due to his personal choice to use cocaine. Since the President had professed that he considered Sheffield to be a man of integrity and moral principles, Lane and the Democrats could no longer propose that a lack of morals and family values were the basic contributing factors in every drug related death.

Casey's death had essentially negated the validity of the Democratic Party's answer to resolving America's drug problems. The Republican's premise that stopping illegal drugs at America's borders while encouraging the youth of America to make the personal choice not to use them, had now been demonstrated as one of the best answers to America's drug problems.

A. Bixby was now caught in a dilemma. If he did not formerly announce Sheffield as his running mate, he would most assuredly be perceived as callous and insensitive to Sheffield's personal family tragedy - a tragedy over which Sheffield had no control.

Additionally, after the President's message affirmed that a lack of family values, ethics, and morality had nothing to do with Casey's unfortunate and tragic death, if Lane did choose to announce Sheffield as his running mate, their campaign would be unable to advocate that raising the standards of family values was the sole answer to America's drug problems. Lane's thoughts of making this a campaign issue were essentially thwarted with Walters' address.

The President had closed any consideration Lane had to profit politically from Casey's death when he appended Casey's tragedy to a matter of personal choice, and absolved the incident as an issue relative to values, ethics, and morality.

Lane's strategists complained, "Walters' address has completely taken away any incentive we might have had to denounce the Republican's efforts to reduce illegal drugs in America. How could Sheffield have been so insensitive to the Democratic Party's illegal drug focus than to permit the President to do that? Didn't he understand what a political benefit this could have been to the Democratic campaign?"

"Apparently not," Lane surmised, "but nonetheless our campaign must rev into high gear. Super Tuesday is almost upon us."

With the realization that his integrity had been restored, Sheffield called Lane to announce that he was ready to rejoin the campaign.

"Excellent." Lane commented without reservation. "Welcome back! Would you be able to join us at 10:00 o'clock tomorrow morning at DNC headquarters?"

"Certainly, Bixby."

"Good," Lane stated. "We're in the midst of Super Tuesday strategy. We need you back, Terrell."

"I'll be there. I'm anxious to resume campaigning."

When Lane announced to his strategists that Sheffield would rejoin the campaign, several in the Democratic National Committee voiced apprehension for his return.

"I think Sheffield has lost his appeal," grumbled one Party strategist.

"So do I," seconded another. "Tragic as was his son's death, I feel that aligning yourself with a running mate whose family history is tainted with cocaine use runs a big risk of turning voters off."

Lane disagreed. Despite their best efforts to persuade him to reconsider Sheffield as his running mate, Lane replied, "After careful consideration of the President's address and of the issues surrounding the death of Terrell's son, I think it would be unwise to consider another running mate. To do so might be perceived as cold-hearted and insensitive to Sheffield's family tragedy."

"Besides," he reflected, "maybe Terrell will bring in a considerable number of sympathy votes. I'll welcome any vote I can get!"

Immediately following the President's address, Wayne Clark returned to his home office where he conferenced a call to the Diego's and to Miguel Thomas. Long into the night, the Onyxitron was kept busy encrypting their conversation. Clark was certain that their distribution pipeline was on the verge of exposure if they did not change their method of distribution.

"Thomas," Clark began, "I'm afraid that it has become too risky to continue to use Ryder trucks to deliver our cocaine. For all we know, Chei Tsai Phat might already have divulged our method of delivery. If he has, the BSDIA will be sure to stop all Ryder trucks and perform a systematic cocaine search. Despite our best efforts to disguise our delivery method, I fear it is too risky to continue business as usual."

"I agree," Thomas replied resolutely. "We have been lucky thus far not to have had a delivery interdicted. We definitely assume too much risk in continuing to use Ryder trucks as our primary means of distribution."

Juan Carlos interrupted, "Do either of you have another recommendation?"

Thomas remarked, "Perhaps I do. We could purchase our own fleet of commercial tractor-trailers and use them to distribute both our refined sugar and our cocaine. To disguise our drug shipment, we could begin to package the coke in the refinery's sugar bags. Packing the bags in boxes we could pallet the boxes just as we do the legitimate sugar products."

"In preparation for delivery, we would load the cocaine shipment in the front quarter section of a cargo container," he said, "then fill the back three quarters of the trailer with the legitimate refined sugar. Using our present transport teams and hiring others, the drivers would make a regular scheduled wholesale sugar delivery, then offload the cocaine at one of our four distribution points."

"Seems like a reasonable plan," Clark said. "Purchasing a fleet of 18-wheelers would be a small price to pay to safeguard our cocaine deliveries."

"I agree," said Juan Carlos.

"How many semis would we need to purchase?" asked Clark.

"The refinery is packaging around 74,000 pounds of sugar a day," Thomas replied, "That's 185,000 tons each week. I believe most big rigs can haul a maximum 40,000-pound load. To transport our weekly sugar production would require that we purchase 10 rigs."

"Since we still have two months remaining before the spring crop of coca leaf is ready for processing, we have plenty of time to purchase a fleet of trucks and get the drivers familiar with our routine refinery delivery sites," Thomas added.

"Seems you've done your homework, Miguel," Clark remarked.

"Well, I have given our distribution system some thought since the President's address. For some time, I have considered recommending this new delivery method of transportation to you. I cannot imagine a more appropriate time now to consider purchasing own fleet of tractor trailers."

"I agree," Clark replied. "Now where do we go from here? And how much do you know about the long-haul trucking industry?"

"I know very little, but two cousins, Cletus and Dewey Tanner, who work at the loading dock and assist Ralph Fiacincio in scheduling and supervising our cross-country sugar deliveries, know the industry well. They are CDL drivers with an acute knowledge of the trucking industry. I will ask their advice on the best vehicles to buy and the best place to buy them."

"I believe a full rig costs around a hundred thousand," Juan Carlos advised, "I'll request that Vicente wire $1.2 million into the mill's account at Apalachee Coastal. That should be sufficient for their purchase without risk of diluting our working capital, don't you think?"

"I would certainly think so," Thomas replied. "That should be more than adequate to make the fleet purchase and to install a diesel fuel depot on the refinery grounds to fuel the outbound trucks."

"Good idea," Clark added. "Let us know if you need any help in setting up the trucking business."

"I will."

"How are the crack sales going, Thomas?" Juan Carlos asked.

"Far greater than our expectations. It seems that American's have a tremendous craving for our crack cocaine," Thomas quipped, laughingly.

"Or had, that is. There was a considerable market for our crack. Almost every ounce has been sold. Next week I will send the couriers out to return the money that has been collected from street sales. I am expecting over $160 million. That's 10 times the dollar amount of what the approximate same gram weight of cocaine would sell for."

"It seems that American's certainly do have a healthy appetite for our cocaine products," Clark said gleefully. "From next year's crop, perhaps we should consider converting a greater quantity of our powdered cocaine into crack."

Cletus and Dewey Tanner were pleased when their boss asked them for their opinion on purchasing a fleet of tractor-trailer rigs for the St. Marks Refinery.

"Best place to go is Atlanta," Cletus offered.

"Right," confirmed Dewey. "There are several company sales lots just a few miles south of downtown Atlanta on I-75. Every time Cletus and I go to Atlanta, we always stop and wander around the lots lookin' at the big rigs. If you're wantin' long lasting quality, you need only go to the Kenworth sales lot."

"Dewey's right, boss. I wouldn't buy nothin' but a KW," Cletus added.

"Okay," Thomas said agreeably. "If you boys aren't doing anything special this weekend, I'll fly us up to Atlanta to shop around."

"Heck, boss. Save yore money. It's only 'bout a six-hour drive. Cletus and I'll drive ya up."

"That's okay, fellows. It'll save us a considerable amount of time to fly. I'll book our flight reservations to leave early Friday morning, if that's okay with you. All expenses are on me."

"Well, heck yeah. That's okay with us. We warn't doing nothing special this weekend no way," Dewey said excitedly. "We'll be ready to go whenever you want."

"I'll let you know as soon as I make the reservations," Thomas concluded.

Thomas purchased three first class tickets on Delta's 10:15 AM flight 206 from Tallahassee to Atlanta. The one hour and three minute flight was anything but routine for the Tanner brothers. This was only their second flight, the first having been to Brazil earlier in the summer. They quickly learned that flying first class meant the offer of as much free alcohol as they could drink before takeoff and during the flight.

The first class stewardess looked on in contempt as the brothers ordered a second double Bloody Mary before their pushback from the gate. After takeoff, even before they had crossed the Florida-Georgia State line, the two were asleep.

Thomas apprised the stewardess, "Be thankful they're asleep. They would just keep you running senseless for drinks and snacks if they were awake."

The brothers were still groggy as they deplaned at Delta's Gate 23 in terminal B at Atlanta's Hartsfield International Airport. Thomas led the pair onto the underground concourse tram and on to the Avis counter in the main terminal building. "Guess you'd better drive, boss," Dewey said. It was more a request than a statement. Thomas signed for a rental car and drove the brothers to check in at the Marriott Courtyard at the South Lake Mall.

After unloading their luggage in their rooms, Thomas suggested they eat a late lunch. "You'll feel better after you've had a good meal," he said to the brothers. "And no more alcohol until dinner tonight!"

"Yes, boss," they agreed.

The men ate a hearty lunch at the Outback Steakhouse, and then headed north on Interstate 75 towards the commercial trucking sales lots. In less than five minutes, they arrived at 'big rig alley' as the Tanners had called it. Dewey and Cletus were now wide-awake as they entered the Kenworth sales center.

"Man, just lookin' at all these rigs is excitin'! " Dewey exclaimed.

"Shore is,' Cletus agreed. "Just bein' here is fun. But actually comin' here to buy a whole fleet of rigs is more excitin' than Christmas!'"

"Okay, guys." Thomas warned. "I know you're excited, but don't appear too eager or the salesman might not offer us a good price."

"Don't worry, boss," Dewey said. "Business is always kinda slow in the wintertime. You don't have to worry about getting the best price. They'll be eager to sell you one rig, much less ten!"

"Just act like you're comparison shoppin'. You'll see," Cletus added.

"Afternoon, gen'lmen," a salesman wearing a Kenworth corduroy shirt identifying him as 'Danny' said. He welcomed the trio into the showroom.

Thomas and the Tanners introduced themselves to the salesman.

"Nice to meet you. Now what can I do for you?" he asked.

"We're just lookin' around," Dewey responded.

"Oh? Exactly what are you looking for?"

"I'd say your 2002 W900L Kenworth will do for starters," Cletus remarked with an air of importance.

"Starting right at the top, huh?"

"Only the best for the boss!" Dewey remarked.

"You must be 'the boss,'" Danny surmised as he shook hands again with Thomas. The Tanner cousins were dressed in their newest pair of Levi's and plaid wool shirts, while Miguel wore a starched blue button-up cotton shirt, khaki pants, and blue windbreaker.

"That's what they call me," Thomas replied.

"Tell me exactly what you need and I'll show you what we have in stock," Danny said.

"We're comparing all makes and models of semis," Cletus answered quickly. We've narrowed our choices down to the KW's and the Peterbilts."

"I see. You're certainly going first class, aren't you?" Danny remarked.

"Like we said, only the best," Dewey again replied proudly.

"Okay then, let's see if I can persuade you to go with Kenworth," the salesman replied.

"How much tonnage are you considering hauling?" Danny asked.

"'Bout 20 a load," Thomas replied.

"Well, the W900L would certainly serve you well. Let's go out to the sales lot and I'll show you our inventory. We have several different colors and equipment packages to choose from. Do you know what specifications you will need?" Danny asked invitingly.

"Shore do," Dewey quickly advised. "We're looking for a 72-inch Aero cab sleeper with a CAT C-15 500 horse diesel. It's gotta have a 12,000-pound front and 40,000-pound rear axle with a 3.55 rear end ratio."

"And a 260-wheel base and an RTLLO18913A tranny," Cletus added. "We want the Airglide 200 suspension and Aluminum front and rear wheels. Also, gotta have a 240 gallon fuel tank for the long hauls."

"Anything else?" the salesman replied. He did not try to hide his amazement that one so poorly dressed would know so much about the trucking business.

Cletus responded quickly. "Yeah, a set-back front axel and 59 inch taperleaf springs. And don't forget the Daylite doors and large front windshield."

"Well, you boys certainly do know the tractor-trailer business!" Danny replied admirably.

"That's why I brought them with me," Thomas responded. "Now let's see if you can fill their orders."

"Right this way, then. You've selected every option but the color."

"The boss gets to do that," Cletus said cheerfully.

Thomas climbed up into a rig that met their specifications and marveled at its roominess. "This really is spacious," he exclaimed. "And complete with a six-foot sleeper."

"That's why you crew with two drivers," Dewey remarked.

"One can sleep whild'st the other'n drives. It'll git you where you're goin' twice as fast."

The salesman could see that the boss liked what he saw. "If there's nothing else I can show you, let's go inside and we'll see if we can make you happy with a good price."

As soon as they were seated, Thomas asked, "Can you color coordinate a trailer to the tractor, say a red cab and red and black trimmed trailer?"

"Of course. What make of trailer would you prefer?"

"Trailmobile," Dewey and Cletus replied in unison.

"Okay, now let's see if I can get my boss to sharpen his pencil and give you a good deal."

"It had better be real sharp," Thomas remarked, "or we may just have to go over to the Peterbilt lot."

"I'm sure you'll find our prices competitive," the salesman said. "I'll get the owner and be right back."

"Hi! Fellows, I'm Marshall Covington. Danny says you're looking to buy a 900L?"

"That's right," Cletus answered.

"And the price had better be right!" Dewey remarked.

"I understand you fellows know the long-haul business. I don't guess there's any use haggering with you then," Marshall said.

"Not if you want to make a sale," Thomas remarked pleasantly.

"Well, a W900L with the specifications you requested retails for $95,450. Add $20,000 for a Trailmobile trailer and, let's see, that's $115,450 plus $9,236 tax. Tell you what, though, I'll make it $99,999 drive off. How does that sound?"

"What price would you make it for if I bought 10 of your rigs today?" Thomas asked.

Covington looked at Thomas quizzically and replied, "You mean 10 complete rigs?"

"Yes, that's right. If you would care to sharpen your pencil a little more." Thomas smiled, enjoying the manager's attempt to disguise his delight at such news.

"Well certainly. Now, let's see. 10 at $99,999.00, that's $999,990. With a 5 % fleet discount, that's $49,999 off. That gets the price down to exactly $949,990.00. Drive off. How does that sound?"

Thomas countered, "How does $925,000 delivered, the first year's tune ups with no labor charge and painted logo's on the tractors and trailers thrown in sound?"

"Sounds like you just bought yourself a fleet of KW's!" Covington remarked excitedly. "Now how will you want to finance this?"

"No financing," Thomas replied. "I'll just write you a check."

"For the whole amount? Today?"

"If that's alright."

"Certainly. I'll just have to call you bank for approval. Just routine, you understand."

"I understand. Here's the phone number. Ask for David Langley."

"Please excuse me while I make the call."

"Hello, long distance for Mr. David Langley, please."

"Certainly, just a moment, please."

"This is David Langley, how may I help you?"

"Hi, Mr. Langley, this is Marshall Covington, with Kenworth Carriers in Atlanta. A Mr. Michael Thomas has purchased a fleet of tractor-trailer rigs from us and would like to write a check for the total amount. I'm just calling to verify that he has sufficient funds to cover the amount of purchase."

"He does," answered Langley resolutely.

"But I haven't even told you the amount yet!" Covington exclaimed.

"I'll assure you, his check is good. Unless it's over 40 million dollars, it doesn't matter what the amount is. I'm telling you that he has sufficient funds to cover it. Mr. Thomas is the owner of the St. Marks Sugar Refinery. He has tens of millions of dollars in our Savings and Loan Company."

Covington replied, "Then I guess a check for $925,000 won't be a problem?"

"Certainly not. Give Mr. Thomas my regards, will you please?"

"I most certainly will," he replied.

"Dog gone!" Covington thought as he walked back to the sales office. "I shouldn't have been so quick to take off an extra 5 %," he muttered to himself. "All said though, $100,000 is not a bad day's profit!"

Covington walked back to office all smiles.

"Everything's all set. I'll order your rigs and have them delivered to...St. Marks, Florida, I believe?"

"That's right," Thomas said as he wrote out the check. I'll send you a camera-ready copy of our company logo to have painted on the rigs. How long before we can expect shipment?"

"Ordering direct from KW and Trailmobile, I'd say two weeks, three weeks tops."

"That's fine. Call me as soon as they are to be delivered."

"Will do. And we do appreciate your business!"

"I had rather thought you might," smiled Thomas.

To celebrate their achievement in the purchase of a fleet of tractor-trailers for the refinery, Thomas and the Tanner cousins enjoyed a seafood dinner complete with Maine lobsters and champagne. As usual, Cletus and Dewey were drunk long before the meal was finished.

CHAPTER EIGHTEEN

I t was Thursday, February 28th. Only five days remained until March's Super Tuesday. The Democratic National Headquarters was a buzz of chaotic activity. It was almost time for "The Big Show" as Lane liked to call it. With a win in the Super Tuesday primaries, Lane felt he could recapture the lead in the presidential race.

During the month of February, nine states and three U.S. territories held either their caucus or primary election. A. Bixby had garnered a majority of Democratic votes but trailed far behind Douglas in the popular vote.

Lane had won the majority of votes only in Iowa, Michigan, and New Hampshire; while Douglas held the majority vote count in Delaware, South Carolina, Arizona, North Dakota, Virginia, and Washington, and in the territories of Guam, Puerto Rico, and the U.S. Virgin Islands. Despite a popular vote majority loss, A. Bixby was virtually assured of winning his party's nomination.

This year's election was unusual. The presidential race was already just a two-man show. The opposing two Republican, three Democratic, and two Independent Party candidates would soon bow out of the race. Their financial backing was menial, and they seemed to be in the race only for a free cross-country meal ticket and for the opportunity to bolster an inflamed ego.

Rather than serve as an election to identify the Republican and Democratic frontrunners, Super Tuesday, for the first time in recent history, was predicted by the media to be a clear indicator of who would win the November election. Lane was unconcerned about the three Democratic soon-to-be also-rans. His campaign was focused principally on defeating Charles Douglas and showing well in all of the caucuses and primaries to be held on Super Tuesday.

Super Tuesday would bring voters in California, Connecticut, Georgia, Hawaii, Idaho, Maine, Maryland, Massachusetts, Minnesota, Missouri, New York, North Dakota, Ohio, Rhode Island, Vermont, Washington, and American Samoa to the polls.

"Win big on Super Tuesday," Lane said, "and we carry a considerable amount of momentum into the state primary elections to follow."

Now, A. Bixby was after those undecided voters in the remaining 41 States whose primary was yet to come. He knew these undecided voters tended to vote for the party candidate who realized the most votes on Super Tuesday. "Everybody wants to feel they voted for the winner. Nobody likes to see his or her vote wasted on a loosing candidate," Lane surmised.

The walls of the DNC conference room were papered with huge state maps. Each county was color colored with either a projected red or blue win. Virtually assured of winning the Democratic Party's nomination, A. Bixby and his strategists had wisely spent over $20 million of their hard money campaign funds on winning the popular vote of each state's largest urban areas. Projecting he would win big in the more heavily populated counties, a large majority of each state map was colored Democratic blue.

The strategists projected Lane as winner in the Northeast. In Connecticut, Massachusetts, Rhode Island, and Vermont, he was favored with 84 to 12 percent of all registered Democrats likely to vote in the primaries.

They also predicted that registered Republican voters in California, Georgia, Maine, Maryland, Missouri, New York, and Ohio favored Charles Douglas by a favor ability percentage of 94 to 6 of all registered Republicans likely to vote.

"To our advantage, these states have a large Democratic voter registration whose registrants tend to cast their vote independent of their party affiliation," Lane stated, "I predict we will have a huge win in each of these states except California. What do you think, Percy?" Lane asked Percy Ableman, his campaign chairman.

"That's exactly what I predict, too," Ableman stated agreeably.

"How do you see the California race shaping up?" Lane asked Terrell Sheffield.

"I believe that California certainly is the hot spot for Super Tuesday's primary election. The energy crisis has voters stirred up as never before, don't you think?"

"Exactly as I see it," Lane agreed.

"We know California's 54 delegate count is greater than any other single state," Sheffield continued. "California voters have a huge influence on the two national party conventions and on the November election itself."

"True," Percy remarked. "Because of Douglas' previously perceived and strongly favored resolution of the energy crisis," Ableman accurately noted, "the Zogby, MSNBC, and Reuters polls have all projected him the winner. They project Douglas will get 32 to 39 percent of votes among all registered voters likely to vote in California. To come out ahead, we must reverse those percentages by next Tuesday!"

"What do you think would be our best strategy to accomplish this, Percy?" Lane asked..

"Because of the three hour time difference between the east and west coasts, the national news media usually projects a winner in the East Coast primaries long before the polls close on the West Coast," Ableman noted. "And that early projection often has a significant impact on late voting West Coast voters." Ableman then invited comment from the others.

"I agree, and would suggest then, Bixby," Sheffield offered, "that we concentrate the last two days before Super Tuesday stumping the principle states of Connecticut, Georgia, Maine, Maryland, Massachusetts, New York, Rhode Island, and Vermont in an effort to be named the projected east coast winner."

At this point, Ableman interjected, "If the media projects you as the predominant East Coast winner, I'm certain that will persuade many of California's undecided to vote for you, Bixby."

Lane remarked, "I agree. Assuredly, then, we must attempt to make the East Coast exit polls project us the winner. Winning there will be the focus of our remaining campaign hours. I say it's now time to start the mud slinging."

A. Bixby initiated a well-planned negative campaign ad strategy. For $4.75 million, his campaign purchased 30-second spots on television stations throughout the eastern United States. The ads were designed to saturate prime time telecasts with negative images of Douglas and the Republicans.

Each half-hour from 6:00 AM to midnight for two days, the ads touched on three sensitive themes predicted to appeal to the moderate and undecided voters. Lane gambled that his ads would entice those voters to vote Democratic on Super Tuesday.

The first ad depicted the Vice President as being soft on crime. The voiceover said,

> Are you tired of hearing that America's felons are being released from prison long before their sentence has been served, then later learn that they have committed yet another rape, robbery or murder? Well, so is A. Bixby Lane. This practice of early release is a Republican indignity, a scourge on America. Vote Democratic. Let Bixby Lane build the prisons needed to hold these criminals for the length of their prison sentence. Vote Republican, and you and your family will remain unsafe on the streets of America.

The second ad depicted the Republicans as failing to achieve their campaign promise to reduce drugs and crime on America's streets.

> How often do you see on the six o'clock news that some thug has robbed a convenience store and murdered the salesclerk for a few dollars to buy drugs? Well, A. Bixby Lane has seen it far too often, and makes more than idle promises to get illegal drugs off America's streets and stop these atrocities. In the last election, Republicans promised they would significantly reduce America's supply of street drugs. Do you think they've succeeded? Bixby Lane doesn't! Vote Democratic. Lane promises to rid your streets and neighborhoods of illegal drugs and make it safe again for all Americans to live without fear of rape, robbery, and murder.

The third ad promoted a fixation that the Republicans were solely responsible for high prices at the gas pump and for the winter's high price of home heating oil.

> Are you tired of emptying your wallet every time you stop to fill up your gas tank? Is it getting harder to pay your home heating bill? Bixby Lane is in touch with the concerns of ordinary Americans. And he has the only realistic plan to solve America's energy crisis. The Republicans have had over two years to fix our energy problems. During their term, the problem has only gotten worse. Bixby Lane has the only plan to reduce high gasoline prices and stop these escalating energy costs. Cast your vote for Lane and keep more of your hard earned money. Vote Democratic.

The ads hit hard in states projected to strongly support Charles Douglas. Released just 41 hours before the Super Tuesday polls opened, the

Republicans had little time to address, much less counter, the false statements proposed by the Democrats.

Usually turned off by negative campaign ads, voters tolerated Lane's tactics because he did not saturate the airways for a prolonged period of time. His negativity had quite the opposite effect. A projected 58% of undecided voters and 42% of moderate Republicans who voted, particularly those in Maryland, Massachusetts, New York, and Vermont, states hit hard by the past winter's high home heating costs, switched their allegiance and voted for Lane in a straight ballot Democratic Party vote.

Edward Walters and Charles Douglas were stunned.

"How could these people have believed any of what Lane's negative ads pronounced? How easily the American electorate forgets the truth," Walters exclaimed.

"How right you are!" agreed the Vice President. "I'm afraid we are in for a long, nasty, hard fought battle this summer and fall."

This observation was no epiphany.

Ralph Fiacincio had been summoned to Miguel Thomas' office.

"Ralph, I have finally received the long awaited call from Marshall Covington. Our tractor-trailers will be delivered tomorrow."

"That certainly is good new, Michael." Fiacincio replied.

"Has our sugar transport carrier been notified that we will no longer need their services after this month?" Thomas asked.

"Yes, they have. With the expectation that we would be begin our own deliveries in April, I gave a 30 days notice to East-West American Transport that our contract will not be renewed at the end of March."

"What about hiring drivers for our rigs, Ralph? How is your recruitment going?"

"Counting the teams you already have, six more long-haul driver teams have been hired. With the pay you are offering, it wasn't hard to attract dependable, experienced drivers. Despite our shipping changeover, I don't anticipate that we'll miss a single day's delivery."

"Excellent," Thomas remarked.

"I have prepared detailed maps for each team to their delivery sites," Ralph continued, "along with the contact names and phone numbers for each delivery location. That should make reaching the destination points much easier for our new drivers."

"By the way," Thomas casually remarked, "on a few of our hauls, I will have some special experimental sugar deliveries that have to be made.

I'll have directions and contact names for these deliveries as well."

"No problem, Michael. Just let me know when and which trucks you will need to add your shipment to. The Tanners will load the pallets for you."

"Thanks, I will."

"I have an idea that may be helpful in distinguishing your special deliveries from our routine refinery shipments, if I might make a suggestion." Fiacincio offered.

"Certainly, what do you have in mind? As critical as these deliveries will be, I've been concerned about insuring that separation, myself."

"Well, you know we shrink-wrap our sugar pallets in three different colored plastic wraps to make it easy to distinguish the pallets of white granular sugar, from the brown sugar and the white powdered sugar."

"Yes, go on."

"We use clear wrap for the white granular sugar, orange for the brown sugar, and green for the white powdered sugar. For your special deliveries, we could shrink-wrap them in, say, red plastic wrap. How does that sound?"

"Great idea, Ralph. And that idea just got you a nice bonus."

"Thanks, Michael. I'll personally supervise your special project sugar palleting and loading myself."

"Thanks. I would really appreciate you doing that. I don't expect it will inconvenience you but about twice a week."

"Believe me, Michael, it won't be any inconvenience at all."

"That's great. I guess that just about wraps up all our loose ends then, Ralph." Thomas laughing remarked.

Thomas was pleased that he now had a plan to incorporate their cocaine shipments into the routine of the refinery's deliveries while insuring their distinctive separation. Fiacincio had inadvertently offered the best plan he could have devised. He would call Juan Carlos, Ortega, and Wayne to inform them of his plan to disguise their cocaine transport, and advise them that their fleet of tractor-trailers would soon arrive.

In less than five minutes, all three were contacted.

"I have good news, Amigos," Thomas began. He then told them how he had surreptitiously found an answer to their cocaine delivery concerns.

"Good news, indeed," Clark remarked. "Be sure you give Fiacincio a nice bonus."

Thomas laughed. "I have already promised him one. His plan is well contrived don't you think? No one will ever be the wiser. Even the

BSDIA's Orca Wave Sonar will be unable to distinguish between the pallets of cocaine and pallets of sugar should a trailer ever be tested."

"Excellent idea, indeed," Juan Carlos remarked.

"Incidentally, Michael Covington called to inform me that our tractor-trailer fleet will arrive tomorrow." Thomas added.

"More good news!" Clark exclaimed.

"Juan Carlos, how is the spring coca crop progressing?" Clark asked.

"It's looking very promising again this year. I expect the coca leaf will be ready to pick by early April or May. I should be able to deliver my first shipment of raw cocaine to Ortega by the first of June. My expenses are going up considerably, though. I am being forced to pay out a lot more bribe money to the local authorities this year to overlook my coca fields. Just the cost of doing business though, isn't that right?"

"Right," Ortega laughed.

"Last year we all amassed a small fortune smuggling our cocaine using Wayne's covert underwater scheme. With this year's crop, we should do even better. Wayne, your plan is simply ingenious!" Diego noted with certainty.

"Thank you, Juan Carlos. It does seem to have worked rather nicely!"

"I'll say," Thomas said.

"How would you feel if we signed on for some extra smuggling duties on the side this spring and early summer while my crop is being processed for shipment to Ortega?"

"What do you mean, Juan Carlos?" Clark asked.

"It seems our operation has had the only successful delivery channel into the U.S. this past year. The Mexicali and Barona Cartels in Mexico and Colombia have had a difficult time smuggling their drugs across the U.S. border. Juan Tierra Barona from Bogotá came to visit me last week with an offer almost too good to pass up."

"He reported that he has 11.25 tons of crack cocaine that he has been unable to smuggle into the U.S" Juan Carlos continued. "The crack is already boxed in 25-pound cases of one-gram packets. He knows we have been very successful in smuggling our drugs into America, although he knew better than to ask how we did so without getting caught. He did ask if we would be interested in smuggling his crack cocaine and distributing it through our pipeline for a 50/50 split. Barona made it clear, we would assume a 100% liability for his half of the sales if anything goes wrong."

Clark did some quick math. "Eleven and a quarter tons has a street value of over six hundred twenty million dollars! A three hundred ten-mil split for us cut four ways, that's over $77 million each. I'd estimate at most, this partnership would occupy only about two months of our time. Considering the smuggling, distribution, sales, and laundering time, I believe no more than that, wouldn't you say so, Miguel?"

Thomas affirmed Clark's time estimates. "I'd say that would be about right. We would need at least one week to distribute the crack throughout our network. We ought to allow about four weeks for sales. Add another week to collect the cash and another two weeks to move it to Grand Cayman, and we're looking at two months tops."

"All in all," Juan Carlos added, "I'd say that forming a partnership to make around $77 mil each for about two months work sounds very tempting indeed."

"What's the down side of a distribution and sales partnership with Barona?" Thomas asked.

Juan Carlos replied, choosing his words carefully. "If anything happened to the shipment or the cash and Juan Tierra didn't get his split, he definitely would hold us, and principally me, since he doesn't know who you are, accountable. If we agree to a 50/50 partnership with Juan Tierra, we would be responsible to pay him his $310 million regardless. To not do so would bring about immediate retribution. And, I'm certain Barona's vengeance, like Clark's, would be inevitable, swift, and terminal."

Ortega remarked, "That's taking quite some risk."

Thomas agreed.

"What do you think, Wayne?" Juan Carlos asked.

"If all goes well, it's easy money. If not, we would knowingly owe Barona his three hundred ten million. Yet, considering that we moved almost two tons of crack this year in less than one week and without consequence, I say it's worth taking the risk. But it's your call, Juan Carlos. You are the only one he can identify. You would seemingly be taking the biggest risk in accepting the offer."

"I agree I'm taking the greatest personal risk. I'm willing to accept that as long as we pledge to combine our deposits in Grand Cayman to cover Barona's split if any unforeseeable problems occur." Diego replied.

"It would be less risky as equal financial partners, Juan Carlos," his brother noted.

"That's right, Ortega. Should we loose either the crack or the sales cash, our combined deposits in Grand Cayman would more than cover the loss. That is, if we enter this operation as equal financial partners."

"Yes," Thomas agreed, "that would relieve you of sole financial risk, though we would have to combine about half of our deposits to cover the $310 million. This way, if we agreed to do this, it would be a risk shared by us all."

Juan Carlos replied, "Yes. It appears we would risk losing around $77 million each if we fail, but we would also stand to make over $77 million each if we are successful. Well, what do you think?"

Clark answered first. "I think it's worth the risk. I'm in."

Ortega responded with a measure of reserve. "I guess I'm in too, although $77 million is about all I have on deposit. I'll be risking everything I have, but I'm willing to accept the gamble."

Miguel, likewise, answered with uncertainty, "If the operation fails, I too, will lose everything I have deposited in Grand Cayman. But count me in."

"It seems it's up to you now, Juan Carlos," Clark said. "What do you say?"

"Since each of you has agreed to an equal partnership in the profits, or in a loss if there is one, I too, say that we chance it," said Juan Carlos. "I'll contact Juan Tierra to accept his offer. Let's be careful and hope that nothing goes wrong. I'll be in contact as soon I receive Juan Tierra's cocaine."

The day after the Super Tuesday primaries found Edward Walters, Charles Douglas, and top Republican strategists in seclusion, developing a counter-strategy to Lane's negative campaign ads and the Democrat's Super Tuesday sweep.

"Historically," Walters noted, "negative campaign ads have tended to dissuade the electorate; yet such ads manipulate the national news media into focusing attention away from the positive qualities of those denounced."

"Yes, that's precisely what they usually do. And partially what they did, Mr. President," Douglas assessed. "The negativity did focus the media's attention away from our campaign; yet the electorate was not dissuaded by the ad's false allegations."

"Unfortunately," Walters asserted, "we were blindsided by Lane and company with their eleventh-hour negative ad blitz. Their strategy certainly worked. The national press has essentially readopted Lane as their chosen one."

"It is my belief," advised the Vice President, "that we must carefully develop a strategy that not only counters Lane's assertions and innuendo, but also convinces those voters in primaries yet to come that the Republican platform remains the best choice for America. Not Bixby Lane and the Democrats. We also must convince those who voted against me in Super Tuesday's primaries to change their vote before the general election."

Agreeing with Douglas, President Walters questioned the RNC's chief strategist. "Don," Walters asked, "considering these assessments, how would you propose that we proceed to best achieve the objectives the Vice President has outlined?"

Donald Perry responded with confidence. "First, let's look at each ad's specific negative content," he suggested. "We know Lane's advertisements are without merit. We need only persuade America that they are. That, I believe we can do. Polarizing the media against Lane will be a more difficult conversion; yet, I believe that, too, can be accomplished."

"After all, both voting America and the media realize that the individual elected as President must do more than speak. He must lead. The public also knows that a popular candidate lacking substance will not make a good leader in times of national adversity. I think that's our best strategy in defeating Lane. We simply need to extol your strengths. Lane's weaknesses will manifest on their own."

"I agree both with your perception and assertions, Don," the Vice President stated. "I want to resolve Lane's negative campaign allegations and regain my credibility as quickly as possible. We have much work ahead of us."

"What then, is our first step?" Douglas asked.

"In general, the American public has little regard for our federal government and for governmental institutions," observed Walters. "All of Lane's proposals thus far call for a greater federal intrusion into their lives. The voting populace just hasn't realized that yet."

"We must refocus our strategy to regain American's trust. I am certain that after your energy speech, you gained an appreciable amount of that public trust. Unfortunately, much time has elapsed. Apparently either that perception has waned or the public temporarily forgot your thorough understanding of the energy crisis and your plan for its resolution."

"I think perhaps it is the latter," Walters continued. "The American electorate is quick to forget one's strengths when bombarded with a constant blitz of false accusations. That is certainly what happened when Lane launched his Super Tuesday ad blitz."

"Mr. President, you are right, of course," Douglas affirmed. "I believe we must refocus our efforts to convince voting America that we are in constant vigilance of their collective well-being. For the next seven months, let's keep the reminders up front with advertisements of our own. I'd like to keep the ads concise, informative, and, most importantly, truthful. To command credibility, I believe we must specifically concentrate on those interests that are especially important to corporate America and to the American family."

"American businessmen are interested in trade relations, a healthy economy, interest rates, the stability of the stock market, and retirement. We will do everything possible to convince them that our platform will provide the most stability for each of these interests," Douglas said. "American families are increasingly interested in education, financial stability and health care. We will structure our campaign message to bolster their confidence in us to meet their expectations in these critical areas."

"I don't feel that either the America electorate or the media will continue to accept Lane's character assassinations and attacks on your political record without questioning his allegations," Walters added.

"I think our best strategy to rebut these accusations is not for me, personally, to attempt to refute them." Douglas stated. "That, the Democrats would expect. I believe it would be far more effective if we used the highly respected Republican political leaders and sports and Hollywood celebrity personalities who have come forward to offer their time and money to refute and question the credibility of Lane's ads."

"I believe that approach would be a wise strategy for two reasons," Perry said. "First, the 1976 amendment to the Federal Election Campaign Act allows private citizens and political action committees to spend unlimited funds on behalf of their candidate. We can use PAC money and the personal contributions of these celebrities to execute a counter-attack plan on our behalf without having to expend your or RNC funds to do so."

"Secondly," Perry continued, "because these individuals have considerable national respect and credibility, using them to question Lane's false accusations will certainly cause the voting public to question the authenticity of the negative campaign ads and rethink their November vote."

"I concur," Walters' said. "Using highly-respected politicians and prestigious celebrities to denounce Lane's ads as blatantly false assertions, allows you, Charles, to take the high road to promote your attributes while not stooping to the same slanderous level as your opponent. Taking this position hopefully will prompt the media to refocus its perception of Lane - and pose you as the true bipartisan candidate most capable to lead the country."

"Continuing to propose a counter-strategy for the Vice President,"

Don Perry rationalized, "I believe our starting point should be to analyze Lane's three contentious negative ads. Let's dissect their accusations and propose the best way to refute their integrity."

"Let's look at the first ad. In it, Lane depicted the Vice President as being soft on crime. The ad also proposed that Republicans in general have induced an indignity on America by allowing the penal system to employ an early release program due to overcrowding in the nation's jails and prisons."

"The ad's first allegation is a particularly easy one to refute," responded Douglas. "I challenge Lane to point to even one occasion where I have ever taken a position that is soft on crime. I have always contended that crime increases in a direct proportion to drug addiction. It has been my further contention that the majority of the criminal acts that constitute crimes are directly attributable to the criminal's need for money to buy illegal drugs."

"In answer to the second allegation," Douglas asserted, "I have never even been asked to comment on crime relative to the penal system and its early release program. Nor have I ever spoken to its impact on subsequent criminal acts and recidivism. More importantly, I challenge Lane to substantiate his claim that the Republican Party has induced an indignity on America by allowing the penal system to employ an early prisoner release program."

Don Perry proposed his counter-strategy. "Considering your compelling arguments, I contend that our rebuttal to Lane's assertion that you are soft on crime will be to challenge Lane to cite specific examples that led him to make such an accusation."

"Additionally," Perry further contended, "I agree with your assertion that we should challenge Lane to illustrate specific examples where Republicans have induced an indignity on America by allowing the penal system to employ an early release program due to the overcrowding in the nation's jails and prisons."

"To these two absurdly false accusations, I contend Lane will have no credible response."

"I agree," Douglas stated, then added, "Since Lane asserted that he is not soft on crime, we will ask him for the specifics of his plan to fight crime. Furthermore, how does he propose to insure that federal funds will be available to build a sufficient number of prisons to hold convicted criminals for the length of their prison sentences? As you contend, I'm certain Lane will have no credible response."

Don Perry next addressed Lane's second assertion that Republicans had failed to achieve their campaign promises to reduce drugs and crime on America's streets.

"I'll address this one," the President replied. "Charles, Rick Tolbert, and I predicted that Lane would accuse my administration, and particularly the Vice President, since he had oversight of the BSDIA, of falling short of its projection to reduce illegal drugs on America's streets."

"In our rebuttal," Walter's proposed, "we will agree that the amount of illegal drugs that do make it past our surveillance efforts continue to have a devastating effect on America's youth. Furthermore, we will reiterate the fact that we are now only halfway through our plan to reduce America's drug problem."

"Our four-year goal was to see a 75% reduction in illegal drugs crossing the U.S. borders. The facts show that in only two years, thanks to the interdiction efforts of the BSDIA, we already see 55% fewer drugs on America's streets. These figures certainly cannot be perceived as a failure of my administration and the Republican Party to protect America from drug-related crime. Far from it."

"Furthermore," the President said, "another positive aspect of our drug interdiction efforts can be seen in the decrease of the drug-related deaths America experiences each year, principally among its young people. In less than two years, we have seen these death rates cut in half."

The President paused momentarily, then continued. "Unfortunately, despite our best efforts to intercept smuggled drugs and to discourage illegal drug use, America's youth are still attracted to the mind-numbing effects of cocaine and other illegal drugs. We will ask Lane to dispute the fact that we simply cannot begin to eliminate America's drug problem until American's make the personal choice to stop their illegal drug use and abuse. I contend, that Lane can not contradict that assertion."

"Additionally," Perry contended, "We will challenge Lane to state the specifics of his contention that he has a better way to end the country's present drug problems. Again, gentlemen, I propose that Lane has no specific drug reduction and interdiction plan, and thus, will have no credible response."

Douglas responded. "I am firmly convinced of one thing. After listening to our rebuttal arguments, voting Americans and the media will conclude that Lane's ad is wrong, dead wrong. Surely, they will understand that until there is no longer a desire to use illegal drugs or until there is no longer a source of supply, the BSDIA has a job to do and will continue to do it with the highest level of excellence."

Finally, Perry led the group in discussion to address Lane's third negative campaign ad. In it, Lane had asserted that the Republicans are solely responsible for high gas prices and for the winter's high energy prices.

Douglas' strategy was simple. "I would propose that we have our spokespersons simply ask Lane two pointed questions: After listening to the Vice President's energy proposal, how specifically, do you contend that Republicans are responsible for America's high fuel and energy prices? And how does your plan differ from the Vice President's proposal to resolve America's energy crisis?"

Perry reviewed Lane's assertion that he had the best plan to reduce American's high gasoline and energy prices. He proposed one follow-up question for Lane. "We have heard the detailed specifics of the Vice President's energy proposal. What exactly are the details of your plan?"

"I am convinced that Lane has no such specific, detailed plan," Don Perry concluded. "Again, I contend that Bixby Lane will have no credible response to these questions."

Juan Carlos Diego contacted Juan Tierra Barona to inform him that he agreed to a 50/50 partnership to sell his crack cocaine, and would assume 100% liability for Barona's half of the sales. In less than 24 hours, Barona landed his 22,500-pound shipment on Diego's private airstrip outside of Barranquilla, Colombia. Transferring the consignment to Diego's 737 took less than six hours. At 9:00 PM, Diego's crew lifted off for the 1,047-mile flight to Cerros. A few minutes after midnight the Boeing aircraft rolled to a stop in the seclusion of the mill's hanger. Before six o'clock that morning, all eleven and a quarter tons had been safely transferred to the second-story chemical laboratory.

It would take four round trips of 72 hours each to move the drug load into St. Marks. Peter Segonyva and Vedonosti Novostey teamed for the first and third transports. Vladimir Kerchenkov and Nicholas Krasnaya piloted the second and fourth.

With the customary stopover at Arroyos de Mantua to recharge the nickel/silver batteries and change the carbon dioxide scrubber, the first three voyages traversed the Caribbean and Gulf of Mexico without incident. On the fourth trip, Kerchenkov and Krasnaya were three hours north of the Cuban base cruising at a depth of 2,900 feet when suddenly their passive sonar detected that they were being actively 'pinged' by a 683-

foot surface vessel located 2.4 miles to their northwest.

With the discovery that the DSRV was under electronic surveillance, Vladimir was glad that both passive and active sonar devices had been installed on the navigational console. While the mini-sub was undergoing instrumentation by Matsujiyama Electronics, Kerchenkov recommended the additional installation of active and passive sonar devices.

As Soviet nuclear submariners, Kerchenkov and Krasnaya knew the advantages for employing both types of sonar. In their request to Juan Carlos to outfit the mini-sub with active as well as passive sonar instrumentation, Kerchenkov stated informatively, "All marine ocean-going surface and submersible vessels navigate with active sonar surveillance. Active sonar instrumentation serves to detect the presence of other marine craft, geographical land masses, and obstructions in the sub's navigational path."

"Likewise, most submersible vessels, particularly military submarines employ passive sonar as well." Krasnaya added.

"I know their addition to the on-board navigational console will be a great expense, but to lessen our risk of detection, I strongly recommend the installation of both active and passive sonar." Vladimir advised.

Krasnaya further pled their case. "An active sonar device will provide us a navigational roadmap, while the passive sonar will alert us when we are under electronic surveillance by either another submarine or a surface vessel."

Fully intending to comply with the submariner's request, Diego nonetheless asked, "Exactly what is the difference between an active and passive sonar?"

Kerchenkov described to Diego in layman's terms how an active sonar device worked. "In its surveillance function, an active sonar emits either constant high frequency or low, intermittent sound waves that travel through the water's fluid medium in search of other vessels or objects in its vicinity. An audible pinging sound is produced when the search vessel's sonar pulses its sound waves."

"Any object within range of the sound waves will be detected as sound wave echoes are reflected back to their sonar's sensors," Vladimir continued informatively. "Active sonar sensors convert the reflected sound waves into digital signals on the sonar's scope and determines the size and distance of the object from the search vessel."

Krasnaya added, "Conversely, passive sonar sensors signal an alert when a vessel is under active sonar surveillance. Passive sonar devices pulse a high-frequency sound wave that is reflected back from an active sonar device. Passive sonar sensors receive the echo and respond with an alarm that its vessel has been electronically targeted by a surveillance craft. Unless a targeted vessel employs passive sonar sensors, it could not detect that it was being 'sounded' by a search vessel's active sonar."

Juan Carlos was only too glad to comply with his commander's request for this instrumentation.

As soon as he heard the warning alert, Kerchenkov hoped that their expenditure of $160,000 for the sophisticated vertical-emission Raytheon passive sonar detector had warned them in time to cloak the identity of the mini-sub before the surface vessel could identify it. "All motors at full stop," he said quietly to Krasnaya.

"All propellers full stop," Nicholas responded.

"Forward lights off," Vladimir ordered.

"Halogens off," repeated Nicholas.

"Start the masking disc," Vladimir ordered.

"CD in and starting."

Since their encounter with the sperm whale pod on their maiden voyage across the Gulf of Mexico, Kerchenkov had purchased a CD of sperm whale communication sounds, purchased perchance for just this precise moment. "Here's hoping the search vessel will think we are just a lone, feeding whale," he exclaimed more to himself than to Krasnaya.

The disc player began emitting the taped sounds of two sperm whales as they communicated on their migration from the North Atlantic into the Gulf of Mexico. The singular wails and moans of the two evoked an eerie mood to the otherwise quiet interior of the DSRV.

"Begin porpoising maneuvers," Vladimir instructed.

Nicholas restored power to the quite-running battery powered electric motors. Alternating power between the aft shrouded propeller and the four ducted side thrusters, the sub's bow rose upwards 10 feet then nosed downwards 10 feet, while maintaining a slow forward motion. As a further disguise, with the side thrusters, Krasnaya alternated a slight port to starboard yaw.

On the surface vessel's active sonar scope, the size of the DSRV and its porpoising motion would make the sub appear to be a lone sperm whale feeding on the plankton 2,900 feet beneath the surface. After detecting a normal whale motion, should there remain any doubt that the object was, in fact, a feeding whale, the leviathan sounds picked up by the search vessel's sonar operator should settle the matter.

After a few minutes of active pinging, the vessel turned southwest toward the Yucatan Peninsula. Vladimir and Nicholas' ruse had been successful. It was fortunate that the vessel had not been an American nuclear powered submarine or the DSRV might have been pursued until a more definitive identification had been made.

Despite the surface vessel's quick departure, Kerchenkov continued deceptive maneuvers for another half-hour. Vladimir estimated they had lost close to one hour of critical travel time. The CO_2 scrubber could maintain an oxygen-replenished atmosphere for approximately 24 hours. Under normal circumstances, this 572-mile leg of the journey would take 22. The extra hour Vladimir estimated it would take to complete the voyage would test the scrubber's maximum oxygen generating capability.

Kerchenkov and Krasnaya had left Arroyos de Mantua at five o'clock in the morning, an hour later than usual. Their routine arrival time at the St. Marks lighthouse and river channel was 2:00 AM. Before 4:00, the sub was usually safely moored in the boathouse.

Vladimir was worried. He said to Nicholas, "Leaving an hour later and running an hour behind time should put us at the mouth of the river around four; only an hour before the marina's charter boats routinely leave port. There's a good possibility we might not make it up-river without being discovered. We're going to be cutting it really close, don't you think?"

"Yes," Nicholas agreed. "It's going to be an interesting voyage."

With the heavy cargo load, inviting extra speed would be difficult. Nevertheless, Nicholas pushed the thrusters to maximum speed. They plowed steadily forward. It was now 3:30 AM. The bottom began its slow ascent. Crossing the Aucilla Ridge, Vladimir scanned the surface ahead, detecting no surface vessels in the Apalachee Bay basin.

By 4:00, they had reached the entrance into the St. Marks River. With the thrusters normally set at a safe speed of 10 miles per hour for the 7½-mile journey upriver, a trip usually taking only 45 minutes at most. Kerchenkov breathed a little easier. Now with a 15-minute safe window, he was certain they could traverse the river and enter the boathouse before the parade of charter boats made their way downriver towards the offshore reefs.

His hopes for an expedient trip upriver were immediately shattered, however, when he realized the river was exceptionally shallow. "Why today of all days," he exclaimed to Nicholas, "is the St. Marks river basin experiencing one of its infrequent low negative tide falls."

Krasnaya stated, "Navigating around the sand and oyster bars of these low tidal waters will certainly make the journey more treacherous, and might require a slower speed to avoid running aground."

"That definitely is the case," Vladimir exclaimed, as the DSRV precariously circumvented the first oyster bar. "I estimate we will have to decrease our speed to 7 miles per hour for the autopilot to safely maneuver around the remaining upriver bars."

The slower speed would increase their travel time to around 60 minutes, approximating a five o'clock arrival; the precise time the charter boats routinely left port. Kerchenkov knew the boats were usually quite punctual in their departure. Hoping the charters would leave a few minutes late this morning; the 60-minute journey upriver, he knew, would seem an eternity.

The deepest draft of the St. Marks charter boats was no more than six feet. With the diameter of the DSRV at eight feet and the negative tidal fall leaving the channel depth now at 30 feet, Vladimir calculated that while traveling at five feet above the river bottom, a depth of 11 feet would remain for the mini-sub to safely pass beneath a charter boat should they meet on the river.

Vladimir wasn't concerned that the two might collide. Instead, he was concerned they would be discovered if one of the charter boats was underway with its sonar activated. Under this circumstance, as the sub passed beneath the boat, a shallow-warning alarm would sound.

Though short-lived, the alarm's report to the Florida Marine Patrol would prompt a sonar search of that part of the river. If the search revealed that no debris could be found on the bottom that could have triggered the alarm, the conclusion would be that some large object had traversed the St. Marks navigational channel. In the right hands, such information might unravel their entire operation.

Kerchenkov could not let that happen. They anxiously watched the sonar and checked their watches. It was 4:56 AM when they made the eastward turn at marker 62. Over a minute ago, their CO_2 scrubber had ceased producing O_2. Only minutes of breathable oxygen remained. If they were not able to open the hatch soon, they would pass out from oxygen deprivation.

Though still five minutes away from the refinery, Vladimir signaled Thomas to open the underwater door. Even seconds now were critical. They could waste no time before ascending for air. Kerchenkov sped toward the riverfront, risking the creation of an underwater wave. Though it was early morning, the wave would easily be detected by anyone on the docks, announcing the presence of an underwater craft. Fortunately, the DSRV's wake went unnoticed.

Approaching Shield's Marina, they could hear the diesel engines of the charter boats idling at berth. It was 5:01. Another 100 yards and they were home free. Their sonar detected the first vessel backing out of its bay, twin screws churning the surface. The DSRV's passive sonar detected no surface echoes as they passed underneath. Kerchenkov breathed a sigh of relief; the charter had not yet turned on its depth finder.

Another quarter mile and the autopilot guided the mini-sub into the boathouse. Ascending as rapidly as possible, the commanders grinned and shook hands while the DSRV surfaced. Opening the hatch, both Vladimir and Nicholas inhaled a deep breath of fresh air. Sweating profusely, they exhaled a literal sigh of relief to at last find the safety of the boathouse and fresh, breathable air.

"I've been worried," Miguel exclaimed. "What happened?"

"You wouldn't believe how close we came to disaster," Kerchenkov said exhaustively.

"Come. Eat breakfast, and then get some rest. Later we'll unload the sub and you can tell me about your adventure."

Vladimir and Nicholas were too tired to eat. They fell asleep instantly, and did not awaken until twelve hours later. After a hearty dinner, they described in detail their tense voyage.

"You certainly were fortunate. Only your skillful maneuvering and precise pre-planning for sonar detection and avoidance saved our smuggling operation. Diego and Clark will be pleased to hear of your planned deception. You've earned yourself a nice bonus," praised Miguel.

"By the way," asked Vladimir, "where is the Stamos?"

"Since I needed to keep the boathouse vacated this week while you made your runs, I had it dry-docked for routine maintenance."

"Good thinking," applauded Nicholas. "You're becoming a regular 'old salt' aren't you?"

"I'd like to think I have blended in quite nicely around the fishing community," Thomas replied with a smile.

For the next six hours, they unloaded the mini-sub and moved the contraband into the safety of the upstairs quarters. After a restful day, the submariners departed at midnight for their return trip to Cuba. This trip would not be as eventful as had been their arrival.

CHAPTER NINETEEN

Miguel Thomas now had all 11.25 tons of Juan Tierra Barona's crack cocaine safely on American soil. Despite their narrow escape on the last transfer, the operation had gone well. So far, they were on track with their projected schedule. It was now time for distribution.

Thomas encrypted a call to Diego and Clark to report on the successful transport of Barona's cocaine into St. Marks. "I have all of Juan Tierra's crack stored safely on the second floor of the refinery. We are now ready to divide and pallet the load for distribution," reported Thomas.

"Wayne, considering the discovery and arrest of your California distribution network, how do you propose to distribute this shipment?" Juan Carlos asked Clark.

Clark replied. "For the past two weeks," he said, "I have worked to restore my West Coast distribution system. As you know, I always have alternative cities through which our drugs can be moved and sold. I still believe that Los Angeles is our best distribution point. I have paid my San Francisco distributor well to become my West Coast lieutenant and to move his operation southward to L.A."

"He has rented a warehouse near Venice Beach through which our West Coast shipments will be distributed. His pipeline through northern California is intact, and he has already established a channel out of L.A. to San Diego and eastward to Nevada and Colorado. The routes in the northeast and mid-western U.S. were not affected by the BSDIA's raid. Neither were Utah, Arizona, and New Mexico. Everything should now be in place to begin distribution."

"Excellent," Juan Carlos exclaimed. "Everything must be in place for this partnership with Barona to be successful."

"Thomas," Clark began, "as soon as we complete this call, I will fax you a map of the location of our new warehouse in Venice Beach."

"Good," Miguel replied. "How do you propose that we divide the 22,500 pounds of crack?"

"I have been thinking about that. Remember that when we distributed our own crack cocaine, though we sold all of our supply in each of the four U.S. markets, our street sales seemed to move faster on the West Coast. I would suggest then that we transport six tons to California and divide the remaining supply, with two and a quarter tons going to New York, one ton to Atlanta, and two tons to Chicago. What do you think, Juan Carlos?" Clark asked.

"Seems reasonable," Diego answered.

"Are you still certain you can disguise the shipments mixed in with the refinery's normal sugar runs, Miguel?" Clark asked.

"I am positive," Thomas answered. "As soon as I receive the California map, all the drop-off points will be identified. I have handpicked our new teams of drivers for the refinery. Except for the California run, the teams of drivers are familiar with their respective distribution routes."

"I do need to report that the West Coast 'husband and wife' team posing as 'Rob and Elizabeth Summers' have quit as one of our transport teams. They said that after the BSDIA made its West Coast arrests they were afraid to make any more deliveries for us."

"I paid them a half million dollars for their silence, and they have moved to Hawaii. Believe me, they will pose no problem; they are too scared to talk. I will use the three remaining couples for the Chicago, New York, and Atlanta routes, and send the Tanner cousins out to make the Los Angeles delivery. They are skilled long-haul drivers."

"That's your call, Miguel. Just remember what we have at stake if anything goes wrong," Juan Carlos cautioned.

"How could I forget? All I have deposited in the Caymans is at risk," Thomas answered.

"Call us as soon as all the shipments have been safely delivered," Clark said.

"I will."

It was the second Friday evening in March. The St. Marks Refinery was closed for the weekend. Thomas alerted the weekend security guards that he and the chemists would be working alone inside the refinery to package a special shipment of research sugar for delivery.

By mid-afternoon Saturday, they had moved all of the 25-pound cardboard boxes to the shipping department. One by one, they loaded the boxes onto pallets, 16 boxes and 400 pounds of crack cocaine to each pallet. By Sunday morning, each pallet had been shrink-wrapped in red plastic and grouped by destination. The eleven and a quarter tons of crack cocaine was ready for shipment.

Thomas had asked the Tanner cousins to make themselves available for work Sunday afternoon. "I need you to load some pallets for me for a delivery that is going out on Monday morning. I also have a special assignment for you if you think you can handle it. If you do, there'll be a nice bonus after you complete the mission," Miguel advised.

"A mission, huh? Can you give us a hint of what you want us to do, boss?" Dewey asked quizzically.

"Sure, I thought you two might like to make a cross-country delivery in one of our new rigs," Thomas answered.

"Are you kidding?" Cletus said excitedly. "You mean you want us to make a long-haul delivery for the refinery?"

"Yeah, sure, Cletus. That is, if you care to make the trip."

"Where ya sendin' us?" Dewey asked.

"All the way to L.A.," answered Thomas.

"Alright! Yeah, boss. I'm game if Cletus is," replied Dewey.

"Well, heck yeah. I wonna go," Cletus answered.

"Okay. There's one request I have of you this weekend, then," Thomas said.

"What's that, boss?" asked Dewey.

"You'll be loading our special research sugar on Sunday. I don't want you two to get drunk Saturday night. If you do, I can't trust that you will be able to drive the forklift on Sunday without fear you might damage the cargo you'll be loading. And I need your skills to load the trailers for me. Can I count on you to stay sober Saturday?" Thomas asked.

"Yeah, boss," Cletus answered. "We shore don't want to do nothin' that would damage yore cargo. 'Sides, we wonna be able to make that long-haul trip you promised."

"Good. Then no drinking Saturday, right?"

"Right, boss," They promised.

True to their word, the Tanners did not drink even a single beer Saturday. They were too hungover from Friday night to want to drink anything, anyway. They slept until late afternoon and then drove into Tallahassee to eat dinner and see a movie. They knew that if they stayed in St. Marks they might be tempted to go to the Front Street juke joint and drink 'another beer or twelve' as they usually did.

It was the first Saturday the Tanner cousins could remember since their senior year in high school that they didn't drink any alcohol. Unquestionably, they wanted to make this cross-country run for the boss. Both were looking forward to getting back out on the road again. They knew that if they showed up Sunday with a hangover, not only would they lose their chance to drive the big rig; they would in all likelihood be fired. They couldn't let that happen. They were making too much money working at the refinery to take that chance.

"Besides," Dewey told Cletus as they discussed their Saturday evening plans, "we can't let the boss down. He's been mighty good to us."

"You got that right," Cletus said.

Miguel phoned the Tanners at one o'clock Sunday afternoon. Half-expecting to hear a groggy voice answer the phone, Thomas asked with reservation, "Uh, are you boys ready to come to work?"

"Shore are," replied Dewey who had answered. "Don't worry, boss," he added. He sensed the trepidation in Thomas' voice. "We didn't drink a single thang yesterday."

"Great," Thomas replied. "We're ready to start loading the trailers as soon as you get here."

"Be there in a minute, boss," Dewey said.

By 5:30 that evening four tractor-trailers had been backed up to the loading dock and were readied for Monday morning's delivery. Skillfully, the Tanners loaded the red shrink-wrapped pallets into the front section of the trailers destined for delivery to the four corners of Clark's distribution network. Behind the red wrapped pallets, the Tanners loaded pallets of clear, orange, and green-colored shrink-wraps containing the refinery's sugar products that were destined for offloading at legitimate wholesale warehouses along the route.

"Fine job, boys," Thomas said approvingly. "Here's fifty bucks. Get yourself a good dinner at Two Rivers Restaurant, then go home and get some sleep. I want you to be well rested before you head out tomorrow. I need for you to be on the road early in the morning."

"We'll be ready to leave anytime you want us to," Cletus replied.

"Eight o'clock will be fine." Thomas answered. "Ralph will be in at seven to have the rigs fueled and ready to go by the time you get here."

"Thanks, boss," Dewey said. "We're lookin' forward to gettin' back out on the road again. Especially in one of these big-rig Cadillacs."

"Good. Just remember, you are not in a race. Drive the speed limit, and be careful. Remember also you are hauling our secretly formulated sugar. Nothing must happen to damage the load. Is that understood?"

"Shore is, boss," Dewey replied.

"I can guarantee you that in our hands yore cargo will be as 'safe as

Mother's milk is to a newborn babe,'" Cletus offered.

"Well, I guess it'll be pretty safe, then," Thomas laughed. "Get on out of here now, and go get some dinner."

"Yes, sir," They replied.

By 8:15, Monday morning the four red and black tractor-trailer rigs bearing the St. Marks Refinery logo were outbound to Clark's distribution points. Within 72 hours, all the crack cocaine had reached its destination sites in L.A., Chicago, New York, and Atlanta. Thomas encrypted a call to Wayne Clark and the Diego's to notify them that the shipments had reached their destination points.

"Were there any problems during the delivery?" Clark asked.

"None. Each team of drivers reported that the drop offs went smoothly."

"Even the Tanner's?" asked Juan Carlos questionably.

"Especially the Tanners," answered Thomas. "Dewey and Cletus radioed me after each drop off along their route to let me know how they were progressing. They followed the map and directions precisely."

"And they weren't suspicious when they delivered the crack pallets in L.A.?" Clark asked.

"Apparently not. They contacted me as soon as the red shrink-wraps were unloaded to let me know that 'my secret formulated sugar' had been delivered without any damage to the cargo. I had preached to them that they had better be extra careful with that load. I don't think they suspected anything."

"Good," Clark remarked. "I'll let you know as soon as I have confirmed with my lieutenants that their deliveries through the pipeline have been made."

Within one week, more than 10 million one-gram packets of crack had been distributed. It would soon infiltrate the streets of America. Clark encrypted a call to the Diego's and to Miguel Thomas to inform them that the second phase of their smuggling operation had been completed.

"Excellent," said Juan Carlos. He had waited anxiously for the call. "In about four weeks we should be ready to collect the street sales, don't you think?"

"Yes, that's about how much time I figured we'll need to sell the supply," Clark affirmed. "I'll keep in touch weekly with the four lieutenants and let you know when the street cash has been collected and boxed and is ready for return."

"Fine," Thomas replied. "I'll have the same four teams ready to return and pick up the cash."

The South Carolina primary was set to follow the day after the Super Tuesday primaries. As a Democratic stalwart in the South, Lane had the upper hand and was expected to win by an overwhelming margin. Douglas was pleasantly surprised when Lane edged him only slightly in the popular vote, even among traditional Democratic voters. Douglas saw a glimpse of hope; perhaps voters were tiring of Lane's negative ads and would no longer be fooled by Lane's false allegations.

The primaries in Colorado and Utah were scheduled to follow three days after Super Tuesday. Implementation of the Republican strategy of taping detailed political responses to counter Lane's negative campaign ads would take longer than the two days remaining before these elections.

During their morning campaign strategy meeting, the Vice President suggested that Lane might unveil a new set of ads. "Considering the effect the Democrat's ads had on the Super Tuesday vote," he said, "Lane is likely to try the same tactics again in an attempt to turn voters in Colorado and Utah away from me."

"I, too, think that is highly probable," President Walters agreed.

"Considering the short time that remains before the election, what are your thoughts, Don?" Douglas asked his chief strategist.

"We know that Colorado and Utah are both Republican strongholds," Don Perry replied. Two long-term elected Republicans represent each state in the U.S. Senate. Despite this fact, I'm afraid that if Lane's negative campaign ads run and we let them go unchallenged, you might lose a close contest in these states."

"My thoughts exactly," agreed Douglas.

Perry continued. "Given the short amount of time we have until election day, I believe that the best way we can counter Lane's negative campaign ads and prevent another defeat at the polls is to call on the four state senators and ask them to tape a short message contradicting Lane's false assertions."

"The message need not be a long rebuttal argument against the ads," Perry proposed. "The senators simply need to make a request to their constituents not to be persuaded by any of Lane's false accusations."

"Sound reasoning, Don. I'll contact the senators personally and see if we can quickly get this rebuttal strategy underway," Douglas said.

"I have a thought," the President added. "Why don't we invite them over to the White House? We'll tape their address right here in the Oval

Office. I believe it would be very effective if the rebuttal was filmed with them addressing their constituents standing beside you and me in the Oval Office."

"An excellent idea, Mr. President," Perry said.

"I like that idea, too. Thank you, Mr. President," Douglas remarked.

Perry turned toward the Vice President. "While you're calling the Senators, I'll have my staff contact television stations in Colorado and Utah and purchase air time. As did the Democrats, we'll run our ads at least once each hour from six in the morning until midnight for the next two days."

"Thank you, Don," the Vice President said. "This may be overkill, but I don't want to take any chances on losing the popular vote in two traditionally Republican states. The media would be unrelenting in their spin on such a loss."

Just as they had surmised, early the next morning Lane began his negative ad blitz. Douglas countered Lane's ads with a short, but compelling request made to the voters by the senators from each of the two key states. Each implored their electorate to ignore the Democrat's ridiculous and patently false campaign assertions. The senators' statements were loosely worded:

> You, the voters of this great state have elected me, and have put your confidence and trust in me as I represent you in Washington. Trust me now when I tell you that there simply is no truth to any of Bixby Lane's false accusations against presidential candidate Charles Douglas. I strongly support Vice President Douglas because I know he is the best candidate to next lead our country. Do not be fooled by Lane's allegations and obvious lies. I ask you to vote for Charles Douglas in the upcoming election. Our future depends on your choice and on your vote. Thank you.

Whether or not the Vice President's counter-ads had been necessary in these two traditionally strong Republican states, he won the election by an overwhelming vote margin. Douglas publicly thanked the citizens of Colorado and Utah for their votes and for having faith in him to lead the country.

His wins in Utah and Colorado renewed his enthusiasm. Douglas resolved that he would mount a rigorous campaign for the upcoming elections in the states of Arizona, Florida, Illinois, Louisiana, Michigan, Mississippi, Oklahoma, Tennessee, Texas, and Wyoming. He had only a few weeks in which to accomplish this task.

Within two days of the Utah and Colorado primaries, the Republican rebuttal ads were taped and ready to air. The spots challenged the integrity of the negative campaign ads and asked the electorate to question Lane's allegations and his empty promises. With a renewed tenacity, Douglas was ready to hit the campaign trail.

In the March 11th Arizona primary, the rebuttal ads directed towards the Arizona electorate by their senator made a substantial impact on the election results. Charles Douglas won the popular vote 82 to 17 percent, with 1 percent of the moderate and liberal votes going to the Independent Party candidate.

On March 14th, the states of Mississippi, Oklahoma, Tennessee, and Texas, each represented by two Republican Senators, were held. Douglas again triumphed with an overwhelming 79 to 18 percent of the popular vote. In Florida, Louisiana, and Michigan, states with two Democratic U.S. Senators, Lane won the popular vote, but with a decidedly smaller margin, 56 to 44 percent.

In Illinois, a state with one Republican and one Democratic U.S. Senator, Lane prevailed with a 53 to 47 percent popular vote. In Wyoming, the two Republican senators elevated Douglas' victory margin; Douglas won 4 to 1.

The March primaries following Super Tuesday had proven to be a big turnaround for Douglas and the Republican Party. The six state wins drew Douglas' popular vote count to within three percentage points of A. Bixby Lane's total.

From the campaign trail, Douglas conveyed his thanks to his chief strategist. "Don, your strategy to use our Republican Senators and national celebrities to tape political endorsements and denounce Lane's negative campaign ads was splendid, a brilliant campaign maneuver."

"Thank you, Mr. Vice President," Perry said. "Let's just see how effective they can be as we move into the remaining primaries in April and May. If these contests follow the March voting patterns, you should win overwhelmingly in those states with two Republican Senators, split the vote in those with one Democrat and one Republican senator, and concede to Lane only in those states that have two Democratic Senators."

Perry's election projections proved correct. On April 4th, Douglas won 4 to 1 in Pennsylvania and lost 3 to 1 in Wisconsin. On the 22nd, Douglas again won by a 5 to 1 margin in Kansas. The month of May, however, found Lane in a better position for reclaiming the lead in the primary elections. Arkansas, Indiana, Nebraska, North Carolina, and Oregon each had one Democrat and one Republican senator. Again, the popular vote was close in the May 5th primaries, but Lane padded his lead by almost 6 percent, showing a 9 percent lead in the overall popular vote.

On May 16th, Lane won 3 to 1 in Hawaii and 4 to 1 in West Virginia, both states with two Democratic Senators. Douglas won overwhelmingly in Alaska, Idaho, Kentucky, and Virginia on the 22nd, cutting Lane's lead to 6.8 percent.

The political messages taped by popular Republican celebrities and the U.S. Senators in states considered as Republican stalwarts effectively destroyed any credibility Lane might have had among the moderate and independent electorate. Without the benefit of hearing the Republican response, these borderline voters might have otherwise been swayed by the ad's negativity.

In those states whose electorate was traditionally Democrat, the rebuttals had little or no political effect. Those who were registered Democrats stayed their party vote in the primaries. In those states, moderate, independent, and undecided voters were easily persuaded by Lane's allegations. As predicted, the press had yet to challenge Lane on any of the points mentioned in the rebuttal ads, despite the constant denunciation and challenge of Lane's allegations by three of America's leading conservative radio and TV talk show hosts.

As close as the popular vote count was through May, Douglas knew that to win in the general election he had to find a way to dissuade those moderate and last-minute decision voters from voting for Lane.

The upcoming month of June would leave only the states of Alabama, Montana, New Jersey, New Mexico, and South Dakota with pre-convention primaries yet to come. Though demographically situated in the Deep South, two Republicans represented Alabama in the U.S. Senate. Montana and New Mexico were split, one and one. New Jersey and South Dakota each boasted two Democratic Senators. If past primary elections were any indication, Lane would hold a slight edge going into these five remaining pre-convention primaries.

Campaigning for the June primaries would be temporarily put on hold for the upcoming Memorial Day holiday. Both Douglas and Lane were preparing for a nationally telecast Memorial Day speech. Lane was again asked to give the keynote speech in Washington D.C.; while Douglas had been offered the opportunity to deliver the Memorial Day address in

Philadelphia on the Independence National Historic Park Mall at the Liberty Bell pavilion.

Rick Tolbert was preparing for a different Memorial Day celebration. Though they talked often, it had been a whole year since he had last seen his best friend, Lincoln Knox. He phoned Knox to see if they could get together for a fishing trip over the Memorial Day weekend.

"Hey, big boy," Tolbert said as Lincoln answered the phone.

"Hey there, yourself, Wyatt Earp," Knox joked, recognizing his friend's voice. "Seems I can't watch the six o'clock news without seeing your ugly mug."

"Not by choice, I'll assure you, my friend," Tolbert countered.

"It's good to talk to you again, Rick. How are you?"

"I'm fine, but I'm a little behind on my fishing."

"I was hoping you would say that," Knox replied.

"And I was hoping you were hoping that I'd say that," Tolbert bantered. "Think you might be able to take a few day's off over the Memorial Day weekend to go to the flats?"

"You bet, especially since you're asking. I haven't been speck fishing since Bill and I went last November. He has been after me all spring to get back up to St. Marks, but business has always seemed to keep me away. I promise it won't this time, though."

"How about reservations?" Rick asked. "Unless we can get a room at Shell Island we may have to stay in Tallahassee."

"The Shell Island Fish Camp has probably been booked since early winter. That's no problem though. Bill wouldn't have it any other way than for us to stay with him. Since his move to Tallahassee, he has built a nice weekend cabin on the Wakulla River just a few hundred yards 'round the bend from the Shell Island Fish Camp. He and Marie spend most weekends at the cabin so it's fully stocked, just waiting for you to come down."

"Sounds good. Tell Bill thanks for the invitation. I'll take him up on it. Just check and make sure it's okay with Marie for us to stay there this weekend. She may already have something else planned for him and the cabin."

"Believe me, when Marie finds out the three of us can get together again, she wouldn't let anything stand in the way."

"Tell her thanks, too, then. Will you?"

"Will do. When do you think you'll be able to come to St. Marks?"

Lincoln asked.

"I expect sometime around mid-afternoon Thursday. What do you say we make a long weekend of it?"

"Sounds good to me. I'll let Bill know so he can ask for Friday off, if he hasn't already done so. Coming to St. Marks on Thursday meets my schedule perfectly. I have a business meeting in Orlando the first of the week, and I had intended to drive from Fort Lauderdale to Orlando, anyway. It's no inconvenience to drive on up to St. Marks Thursday morning. I can meet you at the airport in Tallahassee later that afternoon if you need me to?"

"Right now, I don't think I will, but I'll let you know if I do. I have a meeting scheduled at the Pensacola Naval Air Station on Tuesday and Wednesday. I can get the Navy to fly me over by helicopter after lunch Thursday. I want to take a good look at the coastline on the way over anyway."

"I'll need to check with the St. Marks Police Chief to make sure we can land at the ball field adjacent to the Community Center. It would be nice if you can meet me there and give me a ride back into town."

"I'd be glad to, Rick."

"Thanks. I'm really looking forward to spending a few days with you guys again."

"Same here, Rick. By the way, you'll like Bill's new fishing rig. He's bought a 24-foot Mako Center Console. It's just right for trout fishing."

"Quite a step up from the old Alumicraft we fished from as teenagers, isn't it?" Tolbert remarked, fondly remembering their youthful excursions on the Apalachee Bay.

"It certainly is," responded Knox.

"But I'll bet even today's most modern boat and fishing gear won't help us catch any more fish that we did when we were teenagers, do you think, Lincoln?"

"You're right about that, Rick," Knox acknowledged. "But I don't think we can fish as hard now as we did when we trekked across the Ochlocknee Shoals when we were thirteen."

"You do have a point there, Lincoln."

"I'm glad you can finally find a little time for us common folk, again," Knox admonished his friend in jest.

Rick just laughed. "You know it's not by choice, my friend."

"I know that, big shot. I'll call you after I've finalized everything with Bill. Probably tomorrow. I'm glad you can join us."

"Me, too," Rick said sincerely to his best friend. "I'll talk with you later."

"Count on it. Bye now."

Bill Knox hailed Miguel Thomas as he exited the refinery's third stage centrifugal station. "Say, Michael, if you have a minute, I'd like to ask you a favor."

"Certainly, Bill, I have time. What can I do for you?"

"I've been trying for months to get together with my brother and his best friend to go trout fishing. My brother called last night to say that he and Rick have arranged to take the weekend off and will be in town Thursday. We don't get together often. I certainly would appreciate having Friday off to give me an extra day to spend with them."

"That won't be any problem at all, Bill. You deserve a day off."

"Thanks, Michael. Why don't you come out fishing with us this weekend?"

"Thanks. I might just do that. I was hoping to be able to take the quality control analysts out fishing either Saturday or Sunday this weekend anyway. If we do, I'll give you a shout on VHF Channel 16 when we reach the flats."

"Good. I hope you can arrange to go. I'll be listening for your call."

Though quite easily detected, for the past year and a half, the BSDIA and its allied intelligence agencies had tried unsuccessfully to pinpoint the precise locations of the Diego Cartel's communication transmissions. Despite modern technology, the complexity of the Onyxitron Encryptor's alphanumeric coded signals made it impossible to interpret the message, and difficult to do more than triangulate a general demographic location of the transmissions.

The agencies' intense surveillance had narrowed their search efforts to the general vicinities of the Florida panhandle, to South Florida, and to the Midwestern Caribbean. While in route to St. Marks, Rick Tolbert proposed a reconnaissance of the coastal area of the Florida panhandle to search for any camouflaged land-based or marine transceivers that might prove to be a communication source for these transmissions.

The S-70A Navy Sea Hawk lifted off from the Pensacola NAS a few minutes after noon on Thursday. A direct overhead sun gave Tolbert maximum visibility through the emerald green Gulf water below as he searched eastward along the coastline. His flight along the Gulf coast was unproductive in terms of revealing a covert encryption device.

It was, however, quite productive in identifying the location of schools of baitfish and feeding mackerel in the Apalachee Bay. He would later ask Bill Knox to pass along this information to the local marina operators who could advise the weekend fisherman where they might best troll for Spanish and kings.

A Navy Sea Hawk helicopter was not a common site in the St. Marks area, especially as it maneuvered low over the marshlands towards downtown. The heads of local citizens turned skyward as the helicopter slowly crossed the St. Marks River and Shield's Marina and headed towards the open ball field at the Community Center on Shell Point Drive.

Lincoln Knox watched the helicopter slowly circle the field, assessing its landing site. In a cloud of dust, the blue Sea Hawk settled on the infield. With blades still whirling, the door opened and Rick Tolbert gathered his fishing gear and personal belongings. He saluted smartly to the command crew as the craft lifted off and rapidly rose toward the west.

As the dust settled, Tolbert and Knox embraced in a bear hug.

"It's good to see you again, Lincoln," Rick said as the two shook hands.

"You too, Rick. It's been far too long."

Lincoln and Rick had a genuine friendship. Neither was ever at a loss for words. The inseparable childhood friends had shared the joys and pains of adolescence and formed a special bond that fortunate few ever achieve.

"Let's get going. Bill's waiting on us. He's excited that you could come."

"It'll be good to see Bill again, too, Lincoln. It's nice of him to open his cabin to us for the weekend."

"Nonsense. He wouldn't allow us not to stay with him. It'll give us more time together than if we had to drive back and forth to a motel in Tallahassee."

In less than five minutes, they arrived at Bill's cabin on the banks of the Wakulla.

"Man, it sure is good to smell the salt marsh air again," Tolbert exclaimed as he exited Knox's SUV. "Just being back on the coast certainly brings back fond memories of our youth, doesn't it Lincoln?"

"It certainly does. And I plan on adding to those memories this weekend."

"Likewise," Tolbert agreed.

"Hello, Bill," Rick said as Bill Knox greeted him upon arrival. "It's really nice of you to extend us an invitation to stay with you this weekend."

"Hello, yourself, General," Knox teased as they shook hands. "You don't think I would let the head of the most powerful law enforcement agency in America come down here fishing and stay at a Tallahassee motel, do you? Have you forgotten, who, along with Lincoln taught me how to hunt and fish? I can never repay you for that."

"Well, it will be nice for all of us to spend a little time together again."

"Yes, it will," Bill Knox replied. "I'm glad you could come."

"I am, too," Tolbert said, "Say, I'm getting a little hungry. How about I treat you to dinner at Two Rivers?"

"Sounds good to me," Lincoln answered.

"Me, too," Bill agreed. "Let's get your gear stowed, and we'll head out. After dinner, I want to take you by the new St. Marks Refinery where I work. If the boss is around, I'd like to introduce you to him. His refinery has been a real economic boon for this community."

"That would be great, Bill," Rick replied. "I'd like to meet him."

After enjoying a bountiful seafood platter, they drove to the refinery. Not seeing Thomas' vehicle in the parking lot, Bill did not stop.

"Other than the refinery and a few new houses, St. Marks certainly hasn't changed much since we were in high school," Tolbert noted.

"Not much," Lincoln Knox agreed. "It's still appears to be a sleepy little fishing village."

"Speaking of sleepy, I'm getting that way myself," Rick noted.

"I am, too," Lincoln agreed. "Morning will come early. Okay if we head back now, Bill?"

"Fine with me. We've seen about all that's new in St. Marks anyway."

For a while, they sat in silence on the cabin's screen porch that fronted the river, listening to the evening serenade of the marsh frogs and crickets. While enjoying a cold beer, Tolbert broke their silence.

"This really is a nice change of pace from my duties in Washington," he said. "I can't think of two other persons I'd rather spend the weekend with that you guys. And there's nowhere else I'd rather be right now than here."

"I feel the same way," agreed Lincoln.

They arose before the sun, scurrying around the cabin, cooking breakfast and readying for the day's activities.

"I don't think I've been this excited since childhood," Bill exclaimed. "I can't believe the three of us have finally gotten together."

"It has been far too long," Rick concurred.

By six o'clock, they had finished loading the Mako. After connecting the trailer lights, they headed towards the Shell Island Fish Camp to launch the boat.

"Howdy, Mr. Bill!" Cooter shouted in greeting to the trio as Knox backed the Mako up to the launching hoist.

"Morning, Cooter. How're they biting?"

"Real good, Mr. Bill."

"Any particular place you might recommend to us this morning?"

"They caught the limit yesterday two poles east off the light. Just drift back towards Gray Mare along the spotted bottom. Tide'll start rising 'bout 7:30. Just drift in 'til you find the sawgrass in about three feet of water. A little 'fore eight, they should be bitin' real good."

"Thanks, Cooter. We'll try that. Much obliged."

While Rick hurried inside to purchase a Florida fishing license, Lincoln and Bill filled the ice chest, bought twelve-dozen live shrimp and transferred them to the live well.

Rick emerged from the tackle shop not only with his fishing license, but also with a paper sack full of the hottest colors of shrimp-tail grubs, ¼-ounce red-head weighted hooks, and an assortment of spotted mirror lures. With a sheepish grin he noted that his tackle box needed the update.

"And to think we just use to fish with plain curly tail grubs," Lincoln teased.

"You know how it is." Rick said, "Got to keep up with the latest tackle, just in case I've lost some of my angling skills."

"Very unlikely," Lincoln countered.

As soon as Rick and Lincoln were seated in the captain's chairs, Bill idled out into the Wakulla River. Within a half-mile, they reached marker 62 where the two rivers merged. Once past the 'No Wake' zone, Knox pushed the throttle to two-thirds power, and the Mako leaped out of the water. Quickly reaching plane, the 'Reel Adventure' cruised along at a steady 40 miles per hour as they headed downriver towards the Gulf.

The smell of the misty salt air and the beauty of the marsh in the awakening dawn brought back fond remembrances of his youth. Shouting above the roar of the twin 225 horsepower Mercury outboards, Tolbert said to Lincoln, "I'd almost forgotten how beautiful this is."

"That it is, my friend. Don't wait so long next time to come back," Lincoln said.

"I promise I won't."

Turning his cap around where it wouldn't blow off as they cruised towards the flats, Rick settled back in his chair, counting the channel marker buoys as they gradually decreased in number. Rounding number 21, Tolbert got his first morning glimpse of the St. Marks lighthouse. In the early dawn light, its blinking beacon continued to direct the Gulf's navigational traffic into the St. Marks River channel as it signaled a warning of approach to the shallow water's nearby bars and shoals.

The St. Marks lighthouse was an important icon in Tolbert's personal life. As he directed the Border Surveillance and Drug Interdiction Agency, Tolbert thought of it often. He envisioned that his job was symbolically, not that dissimilar to the function of the St. Mark's lighthouse- persistent in an effort to provide direction and impart warning.

The BSDIA directed America's youth not to become involved with illegal drug use, while it warned drug smugglers to steer clear of America's borders. Tolbert knew that his position as agency head must be performed as steadfast as this beacon of directional warning.

Quietly, Tolbert reflected upon the days of his youth. In countless hours of solitude, he had sat on the porch of their family's cottage on nearby Alligator Point peninsula, peering across Apalachee Bay at the rhythmical flash of the lighthouse beacon. Those were simpler times; a phase in his life when he was unaware there was so much depravity and corruption in the world. Now, he knew better.

Tolbert had to remind himself that he was here to relax and enjoy the company of his friends. Yet, he could not completely dismiss the fact that America was still under siege from the malevolence wrought from an illicit drug trade. He was resolute in his determination to discover and dismantle the drug distribution network that he knew existed within the U.S.

CHAPTER TWENTY

As they cruised past Lighthouse Point and entered the open waters of Apalachee Bay, the orange crest of the morning sun peered over the silhouette of the eastern Gulf horizon. Within minutes, the mist that shrouded the shoreline marsh burned off, and the pelicans, sea gulls, egrets, and herons ascended from their overnight sanctuary. The air was soon filled with the cries of the hungry marine avifauna as they searched the shallow, clear waters for their morning meal.

Quickly locating schools of ballyhoo and menhaden, the birds made steep dives into the Floridian waters and snatched their fill of the schooling fish. The baitfish, churning near the surface, signaled an ebbing tide. The shrimp would now have exited the security of the sawgrass in search of their morning meal of plankton. Bill, Lincoln, and Rick had waited for the churning baitfish, too, as it also meant speckled trout would be on the hunt for their morning meal.

Rounding marker 1, referred to locally as the "bird rack" for the dozens of sea birds that routinely rested there, Bill headed eastward down the 'pole line.' Strategically placed a mile apart in an eastward path across Apalachee Bay, these creosote poles vividly marked the two-mile offshore distance that separated the deeper navigational waters from the shallower inshore shoals and sandbars. At the second pole, Knox steered the Mako northward, skillfully maneuvering the craft through the shallows until the trio spotted patches of sawgrass interspersed on the white sand bottom.

Nearby, seagulls and pelicans dove relentlessly into teeming schools of baitfish. Peering intently into the waters, Bill Knox grinned, pulled the throttle into neutral and said, "Here we are men. Just like old Cooter said." They could see flashes of silver darting among the grass, feeding upon the shrimp and smaller baitfish.

"Cooter was certainly accurate with his directions, wasn't he?" Lincoln noted.

"Boy was he ever," Rick exclaimed. "This seems to be the perfect spot." A slight offshore breeze would serve to propel them along on a steady drift.

"Hurry, Rick, get a mirror lure tied on," Lincoln prompted.

"I'm hurrying, Lincoln. Do you think yellow and red are still the best colors for the morning, Bill?"

"Have been so far this spring," he answered.

"Who's gonna set up the cork and shrimp rig?" Lincoln asked.

"I will," Bill offered. "You guys go ahead and put the artificials on."

To listen to their conversation, one would have thought they were a group of excited teenagers out for a day on the flats. Rick Tolbert looped a yellow-sided mirror lure configured with black dots, red head, and a red dorsal spine onto his 20-pound wire leader. He cocked the bail of his open-faced Shimano and let fly a cast of 40 yards.

"Man, that rod still casts like a rocket launcher," Lincoln noted admirably.

Rick was outfitted with two Shimano reels, each perfectly matched with a spiral graphite, medium-weight, six-foot casting rod. The rod and reel pair had served him well for over 30 years. "It does seem to still have its zing, doesn't it?" Tolbert exclaimed, acknowledging Lincoln's compliment.

He was willing to test new artificial lures, but Rick would never consider abandoning his tried and true casting rods and reels. As he watched the line feed off the Shimano's spool, Tolbert stated with conviction, "A man's fishing equipment is not unlike his shotgun or rifle is it? It's gotta feel like an extension of your arm and hand or it just doesn't feel right, does it, Lincoln?"

"No, it certainly doesn't," Lincoln replied. "I couldn't agree more." Himself, an avid outdoorsman, Knox had his own pair of perfectly matched 30-year old Shimano bait-casting rods and reels.

Bill laughed, enjoying the company of his friends. "You guys wouldn't part with your antique fishing toys for ten technologically advanced models, would you?" Bill challenged.

Both grinned. "'Xpect we wouldn't," Tolbert said, making another cast. He watched as the mirror lure landed with a small splash, settling quickly beneath the surface of the waves. In the early morning low tide waters, he knew he must keep a steady, rather rapid retrieve, or one of the mirror lure's three treble hooks would snag on the sawgrass as it waved to and fro beneath the waves.

After cranking the reel less than a half-dozen turns, a fish slammed the lure sideways. Rick dipped the rod tip slightly, and then jerked his rod upward assuring that the fish was adequately hooked. The rod doubled under the weight of the fish as it struggled to retreat.

"Lincoln, look at this. As soon as the mirror lure began to sink, I began a steady retrieve. I don't think I had reeled five or six times before I got a strike. Better hand me the rubber net. I don't want the treble hooks to get tangled up in the mesh net."

"I'll be glad to be your net man," Bill offered, as he hurriedly placed the rod with the cork and drift line he had just tossed out into an adjacent rod holder. "My hands are free."

"Thanks, Bill. I don't know what this is but it pulls like a good one." In less than a minute Tolbert had netted a 28-inch, six-pound trout.

"Gosh dog, Rick, that's the largest trout that's ever been caught from this boat."

"Just luck, Bill. Casting into the right place at the right time with the right bait. From my perspective, I'd say you really named your boat appropriately. That last cast and retrieve certainly did prove to be a 'reel adventure'," Rick Tolbert punned.

"Just glad to have you aboard, mate," Bill saluted smartly.

"Come on guys. Let's catch a few more," Lincoln said. "Don't forget there's a seven fish limit. Let's see if we can catch a nice box full like that."

Before the two-hour peak feeding time of the rising tide ended, all three had limited out their catch of speckled trout. Throughout the morning, the old friends had engaged in festive banter. There was little difference between the fishing excitement they shared as teenagers and that of this day.

"It's just mid-morning, much too early to go in," Bill Knox noted. "What do you say to a little mackerel fishing?" he asked Rick and Lincoln.

"Sounds good to me," Lincoln said.

"Why don't we try to find those offshore minnow schools I noticed yesterday?" Rick asked.

"I've already plotted the GPS settings you gave me," Bill replied. "Hang on to your hats. Let's make some waves of our own. Shouldn't take but about 20 minutes to reach the deeper waters around outer buoy 24."

Exactly 12 miles due south of the St. Marks river entrance, buoy 24 was appropriately named the "bell buoy." A 24-inch diameter bell served as the buoy's finial. As it bobbed up and down with each rolling wave, the clapper tolled the bell with a distinctive ring that could be heard over a mile away on a windless day.

The early morning hours along Apalachee Bay often find the water masked in thick fog. In the days before modern electronics, many a mariner had been directed to the 12-mile offshore channel marker by the constant tolling of buoy 24's bell. Its distinct sound echoed solace for those lost in the fog, in search of redirection or guidance. The bell helped lost ships set a course for due North and aligned them with the mouth of the St. Marks. Adrift in a sea of fog, many a stranded mariner had experienced welcome relief at the toll of the bell buoy.

For the next three hours, the three friends trolled along the outer banks south of buoy 24. Nothing invaded the serenity of the day; only the rhythmic drone of the outboards and the toll of the bell buoy could be heard. Each caught his limit of four Spanish mackerel, and Lincoln and Bill hit a double on the outriggers on one pass, landing 33- and 37-pound king mackerels. It had indeed been a productive day on the Gulf.

"What do you say we head in now and get a hot meal? Doesn't a hamburger sound more appetizing than the sardines, pork sausages, and cold baked beans and wieners we had packed for lunch?" Bill asked.

"Certainly sounds good to me," Rick said.

"Me, too," agreed Lincoln. "Anyway, it'll give us a little extra time to clean all these fish."

As they reached marker 62, Bill Knox asked, "Say, guys, it won't take but a few minutes. I'd like to run by the mill to show Michael our catch and see if we can persuade him to come out tomorrow or Sunday and join us. I'd like ya'll to see the refinery and meet him anyway."

Lincoln remarked, "Sure. We're in no hurry, Bill. I'd like to see the mill and meet your boss."

"Are you okay with that, Rick or do you need to head on in?" Bill asked.

"I'm fine to do whatever you guys want to do. My staff will page me if I'm needed. Let's go. I'd also like to see the refinery."

"Fine. It's a 'No Wake' zone all the way in. We'll just go slow and enjoy the sights, sounds, and smells of the river."

"Sounds good, Bill. It's nice to be back in saltwater marsh country again. I haven't been this relaxed in a long time," Rick commented. "Please, don't hurry on my account."

Within 10 minutes they had docked at the refinery's wharf.

"Hey, Charlie," Bill shouted to the daytime security guard. "Is the boss around?"

"Yeah, Bill, he just went upstairs to the chemistry lab. Want me to give him a shout for you on the walkie-talkie?" the guard asked.

"Thanks, Charlie. I'd appreciate that if you don't mind."

"No problem. Just a minute."

"Charlie to Michael Thomas. Come in Michael."

"This is Michael. Go ahead, Charlie."

"Bill Knox just docked and wants to speak to you. Just a moment and I'll give him the walkie-talkie."

"Hey, Michael, if you've got a minute I'd like to show you our catch, and introduce you to my brother and his best friend."

"Sure, Bill, I'll be right down."

As Miguel walked down the dock towards the Mako, he exclaimed, "You guys really got in early. Have you limited out already?"

"We have. Wait'll you see."

As Thomas got closer, he was startled as he immediately recognized Rick Tolbert. Despite his best efforts to disguise his astonishment, he could feel the color drain from his face. He only hoped his bewilderment did not draw attention to his anxiousness.

Bill Knox began the formal introductions. "Lincoln and Rick, I'd like you to meet the refinery's owner and manager, Michael Thomas."

"Michael, this big Goliath is my older brother, Lincoln, and this is his best friend, Rick Tolbert."

Regaining some of his composure, Thomas gave each of the men a warm, hearty handshake. "Nice to meet you both," he said in greeting. "So you got your limit today, huh?" Thomas asked with interest, quickly steering the conversation toward fishing.

"Boy, did we ever!" Bill replied as he opened the in-floor icebox. "We limited out with 21 trout that averaged 20 inches and over four pounds each. After speck fishing, we went offshore and caught 12 Spanish mackerel and two kings."

"You really did have a good day, didn't you?" Thomas said.

"We're headed back out around daybreak tomorrow," Knox said. "Why don't you come out and join us?"

"I had intended to, but I began to run a little fever this morning," Miguel lied. "I'll just have to see how I'm feeling tomorrow."

"Yeah, you do look a little pale today," Bill noted. "Well, we'll get out of your way. Just wanted you to see our catch and for Lincoln and Rick to meet you."

"Nice to meet you both," Thomas replied, "I'll give you a shout tomorrow on 16 if we come out, Bill."

"It was nice to meet you, too," Lincoln and Rick replied.

"Hope you get to feeling better," said Bill.

"Thanks, Bill. I appreciate that. And thanks for stopping by. In case I don't feel like joining you, I hope you have good luck again tomorrow and Sunday. Enjoy your weekend."

"Thanks. We will," said Bill.

"Seems like a nice man," Lincoln said as they idled the Mako towards the Shell Island Fish Camp.

"Nice, but awfully nervous," Tolbert thought. "I know I have seen him somewhere before. But where?"

The Memorial Day Celebration in Pennsylvania began at Philadelphia City Hall on South Penn Square. It was a pleasantly warm afternoon on this day that traditionally marked the passage of spring into summer. Huge crowds of celebrants greeted the Vice President's motorcade as it slowly moved south down Broad Street. Charles Douglas and his wife Margie sat atop the convertible's back seat waving enthusiastically to the cheering masses.

Turning east at the intersection of Lombard Street, the parade route continued 10 blocks then turned north on South 6th Street. At Washington Square, Douglas' entourage was greeted by Philadelphia's own modern-day Benjamin Franklin. Transferring into 'Franklin's' horse-drawn carriage, the Vice President and Mrs. Douglas were escorted to the Liberty Bell Pavilion in Independence National Historical Park where Douglas would give his Memorial Day address.

An estimated quarter million celebrants packed the six-block Mall of Independence Park to hear the Vice President commemorate Memorial Day. Most of those along the parade route waved American flags. The crowd shouted "Charles, Charles, Charles," as an informal greeting representative of Pennsylvania's overwhelming choice of Douglas in their primary election. Clearly, Douglas had the support of the people of Philadelphia in his bid to become the next President of the United States.

Pennsylvania boasted a firm and resolute Republican electorate, even as its largest city, Philadelphia, served as the incubator of American democracy. Don Perry and his Republican strategists were certain Pennsylvanians would turn out en masse to receive their anointed candidate. Their assumption proved correct.

A. Bixby Lane had delivered his nationally televised speech in Washington D.C. an hour earlier. All major television and cable news networks broadcast the Democrat's Memorial Day extravaganza. Douglas' speech would likewise, receive maximum national television exposure.

This was Douglas' first nationally televised speech and the most important opportunity to date for Americans to compare the two candidates. This was Douglas' opportunity to demonstrate his historical knowledge and presidential persona.

While Douglas ascended the steps to the speaker's platform adjacent to the Liberty Bell Pavilion, the Ben Franklin look-alike escorted Margie Douglas to the VIP section of the viewing stands. Amidst the cheers and thunderous applause of holiday revelers, Douglas acknowledged the crowd's ovation and waved his thanks for their gracious welcome.

"Thank you. Thank you very much for your warm welcome," he said to the multitude gathered on the Independence Mall. As he began speaking, a respectful silence settled over the crowd.

"My fellow Americans, it is a great personal honor for me to help Philadelphia and all of America commemorate this Memorial Day in remembrance of those who have died in service to our country.

"As we gather here in the birthplace of our great nation, we do so in respect and gratitude, not only for those who have died in military service, but also to our founding fathers who made the initial sacrifices to ensure America's freedom from tyranny. Today, we honor the bold risks these brave patriots took. We remember the courageous spirit they demonstrated as they drafted our Constitution at Independence Hall, and the personal sacrifices they made when they signed our Declaration of Independence at Congress Hall just a few yards from where we are assembled today.

"I stand before you in the shadow of the Liberty Bell, one of our nation's most prominent symbols of freedom. There could be no more fitting historical site for us to recognize our forefathers and all who have given their lives in military service so that we may enjoy life, liberty, and the pursuit of happiness that is granted us in our Constitution.

"Today we assemble to honor all the brave men and women who have paid the ultimate sacrifice for America. They have died so that you and I might live under a flag of freedom, in a nation free of oppression. Two of our country's most beautiful poems superbly illustrate that spirit in our national heritage which validates this Memorial Day celebration.

"'America the Beautiful', in magnificent expression, defines our nation indeed as 'a sweet land of liberty.' Our National Anthem, the 'Star Spangled Banner', penned by Francis Scott Key during a perilous night of battle, reminds us that our flag waves in resolute splendor over 'the land of the free, and the home of the brave.'

"As certain as this is true, we are mindful that our United States would not be a free and independent nation without the brave brotherhood of countrymen who have fought, and who have died to preserve our liberty and ensure for us our freedom. It is only fitting and proper that we acknowledge their patriotic service and unselfish valor in a national day of tribute in which we pay respect and honor to these true American heroes.

"Our freedom did not and does not come without personal sacrifice. The grave markers that adorn the hallowed grounds of Arlington National Cemetery and the other final resting places of our fallen heroes stand as a testament to those sacrifices. It is in honor of those brave soldiers, sailors, airmen, and marines that we gather today.

"On May 5, 1868, General John Logan proclaimed America's first Memorial Day in recognition of the Civil War soldiers who had fallen in battle. That year on May 30th, for the first time in U.S. history, flowers were placed on the graves of Union and Confederate soldiers alike. From that day forward, Memorial Day was called Decoration Day, a day when patriotic Americans decorated the graves of those who had died in battle.

"Ceremonies such as this pay special tribute to those who have lost their lives in service to their country. It is my hope that all American's will consider the true meaning of this day. Without the sacrifices of these fallen heroes, America would not have become an independent sovereignty.

"Today we memorialize over 1.4 million of America's young men and women who have sacrificed their lives for these United States. They left unfulfilled, the hopes and dreams for their own future. And, yet, without personal regard, they willingly laid down their lives so that those very dreams might be realized in the hearts and lives of future generations of their fellow Americans.

"In battle, American soldiers fought with enthusiasm and with the faith that their cause was just. They fought for the stars and stripes. They fought for you, for their families and friends, for those of us safe in our homes, far from the bloodied battleground. We must never forget their memory. We must never lose sight of their sacrifice.

"Let us remember the words of Abraham Lincoln as he eulogized the brave men who died in the Battle of Gettysburg, 'The world will little note nor long remember what we say here, but it can never forget what they did here,' Lincoln said. And so, it is with us today. Our words pale in comparison to the sacrifices of those who died to sustain our liberty.

"As we gather together today under our flag of freedom, we do so with reflection on those who have paid the ultimate sacrifice to bring us to this place, and at this moment in time. Generations of brave Americans have purchased our freedom for us. The heavy price they paid for our freedom, the price of their very lives, must never be forgotten.

"On Veteran's Day we honor all of America's military personnel. It is my hope that none of those men and women now serving in our military would ever have to be memorialized on this day of honor. Yet, we must be mindful that, even as we go about our day-to-day lives, the men and women of America's Armed Forces stand ready to make that sacrifice.

"We must remain vigilant in the honor of America's fallen heroes. In their honor, we must hold true to their patriotism. For these sentinels of liberty, we must remember and never, never forget. So long as there is breath among the living, we must not, we will not, ever forget their deeds or their memory.

"I thank you, the people of a great city in a great state in the greatest nation in the world, for the opportunity to speak to you on this day of remembrance. May God bless you and these United States of America."

For several seconds the crowd stood in reverent silence, reflecting upon Douglas' words and the message his words conveyed. Suddenly a few in the crowd began to clap. Then, in a rolling, thunderous ovation, the crowds along the Mall rose. Spontaneously, pockets of proud citizens chanted, 'Charles, Charles, Charles.'" Douglas turned and saluted the American flag on the right side of the podium. Turning back toward the crowd, he saluted the many waving flags in the swelling crowd.

"How could anyone hearing this speech not be moved to vote to elect this man as our next President?" asked a woman in the crowd. Her sentiments were echoed by others and, surprisingly, by the television analysts.

"Well, folks, you've just heard Vice President Douglas' address," announced one cable network announcer. "You've also heard A. Bixby Lane's presentation this afternoon. If my memory serves me correctly, Lane's address followed along the lines of last year's Memorial Day presentation in Washington D.C. Douglas's speech provided a remarkably patriotic and historical perspective of why we celebrate Memorial Day. The enthusiastic crowds certainly endorsed the Vice President's speech, heartily lifting chants of 'Charles. Charles. Charles.'"

"Which presentation was best illustrative of Memorial Day and its value to our heritage as a people? That the voting public will decide."

"If I may draw another comparison, Katherine," said a second reporter, "Vice President Douglas seemed to hold the upper hand in terms of audience appeal. He held the Philadelphia crowd spellbound with his perspective on Memorial Day. He touched on the importance of educating young American's of this day's historical and patriotic significance. But that's just my unbiased observation. Again, I report, you decide."

Even the national press corps and major networks analysts backed off on their usual effusive praise for A. Bixby Lane. Though reserved in their commendation, they portrayed Douglas' speech as an outstanding presentation of historical perspective. That fact alone was a win for Douglas. Naturally, the Vice President and his Republican strategists were pleased with the political spin.

President Walters called Douglas to add his congratulations. "I'm proud of you Charles. That was an excellent speech and an excellent delivery. Your presentation today assuredly attracted a significant number of undecided voters."

Throughout the primary elections in April, May, and June, Douglas' popular vote count crept closer to Lane's, but the Democratic candidate still held a slight two to three point lead going into the conventions. Douglas had held his own in the June pre-convention primary elections in the states of Alabama, Montana, New Jersey, New Mexico, and South Dakota. In Alabama, the Vice President won with a 28 percent lead over Lane. Montana and New Mexico, each with one Democratic and one Republican U.S. Senator, were equally divided. New Jersey and South Dakota, each of which boasted two Democratic Senators, voted heavily in favor of Lane. In these two states, the Democrat averaged 86 percent of the popular vote.

"Lane has a slight lead going into the national conventions," Douglas said to Perry. "There is no reason to believe that his lead would diminish coming out of the conventions. If we are to believe the November election will go according to the primary vote and if we are to overtake Lane, we must work diligently during September and October to persuade the few remaining undecided voters to vote Republican."

"Three percentage points is not an insurmountable lead," Perry had agreed, "but we need a controversial issue to come to the forefront... something that would cause the electorate to reevaluate their vote." If Douglas could have foreseen the future, he would have seen that 'Mother Nature' herself would provide that issue of controversy.

By the second week in July, all four regional lieutenants had sold most of Juan Tierra Barona's crack cocaine. Within the week, sales would be complete. Another week and the cash would be counted, recounted, and packaged for return to St. Marks.

Thomas contacted the three teams of drivers who had distributed the cocaine to Chicago, New York, and Atlanta. "Stay available and ready to pick up the cash," Thomas told the pairs. "It will be soon, sometime within two weeks."

Thomas called the Tanner cousins in to his office. "Say guys," he said, "how would you like to make another run out to the West Coast for me? I need you to pick up the pallets of sugar that have undergone quality analysis by our California-based chemists."

"Sure boss. Just let us know when," Dewey answered with enthusiasm.

"Should be in about two weeks, I expect," Thomas replied.

"Boss," Cletus asked, "I've got a favor to ask."

"What's that, Cletus?" Miguel asked.

"Would you mind if we went out about a week early where we could do a little sightseein'? We've driven all over California's highways but ain't never had a chance to see any of the sights."

"What did you have in mind?" Thomas asked.

"Well, I thought we might park the rig at a truck stop in L.A. near where we dropped the cargo, then rent a car and tour L.A. and maybe San Diego for a coupl'a days."

"Sounds okay to me, Cletus," said Thomas. "You do have vacation time coming to you. Is that what you want to do, Dewey?"

"Shore is, Mr. Thomas. We ain't had much of a chance to see none of California, 'cept the interstate highways," Dewey replied.

"Well, I'll tell you what I'll do. I'll give each of you an extra thousand-dollar bonus for driving for me, and I'll give you a week off before the pick up date. How does that sound?"

"Sounds mighty good to me," Cletus answered. "We shore do 'preciate it!"

"'Shore do," Dewey added.

"Just promise me you'll pick up the cargo on time and be careful driving it back," Miguel requested.

"We promise we will," Cletus answered for the cousins.

A Tallahassee travel agent helped map out vacation plans for the cousins. By week's end, the Tanners fueled a new tractor-trailer rig and set out for their cross-country trip. Cletus and Dewey took turns driving 22 hours each day, taking only one-hour breaks each morning and stopping only for meal and restroom breaks. Within 48 hours, Dewey reached the Los Angeles city limits.

"Wake up, Cletus. We're almost there," Dewey said. "Get out the map, and call out the directions to the Artesia Freeway truck stop."

"All right, Dewey," replied Cletus groggily. "Take I-10 until it becomes the San Bernardino Freeway. Continue west until the freeway intersects with I-5."

"Okay. He we go."

"I-5 next exit," Dewey remarked a half hour later.

"Turn south on I-5. That becomes the Santa Ana Freeway."

"Okay. What next?" Dewey asked when they were on the Santa Ana.

"Stay on the Santa Ana until you reach California 91, the Artesia Freeway. Stay south and continue four miles until the Artesia becomes the Riverside Freeway. Exit left onto North Brookhurst Road. The truck stop is four blocks on the right."

After arranging for secured parking for the rig, the cousins took a taxi to the Avis Rental Car Service where they had booked a Chevrolet Blazer for the week.

"Which way now? Dewey asked as they retraced their route to I-5.

"Just continue south and look for the Orange County line. Wake me again when we cross the line," Cletus said.

Forty-five minutes later, Dewey woke Cletus. "Wake up, cuz. We just crossed the Orange County line."

"Okay. Okay," Cletus said, looking down at his map. "Now look for the Disneyland Exit at South Harbor Boulevard. Exit right. The Howard Johnson Hotel is the first hotel on the left on South Harbor." Twenty minutes later, they were parked at the Howard Johnson.

"I told you, Dewey. We're just across the road from Disneyland. We can walk to California Adventure and Disney Village or take the shuttle bus."

"I'm dang shore takin' the shuttle," Dewey remarked. "I don't think I'll feel much like walkin' to the gates. We'll have enough walkin' to do when we get inside the parks."

"Let's check in and get some sleep. It's after midnight now."

"You won't hav'ta ask me twice!" Cletus remarked.

The cousins chose to headquarter their California vacation in Anaheim. From there, they could tour Disneyland and the new California Adventure. A tour bus would take them to Universal Studios and the L.A.

sites of Santa Monica, Malibu, and Venice Beach. They planned to drive to San Diego and Tijuana.

For three days, the cousins walked the lengths and breadths of the Disney complexes, California Adventure, and Universal City.

The fourth day they took the L.A., Malibu, and Venice Beach package tour. Next, they toured Hollywood and Beverly Hills. "I shore am disappointed we didn't see no movie stars," Cletus complained grumpily as the tour ended. "I thought we'd see at least one."

"Funny we didn't see no cowboys neither on that Rodeo Drive," Dewey puzzled. "I suppose it warn't much of a place for horses noway. L.A. shore has some strange people livin' in it don't it, Cletus?" Dewey noted.

"Shore does, but not nearly as strange as them weirdoes we saw at Venice Beach. Man, that tattooed skint-headed guy skatin' down the sidewalk shore got touchy when we asked him if he was one of them California gay boys," Cletus remarked. "Shore looked like one to me, wearin' them purple silk shorts and all them ear rangs!"

"Me too," Dewey added. "I was kinda embarrassed when the tour guide said that we probably shouldn't a' asked him that', warn't you?'"

"Yeah," Cletus replied. "Especially when he said, 'How about you boys not asking anyone other than me any more questions from now on. Okay?'"

The last two days of their vacation, the Tanners drove to San Diego to visit the zoo. "They shore have a bunch of weird lookin' animals here," Cletus exclaimed. "I ain't seen hardly none of them back home."

"Me neither. And their pens shore do stink somethin' terrible, too," Dewey noted. "Maybe its best they keep 'em out here in California."

Their travel agent had recommended that they stay the night at the Hotel del Coronado on the Coronado Peninsula across San Diego Bay.

"Oh you'll just love the 'Del'!" she said. "It's simply 'the place' to stay in San Diego. You can't go to Southern California without staying at the 'Del'!"

Easing their way through traffic over the San Diego-Coronado Bay Bridge, the Tanners were surprised when they arrived at the Hotel del Coronado. "I ain't so shore this is a hotel." Dewey exclaimed. "Looks more lik'a English castle."

"Well, the brochure said it was a hotel," Cletus stated. "Come on, let's get checked in. It's 'bout suppertime. Besides, it looks real nice."

"Yeah, nice and expensive," Dewey exclaimed as they registered.

"Lookey here, Cletus, they charge $10.00 just to park! And our room had danged shore better be nice for $275 a night."

"Remember," Cletus reminded Dewey, "the travel agent said we've just got to stay here. 'Everybody of culture stays at the 'Del.'" She said.

"Yeah. So cultured, everybody is headin' off to supper in coats and ties. Cletus, we're wearing cut-off jeans, Budweiser tee shirts, and sandals. Don't neither of us even own a tie. I bet they'll think we're just hicks!"

"Oh, never mind. Who cares? They'll like our money anyway."

Despite their redneck upbringing, the Tanner cousins marveled at the ornate mahogany carvings of the chair rails, walls, and ceilings in the hotel. "Somebody shore was pretty good wid his whittlin' I'd say," Dewey exclaimed to their porter who snickered at the unrefined rednecks as he escorted them to their rooms.

"Must 'a taken quite a while to carve all this," Cletus added.

The porter made no reply and walked away mumbling after he received no tip. "Quite a snippy chap!" Dewey remarked. Shore hope he didn't 'pect no tip just for walking us to our room. After all, we carried our own gym bag."

"I don't know. Some of these California folks are shore hard to figger out," Cletus said.

After they were seated in the ornate dinning room, the cousins stared in disbelief at the menu. "Look how much this here sirloin steak is, Cletus! I dang shore didn't want to buy a whole side of beef. Just a liddl' slice of it."

Their dinner bill, including four Budweisers each came to $112.28. "That's mor'n we spend for a whole week's worth of groceries back home," exclaimed Cletus as he paid the bill.

"Waiter was kinda snippy, too, don't ya' think, Cletus?" Dewey noted as they walked backed to their room. "Don't think he much liked yore tip."

"Yeah, he was, come to think of it. And I give him five whole dollars, too."

The next morning the cousins made the 30-minute drive to the California-Mexico border. An hour after clearing customs they were parked in downtown Tijuana. Another hour and two pitchers of Margaritas later, Dewey and Cletus were well on their way to the 'blind staggers.'

They walked the streets, treating themselves to purchases of handmade leather boots, silver studded belts, and cowboy hats adorned with ostrich feathers. The street vendors took advantage of their inebriated state not to mention their unfamiliarity with the true value of Tijuana merchandise.

Unaware that they were supposed to barter for their purchases, the boys thought the prices were good. They also thought the going price for an hour of sexual pleasure at a local bordello was just right, too. In fact, since they thought the price was so good, they had agreed to come back a second time later in the day.

At dusk, as they were making their way back to their SUV, a young Mexican stopped them and asked if they would like to buy some uppers to keep them awake for their drive back across the border. "Sure, man. We're long-haul truckers. We may want several. Whatcha got? Benny's? Dex's?" Cletus asked.

"Better than that. Some of Mexico's best speed," he said.

"How much, Amigo?" Dewey asked.

"Two dollars a capsule. American."

"That's too much, man," Cletus replied. "We can pay less than that at any American truck stop."

"How about a buck each?" Dewey asked.

"How many you want, Amigos?"

"We'll take twenty," Cletus answered. "That's a nice round number. Are you sure these are real? If they're not, we're really gonna be mad."

"Oh, they're real alright, Amigo. Best speed you've ever bought."

"Okay. They'd better be."

The capsules they bought were not amphetamines as they had expected, but Mexico's purest mescaline, a potent and immediate acting stimulant and hallucinogenic.

After a long night's sleep in San Diego, the cousins drove back to Los Angeles to pick up their tractor-trailer and make their pickup. By mid-afternoon, they were loaded and eastbound on Interstate 10.

Seven hours out of L.A. and an hour west of Phoenix found them near the town of Tonopah, Arizona. For the past 80 miles, the interstate had continued in an almost perfectly straight line. With few curves, it was a monotonous drive. At the wheel, Cletus was becoming drowsy. His usual antics of opening the window and singing to the songs on the radio to stay awake had not worked. The alcohol he had consumed from the day before continued to exert its hypnotic effect.

Still three hours before he was supposed to wake Dewey for his turn at the wheel, Cletus decided to try one of the Mexican stimulants. Taking a swig from his bottled water, Cletus downed one of the capsules. Taken on an empty stomach, the drug began to exert its stimulant effect within 20 minutes. He felt his heart rate accelerate and his mental faculties sharpen. He became more focused, more acutely aware of his surroundings. He felt revived and better able to concentrate on his driving.

"Man, this is some really good stuff," he thought.

His ability to focus and concentrate, however, was short lived. As more of the mescaline was released into his bloodstream, Cletus began to hallucinate. The two-lane highway appeared to narrow. He lost his depth of field and peripheral vision. The mescaline masked his sense of motion. Cletus remained oblivious to the rig's increasing speed; the tractor-trailer sped along at 85 miles per hour, passing every vehicle in his path.

A gasoline-hauling semi in his lane ahead seemed to creep along in slow motion. Quickly approaching the rear of the tanker, Cletus jerked the wheel hard to the left and accelerated past the slower semi. The refinery tractor quickly passed the cab of the gasoline tanker. Cletus had now lost all sense of dimension. Before his trailer had safely cleared the other rig, he jerked the wheel back to the right, jack-knifing his rig into the path of the oncoming tanker. The cab of the gasoline tractor slammed into the side of Cletus' trailer, breaking it off the tractor.

Dewey lurched forward and awoke instantly as the force of the collision began to tilt their cab over on its side. As it did, the bolts holding Dewey's seat belt broke and his side glass window shattered. The tractor began to roll repeatedly. Dewey screamed as he fought to keep his body inside the cab. Thrown partially out the window, he was crushed between the cab and the pavement. Dewey died instantly.

The front wheels of the tanker rode up on the refinery's trailer. The tanker settled hard, slicing a hole in its underbelly. Gasoline rapidly filled the bed of the trailer, soaking its boxed contents. The gasoline suddenly exploded in a huge fireball.

Cletus' seat belt tightly bound his stiffened body as fire quickly filled the cab of his tractor. The tragic event seemed to occur in slow motion. Cletus died a horrible death.

The intense heat from the fire ultimately reduced the metal of both tractor-trailer rigs into a twisted, blackened mass. It was difficult to discern which metal fragments belonged to which vehicle.

The pallets of cash were reduced to nothing more than ash and smoke. Not a single dollar bill remained recognizable. Accident investigators would be unable to determine the container trailer's contents or make an assessment of the value of its cargo.

It would be much easier for Diego, Clark, and Thomas to determine their losses. $310 million - in cash. Half the total sales collected for JuanTierra Barona's shipment vanished in the aftermath of the accident. In their partnership agreement, Barona had been promised he would receive his full share. He expected to be paid in full - his entire $310 million. That had been their agreement; they had assumed all risk, and now the worst had happened.

CHAPTER TWENTY-ONE

It was a hot July Sunday morning when Wayne Clark awoke in his condominium in Miami. As he began to leisurely prepare breakfast, Clark watched the CNN morning news telecast. The scene was an aerial view of a tragic dual tractor-trailer accident near Phoenix, Arizona. An on-the-scene reporter was describing the wreck.

"As we zoom in on this tragic accident scene, you see all that remains of two semi's that collided in the eastbound lane of Interstate 10 late last night. One of the transport vehicles was an Exxon gasoline tanker. The other, a container trailer rig, has yet to be positively identified."

"Arizona State Troopers do know from eyewitness accounts of the accident that the container truck was attempting to pass the tanker rig on the left," the reporter said. "Traveling at a high rate of speed, before it had safely passed the cab of the Exxon tanker, the container trailer abruptly turned back into the right hand lane, and directly into the tanker's path. Unable to avoid a collision, the driver of the tanker hit the container rig broadside, causing it to roll over a number of times. The gasoline tanker exploded on contact with the container trailer."

"As you can see, the accident has completely blocked the eastbound lane of Interstate 10," she said. "One lane of westbound I-10 has been opened for eastbound traffic until the accident debris can be removed and the investigation completed. Troopers reported that the fire continued to burn into the early morning hours. Not until then were responding fire trucks able to approach the scene in an attempt to cool the smoldering wreckage. And not until mid-morning was the mass of metal sufficiently cooled to allow investigators to survey the accident site."

"At this time it is unknown how many people perished in the fire. An unidentified eastbound driver who had been passed by the container rig a few miles back was certain that he identified the logo on both the tractor and trailer as marked 'St. Marks Refinery'."

Clark was speechless, transfixed at the scene displayed before him on television. He broke out in a cold sweat, hoping against hope that if the tractor suspected of causing the accident was from the refinery, it was not the rig returning with their drug money.

"I must contact Miguel and Juan Carlos," he thought. Within seconds, he encrypted a call to both.

"Have either of you seen this morning's national news?" he asked disconcertedly, hardly able to speak.

"No, Wayne." Thomas answered. "What's wrong?"

"I'm not sure, Miguel, but I believe a St. Marks refinery rig has been involved in an accident in Arizona. The whole damn rig is burned to a crisp."

"What?" Diego asked unbelievably.

"Turn on your TV. CCN news. They're still covering the accident."

"Just a moment, then," Miguel said. Both he and Juan Carlos turned on their sets. They watched an on-the-scene reporter talking with an Arizona Highway Patrol officer.

"Officer, were you able to positively identify the tractor-trailer rig that allegedly caused this accident?" she asked.

"No, not conclusively. Due to the intensity of the fire, we have been unable to identify any markings on either the container or the cab of the semi reported to have pulled into the path of the Exxon tanker. Eyewitness accounts though, identify the container company as the St. Marks Refinery."

"Thank you," the reporter said, quickly returning to footage of the scene. "The Exxon tanker was licensed in California. Investigators did find a partial Florida license plate that we know did not come from the Exxon tanker. We are now trying to run the Florida plate through DMV to assist in making a positive identification."

"Please tell me, Miguel, that was just a rig returning from refined sugar deliveries and was not the rig you sent out to return the collected sales money!" Juan Carlos pleaded.

"It has to be the rig that Dewey and Cletus Tanner were driving," Thomas said with a groan. "We don't have any other delivery vehicles out west right now."

"Then don't tell me they had already picked up our load of cash!" Juan Carlos screamed.

"I'm afraid they had," Miguel admitted in anguish. "Cletus radioed me late yesterday afternoon that they had made the pickup and were heading back on I-10."

"Maybe the witnesses were mistaken," Clark said, the slightest hope in his voice. "Try to raise them on the radio."

"Okay. Just a minute," Thomas answered.

"St. Marks base to the Tanners. Base to Tanners. Come in Dewey or Cletus."

"No response." Miguel moaned.

"Our money. $310 million. Gone." Juan Carlos screamed staccato-like.

"It appears that it is," acknowledged Clark.

"What are we going to do?" Miguel asked.

"We're going to pay Juan Tierra his $310 million. That's what we're going to do. We have no choice!" Juan Carlos shouted. "We either pay him or suffer the consequences. If we don't, I'll be forced to live in constant fear of the henchmen he'll send to track me down and execute me."

"Fortunately, we do have $310 million from the other half of the crack sales coming in from Chicago, New York, and Atlanta," Clark noted. "We'll just have to give all of that to Barona and pocket nothing for ourselves."

"I'd rather do that than to try to hide from Juan Tierra," Diego added.

"For your sake, Juan Carlos, we'd just better hope the other cash shipments are transported to St. Marks without any problems," Clark remarked.

"I don't even want to think about them not getting there safely," Juan Carlos stated. "Miguel, when do the other trucks go out to make their pickup?"

"They are scheduled to leave next week," Thomas answered.

"Call us the minute they arrive," Juan Carlos advised. "I won't rest until the cash is safe in your hands."

"I'll call the minute I receive it," promised Thomas.

The Geostationary Operational Environmental Satellite (GOES) imagery was undeniable. An uncommon occurrence for mid-July. It began as a mid-latitude, low-pressure system, seeded by the lower tropospheric African easterlies. Transported westward along the sub-tropical ridge off the Cape Verde Islands through contact with the warm Atlantic waters, the low-pressure system quickly gathered heat and energy.

The hot summer temperatures served as a geothermal heat engine. Moisture evaporated by the ocean's warm surface temperature formed bands of intense thunderstorms. Miami Hurricane Center officials watched with interest and growing concern as wind patterns near the ocean's surface rapidly transformed the weather system into an organized storm with cyclonic circulation.

After intently studying the Center's sophisticated GOES imagery, chief meteorologist Rob Milton turned to his staff. "We'd better keep an eye on this one," he said. "I see no immediate weather patterns in the Mid-Atlantic Basin that would cause this system to diminish."

Less than 400 miles off the Cape Verde islands at latitude 17.870 N and longitude 66.667 W, the Hurricane Center officially declared the weather system a tropical depression. Through NOAA satellite imagery, meteorologists described the weather formation as "a well-organized system of clouds and thunderstorms with defined circulation and sustained winds in excess of 38 miles per hour." It became the eighth tropical depression of the year.

Within 24 hours, NOAA officials upgraded the classification to a tropical storm and named it Bethany. Weather officials noted that Bethany did not appear to be a typical mid-summer tropical storm. Her maximum winds had already increased to 62 miles per hour.

Hurricane season officially runs from June 1 to November 30 each year, averaging 10 tropical storms each season in the Atlantic Basin, comprised of the tropical Atlantic, Gulf of Mexico, and the Caribbean.

GOES imagery substantiated the Weather Center's suspicion that Bethany was an atypical tropical storm. The storm had formed quickly and gained strength rapidly. Within another 24 hours, the weather system intensified to a Saffir-Simpson Category 1 hurricane.

NOAA officials reported that Bethany was now an intense tropical weather system with "a well defined circulation and maximum sustained winds of 88 miles per hour." Bands of thunderstorms now extended over 100 miles from Bethany's well-defined eye. The circulating hot July air had further warmed the thunderstorms, extending the eye wall to over 50,000 feet into the atmosphere. Each day the hurricane strengthened and increased in intensity.

To reach the outer Leeward Islands of the Caribbean, tropical waves travel more than 2,700 miles from the Cape Verde Islands. Moving westward along the 17th latitude at an amazing 42 miles per hour, the hurricane was fueled by the warm tropical waters and its own ferocious energy. NOAA officials warned, "Hurricane Bethany, already 750 miles west of the Cape Verde Islands, continues on its westerly track. With its present speed, the storm should reach Anguilla, Antigua, Barbuda, and Guadeloupe of the northeast Leeward Islands in less than 48 hours."

A Weather Channel meteorologist reported, "At present, weather radar shows no southerly or westerly air masses that could redirect the storm to a northerly course into the Atlantic and away from populated land masses." Residents of the U.S. Virgin Islands, Puerto Rico, Hispaniola, and Jamaica were warned to prepare for the storm to come ashore. With each passing hour, the storm increased in intensity.

As Bethany reached the leeward islands of the West Indies, the Miami Hurricane Center upgraded the classification to a Category 4 storm. Bethany now packed maximum sustained winds in excess of 140 miles per hour and carried a tide surge of 16-18 feet. The residential and commercial infrastructure of Anguilla, Antigua, Barbuda, and Guadeloupe was no match for Bethany's destructive power. The right front quadrant of Bethany's counterclockwise wind struck a full-force blow, devastating the islands.

East End Village and The Valley on Anguilla, St. Johns on Antigua, and Phillipsburg, Grand Case, and Marigot on Guadeloupe were hit hardest. Those structures undamaged by the hurricane's winds were devastated by its tidal surge. Satellite photos of the Leeward Islands showed massive destruction. Little infrastructure remained. It would be days before relief efforts could send aid to Anguilla. Fort-de-France, Martinique, immediately sent aid to Guadeloupe, Antigua, and Barbuda. Americans were stunned to see virtually the entirety of these tropical islands wiped out by the storm.

With greater advanced warning, the U.S. Virgin Islands and Puerto Rico were better prepared for Bethany. Dipping slightly southward as it crossed the Leeward Islands, Bethany gave the islands of the Greater Antilles a glancing blow as it continued on its westward tract.

A high-pressure ridge spiraled northward off the Cordillerea de Merida mountain ridge in Venezuela. Influenced by this southerly airflow, Bethany turned 45 degrees to the northwest as it approached the southern border of Haiti. The full force of the storm struck the Hispaniola west coast. Relentless 148 mile per hour winds slammed into the coastal towns of Jacmel and Les Cayes, leaving behind a massive debris field.

Jamaica next braced for the storm. The National Hurricane center warned Jamaicans that the eye would likely pass directly over Kingston. The Jamaican President urged the island's coastal residents to evacuate immediately, retreating to the higher elevations of the island's interior.

Within seven hours, Bethany's forward storm wall breached the Jamaican coastline. Winds in excess of 145 miles per hour pushed the storm's tide surge over the streets of the city of Port Royal. Jamaicans watched in horror as the news revealed in vivid images the savagery of the hurricane as it rolled through Kingston and to the northwest. Not since 1935 had Jamaicans witnessed the full force of a hurricane with the strength of Bethany.

As the hurricane came ashore, Jamaica's Blue Mountains reduced Bethany's intensity to a Category 2 storm. Continuing on its northwest path, the eye of the storm approached Ocho Rios on the northern Jamaican coast. As the outer wall crossed land and reentered the Caribbean, the winds around the eye would increase in strength and intensity.

As the outer feeder bands of rain approached Ocho Rios, Simone and Santiago Mariquez prepared for the worse. Before the Kingstown television station was knocked off the air, they watched as local reporters announced the intensity of the approaching storm. It was rare for a hurricane to directly strike the Jamaican coast. Jamaicans were unfamiliar with the destructive power of a storm of this magnitude.

When Santiago was four years old, Simone left Sister Margaret's haven for unwed mothers. With the money received monthly from one of A. Bixby Lane's corporate offices, Simone had purchased a condominium for her and their son. Until now, they had led a safe and comfortable life.

Sitting high on the hills overlooking Ocho Rios, the condominium had a beautiful view of the Caribbean. Despite its scenic view, Simone now wished the condominium was situated in a less vulnerable location. Protected by the mountain ridge on the condo's south side, the structure would be most vulnerable to destruction as the eye passed overhead and the winds shifted from the northwest.

"Mom, I'm frightened," the wide-eyed fifteen-year old Santiago exclaimed to his mother. The two had prepared for the approaching storm.

"We'll be okay, Santiago," Simone told her son. "We've put up storm shutters, and we have plenty of provisions in case the electricity goes off for a while. We'll huddle together in the interior bathroom when the storm hits. We'll be safe. Don't worry."

Simone tried to soothe her own worries as she spoke to Santiago. The ominous news reports had frightened her, too, but she tried not to convey her anxiety to her son. From the destruction the hurricane had left in the Leeward Islands and in Haiti, Simone knew newscasters' warnings about the intensity of the storm were no exaggeration.

Simone and Santiago sat on their screened-in porch watching as the outer bands of rain began to fall. At first, rain droplets appeared as those from a routine summer shower. In mere minutes, the rain began to fall in thick sheets, carried horizontally by the intense southeasterly winds.

Simone and Santiago quickly retreated to the drier interior of the condominium. With the windows boarded, they settled in the den and waited for the intensity of the forward storm wall. Moments later, Ocho Rios lost electrical power, and the two were left in virtual darkness. Though it was still mid-afternoon, an eerie gloom settled over the city.

"Maybe we'd better move into the bathroom, Santiago." Simone said as she took her son's hand.

"Okay, Mom." Santiago answered. He held her hand and led her to the inner bath. They had already discussed their plan to huddle in the tub for maximum protection against the storm.

In an attempt to improve their comfort for the long wait she knew they must endure, Simone had placed cushions from the sofa in the tub. For extra protection, they had brought in a mattress from the guest room to cover the tub as they sought refuge. With a battery-powered weather radio and flashlights in hand, mother and son lay side-by-side waiting for the front wall of Bethany to pass.

They listened and waited as 110-plus mile per hour winds battered their condominium. In less than half an hour, the winds and rain abated. The eye wall was passing directly over Ocho Rios. Simone and Santiago moved the mattress aside and exited the bathroom. As they opened the porch door, they were amazed to see a blue sky overhead.

Though the screen wire had been ripped off the porch frame, the condominium structure appeared to have otherwise remained undamaged. Simone hugged Santiago and breathed a sigh of relief. Her sense of well-being was only a temporary respite. Simone's emotions again returned to anxiety as she looked to the south and saw the backside of the eye wall as it drew closer to Ocho Rios.

A sinister-looking mass of black clouds extended from the ground upward as far as she could see. As dark clouds rolled along the squall line, vivid streaks of lightning flashed across the approaching eye wall. Simone noticed that the wind had suddenly shifted to an easterly course and was now beginning to howl over the mountains from the west.

The Weather Channel meteorologist had warned that the approaching rear wall would be the most intense element of the hurricane. Less protected by the open slopes of the hills, their condominium was significantly more vulnerable from this southeastern circulating air mass. The sun began to disappear as the squall line approached. The wind howled with a greater intensity than when the front eye wall approached. Simone was now more afraid than when Bethany first arrived.

"Come, Santiago. We'd better return to the safety of the bathroom," she said, hoping the bathroom would indeed provide them safe shelter.

"I'm coming, Mom," Santiago replied as he rushed into the interior.

In less than five minutes, rain began to pelt the building. From the northwest, the full force of the hurricane struck the condominium broadside. With an increased intensity, 130-mile per hour winds quickly began to peel away the building's corrugated adobe roof tiles, hurling them like missiles into neighboring condominiums. Simone and Santiago cringed as they heard tiles from adjacent buildings hammer the roof and exterior walls of their home.

In less than 15 minutes, the condominium roof was pried away by the fierce winds. Rain fell in torrents into the interior. Simone screamed as the roof disappeared and water began to flood into the bathroom. She turned Santiago beneath her and held him tightly.

"I love you, Santiago," Simone shouted above the roar of the wind.

"I love you too, Mom. Everything's going to be all right," he shouted back.

"Promise me something, Santiago. If anything happens to me, call Ambassador Farley and let him know. The Ambassador will make sure that your father takes care of you," Simone yelled.

"Mom, you're scaring me."

"I'm not trying to scare you, Santiago. I just want you to know that you will always be taken care of if anything happens to me."

"Alright, Mom. I promise I will. Just hold me tight, okay?"

Simone held him close, shielding him beneath the mattress with her body. She clutched the mattress tightly with one hand, knowing the howling wind might blow it away in an instant. As she feared, moments later the force of the wind lifted the mattress, hurling it over the bathroom wall. Rain and debris flooded the interior.

Vulnerable to the force of the storm, Simone lifted one arm desperately trying to shield them from the debris of the storm. Suddenly, a roofing tile from a neighboring building slammed into the bathroom, striking Simone in the back of the head.

As Santiago held his Mother tightly, he felt her body grow limp. As he lay beneath her, Santiago cried as he felt the blood and life drain from his mother's body. With a last gasp of breath, Simone died in her son's arms.

As Bethany left the Jamaican coastline, a tranquil starlit evening followed the stormy afternoon. Despite an overwhelming desire not to leave his Mother, Santiago knew he must seek help. The hurricane had left Ocho Rios without power. Soaked in his mother's blood, Santiago walked the dark residential streets for hours until he encountered a police officer.

Within minutes of telling his harrowing story, they were underway to the Mariquez residence. With flashlight in hand, the officer asked Santiago to wait on the porch steps while he went inside to look for his mother. Finding her body as Santiago had described, the officer confirmed Simone's tragic death.

Though trained to avoid any personal involvement in emergencies, the officer could not distance himself from the tragedy that Santiago had experienced. With teenagers of his own, the officer was determined to help the lad. He stood beside the tub trying to picture the horrible scene that had transpired as the youth witnessed his Mother's death.

Returning to the porch, the officer sat down beside Santiago and placed an arm around his shoulders in an attempt to console him. "Where can I take you tonight, Santiago? Do you have family nearby?" the officer asked.

"No, sir. My grandparents live in Montego Bay. My Mom asked me to promise that I would contact U.S. Ambassador Farley if anything happened to her. He is a friend of ours."

"I will see that you are taken care of tonight. Come, now. Let's go back to headquarters where we can contact the American Embassy by radio. I will also see that your Mother is properly taken care of," he promised.

"Thank you, sir," Santiago said politely.

Though exhausted from coping with Bethany as she rolled through Kingston, Jeremy Farley was instantly alert when the Ocho Rios Chief of Police roused him from his sleep at two in the morning to inform him of this tragic occurrence. The ambassador was dismayed to learn that Simone Mariquez had lost her life in the storm. He was even more dismayed to learn that Santiago had been witness to her tragic death.

The debris field left behind by Bethany slowed his pace to a crawl during the long, cross-island drive to Ocho Rios. Farley arrived at the police station just before sunrise. Santiago had quickly fallen asleep on a cot in the police chief's office. Jeremy Farley was running on adrenalin; there would be no time for him to rest this day. The Ambassador sat down beside Santiago's cot and gently wakened him. "Santiago. It's Jeremy Farley."

"Hello, Mr. Farley," Santiago said groggily.

"Chief Ramirez told me your tragic news. I'm so sorry to learn that your mother lost her life during the hurricane. Are you okay?" Farley asked.

"Yes, sir. I'm not hurt," Santiago answered weakly, "but I'm scared because my Mom's dead."

"Don't be afraid, Santiago. I will contact your grandparents this morning. They will come and pick you up. You will live with them now. That is what your Mother would want you to do."

"Okay, Mr. Farley," Santiago said. Wiping tears from his eyes, he added, "I like my Grandma and Grandpa. I will do whatever you and they say."

"Thank you, Santiago. Your mother would be so proud of you," Farley praised.

"Mr. Farley, during the hurricane I was real scared. Mom held me tight and told me not to be afraid because she would protect me. As she was holding me, she told me to let you know if anything happened to her. She promised that you would make sure that my father continued to take care of me."

"Santiago, I promise you, I will make sure that he does."

Bethany continued its northwesterly course across the Caribbean toward Cuba. The warm seawater re-ignited the storm's intensity. The eye of the hurricane centered on Trinidad and Cienfuegos in the middle of the Cuban island, sparing Guantanamo Bay on the southeastern coast and Arroyos de Mantua on the southwest corner of the island from the brunt of the storm. But for a few loose roof shingles, Bethany left Hector Gomez's boathouse on the Cabo de San Antorrio peninsula unscathed.

An upper-level, high-pressure system streaming down from Canada pushed Bethany from its northwesterly course to the north-northeast. Crossing the Straights of Florida, Bethany now posed an imminent threat to the U.S. coast. Hours before, the Miami Hurricane Center had advised residents of the Keys, Miami, and the whole of the South Florida peninsula to evacuate and move northward, away from the coast.

At 3:30 PM, the full force of the hurricane slammed into the Keys and bore down on the heart of Miami. Reclassified as a Category 4 hurricane, Bethany's winds now exceeded 142 miles per hour. Miamians who had failed to heed earlier calls for evacuation hurried toward safer ground.

Wayne Clark encountered fierce wind gusts and torrential rains as he crossed the Biscayne Bay Bridge and drove away from his CIA office on Brickell Avenue. Despite the intensity of the storm, Clark had returned to his office to retrieve an extra Onyxitron Encryptor and charger that he had left in his office safe. He was afraid he might lose the invaluable communication devise should the building experience heavy damage in the storm. Worst, he feared its chanced discovery.

In an effort to support a rapid evacuation, all traffic lanes along Interstate 75 had been designated as northbound lanes. Nevertheless, traffic along the causeway moved at a snail's pace as late evacuees hurried to outrace the hurricane. Frustrated with the slow traffic ahead, Clark exited onto the less crowded old U.S. Highway 1.

Having circumvented city traffic, Clark sped along the coastal road. Bands of rain and sweeping winds in excess of 70 miles per hour buffeted his Tahoe as he struggled for control. Suddenly, an intense wind shear forced his SUV across a culvert, wrestling the vehicle out of his control. The steering wheel slipped from his grasp, and the right front passenger side slammed into a utility pole.

The air bag inflated, protecting Clark from the initial collision, but his excessive speed had propelled his vehicle forward. It rolled over four times before coming to rest on its top. Knocked unconscious, Wayne Clark hung upside down, supported by his seatbelt and shoulder harness.

There he remained until the hurricane passed. A Florida State Trooper chanced upon his vehicle and radioed for an ambulance. When the trooper surveyed the vehicle for identification, he discovered Clark's CIA registration. The contents of Clark's briefcase were strewn about the interior. Noticing CIA documents and the radio equipment, he confiscated them for safekeeping.

After an extensive emergency room effort to stabilize his vital signs, Clark was moved into the intensive care unit where he remained in a coma. Out of respect for his CIA status, the hospital administrator notified CIA Director Terry Fortson of Clark's condition. Fortson immediately flew a circuitous route around the storm to Miami to check on his Deputy Chief for Caribbean and Latin America Analysis.

Greeting the CIA Director as he arrived at the Miami hospital, the administrator handed him a message and prompted, "Mr. Fortson, after your visit with Mr. Clark, would you please call Florida State Trooper Glenn Owen at this number? He handled the accident scene investigation, and has placed Mr. Clark's personal effects and other items found within his vehicle in safekeeping at patrol headquarters."

"Yes. Thank you. I will," said Fortson. After a brief visit to the bed-side of Wayne Clark, Terry Fortson contacted Trooper Owen. "I'll be right over to meet with you," he told Owen.

Within 10 minutes, Owen met and ushered Terry Fortson and entou-rage into his patrol barracks headquarters. "Sorry that you have to come to Miami under these circumstances, Mr. Fortson," he said. "How is Mr. Clark?"

"Still comatose," Fortson answered. "But his doctors advised me that he should return to consciousness as soon as his brain swelling subsides. They estimate that should be in a day or two. The doctors expect him to make a full recovery."

"That's good news, indeed," Owen responded.

"I believe you have some of Clark's personal effects?" Fortson prompted.

"Yes, sir," Owen continued, pointing to several sealed boxes on the conference table. "When I found these CIA documents and radio equip-ment in Mr. Clark's vehicle, I confiscated them and his personal effects and placed everything under our protective custody until they could be turned over to your agency. I wanted to ensure their protection."

"Thank you very much, Trooper Owen," said Fortson. "I certainly ap-preciate your protection of Wayne's personal effects and CIA property. I will forward a letter of commendation to your Troop Commander in ap-preciation for your conscientious efforts.

"Thank you, Director Fortson. Just doing my job."

Terry Fortson arranged an overnight stay in Miami. The following morning he planned to survey the CIA regional headquarters in downtown Miami and assess Bethany's damage. Escorted to the Hilton where he would reside overnight, Fortson gathered Clark's Assistant Deputy Direc-tors in the hotel conference room for a debriefing.

"Until Wayne is able to return to work, I am appointing you, Robert, as the interim Deputy Chief for Caribbean and Latin America Analysis," Fortson announced.

"Thank you, Director Fortson," Robert Hanner replied.

Fortson handed Hanner the parcel marked "Personal Effects."

"Incidentally, Robert, here are Wayne's billfold, badge, watch, and a few other personal effects that were turned over to me by the Florida trooper that investigated the accident scene. Please secure these for him until he is released from the hospital, if you would."

"Be glad to, sir."

"These remaining parcels are supposedly CIA property. Documents and electronic equipment I believe," Fortson acknowledged as he handed over the remaining carefully wrapped and sealed parcels. "Please examine the contents carefully and have any documents returned to file and the electronic equipment tested for damage."

"I'll have that done tonight, sir," Hanner promised.

Hanner greeted Terry Fortson the next morning as he arrived at the Brickell Avenue headquarters. The Director was pleased to see that the building had survived relatively unscathed.

"Good morning, Director Fortson," he said reservedly.

"Good morning, Robert," Fortson said quizzically. He noticed a perplexed look on Hanner's face. "What seems to be the matter?"

"Uhh, just a little puzzled about something, sir," Hanner began. "It's concerning a radio that was seized from Mr. Clark's vehicle. We found it among the contents of one of the boxes you gave us last night. I've had our Miami electronics experts take a careful look at it, and its complexity has them somewhat baffled. They report that they have never seen anything quite like it before."

Terry Fortson's brow creased in bewilderment as he listened to Hanner's discussion.

"Could you tell me, sir," Hanner asked, "is the agency experimenting with a new communication device which might have been made available only to your staff and the regional directors?"

"Certainly not." Fortson replied. "Let's take a look at what you have."

"Here, sir," Robert Hanner said as he handed the radio to the Director. After initial examination, the radio had been carefully sealed in plastic so as not to contaminate it. "I believe Agent Halpin, our chief electronics expert, can best describe what they have discovered."

"Please, go ahead," Fortson said, nodding at Halpin.

"Thank you, sir," Halpin began. "In 23 years of service to the CIA, I have never seen such a sophisticated communication device. We worked throughout the night trying to decipher its transmission mechanics. Fortunately, its battery charger was found among the boxed contents. After recharging the battery, we were able to activate the radio."

"Please continue," said Fortson.

"Well, like I said, sir, this is one more complicated and sophisticated transmitter. We were successful in transmitting an electronic signal, but could receive no intelligible vocalizations on either an amplitude or frequency modulation receptor - only wavelength sound patterns on an oscilloscope. That's unheard of, sir, even considering the military's most so-phisticated voice communication scramblers."

Halpin continued, "It appears, sir, that this radio has a built-in cloak-ing device that scrambles the voice pattern into an unintelligible garble of numbers and letters. These transmissions are virtually indecipherable without the use of a similar radio at the receiving end of the communica-tion to unscramble the transmission."

"I can assure you, sir," Halpin continued, "someone has paid millions of dollars for production of this device. The only firm I'm aware of that is capable of development of a transmitter of such complexity as this would be the Japanese company, Onyxitron. In support of this supposition, sev-eral of the component parts identified are indeed, those produced exclu-sively by Onyxitron."

"Onyxitron!" Terry Fortson exclaimed. "Isn't that the corporation that manufactured the radios the BSDIA confiscated near Nogales last year?"

"The same manufacturer, sir, but not the same radio. This radio is far more sophisticated than those confiscated in Arizona." Hanner answered.

Halpin continued. "For some time we have known that Onyxitron has been experimenting with communication scrambling devices. From our testing of this radio, apparently they have been quite successful."

"And that's not the most interesting issue we have to report, sir," Hanner added. "It seems that this radio produces the same sound wave patterns that we, the FBI, and the BSDIA have been trying unsuccessfully for over a year now to decipher. We've tried many times to identify a point of origin for the transmissions, again unsuccessfully."

"Are you telling me that this radio is the likely source of the South Florida signals that the BSDIA has intercepted and suspected was com-municating with drug dealers in South and Central America?" Fortson asked incredulously.

"It's a very high probability, sir. If not this radio, certainly one just like it." Hanner replied.

"It appears then," Fortson stated, "that Onyxitron seems to the chosen manufacturer for drug cartel's communication devices."

"It would certainly seem so, sir," Halpin agreed.

"I can't imagine what Clark would be doing with this radio in his pos-session, unless he is working with the drug smugglers. I certainly hope he has a plausible explanation." the Director mused to himself.

"Until we gain further information on this, gentlemen, I want an around-the-clock armed guard placed on Wayne Clark's room and on the

Miami office."

"Yes, sir," Hanner replied. "I will arrange it immediately."

"Clark is a good agent," Fortson added. "It's certainly possible that he has a plausible explanation for having this device in his possession."

Fortson tried to hold at bay the troubling thought that one of his most trusted agents might be guilty of heading the largest drug smuggling ring in American history. "We must remember that Clark remains innocent until proven guilty," he said to those gathered in the room.

"Of course, sir," Hanner replied.

"I must return to Washington immediately," Fortson said. "I'll take the radio back to Langley for further evaluation. Notify me immediately when Clark regains consciousness. I want to interrogate him personally. Do not alert him that we are suspicious of anything. Understood?"

"Perfectly, sir," both Hanner and Halpin replied.

"Good day, gentlemen."

CHAPTER TWENTY-TWO

Terry Fortson was perplexed. He remained mystified as to why Clark had been in possession of such a complex communication device. The only explanation he could imagine puzzled him even further. Was Clark involved in some nefarious drug smuggling scheme? Langley had positively identified the manufacturer as Japan's Onyxitron Electronics. CIA experts had also identified Clark's fingerprints at various locations within the unit.

Halpin and his staff had been careful to wear gloves and not contaminate any fingerprint evidence when they examined the unit. CIA electronics experts at Langley had discovered Clark's fingerprints throughout the interior casing of the Onyxitron as well as the exterior. The Langley findings certainly supported the Director's disturbing theory. Surely, it would be difficult for Clark to explain why his fingerprints had been discovered so readily within the Onyxitron unless the unit belonged to him.

Terry Fortson was resolved to either clear Clark of any suspicion of impropriety or bring him to justice if it could be proven that he was involved in any illegal activity. There would be no whitewash, no cover-up for his Deputy Caribbean Chief. If he should be implicated, Wayne Clark would face the same fate as any drug lord. Fortson feared the evidence would confirm his worst fears.

Thirty-six hours later, Wayne Clark awoke from his coma. The bright lights of the intensive care ward greeted him as he regained consciousness. "Where am I?" he asked groggily of the CIA agent on duty. In preparation of his awakening, surveillance agents had been instructed to respond to Clark's questions only in vague generalities.

"In the hospital, sir," Agent Porter replied. "Just lie still, while I summon your doctor." After notifying Clark's physician, Porter contacted Terry Fortson who made immediate plans to return to Miami.

Clark's doctors ordered a battery of tests to assess his health status. The tests indicated that he had suffered no ill effects from his loss of consciousness. The doctors expected him to make a full recovery.

Clark lay quietly, surveying his surroundings. Hoping he had regained his full faculties, Clark tried to remember. He recalled the accident with clarity. Realizing his memory was intact, Clark made a hasty physical assessment. Though he was sore, he found no broken bones and was happy to find all his limbs properly functional.

Suddenly he remembered that the Onyxitron was in his Tahoe when he lost control of the vehicle. A troubling fear gripped him. He glanced about the room, frantically searching for his personal belongings. Finding none, he feared the worse - the agency had found the Onyxitron. He knew he must contrive a plausible story to explain possession of the radio and he must do so quickly.

Terry Fortson arrived at the hospital within four hours of Clark's return to consciousness. During the preceding 48 hours, the Director had carefully detailed a plan to extract the truth from Clark. Fortson knew his interrogation was paramount to the CIA's integrity.

"Hello, Wayne. Welcome back," Fortson began, smiling warmly as he walked to Clark's bedside and shook hands. "I was so relieved to hear that you had regained consciousness. You gave us all quite a scare, you know." Fortson spoke in a fatherly tone. Clark searched the Director's eyes for any hint that this was just a social visit. He found none. Though Fortson smiled, the coldness in his eyes belied his kindness and the warmth in his voice.

"Sorry to have done that, sir. It's nice of you to come," Clark responded, trying to relax his voice. Looking into Fortson's steely eyes, Wayne Clark knew any pretext of deception would be useless. He was certain his ruse had been discovered. Just how much the Director knew about his smuggling operation, Clark could not determine from Fortson's demeanor. He felt his mouth become dry and his breathing labored. If forced, he would admit as little possible in an effort to retain at least a portion of his acquired wealth.

Clark's obvious apprehension in seeing Fortson conveyed the one signal that the Director had hoped he would not see. Clark was tense; not at all relaxed as would be someone with nothing to hide. Even before he began his interrogation, the Director knew Clark's visible anxiety evidenced his guilt. Of what, and to what extent, he did not know. It would not take him long to find out.

"Agent Anson," Fortson called, glancing towards the corridor door of the intensive care unit. One of Clark's Deputy Assistants entered the room holding a cardboard box. With the slightest trace of a smile, Fortson said,

"Clark, here are your personal effects. The trooper who chanced upon your accident secured these and a few other items found in your vehicle."

Staring intently at Fortson, then at the box, Clark simply replied, "Thank you, sir."

Maybe it's not in there. Clark thought. Maybe they didn't find it. Maybe the radio was thrown from the Tahoe during the accident and hadn't yet been recovered. Maybe things aren't as bad as I think they are. Maybe. Just maybe. Please let it be so, he prayed silently.

As if he were reading Clark's thoughts, Fortson turned towards the door and called out in a more intense voice, "Agent Halpin." Halpin appeared, not with a box in hand, but holding the Onyxitron Encryptor. Clark's heart sunk, his eyes widened, and his expression immediately changed to a look of dismay as Halpin handed the radio to the Director.

"Care to discuss this?" Fortson asked coldly, holding the radio up for Clark to see. The Director knew Clark's next few responses would either establish his innocence or confirm his guilt. Almost from the moment he regained consciousness and remembered the Onyxitron, in the likely event he would be asked, Clark had rehearsed his response to Fortson's question.

"Oh good. You have it," he said quickly with feigned relief. "I was afraid the radio was lost. I just came across it last week and had returned to the office to retrieve it, just in case the storm damaged our building. I don't quite know what it is, other than a uniquely designed radio, but I felt it important enough to risk returning to the office in the midst of the hurricane to retrieve."

"Yes, as you say, it is quite unique," Fortson replied. "Why don't you describe the CIA analysis, Agent Halpin?" the Director invited.

"Langley reports that it is the most sophisticated and technologically advanced communication device that we have ever encountered," Halpin offered.

"How did you say this came into your possession?" Fortson queried. His voice switched from intense interrogator to friendly inquisitor.

"I didn't, sir. I only said I received it last week," Clark said in a hurt voice.

"Please continue, then," Fortson invited pleasantly.

"Well, just last week, when we arrested Constantine Destrosky off the coast of Honduras, I found this radio in his possession. I've tried unsuccessfully to communicate with any of his Bulgarian compatriots. I kept the radio in case anyone tried to communicate with him. I didn't recognize any markings on the cover when I inspected it, so I thought it might be valuable to the Agency. That's why I returned to the office to retrieve it."

"Did you say you inspected the radio inside and out?" Fortson questioned.

"No, I didn't disassemble it." Clark replied. "I was afraid I might compromise the integrity of some of the integral components." Clark became extremely nervous. Fortson had blindsided him with that question. His response had been extemporaneous, and as soon as he said it, he knew it was the wrong answer. He suddenly turned ashen.

This was not the answer and response Fortson had hoped Clark would give; yet it was what he had feared he might receive. He had caught his Deputy Chief in a lie. Desperately hoping that his interrogation would exonerate Clark of any wrongdoing, the Director was nevertheless prepared to deal with this result. Knowing Clark's innocence was now seriously in question; Terry Fortson knew he had to press on discerning the truth.

A faint smile crossed the Director's face. Fortson glanced at Halpin, who knew the Director had just opened the one door that would lead to Clark's downfall. Halpin also knew the Director would be unrelenting in his pursuit of the truth. Fortson would no longer afford Clark the courtesy of perceived innocence. It would now be a full criminal interrogation.

"There's seems to be a little problem with your answer, Clark," Fortson said.

"What do you mean, sir?" Clark asked as incredulously as possible.

"If you didn't open the radio, would you care to explain how your fingerprints were found throughout the interior of the case and on the rechargeable battery?" Terry Fortson asked icily.

Clark said nothing. He just lay there, staring at the ceiling.

"So you have nothing to say for yourself?" Fortson chided.

"What do you want me to say?" Clark asked diffidently.

"We know this radio is likely the source of transmission of signals we have been monitoring for the past two years between South Florida, the northern Florida panhandle, and somewhere in Central America. When we found your fingerprints in the case, we concluded that you must be a part of that communication triangle."

"You're wrong, Mr. Fortson. So what if I forgot that I had opened the case? That doesn't make me guilty of anything other than a poor memory. I guess the accident just made me forgetful."

"Nice try, Clark. I once considered you a friend, as well as one of my most trusted agents. You belied that trust, and now I am quite disgusted with you. You're a disgrace to the CIA. I've half a good a mind to let Halpin and Anson have about an hour alone with you. I'm quite certain they can refresh your memory."

"Oh, please do, sir," Halpin jokingly pleaded, rubbing his hands together as if in expectation. "Leave us alone with him for a while. We'll wrangle the truth out of him!"

Clark looked around wild-eyed, expecting an attack any second from one of these brutes. "Okay, okay. I'll talk," he said.

"Mirandize him first, Anson," the Director said.

"My pleasure, sir." Anson read Clark his Miranda rights, then remarked in disgust, "You certainly are a disgrace to the CIA, Clark. Your possession of this radio alone is evidence that you're involved in a widespread drug smuggling scheme."

Fortson made it clear to Clark. "You know you're going to prison, Clark," he said. "What you say now may well determine where you spend a significant portion of the rest of your life. Will it be in Leavenworth with the criminals you helped arrest and convict? Or at a minimum-security prison away from the threat of danger of those you sent to prison? It's your choice, Clark and I'm in no bargaining mood. It would be best for you to just come clean."

Clark knew he was defeated. Hoping for a lighter sentence, he cooperated with the Director's every question.

"My partner is Juan Carlos Diego," he began. For the next half hour, excluding the St. Marks role in the partnership, Clark gave every detail of their underwater smuggling operation except the St. Marks details role.

He implicated the Belizean plant and its smuggling role. Clark discussed the Cuban stopover and its vital role in the smuggling plot. Clark chose not to implicate Miguel Thomas. He hoped to forewarn Thomas with his one permitted phone call. He also hoped Thomas would move and protect his money. Surely, Thomas would do this for him in exchange for not implicating him.

I'm still relatively young, Clark thought. Maybe, just maybe, with good behavior, I can get out of prison and enjoy some of my money. Thomas was now his only hope for the future. A future once assured of fabulous wealth had been ruined by a freak storm and a simple traffic accident.

Clark explained that his part in the smuggling scheme was to distribute their illegal drugs through his distribution network. When asked how they smuggled their drugs undetected into the U.S., Clark informed Fortson that they employed a submarine to deliver their drug cargo. In his confession, he lied when stated that they offloaded their cargo onto local fishing boats working out of the Tampa area.

When pressed, again, he lied. To protect the St. Marks refinery, Clark said that Diego was in charge of the maritime drug smuggling operation, and that he only managed the distribution network throughout the U.S.

"I swear, sir, I don't know anything else about Diego's submarine operation. All I can tell you about is my distribution pipeline throughout the U.S. Sir, I'm coming clean with you. I'll tell you everything I know. Will you tell the AG that I cooperated with you?"

"That I promise, Clark, but I can give you no assurances of how he will perceive your cooperation," Fortson replied.

Next, Clark identified the Atlanta, New York, California, and Chicago lieutenants who were his national distribution network operatives. Swearing that he had told them all he knew, Clark was transferred to the Miami FBI office where he was taken into federal custody. There, he was permitted his one phone call.

"Please, oh please, answer the phone, Thomas," Clark cried as he dialed Thomas' number in the living quarters at the St. Marks refinery. He was lucky. It was dinnertime. Thomas was just sitting down to eat.

"Thomas, this is Wayne Clark. Don't talk. Just listen." In his two minutes of permitted phone time, Clark informed Miguel of his arrest and of his interrogation by the CIA Director. Wayne explained his answers and why he had not implicated him. He gave Thomas his account number at Grand Cayman Capital Trust.

Miguel Thomas listened attentively. He told Wayne Clark to "take it easy" and assured him that he would transfer his money immediately. Thomas promised Clark that he would stay in touch. Michael Thomas knew he must act quickly and decisively.

Bethany had tracked its way across Miami northwards through South Central Florida. Steered to the north-northeast by a mid-western clockwise high, Bethany finally exited the Florida coast at Jacksonville. Downgraded to a Category 1 storm shortly after it broached land, Bethany nevertheless pelted coastal communities with six inches of rain and an eight-foot high-tide surge. The accompanying tide wall flooded communities already damaged by the hurricane force winds. Floridians had not seen this extent of damage since Hurricane Andrew a decade earlier.

A. Bixby Lane was on route to Orlando even before Bethany exited the north Jacksonville barrier islands. He had scooped Douglas and the Republicans with his presence in the disaster area. Members of the national press corps and cable networks had been invited on A. Bixby's impromptu trip.

Their cameras and microphones captured his every word. Lane questioned the President and Vice President's absence. "To the residents of Florida whose lives have been devastated by Bethany," he spoke into the cameras, "I promise my full cooperation from within the U.S. House of Representatives. I believe in helping Americans affected by such disaster rebuilt their homes and restart your lives."

"With the hurricane hardly off the Florida coast," one network anchor reported, "A. Bixby Lane is on the scene, surveying the resultant damage, and offering aid and comfort to Bethany's disaster victims. Lane has already promised to promote legislation to provide low-interest federal loans to those who have lost so much in the aftermath of this hurricane."

Moments later in the Oval Office, only a token moment of airtime was given to Edward Walters as he signed a Federal Emergency Management Agency directive declaring Florida a federal disaster area. The declaration would release millions of disaster relief dollars to provide manpower to aid Florida in its cleanup efforts, and provide the low-interest reconstruction loans to disaster victims that Lane had promoted.

"As requested by Florida Governor Gerrett Newton, I am designating the state of Florida as a federal disaster area," Walters pronounced. "I send assurances to Florida residents impacted by the storm that the full resources of the federal government are now at your disposal. This afternoon, along with Governor Newton, FEMA officials will survey the scope of Bethany's damage. In a cooperative effort with the Florida Emergency Management Agency, the federal government will help you rebuild your homes and restore your local communities."

Despite the President's declaration, the national media continued to designate a significant portion of its coverage to Bixby Lane's on-the-scene activities. For two days, Lane toured coastal communities devastated by the hurricane. It made little difference to the media that most of those whose property was destroyed by the storm had already received a FEMA number, legitimizing them for federal disaster aid.

Conducted only one week before the Democratic National Convention, Lane's cross-Florida stops were again deemed "among the Senator's finest hours." Little did Lane know that his political career would have few remaining 'finest hours'.

Edna Parrish, the switchboard operator for the Northeastern Export Company, took a strange long distance phone call. "Please have Mr. Bixby Lane call Betisto Mariquez at 01-0989-5555 in Montego Bay, Jamaica, as soon as possible." She had no idea that the export company was a subsidiary wholly owned by the Democratic Presidential candidate. She called Ed Gaines Ferguson, the company CEO, and informed him of the unusual message.

"What's that mean?" she asked of the CEO.

"I'm not sure," he replied, "but I'll handle it."

Other than the company's legal counsel, only Ferguson knew that Bixby Lane owned the company. He had never questioned Lane's request that he do so, but for almost sixteen years, Ed Gaines had been curious why Lane had requested that he send two monthly company checks in amounts of $7,500 and $2,500 to the Sister Margaret Child Care Mission in Jamaica.

Ed Gaines had his suspicions, and now perhaps he had his opportunity to find out why. Ferguson had tried unsuccessfully for years to persuade Lane to sell him the export company. Now he was certain that if his suspicion was correct, he would have no problem persuading Lane to sell, and sell quickly.

Santiago's grandfather answered Ferguson's phone call. "Mariquez residence," he said.

"Hello, Mr. Mariquez. My name is Ed Gaines Ferguson. I am the CEO of the Northeastern Export Company. I believe you left a message for Mr. Bixby Lane to call you as soon as possible?"

"Yes. I did."

"Mr. Lane is unavailable to talk to you at the moment. He asked that I call on his behalf. He wanted me to ask what he could do for you."

"Well, I wanted to tell him that his son's mother, our daughter Simone, died this week in the hurricane that came through Ocho Rios. His son, Santiago, was unhurt and is now living with us in Montego Bay."

Acknowledging no surprise at the announcement that Lane was father to another son, Ed Gaines feigned a mournful reply, "I am so sorry to hear that, Mr. Mariquez. I am sure that Mr. Lane will also be very distressed to hear the news." He now understood why Lane had requested that he send $10,000 each month to Sister Margaret's Child Care Mission. His suspicion had been correct. "So Lane has a son in Jamaica born out of wedlock," he mused. "How interesting!"

"Thank you for the information, Mr. Mariquez. I will inform Mr. Lane right away of Simone's untimely death. Incidentally, I am the one who has forwarded Mr. Lane's checks each month to Sister Margaret's Child Care Mission. Would you now want the checks forwarded to you in Montego Bay?"

"Yes, please. That is the other purpose for my call. Before she died, Simone promised Santiago that his father would continue to provide for him according to the terms of his signed agreement."

"And I promise you and Santiago that he will continue to do so," Ferguson said as he wrote down Betisto Mariquez's address.

"If you can promise that, Mr. Ferguson, there is no need for Mr. Lane to call," Betisto replied. "All I want is assurance that Santiago will be well-cared-for where he can have hope for a bright future."

"Believe me, sir, you have my assurance on that."

Ferguson dialed Lane's office. "I'd like to leave a message for Mr. Lane," he said. "Please have him call Ed Gaines Ferguson as soon as possible. He has the number. I have a message for him that is a matter of extreme personal urgency. I need to talk with him today."

"I'll give him the message, sir," replied a Lane campaign operative. "He should be able to return your call within the hour."

"Hello, Ed Gaines. I understand you have an urgent personal message for me?" Lane asked questionably.

"Hello, yourself, Bixby. Yes I do. Are you sitting down?" Ferguson queried.

"Yes I am. Why do you ask?" Lane queried with some hesitation.

Ferguson answered abruptly. "I just received a phone call from Betisto Mariquez. You do know who he is, don't you?"

"Uhh, Yes. Yes, I do," Lane said haltingly.

Ferguson continued, "He asked to speak to you. I told him you were unavailable, but I would glad to take a message. He asked me to inform you that Santiago's mother, Simone, died this week from injuries she received when Bethany passed through Ocho Rios. He also wanted to let you know that your son, Santiago, is unharmed and is now living with them in Montego Bay."

There was nothing but silence from Lane. Hearing no response, Ed Gaines remarked, "Uhh, hello, Bixby. Are you still there?"

"Yes. Yes, I'm still here," he said almost in whisper.

"I suppose that you're just a little stunned to learn that someone else knows you are the father of a son born out of wedlock," Ferguson exclaimed, adding insult to injury. "I also expect that you are quite shocked to hear this from me."

"Yes. Yes, I certainly am," Lane admitted although he displayed no remorse in learning that the mother of his illegitimate son was dead.

"Shocked that Simone is dead or that I know you have an illegitimate son?" Ed Gaines asked sarcastically.

"Both, quite frankly," Lane lied. "Uhh, say, listen, Ed, I'm sure you understand my concerns for keeping this information confidential, don't you?"

"Why, of course I do, Bixby. I'm quite certain that if this information became public knowledge, it would have, shall we say, quite a negative impact on your campaign," Ferguson laughed. "Would it not, Bixby?"

"Of course it would. Uhh, I certainly hope you will keep this bit of information to yourself, Ed Gaines," Lane said pleadingly.

"That all depends," Ferguson replied.

"Uhh, depends upon what?" Lane asked hesitantly.

"On whether you are now interested in selling me the company," Ferguson quipped.

"Ed Gaines, it seems I suddenly have an extreme interest in divesting myself of ownership of Northeastern Export," Lane quickly replied.

"I had rather thought you might," Ferguson said flippantly.

"I'll direct the company attorney to draw up the necessary papers today," Lane promised.

"Today would be fine," said Ferguson.

"And, incidentally, write this address down. You do understand that you now need to make arrangements for another entity other than Northeastern Export to forward Mr. Mariquez the money he's expecting each month for Santiago's care."

"I understand perfectly," Lane said.

With the assistance of the Belizean government and a dozen of its military officers, Rick Tolbert and a contingency of BSDIA agents invaded the Belizean sugarcane processing plant. Caught completely off guard, Ortega Diego, his 'chemists,' Peter Segonyva, and Vedonosti Novostey were arrested.

The processing facility was placed under the protective custody and temporary management of the Belizean government. The sugarcane mill had too great an economic impact on the Corozal economy to simply cease operation. Its payroll essentially supported the entire economy of Cerros;

to close it would have devastated the financial infrastructure of the district. The legitimate end of the sugarcane processing business brought in a considerable profit.

Government officials were astounded that such an elaborate smuggling setup was uncovered within the confines of the processing plant. Even Rick Tolbert was amazed at the proficiency of the easily-disguised operation. He was disappointed, though, that the transport submarine was not discovered at the facility.

Although he had arrested two of the submarine commanders, neither they, nor Diego, nor his chemists were cooperative. Even when promised a substantially reduced sentence to divulge information about the present location of the mini-sub, none would do so.

"All else considered," Tolbert thought, "it has still been a pretty good week's work for the BSDIA."

Seated at his dinner table, Juan Carlos stared at the television in stunned disbelief as a CNN Special News Report interrupted its sports programming. "Busted!" read the caption below the pictures and names of Wayne Clark and Juan Carlos's brother, Ortega Diego.

CNN news analyst, Kristina Myers began her report, "BSDIA Director Richard Tolbert disclosed at a press conference that ended just a few minutes ago, that with the arrest of Wayne Payton Clark, Ortega Diego, their principle cocaine processors in Belize, and network distributors in the U.S., America's largest drug smuggling ring has essentially been dismantled. In their raid of the drug network's principle U.S. distribution centers, BSDIA agents recovered an astounding $310 million in cash. Neatly wrapped and packaged, and ready for transport out of the country."

Myers continued. Her narrative described the events leading to the arrests of Clark and Diego and detailed their roles in the smuggling organization. "Ortega Diego, the brother of the notorious international drug smuggler, Juan Carlos Diego, ran the drug ring's cocaine processing plant in Belize. From there, Juan Carlos' cocaine was smuggled into the U.S. by submarine transport."

"Until his arrest," Myers said, "Wayne Clark served as the CIA's Deputy Chief for Caribbean and Latin American Analysis. At today's BSDIA press conference, CIA Director Terry Fortson expressed shock and dismay that one of his most trusted operatives had lead a double life as one of the ring leaders of the largest drug smuggling operation ever discovered in America."

"Tolbert concluded his press conference by saying that with the raid on the Belizean cocaine processing plant, the arrest of Ortega Diego and his cocaine processors, and the arrest of Wayne Clark and key players in the distribution network, the BSDIA has all but closed down Juan Carlos Diego's smuggling empire."

Too stunned to speak or even move, Juan Carlos stared blankly at the television, trying to convince himself that perhaps he really did not see or hear what he thought he had just seen and heard. "No. No. No," he finally screamed. "Surely, it can't be true. I'll call Ortega. I know he'll answer the phone." Hurriedly he dialed Ortega's private office number at the mill. A recorded message left by Rick Tolbert greeted his call.

"Hello, you have reached the office of Ortega Diego. I'm afraid he's not here now to receive your call. Mr. Diego is presently in the federal penitentiary at Leavenworth, Kansas. If you would like to leave a message he should be able to return your call in about 50 years."

Diego slammed the phone down, letting out a stream of expletives. Next, he placed a call to Miguel Thomas.

In less than 48 hours, Lane's attorneys had drawn up the necessary legal papers for the sale of Northeastern Export Company. Ferguson was finally the owner of the company he had built; the company that, over time, had helped to make A. Bixby Lane a wealthy man. Despite finally having ownership of the company he had tried for years to purchase, Ed Gaines Ferguson was still a frustrated and angry man.

Ferguson still harbored resentment for Lane's longstanding refusal to give him any share of the considerable annual profits realized by the company. Each year they had argued over giving Ferguson even a small bonus. Though Lane paid him an excellent salary, like other corporate CEO's, Ferguson felt he should have automatically received a bonus consistent with his hard work and the company's profits. He had stayed with Northeastern Export with the dream that one day he would have the opportunity to purchase the company from Lane.

Today, that dream had finally become a reality. Today should have been a happy day. But it was not. Ed Gaines still seethed over the bonuses Lane had denied him; bonuses he was certain would have paid a substantial amount of the purchase price of the mill. It was payback time. Ferguson wanted to show Lane what it had been like over the years to be denied a share of the mill's profits.

Suddenly, he smiled. It was two days before the Democratic National Convention, which had been billed as if it were Lane's coronation day, the defining moment of a future president. Ed Gaines Ferguson was determined that he would dethrone the would-be king. He would take this moment from Lane as Lane had taken priceless reward from him.

With equal disbelief, Michael Thomas had watched the same CNN Special News Report as Juan Carlos Diego. CNN had just returned to its regular sports programming when Thomas' phone seemed to ring with a certain urgency. Before he could even say so much as "hello," Juan Carlos shouted at him. "Thomas, Thomas. Have you heard the news?"

"Oh, are you referring to the CNN Special News Report?" asked Thomas facetiously.

"Yes, of course, the CNN News Special!" Diego screamed, failing to note Thomas' sense of amusement at his question. "What are we going to do?"

"You mean, what are you going to do, Juan Carlos? Have you forgotten that you still owe Juan Tierra Barona the principle amount of his $310 million?"

Juan Carlos did not immediately answer. Distraught at having just learned that their smuggling empire had suddenly crumbled, he had all but forgotten about his debt to Barona. Finally, he replied, "I'm so upset, I haven't thought about that. I can't pay him back. My expenses have been so great that without the partnership's financial help, I don't have enough money to even begin to repay Barona. Can you help me, Miguel?"

"You know I have less than $80 million in Grand Cayman. I'll loan you that if it will help," Thomas replied nonchalantly.

"That won't be enough. Even with your and Ortega's money, I would still be about $100 million short. Perhaps Barona will let me owe him the balance," Diego reasoned.

"Hardly," Thomas stated unequivocally. "Remember his stipulation when we agreed to sell his cocaine? 'Either pay me my money or return the cocaine. Or else.' I think we both know what 'or else' means," Miguel said solemnly.

"Yeah. I think we do."

Frantic to devise a plan to repay Juan Tierra, Diego remarked hopefully, "Maybe we can get Clark's money out of Grand Cayman Capitol Trust. Yeah, that's it! We'll wire his money and mine on to Juan Tierra."

"Not without Wayne's account number you won't, and I don't think he's of any mind to help you out right now," reminded Thomas. "What are you going to do?"

"Maybe I can reason with Barona. Promise to pay him back next year," Diego said optimistically.

"Good luck!" Thomas said. "Do you think a promise will buy you any time when Juan Tierra knows your smuggling and distribution system is in shambles?"

"You're right. I guess I have no choice but to seek asylum somewhere. At least until I can think of a way to repay Barona."

"You can always come to St. Marks and hide out," Thomas remarked casually. "No one, especially Juan Tierra, would ever think of looking for you here."

"You are right, Amigo, that would certainly be the safest place for me to go into exile. Nobody, not even Rick Tolbert, would think of looking for me there," Diego said.

"I think you ought to consider it," Thomas said suggestively.

"That's probably my best option, but being on the FBI's Most Wanted List, I hate to even consider coming to America. I think first I'll try to hide out somewhere in Central or South America, or in Mexico. If that doesn't work out, I will call you to make arrangements to come to St. Marks."

"When you are ready, come, Amigo. Vladimir Kerchenkov and Nicholas Krasnaya are safe here. You are welcome to come and join them," Thomas urged. "If you don't feel safe elsewhere, give me a call and we'll make plans for them to transport you here in the mini-sub."

"Gracias, Amigo."

CHAPTER TWENTY-THREE

The Democratic National Convention began as an event of celebration. A festive mood prevailed among conventioneers in Phoenix. The downtown avenues and the Phoenix Convention Center were festooned with Democratic blue. Street vendors hawked donkey emblem souvenirs in every conceivable manner of sale.

The Democrat faithful bought the souvenirs by the bagful. It would be a convention to remember for decades. They all wanted a piece of history. The DNC was certain they would retake the White House come next January. By their calculations, the Democrats estimated they would gain four senate seats. Already holding a majority in the House, they projected they would control both houses of Congress.

For two days, conventioneers eagerly awaited the official state vote count. Though already assured the nomination, A. Bixby Lane watched from his hotel suite as the votes were tabulated. For weeks he had prepared his acceptance speech. After officially receiving the nomination, Lane hastily made his way to the Convention Center to receive the accolades of the delegates. This was A. Bixby's shining moment and yet another opportunity for national television exposure. The nation awaited.

U.S. Secret Service agents escorted Lane as he strolled through the underground passageway on route to the convention floor. On closed-circuit televisions strategically placed around the convention center, the conventioneers watched Lane's approach to the stage. FOX News reporter Paige Jacobs had stationed herself in the outer corridor. She shouted to Lane as he prepared to ascend the steps to the stage, "Mr. President! Or at least the next 'Mr. President,'" she said, "Will you take a moment to say 'hello' to the FOX News nation?"

Lane paused for the cameras. "Of course," he said graciously. He put his arm affectionately around her shoulder and smiled for the cameras. "Mr. President," she repeated as she held her mike for Lane to respond to her question.

"Not quite yet, Paige, but it appears I'm well on my way," he boasted.

"Yes, it would seem that all of American is only moments away from discovering your true Presidential attributes," Jacobs acknowledged. "Senator Lane, a major plank of your Democratic platform is your assertion that Americans must establish strong principles of character and morality as they develop a family values system."

"Yes, I have long advocated that in order for America to become a strong, moral society, American's must display a high standard of character and must establish a strong system of family values," he said, delighted at the reporter's mention of one of the key themes he would underscore in his upcoming speech.

"And you example your family and your life in doing so?"

"I do. I do," Lane professed, smiling broadly for the camera.

"Then, would you care to share with America why you have not disclosed the fact that you have an illegitimate 15-year-old son living in Jamaica?" Lane's arm fell from her shoulder. He took a step backwards.

"Whatever are you talking about?" He looked at her incredulously. "I have no son other than Augustine Bixby, Jr." The color faded from Lane's face. He appeared to grow faint. On the convention floor, Lane had been announced. The crowd eagerly awaited the acceptance speech from their party's anointed one.

The Secret Service agents grasped Lane's arms and assisted him as he ascended the steps to the stage. Gasps of surprise and cries of despair were heard around the convention floor as Lane stumbled to the podium as if in a drunken stupor. He was visibly shaken. He couldn't speak. He stared blankly around the convention center, trying to regain his composure. Finally, Lane muddled a semblance of an acceptance speech.

Americans just tuning in to the convention were shocked at his demeanor. Those who had seen the earlier interview were left stunned, both by the reporter's question and by Lane's reaction to the question.

Within 24 hours, America knew the truth; the whole truth. Every half hour FOX News retold the story. They detailed how Lane's Jamaican fact-finding mission on trade relations while a member of the British West Indies Trade Relations Committee 16 years earlier had led to his dalliance with a young Jamaican waitress who had borne Lane's illegitimate son.

FOX replayed Lane's return interview at Washington National where he had been asked to describe their trade relation's venture. Americans were sickened to see Lane's wry smile as he had exclaimed for the cameras, "In our short trip, we discovered much of Jamaica's natural beauty."

The Democratic National Convention ended in confusion on the grandest scale. Lane's staunchest political allies attempted unsuccessfully to lessen the impact of his infidelity. The American people simply would not tolerate another cover-up of this magnitude. Never again would moral America elect a presidential candidate with such amoral character. Americans attacked Lane's infidelity with a vengeance. The public outcry did not go unnoticed by the news media.

Many of the same press corps that had lavished the candidate with generous coverage and praise now denounced his credibility. Bixby Lane had lost more than his bid for the presidency; his political career was over. In a nationally televised broadcast, Lane tearfully renounced his candidacy and withdrew from the presidential race. The Democratic Party was left in shambles.

Despite his best campaign efforts, even the affable Terrell Sheffield was unable to overcome the damage A. Bixby Lane had brought to the Democratic Party. In a resounding 72 percent of the popular vote, Charles Douglas was elected President of the United States in the November election.

In his congratulatory phone call to Douglas, the gentlemanly Sheffield praised Douglas for a well-deserved win and pledged his cooperation and that of the Democratic Party.

"America has seen enough congressional bickering," Sheffield acknowledged. "It's time for bipartisanship to portend something other than just lip service. It's time to put aside our differences and for once, seek a legislative agenda of issues that are in the best interest of America and of all Americans. To this end, you have my pledge of support."

Douglas foresaw that this was the dawn of a new day in American politics. Edward Walters watched with pride as his Vice President took the Oath of Office. Though his neurological problems had worsened, Walters descended the Capitol steps to watch Douglas assume the highest office in the land. Content in the knowledge that his prodigy would continue his executive philosophy of compassionate conservatism, Walters took great pride in his own term as President and the success of his Vice President.

"The American electorate has demonstrated that principled men of decency, honor, and character are of foremost importance in American politics," Edward Walters said proudly to Claire as Charles Douglas completed his oath.

Miguel Thomas, Kerchenkov, and Krasnaya were watching the Pro Bowl game on CBS when the phone interrupted their evening.

"Buenos Nochas, Miguel," Juan Carlos said as Thomas answered.

"Juan Carlos," Thomas replied, "It's good to hear from you! It's been almost five months since we've last talked."

"Yes, I know, Miguel," Diego began. "I'm tired of running and hiding. I'm ready to come to St. Marks. I've finalized my plans."

"Excellent, Amigo. What are they?"

"My private jet will fly me to Cuba where the submarine can transport me to Florida," Diego replied.

"That sounds like a simple enough plan, Juan Carlos," said Thomas.

"Simple, but expensive. It will cost me $15 million dollars in payoffs to do so, but I have finally received permission from the Castro government to allow me to land in Cuba. I have talked with Hector Gomez. He has agreed to provide me with housing until Vladimir and Nicholas can transport me to St. Marks. How soon do you think they can be underway to pick me up? The sooner, the better."

"They're sitting right here with me. Let me ask them," Thomas answered.

"They say they can leave as soon as ten o'clock tomorrow night. Does that give you enough time to reach Cuba?"

"Yes, plenty of time. I will fly to Cuba early in the morning. I'll be waiting on them around 8:00 PM, day after tomorrow at the Arroyos de Mantua boathouse."

"Good," said Thomas. "It has long been my desire that you would some day be come to America. I am very excited that you are coming. You can't imagine how much I am looking forward to your arrival."

"Thank you, Amigo," said a dejected Juan Carlos. "Even under the circumstances, it will be good to see you, again."

"I assure you, Juan Carlos, when you finally arrive, the pleasure will be all mine!"

The following day, while Vladimir and Nicholas slept in preparation for their 10 o'clock departure for Cuba, Thomas' condominium was a blur of activity as he prepared for Juan Carlos Diego's arrival.

Shortly before 10:00 PM, the sub commanders backed the mini-sub out of the boathouse, beginning their roundtrip voyage to transport Juan Carlos back to Florida.

Reclining under his beach umbrella from the hot sun of Sandy Bay, Thomas sipped a cold Corona and lit a Montecristo Robustos. Oh, how he cherished this moment. He had awaited this day for his entire adult lifetime.

Earlier that morning after Vladimir and Nicholas had departed, Thomas drove to Tallahassee and boarded an early morning flight to Miami. By early afternoon, he arrived at Anthony's Key Resort on the Bay Islands off Roatan, Honduras. Here he would finally be able to execute the plan he had worked years to carefully design. Thomas dialed the number of the BSDIA headquarters in Washington, D.C.

"Richard Tolbert, please," Michael requested of the operator who answered his call.

"One moment please, and I'll connect you with his office."

"Director Tolbert's office," the secretary answered.

"Good afternoon. My name is Michael Thomas. I'd like to speak to the Director, please."

"I'm sorry, sir, but Mr. Tolbert is in conference. Would you like to leave a message?"

"Yes, please," said Thomas casually, "But I might suggest you give him the message immediately. Tell Mr. Tolbert that if he would like to know how he can capture Juan Carlos Diego, I can tell him how he can do so."

"One moment, sir," the secretary said. "I'm sure the Director won't mind my interrupting his meeting with this message."

"No, I don't imagine he will," replied Thomas, puffing on his fine Cuban cigar.

"Mr. Thomas, this is Rick Tolbert. I understand you have some information that might lead to the capture of Juan Carlos Diego. Do I understand correctly?"

"Yes, you do, Mr. Tolbert," Thomas said.

"Michael Thomas. Michael Thomas. Your name sounds familiar. Have we met?" Tolbert asked.

"Indeed, we have. You have a good memory. I believe my former employee, Bill Knox, introduced you to me when you and his brother, Lincoln, went trout fishing with him at St. Marks."

"Yes, I remember distinctly. I believe you weren't feeling very well when we met."

"That was just a ruse, Mr. Tolbert, in case you recognized me."

"I'm not sure I understand."

"You soon will, Mr. Tolbert."

"Please call me Rick," Tolbert advised. "As we departed, I felt there was something familiar about you. But I just couldn't quite put my finger on when or where I might have previously met you."

"I'm not surprised that you didn't recognize me, Rick. It has been over 15 years since we last met, and I was a lot younger looking then."

"I apologize, Michael, but I just can't remember the circumstances of that meeting," Tolbert advised.

"No apologies necessary. Before we discuss how you can capture Juan Carlos, I would like for you to know all the details leading to this phone call," Thomas said.

"Please continue, Michael. I have all afternoon."

"I was born in South Carolina. My father was in the Marine Corps. While I was in college, my father was honorably discharged from the Corps and was recruited by the DEA. Because he spoke fluid Spanish, he was assigned to a Caribbean task force charged with infiltrating South and Central American drug rings and supplying smuggling information to the DEA. He did such a good intelligence job," Thomas explained, "that he was singly responsible for providing the information that lead to the interdiction of hundreds of millions of dollars of Colombian drug shipments. One night in South Carolina, while he and my mother were returning from dinner, their car exploded and they were both killed."

"I'm sorry," Tolbert interjected.

"I was still a senior in college, and at the time I knew little of my father's work in the DEA. I only knew that he was gone from home quite a lot. Shortly after I graduated, I surreptitiously learned of my father's work for the DEA. I became certain that my parent's accident was indeed no accident at all. I learned that the explosion was, in fact, an attempt on my father's life for his success in gathering DEA intelligence information."

"Yes," Tolbert interrupted, "I now remember the case well. I had just started work for the FBI and was assigned to investigate the accident. The report of our investigation pointed to Juan Carlos Diego as the one responsible for ordering the assassination."

"The information in that report is what I came upon quite by accident," Thomas said.

"I guess there's no use asking how you happened upon the report."

"None, sir. That information must and will remain a mystery."

"Fair enough," Tolbert replied. "I attended your parents funeral and remember how staunchly brave you appeared to be in the face of the adversity of loosing both your parents in such a tragic way."

"Thank you for noting that."

"There's one small point in your story, Michael, that I can't quite reconcile."

"What's that?"

"Very simply, wasn't your father's name Thomas Miguel Michaels?"

"Yes, it was. I am Thomas M. Michaels, Jr., but I have gone by Michael Miguel Thomas to protect my real name. The day I learned the truth of my parent's death, I swore revenge against Juan Carlos Diego. I reordered my names to be better able to seek my revenge. When we met in St. Marks, I thought you might have recognized me. Frankly, I was afraid I might be unable to bring about my planned revenge if you started asking too many questions."

"That's why I tried to distance myself from you as soon as possible when we met," Thomas explained. "I still had a plan that was unfilled. It was a plan I was determined to carry out."

"This only explains part of why I called you," Thomas said.

"I'm intrigued," Tolbert prompted. "Please continue."

"My plan was not to seek my revenge by murdering Juan Carlos. Once I infiltrated the inner core of his 'family,' I could have done that anytime. For what he did to my parents, simply killing Diego would have been too easy on him. I wanted him arrested. I wanted him to suffer. I wanted to destroy him, his financially empire, and his entire drug smuggling operation. Only by accomplishing all three would I feel I had revenged my parent's death."

"I took me only a short time to plot my revenge," Thomas said. "But it took me 12 years to put my plan into effect. Shortly after I learned the truth about my parent's death, I began to think about how I could seek my revenge against Diego. To get to Juan Carlos, I knew I had to leave the U.S. and get into his smuggling backyard."

"I became a student of drug smuggling," Thomas confided in Tolbert. "I soon learned that a significant part of Juan Carlos' drug shipments were transported across the Colombian border into Panama. This was Diego's front for transporting his drugs out of Central America. At the port of La Palma, Diego's drugs were hidden in raw ore cargo containers and shipped overseas to the U.S."

Tolbert listened, amazed at Thomas's dedication to his cause.

"I took a job at the La Palma shipyards and soon became the chief load engineer for Diego's drug shipments. Before long, Juan Carlos took me to Colombia and made me one of his most trusted lieutenants. When the BSDIA intercepted three of Diego's largest drug shipments two years ago, he and Wayne Clark entered into a drug smuggling partnership establishing the Belize mill as their cocaine refinery. Their strategy employed use of a submarine to transport their drugs into the U.S."

"I will admit," Thomas told Tolbert, "that it was a very simple and effective scheme. His U.S. port of entrance for the submarine was the St. Marks Sugar Refinery. You were docked less than 50 yards from the minisub when Bill brought you to meet me."

"I wish I had known it at the time. I would have put Diego out of business that very day," Tolbert exclaimed.

"Yes, but only out of business. Remember my plan included not only destruction of his drug and financial empire, but his arrest. By waiting until now, you have the opportunity for all three."

"How so, Thomas?" Tolbert asked.

"Juan Carlos is a scared man. Scared and on the run. Last year, Diego entered into a partnership with Juan Tierra Barona for us to sell over $620 million dollars of his crack cocaine. Crack that Barona had been unsuccessful in smuggling into the U.S. The partnership was to be for a 50/50 split of the profits."

"Remember the two tractor trailer rig accident last summer near Tonopah, Arizona, where a container trailer and a gasoline trailer collided?" Thomas asked.

"Yes, I remember seeing the CCN reports," Tolbert replied. "If I remember correctly, the two rigs were burned to an almost unrecognizable pile of rubbish. And yes," he suddenly remembered, "wasn't the rig that allegedly caused the accident identified as from the St. Marks Refinery."

"Right you are," replied Thomas.

"Our rig contained over $310 million dollars in cash, cash that was to be used to repay Barona his half interest for our partnership. Clark, the Diego's, and I had entered into an agreement for an equal share of the profits, or the loss if anything happened to either Juan Tierra's crack or the money from sales."

"With your arrest of Clark and Ortega, Diego could not come up with the $ 310 million to pay Barona back. Since Juan Tierra does not know the identity of Juan Carlos's partners, Barona is looking only for Juan Carlos. He has promised to kill him. Juan Carlos has had little choice but to seek asylum. He has been on the run now for over five months, and said he has run out of hiding places in Central and South America."

"When Diego called, I persuaded him that it would be safe to seek refuge in St. Marks, away from Barona," Thomas continued. "Juan Carlos is tired of constantly looking over his shoulder for Barona's henchman.

Though he has great trepidation in coming to the U.S., he has finally reconciled that St. Marks will be his best place for refuge."

"At 10:00 PM last night, Diego's other two sub commanders left St. Marks for the 22 hour journey to Arroyos de Mantua on the Southwest Cuban Peninsula de Guanahacabibes. Juan Carlos will join them there. Around 4:00 AM, after they've had a few hours sleep, they will return to St. Marks. I am expecting them to arrive at the St. Marks Refinery around 2:00 AM day after tomorrow. If your interested, I'll tell you how you can capture him."

Tolbert laughed, "Oh, I'm very interested."

"Just get to the refinery around midnight," Thomas said. "The night watchman's name is Gus. Other than the 'chemists' working on the second floor, neither Gus nor anyone else working at the refinery is involved in the smuggling scheme."

"When you reach my second floor condo, take the south stairs down to the boathouse dock. The switch to the left of the entranceway opens an underwater door into the river. When the sub is within 100 yards of the boathouse, it will signal you to open the underwater door. The red light bulb over the boat slip will begin flashing and a pulsing buzzer will announce the sub's arrival. You need only press the switch to open the entranceway. I'll assure you, you'll find a very surprised Juan Carlos and company when they open the hatch!"

"Thank you, Thomas. How can I, rather, how can America thank you for your assistance in bringing Juan Carlos Diego and his smuggling empire to justice?"

"I think I know a way," Thomas replied.

"How's that?"

"I am concerned about my perceived criminal activity involvement as a member of Juan Carlos Diego and Wayne Clark's drug empire. In my long-term efforts to bring about the downfall of their drug smuggling organization and to ultimately bring Juan Carlos to justice, I would like for you to request that the Attorney General and the President absolve me of any criminal activity."

"Consider it done." Tolbert replied assuredly.

"Thank you, Rick. I was hoping you would say that."

"I do have a concern, though," Tolbert remarked.

"What's that, Rick?"

"A concern for your safety after this story breaks. Does anyone in the cartel know your real name?"

"No, Rick. They know only my 'assumed' name. I have been very careful not to disclose my real name to anyone."

"That's very fortunate for you, Thomas. After the details of Juan Carlos' arrest are made public, and Wayne Clark learns that you have betrayed him, I'm certain that both he and Juan Carlos will try to implicate you. Since they know you only as Michael Miguel Thomas, they will not be able to do so. I promise you, Thomas, only the AG and the President and I will know the full details of this incident. I will explain your necessary involvement in the drug smuggling partnership, and your 15-year undercover effort to bring about the downfall and arrest of Juan Carlos. I can assure you that Thomas Miguel Michaels, Jr. will have complete amnesty and anonymity."

"Thank you, again, Rick. I was hoping that would be the case. And thank you for helping me bring Juan Carlos Diego to justice. Soon my parent's death will be revenged. There are two other favors I would ask of you, Rick," Thomas said.

"What are they?"

"First, on my dining table are the legal papers assigning ownership of the St. Marks Refinery to the mill's employees. I have designated Ralph Fiacincio and Bill Knox as co-CEOs. I trust the government will find the terms of transfer of ownership legal."

"I promise you, Thomas, I will implore Florida's Attorney General to see that it is, and if not, to find a way that it can be done. That is most commendable of you."

"Thank you, Rick. The refinery's employees are good, hard working people," Thomas said sincerely. "They deserve to share the profits of the mill."

"Secondly," Michaels requested, "Write these numbers down if you will, Rick. N9827L6. I have transferred Wayne Clark's $217 million out of Grand Cayman Capital Trust and into this numbered Swiss account. I trust you will be able to find a way to transfer a significant portion of these funds to your BSDIA operating budget."

Tolbert laughed, "I'm quite sure Congress and the Office of Inspector General will have their say as to the distribution of these drug funds, but I'm sure we'll get our share. On behalf of President Douglas and the BSDIA, 'many thanks' for your efforts to bring down Juan Carlos Diego and his drug empire."

"I'll assure you, Rick. The pleasure is all mine!" replied Thomas.

"Are you sure you do not want to enter the federal witness protection program?" Tolbert offered.

"No, Rick. I am content to reside right here in this tropical locale for quite some time."

"I understand. Incidentally," Tolbert asked, "how's your bank account? Do you have enough money to take care of your needs?"

"Oh. I have a few dollars put aside," Thomas replied with a smile.

As the mini-sub surfaced in the boathouse of the St. Marks Refinery, a broadly smiling Rick Tolbert greeted a very surprised Juan Carlos Diego and crew as they opened the hatch.

"Buenos Dias, Juan Carlos. Welcome to the United States." Tolbert greeted Diego affably as the underwater door closed, effectively sealing the fate of the notorious drug smuggler. With the boathouse dock ringed with heavily armed BSDIA agents, Diego, Kerchenkov, and Krasnaya had little choice but to surrender. They quickly joined the 'chemists' who had previously been rounded up and rushed off to the Florida Penitentiary in Tallahassee.

Earlier in the evening, Navy Seals stationed at Guantanamo Bay had moved onshore at Arroyos de Mantua, setting charges that destroyed the submarine's mid-point way station. With this, the drug smuggling empire of Diego and Clark came to an abrupt and permanent halt.

An exhausted Rick Tolbert walked out to the refinery dock to stretch his tired body. A full January moon brightly lit the adjacent salt marsh. Oblivious to the cold night air, Tolbert stared pensively at the tranquil marshland stretching southward toward the Gulf. As often as he had navigated these Gulf waters in youthful exploration, never could he have imagined how the St. Marks lighthouse could have so inevitably directed this course of his adult life.

Tolbert reflected on the symbolism of this bastion of navigation. Like the BSDIA, it provided directional warning. In navigation as in life, when warned that continuing a steadfast course will ultimately lead to peril, most heed the warning and change direction.

Wayne Payton Clark and Juan Carlos Diego chose to ignore the warnings of the BSDIA. The rhythmic signal of the St. Marks lighthouse directed their drug smuggling venture to Florida where their own unrelenting greed, and the inexorably planned vengeance of Thomas Michaels ultimately brought them to justice.

Printed in the United States
1244400003B/31-39